The Moonflower Vine

The Moonflower Vine

A Novel

JETTA CARLETON

Foreword by Jane Smiley

HARPER ⬤ PERENNIAL

NEW YORK • LONDON • TORONTO • SYDNEY • NEW DELHI • AUCKLAND

HARPER ● PERENNIAL

The resemblances between the characters in the book and my own family are their environment and occupation, their love of God and each other. This much is the truth. The rest is fiction.

A hardcover edition of this book was published in 1962 by Simon and Schuster, Inc.

P.S.™ is a trademark of HarperCollins Publishers.

HarperCollins books may be purchased for educational, business, or sales promotional use. For information, please e-mail the Special Markets Department at SPsales@harpercollins.com.

FIRST HARPER PERENNIAL EDITION PUBLISHED 2009.

Library of Congress Cataloging-in-Publication Data is available upon request.

ISBN 978-0-06-167323-8 (Harper Perennial edition)

15 16 17 18 /RRD 20 19 18 17 16 15 14 13 12

*This book is for my father and my sisters
and in memory of my mother*

FOREWORD

Jane Smiley

Most novelists, no matter how popular, fall into obscurity. Charles Dickens was unread for a few decades after his death; Anthony Trollope, almost unbelievably prolific, had to be resurrected in the 1940s. Who is obscure these days? Ever heard of Rhoda Broughton? Ever read Sumner Locke Elliott or Camilla R. Bittle? And yet, through the vagaries of reader affection and publisher loyalty, a few novels keep turning up. One of these is Jetta Carleton's *The Moonflower Vine*, published here in a new edition for the first time in twenty-four years.

When *The Moonflower Vine*, set in the early part of the twentieth century in rural Missouri, was published, author Jetta Carleton had a strong sense that it was different from the general run of novels then on the market. She remarked in the biographical note to the *Reader's Digest Condensed Books* version, "It's really so unfashionable to like anything anymore, and I like a good many things. The Angry Young Men are in vogue now, but I'm a Glad Old Girl." Perhaps Carleton, nearly fifty, was thinking of Norman Mailer, James Baldwin, and Gore Vidal, writers some ten or twelve years younger than she was, who had made their reputations defying the system. But Carleton, who worked on *The*

Moonflower Vine for some six years, was far from unsophisticated. After graduating from the University of Missouri and working in radio in Kansas City, she had gone east to work in advertising. In 1962, she lived in Hoboken, New Jersey, was married to an advertising man, and worked in Manhattan. She wrote Ivory Soap commercials for television—in other words, she was at the top of a quintessentially modern profession. Her family back in Missouri viewed her as madly sophisticated—her grandniece, Susan Beasley, remembers, "She was outgoing and witty, and the star of our family, the exotic one. We always knew which TV commercials were hers because they sounded just like her; she was very original in the way she expressed herself. She was delightful, she loved to laugh, and she loved a good time."

No doubt Carleton herself knew that *The Moonflower Vine* was far from a nostalgic piece of sentimental Americana. It was complex and daring when it was first published, and it remains so in the twenty-first century—a delicate and loving exploration of some of the most sensitive topics of family life, presented in a straightforward style that is remarkable for its beauty and moral precision. *The Moonflower Vine* is one of those books that readers wish had a sequel. Even Robert Gottlieb, one of the most experienced editors in publishing, felt this. In 1984, he wrote, "Of the hundreds upon hundreds of novels I've edited, this is literally the only one I've reread several times since its publication. And every time I've read it, I've been moved by it again—by the people, by their lives, by the truth and clarity and generosity of the writing and feeling."

The Moonflower Vine opens with an overture. We are introduced to the Soames family, down on their small farm in rural Missouri. Matthew and Callie, about seventy, are hosting three of their daughters—Jessica, about fifty; Leonie, in her late forties; and Mary Jo, a good deal younger—for their annual summer visit. The weather is hot. The farm is without most conveniences, as it has always been, and there is the sense that the daughters enjoy their yearly visits because they know they will leave soon and go back to their own lives, but part of the novel's force is in the fact that we see nothing of those lives. On the last day of the visit, various inconvenient neighborly obligations threaten, and then kill, the Soameses' family-oriented plans to have a picnic at the old bee tree and gather honey. Reluctantly, they do what they all know must be done, until at last they escape the neighbors and relatives and go home to enjoy the annual evening blossoming of the moonflower vine (a night-blooming relative of the morning glory). Carleton's storytelling is leisurely, as befits the heat and the circumstances. She tempts the reader to wonder about the Soames family, but also lulls the reader into thinking that Matthew and Callie are a simple, old-fashioned married couple and that their daughters' lives, too, have been your basic American lives, just the sort you might find in a G-rated movie about the rural Midwest.

As the structure of the following sections carries the story forward, though, through the point of view (though not the voice) of each of the family members, things turn out not to have been what they appeared to be: the close-knit family life of the Soameses is as idiosyncratic, and as much of a triumph over adversity, as that of any other family, viewed steadily and viewed honestly. What emerges is a remarkably true narrative, but one that is never partisan or small-minded—the anatomy of a family carried out with simultaneous honesty and love.

The promise of the novel, as an art form, is always that a story will be told with full complexity and, as Edith Wharton once observed, with each element so "thoroughly thought through" that the reader cannot imagine that anything about it is missing or unknown to the author. Such completeness must be an illusion, but it is the essential illusion of all successful novels—even parts of the story that the narrative does not address seem to have been understood and considered by the author. It is in this that *The Moonflower Vine*, only 336 pages long, seems to excel.

The real subject of *The Moonflower Vine* is romantic love. The narrator explores the romantic choices that each character makes, placing these squarely in the context of each character's history and sense of himself or herself. And even though Matthew, Leonie, Jessica, Mathy, and Callie mean well and feel strong bonds with the other members of their family, their choices invariably strain those bonds. It is Matthew who sets the tone with his almost tragic sense of his own shortcomings—even when he wins Callie, whom he considers the most attractive and desirable girl he knows, he cannot reconcile himself completely to family life or to the small world that he lives in. Aware of his own failings, he grows stricter and more forbidding, and the girls find themselves drawn to young men who offer the possibility of escape. Carleton is remarkable in that she is equally adept at portraying each of her character's temperaments: Mathy, the wild one, is convincingly and delightfully anarchic; Leonie, the good girl, is painfully aware that goodness does not make her lovable; Callie is a little intimidated by her husband, but nevertheless understands him perfectly.

The portrayal of Matthew is a feat of empathy. He fears temptation and always tries to rise above it—his position in the town and his religious beliefs require absolute rectitude. Both the desire that drive him and the guilt that consume him are honestly and convincingly portrayed.

All of these passions are set in a beautifully realized natural landscape of plants, flowers, animals, the weather, the contours of the land. The Soames farm is nothing special and has never thrived, but it has given the daughters an education in the beauty of the natural world that often serves to comfort and inspire them. At one point, the girls pick lettuce where Matthew had planted it early in the season, at a spot where he'd burned brushwood, and "the soil enriched by this pure compost, yielded an enormous crop." Nature also gives their mother a sense of fulfillment: "Callie found the summer complete. Sometimes it seemed to her that she could ask for nothing more than this—the long busy days and the warm sweet nights, when the smell of honeysuckle filled the air and her husband sang on the porch with their daughters." Some novelists, with their close and loving observations of the day-to-day activities of their characters, end up drawing detailed portraits of ways of life that later disappear. Their novels become artifacts of vanished places and lost worlds. Carleton clearly understood that *The Moonflower Vine* was something of a time capsule: the members of the Soames family, in spite of themselves and their temptations, continue to exist in a miniature Eden, where the earth is capable of astonishing displays that the characters sometimes are lucky enough or sensitive enough to observe.

Novelists who write a single, excellent novel are a rare breed. The most famous American novelists to have done so are Harper Lee and Ralph Ellison, both of whom, like Carleton, drew principally on their own experiences for their stories. Both Lee and Ellison explored the private ramifications of a political topic, racism, and they did so to great and successful effect, awakening their many readers to not only the pervasive injustice of prejudice, but also to its psychological cost. Lee and Ellison seem to have balked at their huge success, however. Lee is reported to have said that the reception of *To Kill a Mockingbird* was "in some ways . . . just about as frightening as the quick, merciful death I'd expected." Ellison even went so far as to report that a house fire had destroyed hundreds of pages of his second novel, when, as it turned out, those pages did not exist.

The Moonflower Vine, in contrast to *Invisible Man* and *To Kill a Mockingbird*, explores the ramifications of passion, and seems to fit neatly into the category of novels that are private, not political. Carleton's own remarks for *Reader's Digest* promote this view, and it is tempting to read the novel as a lovely little story of the private life of a single family. But the novel keeps turning up again because Carleton does hone in on perennial themes of American life: religion, sexuality, women's ambitions, small-town life, and the pastoral landscape. Indeed, these very themes, still private in 1963, were soon, thanks to the women's movement, to become political. The controversy that Carleton manages to dampen down by using a tight focus, a sympathetic style, and a very particular setting would, ten years later, be impossible to contain.

Beasley recalls that the older members of her family were shocked, and to a degree dismayed, by what Jetta had written (the younger members "thought it was wonderful," however). In 1962, a sea change was in the works in the way women's lives were to be considered. Around the time Carleton published her novel, Gloria Steinem had a controversial article in *Esquire* about women's life choices. And Betty Friedan published *The Feminine Mystique* in 1963, as *The Moonflower Vine* was finding an audience among readers of the *Condensed Books*. But Steinem was twenty years younger than Carleton, and Friedan was eight years younger. Carleton managed to write her novel in a nonpolitical way; her subject matter has become political in spite of her efforts.

To Kill a Mockingbird, *Invisible Man*, and *The Moonflower Vine* all share one characteristic: they succeed because they are deeply intimate portraits, strongly felt, based on autobiographical material. Readers love them because of their authenticity; because, in some sense, propriety *might* have prevented them from being written, but did not. They are startling, in part, because they are not confessional—the novelist withdraws herself or himself from the material in order to examine it with more objectivity. Each novel seems "true" with a power that a memoir or a nonfiction account might not possess. A first novelist, even a sophisticated one like Carleton, might not anticipate the sense of self-exposure such novelistic intimacy engenders. Other novelists (Dickens comes to mind) don't get to the autobiographical material until later in their careers, when they are used to the public eye, and used to the profession of writing.

That Carleton seems to have worked on a subsequent novel for many years (according to Susan Beasley) adds greater poignancy.

None of Jetta Carleton's living relatives have seen the novel or know where the pages are. It is possible that the manuscript was with her papers, and these were lost in the tornado (a piece of characteristic Missouri irony) that destroyed the town where they were stored in 2003. But *The Moonflower Vine* is ours to enjoy, and we are lucky to have it.

Jane Smiley gratefully acknowledges the assistance of Susan Beasley and Carlin Landoll, Jetta Carleton's grandnieces, in writing this foreword.

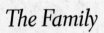

The Family

1

My father had a farm on the western side of Missouri, below the river, where the Ozark Plateau levels to join the plains. This is a region cut by creeks, where high pastures rise out of wooded valleys to catch the sunlight and fall away over limestone bluffs. It is a pretty country. It does not demand your admiration, as some regions do, but seems glad for it all the same. It repays you with serenity, corn and persimmons, blackberries, black walnuts, bluegrass and wild roses. A provident land, in its modest way. The farm lay in its heart, two hundred acres on a slow brown stream called Little Tebo.

The nineteenth century had not yet ended when my parents, Matthew and Callie Soames, first came to the farm. They arrived newlywedded, with a teakettle, a featherbed, and a span of mules. Later they went to live in a small town, where my father taught school. Sometimes they came back to the farm for the summer. After many years they came home to stay. They painted the house and propped up the old gray barn, bought a bull and a butane tank, and lived here the year around, as happy as if they were hale and twenty instead of a frail old pair who would not see seventy again.

My sisters and I used to visit them on the farm. We came each summer—Jessica from deep in the Ozarks, Leonie from a little town in Kansas, and I from New York, where I worked in television, then a new industry, very mysterious to my family. To me, and somewhat to my sisters, these visits were like income tax, an annual inconvenience. There were always so many other ways we could have spent the time. But, old as we were, our parents were still the government. They levied the tribute and we paid it.

Once we got there, we were happy enough. We lapsed easily into the old ways, cracked the old jokes, fished in the creek, ate country cream and grew fat and lazy. It was a time of placid unreality. The lives we lived outside were suspended, the affairs of the world forgotten and our common blood remembered. No matter that our values differed now, that we had gone our separate ways; when we met like this on familiar ground, we enjoyed one another.

I remember particularly a summer in the early fifties. Jessica's husband and Leonie's had stayed behind that year; one was a farmer, the other a mechanic, and neither could get away at the time. Only Leonie's boy had come with her. Soames was a tall, beautiful, disconsolate child who had just turned eighteen. In a few weeks he was leaving to join the Air Force, and Leonie could hardly bear it. Once he was gone, there was so much he would have left undone, so much unsaid, that neither of them would ever again have a chance to do or say. It was a sad time for them. For the rest of us, too, especially as the war was still going on in Korea. The war itself troubled us deeply, and it gave his leaving a special gravity. We could not think of one without the other. And yet, here in deep country, remote from the outside world, it was possible, for the moment, to think of neither. There was no daily paper. Nobody bothered with the radio. The little news that came our way seemed unreal and no concern of ours. Only the planes roaring over each day from an airbase on the north reminded us of danger, and soon even they lost their menace. Their shadows slipped across the pasture and yard like the shadows of clouds, hardly more sinister. The farm was a little island in a sea of summer. And a faraway war where young men were dying troubled us less than the shooting of one old man.

This had happened close to home, a mile or two up the road. A recluse farmer named Corcoran had been shot by his only son, a poor creature recently discharged from the army. My parents found the old man the next morning, rolled under a bed like a rug in summer and left there to die. He was still, though barely, alive. They drove him twenty miles to a hospital, my mother sitting in the back seat with the old man's head in her lap.

All this had taken place just before our arrival. On our last day but one, we were still talking about it.

"Poor old thing," said my mother, "be a blessing if he could die."

"Yes, it would," said my father. "Nobody to care for him at all."

"He was a grouchy old thing, but he doesn't deserve to suffer."

"How old is he?" I said.

"He must be seventy, at least," said my mother. The way she talked, he could have been her grandfather.

"Have they caught the boy?" said Soames.

"Not yet."

"Wonder how come him to do that."

"I don't know," said my father. "Some say the old man was pretty hard on him."

"There were all kinds of tales!" my mother said. "About his daddy chainin' him in the smokehouse and all that. I never believed 'em."

"Idle gossip," said Dad. "The old man had a way of antagonizing people and they had to get back at him. He was rough and crude in his ways, but he wasn't mean."

"No, he wasn't. The boy was just odd, that's all. He wasn't quite right. I don't know how he got into the army."

"It figures." Soames grinned and got up.

"Oh, you're a sight!" Mama said, patting him on the seat of his jeans. "My goodness, we forgot to heat dishwater."

So ended the symposium on neighborhood violence. We pulled ourselves up from the table, all of us stupefied with food. We had dined on roast tenderloin, peas in pure cream, sliced green tomatoes browned in butter, and burnt-sugar cake for dessert. My mother set a country table, and dinner was at noon.

"That sure tasted good," said Jessica. "I wish I had three stomachs, like a cow."

"Me, too," Leonie said. She ate the last fried tomato off the platter.

"On top of cake?" I said.

"I always have to finish off on something salty."

"You'll get as fat as pig," said my father, patting her shoulder.

"Where are you going now?" said Mama.

"Just out on the porch," said Dad.

"Well, don't forget, you have to go in town this afternoon to get ice—you or Soames one."

"I'll go, Grandma!" Soames never missed a chance to drive my little car.

"Why, honey," said Leonie, "you don't want to go running off to town, do you? Why don't you stay home like a good boy and work on the barn roof? Mother would be so proud if you'd just finish your job."

"I'll finish it."

"Well, never put off till tomorrow what you can do today. You know tomorrow we're going to cut the bee tree."

"I know it."

"And there's a whole bundle of shingles you haven't touched yet."

"I know that, too, Mother. I'll get around to them."

"Not if you go running off to town."

"Aw, let him go," said my father. "It gets hot up there on that roof, doesn't it, boy? We'll both drive in after a while."

"Don't wait too late," Mama said. "We want to get our cream made before the moonflowers bloom."

"We'll be back in plenty of time."

"Well, be sure." She turned back to us. "We ought to have two dozen blooms tonight! I counted the pods this morning. I never see so many! Well now, girls, what are we going to take on our picnic tomorrow? Let's decide."

We discussed it as we washed dishes. Down in the woods my father had found a hollow tree where the bees had hived. Tomorrow we were going to smoke them out, chop the tree, and take the wild honey. In the course of it, we would also fish and swim and cook our dinner by the shady creek. Our father and mother planned it as an all-day excursion, a jolly windup of our two weeks at home. As we debated the respective merits of French fries and potato salad, the telephone on the dining-room wall rang two shorts and a long.

"That's our ring," said Mama.

"I'll get it," Dad called. A minute later he came to the kitchen door. "Mama, it's Jake Latham. He and Fanny and the Barrows and some of them are going over to Corcoran's place tomorrow. Jake says his timothy is dead ripe and ought to be shocked. He thinks the peaches need picking, too."

"Oh, he does, does he?" Mama's smile was mildly ironic. "It's about time they did a little something for him. This'll be the first time."

"Well, better late than never. *Absit invidia.*"

"I reckon they wanted us to come and help."

"That's what they want."

"I guess you told 'em we couldn't."

"I said I'd see."

Mama looked at him as if he'd gone soft in the head. "But we're going to cut the bee tree tomorrow!"

"I know, but—"

"Didn't you tell him that?"

"No—"

"Why not?"

"Well," Dad said, squirming, "I don't know that Jake would think a bee tree much of an excuse."

"Oh foot, who cares what Jake thinks!"

"We don't want to appear uncooperative," Dad said primly.

"Appears to me it's them that's uncooperative. They never done anything for him before. Well, anyway, it's nice they're doin' it now. I wouldn't mind helpin', but can't they wait till Monday?"

"I asked Jake. He said that didn't suit *him.*"

"Well, tomorrow doesn't suit *us.* We've got our plans all made."

"I know," Dad said, looking worried. "I hate to go tomorrow, but I don't see how I can refuse. You folks go ahead with your picnic, and I'll go on over to Corcoran's and help."

"That wouldn't be fair," said Jessica. "Why don't we just all go. Your big girls can help."

"No sir!" said Mama. "Ain't any of us goin'. Ain't any use in lettin' them spoil our day. There's plenty of them to do the work, without us, and for once they can just do it."

"They'll think we're mighty selfish," Dad warned.

"Then they'll just have to think it. That's the price we'll have to pay."

"All right. If that's how you feel, I'll say no more." Dad put on his hat and went out with an air of noble resignation. He was vastly relieved.

We finished the dishes, and Mama went upstairs for a nap. Soames had gone back to work. Leonie went out to tell him what a good boy he was.

"Poor ol' Leonie," said Jessica, "looks like she's going to *force* him to finish that roof."

"Not if she encourages him to death," I said. "If she doesn't shut up, he'll get mad and quit, like he always does."

"Yes," said Jessica, "and then he'll feel guilty, poor young'un."

"And have to be mad at her."

"And she'll think he doesn't love her or he'd have done what she wanted him to. Oh dear."

"Just like the voice lessons," I said. Leonie had pleaded, nagged, encouraged and commanded, tried every stratagem known to mothers to turn Soames into a singer. She was right, of course, for Soames had a fine voice. He might have been really good if he'd worked. But he wasn't interested in singing or in anything much, except flying.

"Poor kids," said Jessica. "I feel so sorry for both of them I can't hardly stand it."

"Well, let's get her back in the house if we can and make her leave him alone. I'll play the piano. That ought to do it."

We went into the front room to the old battered piano and dug out some very back issues of *Etude* Magazine. I attempted a composition called "Cupid's Appeal," a great favorite of mine in my youth. It took me a while to arrange my fingers, and the melody tended to get lost between chords.

Leonie came in with her hands over her ears. "Ow-wow!" she said, like Amos and Andy. "Move over!"

She polished off "Cupid's Appeal" in a competent manner and played some other pieces in the back, including the songs—all of them full of *Hark!* and *Ah!* and sorrow at eventide—which Jessica and I rendered in appropriate mood. We thought we were pretty funny. In the midst of it, a stray beagle who had hung around the yard all week began to howl.

I went out to comfort him. "Poor thing, I wish you knew where you lived."

"He's a sad crittur," said Jessica.

"He's a nice little dog. I like him."

"He's got fleas."

"He can't help it."

"Whatever happened to the one with the beard?" said Jessica.

"A dog with a beard?"

"Well, he was kind of a dog. I mean that funny-lookin' boy you brought here last summer."

"Oh, him! I didn't bring him—he just came. He was on a walking tour."

"Talking tour, I'd call it."

14

"I remember him," Leonie chimed in. "He wore tennis shoes."

"And no socks," Jessica added.

"And he smelled funny."

"One of those dirties she takes up with!"

They beamed at me in devilish glee, off on a tear again about the company I kept. They never could understand the wild-haired anarchic types that seemed to gravitate to me, and I didn't always appreciate them myself.

"Remember him and the sorghum?" Jessica said. "He kept spilling it in his beard."

"And getting his beard in his plate!"

"There was always a swarm of flies after him."

"Now stop it!" I yelled. "He was very intellectual."

"Intellectual!" Leonie reared back indignantly. "He *sneered* at *Shakespeare!*"

"Sh! You'll wake Mama!" Everybody broke out giggling again for no special reason.

"I'm so hot," said Jessica, "I'm foamin' between the legs. Let's go down to the bathtub."

The only bathtub on the farm was a wide place in the branch. Taking some towels and a cake of Ivory, we strolled down through the east pasture to where the little stream nibbled its way through a deep ravine. At one spot, my father had hollowed a spring out of the bank and kept a cup hanging on a birch limb. He believed in the therapeutic value of spring water, wild honey, and sunshine. We slid down and squatted on our heels in the sand. It was cool and sweet-smelling down there.

"Have some branch water," said Jessica, handing me a cupful. "Good for the kidneys."

She and I had a contest to see who could hold the most. Neither of us had ever heard of internal drowning. Leonie finally made us stop. "You'll be peeing in the bathtub," she said. We waded on down to where the stream widened into a pool. The water was deeper here, so clear you could see leaf shadows on the smooth sandstone bottom. We hung our clothes on the buckbrush, and Jessica waded in, screeching as the icy water came up around her middle. Leonie stepped in delicately, splashing water on her wrists and the backs of her knees. My foot slipped and I fell in. After a bit we got used to the cold. We soaped and dunked and splashed, cavorting like three little boys instead of grown-up women. Jessica was almost fifty and Leonie not far behind. I was close to thirty. But none of us acted our age or felt it. We mostly behaved like retarded children, because our parents liked us that way.

Our bodies glowed with the sting of the water. "Aren't we pretty?" I said.

We stopped splashing and looked at each other. "Why, yes we are," said Jessica. "We're real nice."

Though she was overweight and I was skinny, all three of us were smooth and unblemished and the skin fit snug on our bones. Out here in the open, lacy with sunlight, we were beautiful, and it seemed the natural thing to say so. We climbed out and sat on a flat rock, rubbing ourselves warm with the big towels.

"I wish Mama and Dad would put in some plumbing," said Leonie. "Wouldn't you think they'd want it?"

"Well, I don't know," said Jessica. "They've been without it for seventy years, I guess they don't miss it."

"They could get used to it."

"Why, what's the matter with this?" said Jessica, imitating my father's tone. "Why, this is good enough for anybody!"

We laughed, and I thought of the town where I grew up, where only the banker and the grocer could afford a septic tank and the constant repairs of a pump in the basement. The rest of us got along the best way we could. I remember the kitchen on a winter morning—coal buckets underfoot, the bucket for slops near the door, water boiling on the big black range, my father shaving at the kitchen table, and I in my petticoat, washing myself in the gray enamel pan (my neck and under my arms), while my mother fried the bacon and grease burned on the stovelids. The kitchen was not a gracious room. It was bathroom, dining room, laundry and dairy, each in turn or all at once. Not that you thought very much about it. Not, that is, till you visited in the city. After each exposure to other folkways, it was harder to sit in the outhouse at ten below or tolerate that functional urn in the bedroom.

This was in winter. In summer, life expanded with the sunshine. You could bathe upstairs, do the laundry outside in the shade of the peach tree. You could iron in the breeze on the back porch. The house grew taller, wider, prettier. Heating stoves went out to the smokehouse and flowers came in to the tables. There were still the water buckets to fill and the slops to empty. But no coal to carry in, no ashes to carry out. And there was no need for the chamber pot; one went out to the toilet before going to bed—a pleasant excursion on a summer night.

16

"Well, anyway," Leonie was saying, "I wish they'd modernize the place a little, if they're going to stay here."

"They can't stay here much longer," said Jessica.

"They think they can."

"I know, but they just can't. Bless their hearts, they're too old. Anyway, plumbing wouldn't be half as much fun as this."

The sun trickled down through the oak leaves. Away off in the woods a cardinal told us what a handsome bird he was. "Pretty-bird, pretty-bird!" he said over and over. Jessica sat on a blue towel, hugging her knees. Her skin was still rosy from the water and her round cleft rump like a great peach. She looked like Boucher's Diana or a bather by Renoir. But she would have laughed if I'd told her, and said Boo-shay didn't know boo-cat, or something to that effect. Jessica was not about to pretend that she was anything but what showed up in clothes—a plain, middle-aged woman, rather dowdy and in need of a girdle.

I looked at my other sister, sitting in the sunlight, brown and glossy as a warm brown egg. She was the one with enviable pigment, a dark-skinned blonde whom sunlight loved. As her skin tanned, her hair turned paler and paler. It streamed over her shoulders now, fine and silvery as young corn silks. No woman who looked like that, I thought, deserved the nature of Carry Nation. But Leonie's was something like that. More than the rest of us, Leonie bore the vestigial burning passed down from our forebears, a hellfire breed who preached a trail through Indiana and Kentucky, hacking the wilderness with the Word of God. If in their zeal the apple sapling fell with the poison oak, that was right, for it was the Word of God that felled it. The Holy Book was the law and the light and the way, and it was not love. And nothing could sway those ember-eyed fanatics, chopping their way toward Missouri and the twentieth century—just as nothing swayed Leonie. She had this burning, this ax of God. But hers was a hard way, like theirs, and defeats were many. When the blight of doubt fell on her, it was pitiful to see. Two weeks ago when she came to the farm, her face sagged with worry and her eyes were hollow. But the gentle days and the cream and laughter had rounded and smoothed her and made her beautiful again. Sitting naked on the rock, combing her long blond hair, she looked like a Lorelei, and I told her so. She took the compliment with a shy smile, not believing but pleased that I gave it.

"I expect Mama's awake by this time," she said. "We ought to get back."

"I suppose we should."

But nobody stirred. We watched a leaf tilt down slowly and land on the water. Another followed. A locust ripped a little hole in the silence with his serrated cry.

"Autumn . . ." said Jessica. We let it drift away on the warm air.

After a while we dressed and took the long way home. Climbing a slope, we came out on the high meadow we called the Old Chimney Place. A few soft bleached bricks marked the spot where a house had burned, years before our time. Jessica and Leonie could remember when the chimney stood tall, visible from the road.

"Remember," said Jessica, "how we used to mark off rooms inside the old foundation?"

"With clover chains," said Leonie.

"And decorate them with daisies?"

"Yes, and Queen Anne's lace and chigger weed."

"And how the chiggers decorated us!" They laughed. "There was a plum thicket here—we used to eat them before they got quite ripe, remember?"

"We got so sick and Mama got so mad! It was nice here then."

"That was a long time ago."

"Yes . . ."

"Mathy had a playhouse here," said Jessica. "Remember the times we found her here when she didn't come home after dark?"

"I remember!"

They smiled at each other and moved on ahead of me, lost in times that I had little part in. I had not shared their childhood. They had another little sister, long before me. This was Mathy, the third daughter, whom I remembered only dimly. She went away when I was three. But Mathy had a child, a boy named Peter, born when I was five. Through him I knew something of her nature. Peter was very like her, so they told me—fine-boned and dark, with bright dark eyes; quick and antic and imperturbable, and, like his mother, fascinated by the world. Peter loved trees and stones and dug-up bones and most especially the intricate mechanism of anything that crept or flew—bugs, beetles, butterflies. He had made them his work. He was studying in Europe now on a fellowship, at the University of Leyden. We were all terribly proud of Peter.

Jessica and Leonie came back around the old foundation, still talking of Mathy. "It must have been a hard life," Leonie said. "I wouldn't have liked it."

"Neither would I. But I think she was happy."

"I hope so. I really do hope so!" Leonie looked up earnestly, as if Jessica might doubt her.

"I wish Peter were here," I said, watching a ladybug climb up a stem.

"I wish I were there!" said Leonie. "I'd give anything to see Europe."

"I'll take you some day—if it doesn't blow up first. Wouldn't it be fun to be there with Peter?"

"Oh, wouldn't it!" she said. "Did he write you about his vacation, that trip he took? He writes the most marvelous letters."

"And lots of them."

"I hope Soames will do half as well. Last summer when he was away, I got one little postcard." Her face clouded briefly and brightened again. "Peter sent us cards from everywhere. London, Venice, Denmark. Just think, he's seen Elsinore!"

"Yes, he wrote me."

"Elsinore! All those places you read about in literature! And Peter appreciates it so."

"Yes, he does."

"I wish Soames were like that." Again that look of hurt perplexity came into her face. "Oh, when I *think!* If only he'd kept on with his vocal lessons—he could have studied in Europe, too. Italy—Paris—! If only I could have found some way—if his father had been any help—" She turned away, her pretty face clenched in frustration.

A faint "Hoo-hoo?" came drifting through the woods from the direction of the house. "There's Mama," I said. "We'd better get on back before she comes looking for us."

We set off down the slope, passed through a strip of woods, and came up through the orchard among the silvery arthritic trees, their joints swollen and calcified with time. Here and there my father had set new trees, replenishing his grove. Nothing was allowed to die.

"There goes the mail carrier!" Jessica said, as a car drove up the road. "He's late today."

"Maybe we'll hear from Peter," said Leonie. She hurried to the mailbox, where Mama stood with a letter in her hand. "Is it from Peter?"

"I think it's from Ophelia," said Mama.

"Oh, shoot."

Ophelia was a second cousin of ours. She and her family lived south of the farm, some forty miles away. Mama opened the letter and handed it to me. "Read it, Mary Jo. I never can make out her writin'."

I peered at the letter and held it out at a distance. Ophelia's script was like an abstract painting; you had to back off and squint to make something of it.

"'Dear Cousins,'" I read, "'haven't heard from you folks in a while. Wonder if you are still alive and kicking, ha! Well, Ralph and me are about as well as common. With the help of Jesus. Ma complains some. She is poorly this summer. I don't know how much longer we will have her with us.'"

"Poor old Aunt Cass," Mama said, referring to Ophelia's mother. "Her mind wanders. But my land, for one her age, she's stronger than I am."

"She smells it, too," I said. "She was pretty ripe when we were down there last summer."

"Why, Mary Jo!"

"Well, she was—all of 'em were. Ophelia and Ralph holler and carry on at those holiness meetings and work up a good sweat and never take a bath."

"They're washed in the blood of the Lamb," said Jessica.

"It's no substitute for Lifebuoy."

"Hush that, both of you," said Mama. "You ought to be ashamed. What else does she say?"

I squinted again. "'If the Lord wills, Ma will be ninety-six her birthday. We are looking for you folks down that day. You promised you would come and bring the girls.'"

"I could kick myself," said Mama. "I did promise, when we's down there Decoration Day. I'd forgot all about it. Why couldn't she!"

"Because she's got a memory like an elephant," I said.

"And that ain't all," said Jessica. Ophelia was rather large. "When is Aunt Cass's birthday, Mama?"

"Tomorrow!"

"Oh no!"

"Ain't that just the way of it!"

"We don't have to go, do we?"

"We'd ought to."

"We can't—we're going to cut the bee tree."

"But I promised!" Mama wailed, looking at us in despair.

"Well," said Jessica, "you can break that kind of a promise. God won't hold it against you."

"Yes, but Ophelia will. She'll be plumb mad. And Aunt Cass is so old—this may be her last birthday."

"Mama, do you realize we've been going to Aunt Cass's farewell parties for the last nine years?"

"Well, I know, but—"

"And we may be going another nine, if these all-day powwows don't get her down before then. All that cryin' and kissin'—"

"Cousin Ralph and his wet mustache!" I said.

"—and shoutin' and singin' hymns!" Jessica went on. "If Ophelia's so worried about her ma, she better cut out the celebrations. She just has 'em because *she* likes 'em."

"I guess that's true," Mama said. "But you can't hardly blame her. It gets awful lonesome down there."

Jessica snorted. "Why, Mama, they don't get lonesome! They go to those tent meetings and drive into town and Ralphie and the grandchildren are always coming to see them—they have a dandy time."

"Ophelia *says* they're lonesome."

"She's just playing on your sympathies. She knows she can do it. She has you and Dad running down there all the time. And the trip's hard on you, you know it is."

"Well, yes," Mama conceded. "But next time I see her, she's going to want to know why I broke my promise. What excuse will I give her?"

"Tell her we were going to cut a bee tree—just tell her the truth."

"The truth's hard for some folks to understand."

"Then make it easy on Ophelia. Lie!"

Mama looked at us thoughtfully. "I reckon I just will."

We laughed and I kissed her on the cheek. It had the soft worn feel of old linen. (I never could get used to mothers who were young. Mine was middle-aged when I was born, and crisp young mothers never seemed authentic.)

"Besides," said Mama, "if we's to go away off down there, we wouldn't get back in time for the moonflowers."

That crisis passed, we settled down to peel peaches in the parlor. It was cooler in there. Mama wanted to make preserves before supper. We didn't need more preserves, but she enjoyed the work. Every morning of our vacation she greeted us with shining face.

"Now today we're not going to work—we're going to do just what we want to do!" And every day it turned out that we just wanted to wash all the quilts, or scrub woodwork, or make another batch of preserves. It had been like that all our lives. Our mother ruled us with a practical hand, the broom and fruit jar her badge of office, the washboard her shield and buckler. We were allowed to study, as our father was a schoolteacher, but we were rarely allowed to read. Shouldn't we instead be doing something? And wouldn't we rather? Mama needs you—let's clean the smokehouse —hurray! My mother loved her work, and never so well as when she had us to help her.

Age had done nothing to diminish her passion. Here she was at seventy, keeping house as assiduously as ever. She had none of the conveniences at the farm. But bless her, she had someone to help!

She had a friend whose name was Hagar, a leathery little old maiden lady who lived on the next hill. Miss Hagar had moved there some years ago with an aging father. When the old man died, Miss Hagar stayed on on her rundown farm, as lonely as her namesake. Oftentimes we beheld her single in the field, a solitary reaper in sunbonnet, faded gingham, and a man's old shoes. A rough, shy, stolid little creature who fended for herself and asked no favors. She did a man's work more easily than woman's. She smoked a pipe. Aside from a certain female relish of "natural sorrow, loss, or pain," there was hardly a feminine trait about her. But she was devoted to my mother. Several times a week she came to visit, and the two of them gathered and canned and cleaned and talked, cozy as cats in a warm barn.

She was an odd companion for my mother, who smelled of sachet and wore ribbons in her petticoats. My mother put ruffles at her windows and doilies on her tables; she longed for the Victorian elegance of plush, cut glass, long velvet portieres, and a fine white house in town. A big house on the corner, with a porch all around, a great green lawn, and a boy to come Saturdays and trim the hedge. She would have been quite at home with servants.

Yet on the other hand, my mother had plowed a field in her day and was not ashamed. She had country values. She liked crops and fat cattle, jars glimmering red and gold and green in the cool earth-smelling dark of dirt cellars. She liked the kitchen filled on Sunday with relatives and old friends. And she liked a good visit, a conversation heavy and rich with death and loss and pity.

Miss Hagar was her woman, far more than ladies she had lived

22

among in town. Those ladies, most of them, played bridge and gave luncheons. They called things by fancy names and bought gadgets and listened to serials on the radio. My mother scorned such women, yet they made her ill at ease. Because her grammar was faulty and her values were not, she was made to feel out of place.

Lonely for her own kind, she kept a good deal to herself. She tended her house, raised her children, and for forty years waited for her husband. Morning after morning she rose and cooked his breakfast and saw him off to school. Evening after evening she sat beside him, watching him as he worked. The wind mourned in the chimney, the kettle sighed, the rocker creaked, and he said never a word. He had work to do; he must not be interrupted. She sat motionless to still the rocker. The clock ticked, the kettle sighed. And she slipped off to bed. She was lonely for forty years. But she loved him and she waited.

Her children grew up with flawless grammar and strange rebellions. But she loved them and was patient. All of them went away, one of them died. But at last, incomplete as all things are, but recognizable withal, the joy she waited for came about. She could come back to the good creek farm. Her husband was all hers at last. Her children came home to her in summer. And she had a friend, devoted as a good servant, who loved to talk of death and disaster and could not read a word.

"Miss Hagar went to town this afternoon," Mama said, glancing up from her peaches. "I don't know what for. It must have been important—she hasn't been to town more than three times all summer."

"Too bad she didn't know Dad was going," said Jessica. "She could have gone with him."

"She wouldn't have, anyway. We're always askin' her to go in with us, but she's afraid she'll be some bother to somebody. Won't hardly let you do a thing for her. And land-a-livin', as much as she does for us!"

"She sure is a help."

"And won't take nothin' for it. We try and try to pay her a little something, but she won't have it. Papa takes her up a box of groceries once in a while, or a sack of feed." Mama glanced up again. "Where *is* Papa? I wish he'd go on in and get that ice."

"He's already gone," I said.

"Are you sure?" said Leonie. "I thought Soames was still here."

"I guess Dad went without him."

"Really?" Leonie went to the back door and looked out. "I can hardly believe it," she said, coming back. "Somebody went to town and Soames is still here working!"

"He sure is doing a good job on that roof," said Mama. "Listen—don't that sound pretty?" Soames had begun to sing.

"Oh yes, he'll sing now—when he thinks nobody's listening." Leonie's face was wistful as the clear sweet baritone soared from the barn roof, dreaming of Jeanie with the light-brown hair. She had such hopes for that voice.

Mama sighed contentedly. "Such a sad song. Makes me think of poor Mr. Corcoran." And she told us once again how they had found him that morning when they drove up to take him a pound of butter . . . not that the old man seemed to appreciate what they did, but it was just his way . . . and she couldn't bear for him to eat so poorly, such an old man living all alone like that with no one to look after him. Her dry little domestic voice droned like an old ballad, full of love and woe.

A breeze lifted the lace curtains, dallied a moment, and vanished into the stillness of the old farmhouse. My sisters and I rocked and fanned, stretching our bare legs over the flowered carpet, under the pictures of Christ walking on the waters and praying in Gethsemane. The miracle went unremarked and the passion in the garden did not move us, abandoned as we were to the profane pleasures of disaster in which we were not involved and the serenity of the long warm afternoon.

Jessica fanned her legs with the hem of her dress. "My, but it's hot. I could use another bath already."

"Yes, it's hot," said Mama, turning her collar inside. "Put your dress down, Jessica. I can see right up you."

"Well, Mother, that's all right. You know what's up there."

"Ah! What if somebody came up on the porch?"

"If they slip up on us without honking, it serves 'em right."

"Remember last summer," I said, "when the preacher came to the back door and caught you trying on that old corset? Boy, was he surprised!"

Mama said, "I told you the back porch wasn't no place to try on a corset!"

"Where would you have tried it on?" said Jessica.

"Upstairs, of course."

"But it was hot upstairs. And anyway, the preacher had no business out here in the first place. Way out here in the country in the middle of a hot afternoon. We're already saved, and he knows it. He should have been home readin' his Bible or accommodating his wife."

Leonie and I giggled, and Mama said, "Jessica! Shame on you."

"She looks like she could use a little, poor thing."

"Now you stop talking like that. It's not nice."

"Okay, Mother." Jessica grinned. "But she doesn't look like she gets much, does she?"

"Now hush that!"

We snickered and stretched and yawned. Leonie went out to the back porch and brought back a pitcher of iced tea. We sprawled in our chairs and rattled the ice in our glasses. The air was sweet and spicy with the smell of honeysuckle and cedar. At the windows the white curtains filled and wilted and filled again, easy as breathing. The sound of hammering peppered into the warm air intermittently from the barn roof.

The afternoon ran slowly, heavy like honey, sweet and golden and not oppressive. We rocked, and the ice clinked in our glasses, and the curtains rose and fell. And I thought without really thinking in words of those moments in Chekhov, when the pace of the play slows down to a stasis. The woman in the swing moves forward and, after a long time, back. The doctor (for there is always a doctor) sags in his chair, too heavy with unhappy wisdom to stir. Daughters or uncles lean against trellises in a trance of frustration. And the stillness and the heat and the boredom of the provinces weigh the play down until it scarcely moves.

The crunch of wheels on the sandy road broke into the silence. "There's Miss Hagar," said Mama. "I thought it was about time." We followed her out to the yard. "Maybe she's heard something about Mr. Corcoran. Hoo-hoo!" she called.

Her friend drove up in a creaking hack, sitting tiny and erect, feet together and knees apart, under a black umbrella. "Ho!" she said to the horse. The horse came to a stop with a long sigh of relief. His knees went slack, the back caved in, and the neck sagged slowly, like a licorice stick in the heat. When his nose touched ground he began contentedly to nip grass. "Howdy," said Miss Hagar.

She laid her pipe on the seat. She could never bring herself to smoke in front of my mother. "Are you hot any?" she said, grinning around her hard little yellow teeth. We said we were.

"Any news?" said Mama.

"Ain't anybody heard ary word since yesterday. They said he was about the same. Some bad."

"Poor old thing."

"Goddamighty, I don't see how he lived at all."

"Neither do I. Guess they haven't caught the boy yet?"

"Not yet. Somebody said they seen him down around Osceola the other day. Others says he's around here somewheres."

"My, I hope not," said Mama.

"He ain't nothin' to worry us."

"No, I guess there's not any more harm in him. Him and his daddy just had something to settle among themselves. Makes me feel a little juberous, though, knowin' he might be around here somewhere. Ain't you awful nervous up there by yourself?"

"I ain't a-skeered of him."

"I reckon I oughtn't to be, the poor boy. Jake Latham called up this morning. Some of them are goin' over there tomorrow and do some work."

"I heered. Hell, I went over there the other day myself and laid by a patch of corn for him."

"Why, that was nice."

"It don't take no whole gang of folks, what little crop he's got. I got a idy Jake wants to show out a little. I hope you told 'em to go to the devil."

Mama smiled. "Well, we told them we wouldn't be able to come tomorrow. It's the girls' last day."

"I thought it was. You wouldn't want to be workin' over there all day, the last day they's home."

"That's right."

"You prob'ly got plenty to do without that."

"Yes, we'll be busy."

"Prob'ly too busy to cook for yourse'ves!"

"Well, we'll be busy, all right."

"That's what I figured." Miss Hagar paused, and her rough brown face, normally as expressionless as an oatmeal cookie, took on an eager shine. Her mouth pulled into an embarrassed smile. "I want to invite you folks up to my house tomorrow to eat dinner with me!"

"What!" said Mama, forgetting her manners in her astonishment. In all their acquaintance, Miss Hagar had never entertained.

Miss Hagar jerked her head toward the back of the wagon. "I'm a-fixin' to make ice cream for ye!"

We looked, and there in a wet gunny sack lay a chunk of ice, a

26

luxury for Miss Hagar. She had driven all the way to town to buy it.

"My goodness!" said Mama.

"I got a old hen in the coop, fixin' to dress her in the mornin'. And I'm gonna bake a cake!"

"Why, Miss Hagar!"

"It won't be as good as you'd make for yourse'f, but maybe ye can eat it."

"Why, you shouldn't do all that, just for us."

Miss Hagar beamed. "Aw, hell, it ain't much."

But it was quite a bit, and Mama knew it. Miss Hagar must have studied and planned and saved for this event all summer. "I don't hardly know what to *say*, Miss Hagar. We'd like just awful well to come. But you see—" She hesitated, and the smile wavered on Miss Hagar's face.

"You already got something planned?"

"Ye-es, I'm afraid we have—"

"Oh."

"Mr. Soames found a bee tree down by the creek, and we thought we ought to go cut it."

The smile revived. "Well, that hadn't ought to take all day. If you go down there first thing in the mornin'—"

"Well, of course we *could* do that—" Mama stopped, hoist on a genuine quandary. Miss Hagar plainly set great store by the honor of our presence, and she had never asked for anything before. Mama looked around at us, her face woeful. Then she turned back to her friend. "I'm awful sorry, Miss Hagar, but I just don't think we can come."

"Oh." The little brown cookie face settled into inscrutability as before. "Well, it was just a idy."

"And a good one, too. I'm *so* sorry, Miss Hagar."

"It's all right."

"Any other day we'd have been so glad to come."

"Glad to!" we echoed.

"But I don't know—tomorrow bein' their last day and they ain't home but such a short time . . ." Her voice trailed off, and we stood in silence, humbled by Miss Hagar's mute disappointment.

"Reckon I won't see you girls no more," she said. We said we guessed not. "I'll say goodbye to ye, then."

"Can't you come in awhile?" said Mama.

"No, I've got to get home and do the chores." She picked up

27

the reins, the horse gathered himself together, and the hack creaked on down the road. The little chunk of ice wept steadily into the dust.

Mama watched her down the hill. "Poor old thing," she said. There were tears in her eyes.

"Mama?" said Jessica. "We could change our minds. We don't *have* to cut the bee tree."

Mama turned and looked at us, and her dim brown eyes swam with tenderness. "Yes, we do," she said.

As we turned toward the house, a magnificent uproar arose from the barn lot—a whoop and a holler, the *vroom!* of a motor, and a great squawking of hens.

"Mercy! What's all that racket!"

It was Soames, chasing chickens again in my little car.

"Stop that!" Leonie yelled.

Soames slammed on the brakes, spun the car around and roared toward the fence, coming to a halt six inches away.

"You stop that!" she yelled again.

"I've stopped." He sat grinning like a fiend, naked to the waist and looking all of a piece with the small open car, like some mechanized centaur.

"I could just spank you!" Leonie said. "You'll make Grandpa's hens stop laying."

"Aw, Mother, they like to be chased. They think it's some new kind of a rooster."

"You've always got to fool around. You ought to be up on that roof finishing your job."

My father drove into the lot at that moment, causing another stir among the chickens. Soames jumped out and helped him carry the ice to the smokehouse, where they bedded it down in a washtub.

"There now," my father said, "as soon as you womenfolks get the ice cream ready, we're ready to start cranking."

He sat down on the well curb and fanned himself with his hat. At seventy-two he still had most of his hair—very fair hair turned gray and looking much as it always had. His face was still lanky and severe, but the laugh lines had deepened around his mouth. He had mellowed. He let us sleep now till six-thirty. An indulgence. "My-o, look at the windfalls," he said. "You girls haven't been on the job."

We ran to the peach tree in the corner of the yard and picked up the clingstones. They were soft and heavy, and the juice ran

28

down our chins as we ate. Soames went back to fondle the car. It was a red MG, which I had bought the minute the British devalued the pound. There weren't so many around in those days, and Soames had never seen one before. It was his darling. In the evenings he drove it into Renfro, the nearest village, and parked on the square, where the little girls converged on him in hysterics of admiration. Ol' six-foot Soames and an English car were quite a combination.

"Can I have it again tonight, Aunt Jo?"

"I don't care. Just so your girl friends don't stick up the dashboard with their bubble gum."

My father aimed a peach pit at two bluejays squabbling in the tree. "Get out of there!"

"Wait'll I get my slingshot, Grandpa!"

Soames bounded out of the car and fired a stone into the branches. The jaybirds scattered toward the orchard, screaming *Thief!* The peach leaves settled into place again, fixed in the still air like geranium leaves in pale apple jelly. Beyond the orchard the sun grazed the treetops on the Old Chimney Place. Shadows began to flow across the yard.

"Let's go down to the creek!" said Leonie.

"Not *now!*" said Mama.

"I think I've got a fish on my line—a big catfish!"

"But you wouldn't get back in time. The moonflowers are going to bloom."

Leonie squinted at the sun and looked across at the vine. "Ah, the shade isn't near over there yet. We can make it if we hurry."

"Now, Leonie, it's later than you think," I reminded her.

Somebody always had to say it. Leonie's bad timing was a standing joke. Like all zealots, she wanted so passionately to do whatever it was she wanted to do that time must certainly accommodate her. In this unshakable belief, she missed trains and burned dinner and never knew how a movie started. They couldn't even get her off to the hospital when Soames was about to be born. She insisted they had all day. She went right on tying bows on the baby basket—she wanted everything to be just perfect—and set out for the hospital in her own good time, and Soames was born in the front seat. Leonie never learned.

While she was arguing with us, idly, by habit, the shade crawled across the yard and up the front of the smokehouse. I went over to look at the vine. It swarmed over the smokehouse roof and into the walnut tree, a thicket of heart-shaped leaves and long tight pods. All this had come from the brown pebbles dropped in the earth in spring, seeds as hard as a nut and so protective of the life within that you must saw them with a file to let it out.

Out of the corner of my eye I caught a movement. I turned quickly. Nothing stirred. The vine hung immobile. But I knew. It was beginning. I called to the others. They hurried across the yard, my mother snatching up the folding stool as she ran. She sat down to watch the show. My father squatted on his heels beside her. Little by little we stopped talking. The silence grew intense. Now, the next instant, the flowers would begin to open.

"There!"

"Where?"

"No, I guess not. Not yet."

The watch resumed. Soon, now, a stem would tremble, a faint shudder run through the vine, sensed more than seen. A leaf twitched. No, you imagined it. But yes, it moved! A light spasm shook the long pod. Slowly at first, then faster and faster, the green bud unfurled, the thin white edges of the bloom appearing and the spiral ascending, round and round and widening till at last the white horn of the moonflower, visible for the first time in the world, twisted open, pristine and perfect, holding deep in its throat a tiny jewel of sweat.

"Oh, look!"

"There's another!"

"Three of them—four!"

The vine stormed to life, and the blooms exploded—five, twelve, a torrent of them, tumbling their extravagant beauty into the evening air.

"Twenty-two, twenty-three, twenty-four—twenty-four of them! Mama, you were right!"

"I never saw so many at one time."

"It's a good year."

"How beautiful they are!"

"And gone so fast."

"But so beautiful now!"

The big spendthrift blooms extended themselves, stretched tight as the silk on parasols. In the dusk they would glimmer weakly, limp and yellowed as old gloves after a ball. But not now. Now the starred blossoms burned white against the dark vine and filled the air with the sweet, faintly bitter scent of their first and last breath.

We lingered, hoping for one more tardy bloom. But that was

all for today. The lights had come up. The performance was over. We turned, smiling at each other, feeling lighter in some way, shriven and renewed. The blooming of the moonflowers was a kind of miracle, and like all true miracles it had the power of healing.

2

We ate our supper in the yard that night. As we gathered at the table, my father said, "Bless this food, O Lord, to its intended use. . . . Bless our loved ones, wherever they may be, and grant, O Lord, that we may follow in the paths of righteousness . . ." What he meant was that he was grateful for the good smells and sounds of the summer evening, for the star impaled on the lightning rod, for fresh tomatoes from his garden. But he would have felt it pagan to state his pleasure in such plain terms. He said it in his own way, and no doubt the Lord can translate; He must have a lot of it to do in a day's work. ". . . and at last gather us to Thyself in Heaven, our Home. We ask it in Christ's name. Amen."

There was a slight shuffle as we waited the decent interval between Amen and the passing of the bread.

"Now fill your plates," said Mama, "and don't forget to save room for cream." She seemed to feel it a nicety to call ice cream merely cream.

Nobody saved any room. But after the ham and tomatoes and sweet corn, we ate most of a gallon of peach ice cream. Leonie poked around in the freezer. "Jessica, come on now, there's still some left."

"Okay, dump 'er in here," said Jessica.

"You'll make yourself sick," said Mama.

"Oh, I don't think I will. Boy, we sure got it full of vanilla tonight."

"Yes, it's strong, isn't it. It's that new bottle I got from the Jewel Tea man." I suppose there never was a peddler who couldn't sell Mama something.

Jessica began to sculpt her ice cream with her spoon. "You're playing in it now," said Mama. "You've had enough."

"There's still some left in the freezer."

"Why don't you take it up to Miss Hagar?" my father said.

"Why, that'd be nice," said Mama. "One of you run up there and take it."

Soames and I climbed into the MG, I with the ice cream in my lap, and drove off into the night. It was very dark. Sitting low in the open car, I felt the night tower over us, close in over our heads, and chase after us down the lonely road. I thought of "the business that walketh in the night," that Gothic notion of pestilence, and I felt goosebumps rise on my flesh, though whether from fright or pleasure I couldn't tell.

A little before Miss Hagar's place, a lane turned off in the other direction, between two rows of cedars. This was Mr. Corcoran's lane. It led up to the old brick house where he had lived in lonely hostility and where the boy had shot him.

"What a place for a murder!" I said.

Soames slowed down. "Let's go up and have a look."

"Up to the house?"

"Yeah!"

"There's nothing to hurt us—come on!"

He swung around the mailbox into the thick cemetery gloom of the cedars. The small car bounced over the rough road. At last the high brick house appeared in the headlights, blind-windowed, secret and forbidding. We sat there for a moment without talking. The cedars whispered around us. Except for that sound and the small isolated throb of the motor, the silence was intense. In the dark night the crazed boy had come, furtive and deadly. I thought of a door opening noiselessly, a face at the window—

"Let's get out of here!" said Soames.

We skittered down the lane and up the road toward Miss Hagar's. The thought of her stolid calm was reassuring.

"I'll only be a minute," I said as we reached the house. Taking the freezer, I walked up to the door and knocked. There was no answer. Since the lamp was burning I assumed she must be awake, and knocked again.

"Who is it?" a small voice said.

"It's me."

"Who?"

"Mary Jo—Mrs. Soames's girl."

"Oh! I'm comin'." There was a scraping sound, like the moving of heavy furniture. A bolt slid, and Miss Hagar stood in the doorway. A blast of heat thrust outward into the darkness. "My gracious, I didn't have any idy who it could be!"

"I'm sorry, Miss Hagar—did I wake you up?"

"I was just dozin'. Come in, come in!"

"I can't stay. We just ran up to bring you some ice cream."

"Thanky. This'll taste good, a night like this. Come in; I'll scrape it out in a dish."

"Oh, don't worry about that."

"Don't you want to wait for the freezer?"

"We can pick it up another time."

"Come in awhile, anyhow," she urged.

"It's late, I think we'll run along."

"Oh, stay—can't you?" Her hand reached out, as if to pull me in, and as she stepped down onto the doorstone, I saw into the room. A heavy chest sat slantwise to the door, and the windows were sealed with paper. Against the bed stood a hatchet. Miss Hagar was afraid! "Well—I guess I can stay a few minutes," I said.

"Here—set down in the rocker—pull it up to the door."

The heat in the little room was sickening. I felt myself turn green and mossy like a mullein leaf. Mopping my face, I made conversation, while Miss Hagar sat on the edge of the bed and ate right out of the freezer, gulping the coolness. As I talked, I thought of her lying through the lonely night in this airless house, listening for the furtive sound at the window, the deadly footfall. And I thought of our house on the other hill—wide open, breeze in the curtains, laughter sounding in all the rooms, and lamplight spilling into the yard to make a moat of cheer and safety.

"Miss Hagar, why don't you come home with us and spend the night?"

The little brown face peered wistfully over the ice cream freezer, and I saw her waver.

"Thanky just the same," she said. "But you folks like to be by yourselves, and it's right that you should be." She said it without a trace of reproach.

After a while, Soames and I drove home without her.

"You go right back up and get her," said my mother. "And this time, don't take no argument."

Back we went and brought Miss Hagar home with us. We put her to bed on the old spring cot in the dining room. The rest of us tried to sleep upstairs. But even in our big open house, it was hot that night. Not a breath of air. Before long we were all up, changing beds, shifting around like corn in a popper. Soames decamped to the front porch with a quilt. Jessica and I set up two army cots in the yard. Mama padded around with a flashlight, like some busy household ghost, trying to make us all comfortable. By that time, a melted yellow moon had come up and there was thunder in the distance.

An hour later a wind began to blow and the rain came. The whole household rose up again and rushed around in the dark, closing windows and banging things. Soames ran out and drove my car into the corncrib. Mama sent Dad to put the washtub under the drain. The rain crashed against the house and the air turned cold. Since everyone was wide awake, we lighted the lamps and made hot cocoa.

"Goddamighty!" said Miss Hagar, grinning over her cup. "If this ain't a sight on earth!"

After a while my father went out to the back yard. "It's passing over," he called. "Mighty pretty out here now." I went out and stood beside him, barefooted in the wet grass. The rain had blown east, rolling the clouds in a heap beyond the orchard. Over the woods in the west, the moon hung white and cool, washed clean by the rain. Suddenly my father said, "Look, daughter!" and pointed to the east. There against the clouds stood a rainbow. It was pure white.

It was almost three in the morning, yet there was the ghost of a rainbow, arched over the woods. Under that soaring image of moonlight, the farm lay like a little crèche edged in silver. The white feathers of roosting chickens glimmered in the curved wet leaves of the peach tree. The dripping fence glittered. The new shingles made a silvery patch on the dark heap of the barn.

We called to the others to come out and stood hugging our arms in the cold air. My mother wore a white shawl over her head. My father shelled an ear of white corn, to keep busy, and the kernels glistened, dropping into a silver pan. For a long time nobody spoke. Behind us the wind rummaged among the leaves of the moonflower vine.

"Tomorrow will be a fine day," my father said presently.

One by one the others went back to the house. Only my father and I were left, watching the moonbow. "Did you ever see one before?" I asked him.

"Never before. We are privileged," he said.

34

When the last glimmer dissolved in the black air, we went inside.

That night I dreamed that my father died and we buried him in the vegetable garden. The dream woke me, and I lay for a while recounting it to myself. It seemed most natural to bury him, not under formal sod or a marble block, but among the carrots and onions, with his feet in the strawberry bed. It was a droll sweet thing, like some long-cherished family nonsense. As the garden reverted to its natural state, so would he, both of them changing slowly into pepper grass, mullein, and wild primrose. He would be at home there among familiar things; he would sleep peacefully.

3

"Girls?" Our father's schoolbell voice clanged at the bottom of the stairs. "It's late—better get up!"

"The gospel according to Matthew," said Jessica, rolling out of bed. We ran to the stairway to say good morning.

"I'm loaded for bees—got the ax and washtub in the car. If you're going to cut a bee tree with me, you'd better come on!"

"We'll hurry."

"It's a beautiful morning," he called as a parting shot.

I ran to the window and looked out. It was the prettiest morning I ever saw, and I've seen a lot of pretty ones in my day. I get up looking for them. We threw on our clothes, shivering in the delicious chill, and hurried downstairs. The kitchen was empty, but a fire mumbled in the woodstove and the room smelled of fresh biscuits. Sunlight bounced off the silverware and danced on the ceiling. Mama was outside, tidying up the moonflower vine. With a brisk unsentimental hand she stripped off the old yellowed blossoms.

"Have to get these out of the way, to make room for the new ones tonight. Gracious, baby, you'd ought to have a dress on. Aren't your legs cold in them little short pants?"

"Yes!" I said. "I like it." I stuck a marigold in her hair and ran down the path to the john.

While we were eating breakfast, Mama dug out some old lace curtains for us to wrap around our heads. Protection from the bees, she said. About that time, Soames came in and announced that the barn roof was shingled.

"You finished!" Leonie jumped up and threw her arms around him. "You're a good boy! Now aren't you proud? Doesn't it give you a good feeling to finish something? Next time you start a job, you just remember this wonderful feeling of satisfaction!"

"I don't know why you're makin' such a fuss," said Mama. "I knew he'd finish it—he said he would."

"Yes, but he doesn't always—"

"Well, he did this time. You girls hurry up now and wash the dishes. Soames honey, bring Grandma the picnic basket out of the smokehouse. Let's get started."

"I think I'll make cookies!" said Leonie.

Mama, Jessica, Soames and I turned on her of one accord. "Now?"

"A reward for Soames!" said Leonie.

"Aw, Mother!" he said.

"Some of those little ginger cookies you're so crazy about."

"Ain't it a little late?" said Mama.

"It won't take but a minute."

Mama looked at her and glanced over at us and kind of smiled. "Well, go ahead. We're not in that much of a hurry, I guess."

"Oh, good! I'll have 'em done in two shakes."

Jessica looked at me and winked. "Let's paper the kitchen before we go."

"And piece a quilt!" I said.

"It won't take but a minute."

Leonie looked around with a hurt innocent face.

"We're teasing you, hon." Jessica gave her a little hug. "You go ahead with your cookies. We'll help you."

We banged around the kitchen with rolling pins and pans, and Jessica put on a lace curtain and sang "Here comes the bride." We were making so much noise we hardly noticed that the dog was barking his head off.

"Now what's the matter with him?" Jessica said, glancing out the window. "Oh, shit!"

"Jessica!" said Mama.

"Here comes the preacher!"

"Oh my goodness, he'll stay all morning!"

"Run and hide—he'll think we're gone!"

We ran for the front room, pulling Mama with us. "We hadn't ought to do this," she protested.

"Sh!"

"It ain't right."

But she stood there as the dog barked himself into a frenzy and the preacher came up, paying him compliments in a bold voice. He knocked at the back door, waited a moment, and knocked again. "Good dog," he said. The barking tapered off and the dog's tail beat a tattoo against the house.

"Brother Soames?" called the preacher. There was a long wait. "Anybody home?"

"We ought to let him in," Mama whispered.

There was another knock, a long wait, and a halfhearted tap. The preacher went down the steps. "Git," he said mildly to the dog.

"Poor little thing," Mama said. "It's like Jesus knockin' at the gate and won't nobody answer. I'm going to let him in." And she marched off to the kitchen. "Hoo-hoo?" she called. "Oh, Brother Mosely! I *thought* I heard somebody."

"Good morning, good morning! I didn't think nobody was home."

"We were all in the front," Mama said. It would not be her fault if he thought she meant the front yard. "Can't you come in for a minute?"

"Or an hour or two," Jessica whispered.

"Thank you," the preacher said. "I hope I caught your good husband at home."

"Yes, he's around here somewhere. Come on in here where it's cooler." We made a dash for the front door, but she caught us as we hit the porch. "Oh, come in, girls," she said, as if we had been outside the whole time. "Here's Brother Mosely—you remember Brother Mosely."

We filed back in and shook hands. The preacher, a meager young man, sway-backed in the pride of his calling, blessed each of us in turn. "Glad to see you again, God bless you, mighty pleased to see you." He passed a few witticisms on female charm and, having dispatched that duty, arranged his features in a solemn look.

"Well, I've come on a sorrowful mission," he said, and there was a weighty pause. "Sad news, I'm afraid. Brother Corcoran has gone to his long home."

"Ah!" said Mama, putting her hand to her cheek.

"He's at rest now. His sufferings are over. The boy's in jail in Clinton."

"Poor boy. Papa?" she called, seeing my father pass the window. "Mr. Corcoran's dead."

"Is that right!" Dad came in with an ear of corn in his hand. "Good morning, Brother Mosely."

"God bless you, Brother," said the preacher.

"When did it happen?"

"Yesterday afternoon, late. I was with him at the time."

"I'm glad the old fellow didn't die alone."

"I've been going over to pray with him every day," said the preacher. "I hope I give him some help."

"I'm sure you did," said my father.

"Brother Corcoran wasn't much on church."

"I'm afraid not. Don't know what church he rightly belonged to."

"No, but he ought to have a funeral like anybody else, and I'm aimin' to preach him one."

"Yes, we must give the old soul a Christian burial. I presume we'll have to arrange for a plot."

"No," said the preacher, "he already had one, I found out. Down by Cole Camp."

"Clear down there!"

"Yes, he come from down there, and we'll take him back. But I thought the services ought to be at Renfro, so what friends he had could come. Won't be many there, I don't reckon."

"Not many."

"Just you folks and a few of the neighbors. I'm dependin' on you for the music."

"Yes, I'll arrange for a choir. When are you planning to have the funeral?"

"About three-thirty," said the preacher.

There was dead silence.

"Three-*thirty*," said my father.

"The body's comin' in on the three o'clock train."

"To*day*?"

"There didn't seem no reason to keep him."

My father and mother looked at each other. They had tried so hard to protect this day. Right or wrong, they had held out against neighbors and duty, friendship and pity. But there was no holding out against death. My father turned back to the preacher.

"I'll be there," he said.

"We'll come," said my mother.

"Fine," said the preacher. "I knew I could count on you folks. I must run on now and get somebody for pallbearers. Shall we have a prayer?"

We bowed our heads, and I counted backwards from a hundred. ". . . and keep us in Thy way, O Lord. Help us to walk in the path of righteousness for the sake of Him who give His life for us . . ." Finally the young preacher pronounced a solemn Amen and picked up his hat.

"Oh, shoot," said Mama, as he went through the gate. "It's such a pretty day!"

"Yes," Dad sighed.

"And buried away down at Cole Camp! We won't even get home in time for the moonflowers!" She looked wistfully at the picnic basket. "I reckon we wouldn't just have to go—it ain't like he was a real close friend."

"No, but there won't be a handful, counting us. I'd feel bad if we weren't there."

"I guess I would, too." Mama sighed. "Well, no use brooding about it. You get out your suit, Papa; I better press the pants. And you children—" She turned to us in defiant tenderness. "You children don't hardly know him at all. You go on with your picnic. You don't have to go to no funeral on your last day home."

"That's right," said Dad. "The moonflowers will open before we get back. You stay here and have a good time."

My sisters and Soames and I glanced at each other. It would be lovely in the woods today, and twenty buds hung on the moonflower vine, ready to bloom.

"Nope," said Jessica, "it wouldn't be fair. If you have to go to a funeral, we're going with you."

So there went the picnic. We put away the basket and pinned up our hair and rushed about pressing dresses. Somewhere along in there, Leonie finished her cookies.

"One of you run up and tell Miss Hagar," Mama said. "She'll want to go, sure, and I reckon we can all squeeze in the car."

"Soames and I can go in mine," I said.

Mama glanced out at the red sports car. "Well, I don't know—won't it look a little out of place at a funeral?"

"Take it!" said Jessica. "It'll jazz up the procession. Try to get right behind the hearse."

"Oh hush, Jessica, I'm tryin' to be serious. I guess you'll have to take it, Mary Jo. But wear something on your head!"

"Like what?" I said.

"Like a hat. You've got a hat, ain't you?"

"Not with me. I didn't bring one." None of us did.

"Well, you can't go to a funeral without a hat."

"Everybody else around here does."

"I don't care, it don't look nice. Run upstairs and get that box on the chifferobe. You'll just have to wear one of mine."

I brought down the box and we tried on the contents—summer hats, winter hats, old ones and new.

"Maybe I could get by with this one." Leonie scowled at herself in an Empress Eugenie.

"It's moulting," said Jessica. "You'll have to take off the feather. This one doesn't look bad on me."

"You've got it on backwards," said Mama.

"It looks better that way."

"Then wear it backwards. But hurry up, all of you. And stop acting so silly!"

By a quarter till three we were ready to go. Jessica and Leonie and I put on Mama's hats and, feeling like the Three Weird Sisters, marched out to the cars.

"You're kidding!" said Soames.

"I didn't hardly reckonize you," said Miss Hagar.

"You look sweet," said Mama.

"All right, all right, come on," said my father, "it's getting late. Soames, you stay behind me." He didn't want Soames hotrodding on the way to a funeral. Soames and I grinned at each other as I climbed in beside him. Dad drove off sedately, and as sedately as we could, we followed. We crept up the hill past the Old Chimney Place. Doves, sitting sweet and stupid in the middle of the road, barely bothered to get out of the way. The little car chugged and lurched, unaccustomed to the petty pace.

"I'll never get out of second!" Soames complained.

"Ho hum," I agreed, settling back.

The road to Renfro wound in and out, past Latham's broomcorn patch; smack through the middle of Barrow's property, between house and barn; past Bitterwater School, where my father used to teach; across a bridge spanning Little Tebo. The planks clattered alarmingly, loose as ever. It was all so familiar. In all those years nothing had changed but the names on some of the mailboxes. Now that I thought about it, I doubted that I had changed much either. I had tried; I had run away as far as I could. Yet here I was on the same old road. And it didn't make much difference that I rode now in my own car, my bright symbol. I was still following my father, keeping the pace he set.

"Here comes your dog, Aunt Jo!" Soames's voice brought me out of my reverie.

I looked over my shoulder. Here came the hound, ears in the air, tongue trailing like a banner. He had followed us half the way to town.

We stopped and Soames threw a rock, but he might as well have saved the effort. The dog paid no attention. Wild with joy, he caught up with us, bounded into my lap and covered my face with kisses. This was the story of my life. I was the beloved of all things lost, strayed, misfit, and unwanted. They followed me, like my background. I couldn't lose either one.

"What'll we do?" I said, pushing the dog out.

"Take him with us," said Soames.

He dumped the dog back in my lap, climbed under the wheel, and took off for town like a bat out of hell. We didn't slow down till we hit the square.

"Watch it, Jackson!" Soames slammed on the brakes, missing a pickup truck by inches. "Hey, I thought we were going to be the only ones here."

We stared up the street. All the way to the Methodist Church, the street was parked solid. There were cars clear around the square. Everyone in the county, it seemed, had turned out for the funeral. We had forgotten that old Mr. Corcoran had not died a natural death. He was murdered, and murder had made him famous. The churchyard was jammed with people, children ran back and forth. Except for the presence of the hearse, it looked like a basket dinner. Death is always a social occasion, and this one was a jubilee.

Soames pulled in beside Dad's car and I tried to hide the dog.

"Good *night!*" said Jessica, climbing out. "We could have stayed home and never been missed."

"Yes," said my mother, "but most of these folks just come out of curiosity. That ain't the right way. Can't you children park that car somewhere out of sight— My land! What are you doing with that dog!"

We backed up and drove around behind the church, squeezing in close to the wall. Soames tied the dog to the car with his necktie. We couldn't find anything else.

The church was crowded by the time we got in. My father went up to the choirloft, Leonie to the piano. The rest of us had to sit in the front pew, staring into the casket. Old Mr. Corcoran lay a few feet away, stern and disapproving against the cheap satin, his long bristly nose pointed upward in contempt.

I glanced around. "Where's Soames?"

"I don't know," Jessica said. "Oh, there he is, in the choir!"

"Did Leonie make him go?"

"I don't think so."

"Brothers and Sisters—" The preacher stood at the pulpit surveying with solemn pleasure a crowd such as he'd never drawn in a month of Sundays. "Brothers and Sisters, rise with me as we pray."

The congregation creaked to its feet. From the back row, a child's voice piped up. "I want to see the man!" She was noisily shushed, and the prayer began.

I counted backwards from a hundred, all the way to zero, and Brother Mosely was still invoking the Lord. Over and over, his earnest voice soared in thunderous tremolo and descended in a minor key. I shifted my weight. My sunburn itched, and one ear hurt where Mama's hat rubbed against it. I sighed discreetly, longing for the golden weather outside. In all this crowd, who would have missed us? But my mother was right. Though many came here in celebration, few came to mourn. And that was sad, for here lay a man who must have found life good at one time or another, and felt joy and sorrow like all the rest of us. Yet there was no one to miss him, no one at all, except Brother Mosely and my parents. They would miss him a little, not because he had done much for them, but because they had done a little for him.

". . . we ask it in Thy name, Amen."

We gratefully sat down. At a signal from my father, the choir rose again, Leonie played an introduction, and they began to sing.

"Abide with me: fast falls the eventide."

The old hymn wavered through the church, the ill-assorted voices marshaled into line by my father's cracked, authoritative bass.

"The darkness deepens; Lord, with me abide:
When other helpers fail and comforts flee—"

They had gone about that far when the dog raised his voice. Tied in the car and left behind, he was moved to self-pity by the music and gave expression in a long lugubrious howl. The preacher glanced up in dismay. A titter ran through the church. Beside me,

Jessica made a choking noise and poked me with her elbow. On the other side, my mother twitched impatiently, drawing herself up. She knew whose dog it was, and there wasn't a thing she could do about him without letting everyone else know, too.

The mournful howls continued. Succumbing to competition, the choir began to falter. One by one they choked up, ducked their heads, and stopped singing, till only my father and Soames were left. Dad's face was livid. He stumbled over the words, lost his place, and started again, and at last, floundering hopelessly, gave up. Soames sang on alone.

At first it was hard to hear him, the church was so sibilant with laughter. But he stood there, young and steadfast and unperturbed, looking like one of those angels of the Lord in ecclesiastic art, tall and fair, masculine and guileless, and his easy voice poured over the crowd like a benediction. Little by little they grew quiet. The dog was shamed to silence. As the last echoes of the hymn died away, the only sound was the twittering of sparrows in the yard. Soames stood for a moment motionless. Then he turned his head and smiled at Leonie, as if there were no other in the church but her.

Suddenly it seemed to me that I looked back from a great distance on that smile and saw it all again—the smile and the day, the whole sunny, sad, funny, wonderful day, and all the days that we had spent here together. What was I going to do when such days came no more? There could not be many; for we were a family growing old. And how would I learn to live without these people? I who needed them so little that I could stay away all year —what should I do without them?

I looked at them—my mother, still a tyrant, with her broom and her fruit jars; my father, softened by age but only as a stone is softened by its moss; Leonie, running counterclockwise to the world; funny old Jessica with Mama's hat on backwards—and I knew I liked them better than anyone else alive. Then I looked at Mr. Corcoran and began to cry.

The service went on for more than an hour. But at last it was over. The undertaker wheeled the casket into the vestibule, and the old man lay there in state, waiting the long file of the curious, who had come to gaze pop-eyed on the fact of murder.

We were the last ones out. Like relatives we filed out slowly and stood in an indecisive huddle as the undertaker, with a brisk "Okay?" to my father, snapped the lid shut and packed the last of Mr. Corcoran off to eternity.

The worn stones of the church lay in shadow now. It was after five. Around the square and up and down the streets, engines sputtered.

I turned to my father. "Do we *have* to go to the cemetery?"

He hesitated. Cole Camp was miles away. "I just can't think of the old soul lowered into his grave without somebody there."

As he spoke, the hearse crawled forward, followed by the preacher's Ford. Another car fell into line, followed by another and another. As the hearse turned onto the highway, it was followed by a train reaching half around the square.

"Well," said my father, "if all of them are going—"

My mother looked at him thoughtfully. "If you think it would be all right, if we hurried, we could still get home in time—"

We heard no more. Our solemnity near the breaking point, we started down the steps. By the time we reached the cars, we were what you might call running. Soames and I took off first. As we turned onto the country road, he rose up in the seat and gave a Comanche yell.

Over the hills we went, hellbent for leather, my father right behind; across the bridge, past Bitterwater, through Barrow's farm, and down the hill, around the corner, up our lane, into our barn-lot—dust flying, hens squawking, all of us shouting, and the first moonflower just beginning to bloom.

"We made it!" my mother cried.

I'll remember it the rest of my life.

Jessica

1

To his daughters as they grew up, Matthew Soames was God and the weather. He was omnipotent and he was everywhere—at home, at school, at church. There was no place they could go where the dominating spirit was not that of their father. And, like rain or shine, his moods conditioned all they did.

With other people around, he was pleasant as could be, full of laughter and witticisms and conversation marvelous to hear. Ladies often said to them, "Your father is just the nicest man!" The girls could hardly help observing that he turned his sunny side to his public and clouded up at home. There, he was often preoccupied and short-spoken, indifferent to his children except to command or reprove. "Daughter," he called each of them indiscriminately; it was a little more authoritative than the given name, which might not occur to him at the moment anyway.

"Papa's nicer to other people than he is to us," Leonie once said.

"Yes, sometimes he is, honey," said her mother. "But he's got to be. Your Papa's an important man in the community. That's the way he's got to act."

His importance might have been a comfort to the girls if it

47

hadn't been such a nuisance. There were so many things they were not allowed to do "because it wouldn't look well." And they couldn't get out of his sight and do them, because he was everywhere. For the most part, they resigned themselves to the situation and did as Papa said. The purpose in life, he said, was to work. "*Laborare est orare*," he said; and work meant to study your lessons and help Mama.

They had many good times in between. Relatives came often to visit. On the farm they could play in the woods and go fishing. When they moved to town they had girl chums and Sunday School parties. They had no toys to speak of (one doll, handed down from one to the other); but living as they did a good deal out-of-doors, they didn't need such props. They played with what they had or found or made up and enjoyed themselves hugely. But very early they understood that playing was somewhat suspect, allowed through indulgence, a trivial pastime soon outgrown, and only about twice removed from sin. Pleasure was only once-removed. The girls grew up before they realized that pleasure was not an ugly word. In their father's vocabulary it meant joyrides, dancing, card games, cigarettes, and other things too dreadful to define.

Recreation, however, was honorable. Their father spoke of it with respect. It was an abstraction, smacking of education, and good for you, like boiled turnip tops. The girls weren't sure just when they were having recreation. But they knew when they had fun. And the most fun was when Papa looked up from his work, every month or so, and saw that they were there. Then, sitting around the heating stove on a winter evening, they might pop corn and listen to stories of his boyhood. ("My-O, did we work when we were kids! Pa used to get us up at four-thirty in the morning to go shuck corn!") Sometimes they sang together, with Leonie playing the piano. Their father called it recreation, but they enjoyed it just the same.

They cherished these moments like little gifts. Such largess was more than their due. Papa was not obliged to do them this favor. Papa was *busy*. He had papers to grade and lessons to plan. He had meetings to attend and a thousand and one things to write off for: library books, maps, chalk, and music for the Glee Club. Or he had choir practice at the church, a deacons' meeting, and his class to teach. He had to milk the cow and spade the garden, put up a heating stove or take it down, clean the henhouse or a sparkplug, and patch a tire on the Model T. On Saturday, like as not, he had to drive to Clarkstown to see the County Superintendent, or down to the farm to see why the tenants hadn't paid the rent.

His excessive busy-ness took precedence over anything else and often interrupted other plans—such as the time they'd planned to surprise him on his birthday. This was after they had moved to town and learned about birthday parties. They had baked him a cake and Mama let them buy candles. She even let them decorate the dining room. They had spent hours in secret, coloring strips of paper with their Crayolas and pasting them together in interlocking rings. That afternoon they ran home from school and strung them around the room. They got out the best tablecloth, set the table just so, and put the cake in the middle. Everything looked fine. They could hardly wait for Papa to get there. About five o'clock the telephone rang. Papa's teachers had just sprung a surprise on him at school—a covered-dish supper spread out in the study hall, with a great big cake. He wouldn't be home for supper.

Mama explained that the girls had also planned a little surprise. But of course Papa couldn't disappoint his teachers. Jessica and Mathy cried, and Leonie got stomping mad. Mama finally had to bawl her out. "We'll surprise him tomorrow night," she said. So they put the cake away and took down the decorations, and the next night they tried again. But it didn't work. In the middle of supper, Mathy, who was seven years old and too big to cry, burst into tears and smashed her fist right into the birthday cake. Papa lectured her about losing her temper and wanting her own way all the time. She finally shut up, and they all tried to eat the cake anyway, but they couldn't.

That night Mama came upstairs and gave them a good talking-to. She was nice about it, but she made them go and tell Papa good night and tell him they were sorry. It nearly choked them, but they did it. Papa forgave them, as the Heavenly Father does.

In such manner they learned to accept him as one accepts the weather. Though they might complain of him sometimes, there wasn't much they could do about it, or expected to do. He was threat and authority, the no-sayer, the stern enigma. But their mother had taught them their father like a creed, and their belief in him was profound.

As for Matthew, he loved his children, but in an abstracted way, with perhaps a little less direct concern than for calves or baby chicks. Once they reached school age, he tended to forget they were his. Five days a week they blended into a group of other children whose esteem was more important. Not to seem partial to his own, he treated them with elaborate objectivity.

This was partly in self-defense. For if they could never escape from him, neither could he escape from them. In all his years of teaching, there was hardly a time when he could stand up in a classroom without confronting one or more of his own daughters. The schoolroom clothed him in authority, transformed him nobly each morning. Yet always before him was a little face that had seen him a few hours earlier in his nightshirt, or coming in from the barn in his dirty coat, smelling of milk and manure. Being a public figure and a father too was troublesome.

But this was a minor flaw in his life. Though he often longed for wider horizons, travel, greater knowledge, more time to achieve his goals (he had started late), he was for the most part intensely happy. He loved his work. A schoolhouse was his principality. All he did therein was meat and drink to him and "fire and horse and health and holiday," as Emerson put it, and he would not have changed places with anyone in the world.

However, "a bell and a plough have each their uses," and Matthew loved a school only a little more than a farm. He had held on to the place near Renfro—an expensive proposition, as taxes were high and tenants not easy to come by, especially during the war, when nearly everybody deserted to the city. He had no time to work the place himself; when he wasn't teaching he was attending summer school. Some years a neighboring farmer put in the crops for shares; some years the place lay fallow; and all years it demanded upkeep, like an expensive mistress.

Sometimes he had to be almost secretive about the attentions he paid it. For, though Callie loved the place as he did, she couldn't help fussing a little. "You ought to buy a new overcoat," she would tell him. "You look awful shabby to be the superintendent of schools." Or, "Now, I don't care—Jessica's going to graduate in a new dress. If the farm don't get that new fence this year, it'll just have to wait!" Somehow, Jessica had her dress and the farm had its fence. But it was touch-and-go all the time, and Matthew worked like a trooper.

2

One spring soon after the war, the house they rented in Shawano was sold from under them. The new owner demanded immediate possession. There were only two other rentals in town—the big Cooper place, which was too highfalutin and just plain too high, and a humbler house which would not be empty till fall. Matthew was seized by a lovely notion. He was weary to death of books and blackboards. Why not, he said to the family, move down to the farm for the summer?

His two oldest daughters had ninety reasons between them why they shouldn't go. Leonie, an elegant young lady of sixteen, hated to leave her girl chums and her piano teacher. Jessica, who was eighteen and about to graduate, wanted to go to Clarkstown to summer school. Her best friend was going, and they wanted to be roommates and take teacher's training, learn to play tennis, and go to ice-cream parlors and picture shows. Her father explained that he couldn't afford to send her; the farm needed new fences and he'd have to buy or rent a team for the summer—that sort of thing. Anyway, her mother said, she had to go along and help. "Mama's not as strong as she once was." (Callie was not quite forty and as tough and limber as a hickory sapling. But being limber, she bent easily. When she bowed with the weight of one of her sick spells, they all trembled with fear that she would never straighten. Since the age of thirty she had hinted that death was around the corner.)

Jessica's real reason for wanting to stay in town was one she could not reveal. She had discovered boys. A late discovery, since Matthew and Callie guarded their daughters like farmers guarding prize pumpkins. The girls never went on dates. Jessica had tried it once, in a tentative way. A boy walked home with her from a party at the schoolhouse. Matthew saw them leave the building, but acknowledging reluctantly the facts of life, he let them go. Unfortunately, he arrived home before they did, by a margin of some ten minutes. He was waiting at the door. He curdled the air with his anger, embarrassed Jessica to death, and scared the boy out of his adolescent wits. Since the word quickly got around, any

51

boy in school who had even looked at "Prof's" daughters no longer dared to.

But there came a night in spring, during senior play practice, when a boy named Marvin, more reckless than most and possibly on a dare, caught Jessica in the dark by the water cooler and kissed her. She was terrified—until she made quite sure that her father knew nothing of it. She promptly fell in love. Hopelessly. There wasn't a thing she could do except look at Marvin. But even that was a comfort. Down in the country she wouldn't even see him on Sunday!

Her pleas and Leonie's fell on deaf ears. Papa either scolded or teased them.

"Why, you girls need to hoe some corn!" he said one evening. "You need to get up at four in the morning and milk the cows!" He pulled Jessica down on his knees, though she was too long-legged for lapsitting. "I'll let you slop the hogs this summer!"

"Oh, Papa!" she said, exasperated. She laughed because he expected her to. She was a tall slim girl with a face as clean and plain and virtuous as a cake of soap. Her hair hung down her back, soft-brown and shiny, held back by a big bow-ribbon. When she did it up, like other girls, Mama and Papa said she looked too old. She didn't care. She didn't like to do it up anyway; it made her feel too formal.

Matthew squeezed her face between his thumb and finger. "You'll have to watch out about that nose this summer. We may have to fix up a little awning to protect it from the sun."

"Oh now, Papa! It's not that big." Jessica hid her face on his shoulder. Her high thin nose gave her a sort of classic beauty, but no one had ever told her so. They only teased her, especially her father, who felt he had a right to tease her, since it was his nose.

He looked down at the little girl sitting on the floor. "Now Mathy's anxious to go to the farm. Aren't you, girlie?"

The little girl looked up with bright solemn black eyes. "I love the farm. I can't wait to get back."

"What are you doing there?" said Matthew.

"Pressing a four-leaf clover."

"I don't think the Bible is any place for that."

"It's the biggest book I could find."

"Use one of those picture books," said Callie, glancing up from her mending.

"All right." Mathy carefully lifted her clover leaf and carried it to the bookcase, where the bottom shelf was filled with the *Picture*

Index of Mythology and World Literature in twelve volumes. Matthew had bought it from a traveling salesman who, like all born salesmen, was part evangelist, part bully. Matthew simply hadn't the courage to say no. To himself and to Callie he argued that the books would be educational for the girls. The girls found them quaint and uproarious.

Mathy pulled out Volume One and turned to some engraver's version of Andromeda, fat and nude, chained to the rock. "I'll put this on her like a fig leaf," she said, and fixed the leaf strategically in place.

"Where did you find out about fig leaves?" said Callie.

"I don't know."

Callie glanced at Matthew with a shrug. They never knew what Mathy would pick up or where. She read a good deal. Sometimes she read the same book over and over. There was one called *The Tree-Dwellers*, which she found on the third-grade shelf, a story of a little boy in the time of the woolly mammoth. Mathy monopolized the book till at last the teacher spoke to Matthew about it. Shortly thereafter the book disappeared. Matthew found it one rainy morning in one of his rubber boots. Mathy was given a lecture on the Eighth Commandment and made to stay indoors all Sunday afternoon. She returned the book next morning and made her apology to the teacher. Within a few weeks, the entire text of *The Tree-Dwellers* appeared on the walls of her room. She had copied it in longhand, word for word, in her Big Chief tablet. Matthew spoke to her sternly, but the pages stayed on the wall. He had a feeling he had lost the round.

Mathy put the big picture book back on the shelf and climbed into Jessica's lap, so that both of them were sitting on Matthew. "Papa, when we move to the farm, can I ride down on the furniture wagon?"

Matthew laughed. "You can if you *may*."

"*May* I ride down on the furniture wagon?"

"We'll have to ask Mama about that."

"Mama, may I?" Mathy flung herself across Callie's lap.

"Oh, my goodness!" Callie said, picking her off like a piece of lint. "You'll fall off the wagon and break your neck."

"No, I won't. I'll be careful."

"I can't let you ride down there like that—just you and them men that moves us."

"Well, why can't Jessica and Leonie ride on the wagon, too?"

Leonie turned around from the piano, where she was practicing her new piece. "I don't *want* to ride on the wagon."

"Why not?"

"It's undignified."

"I think it would be kinda fun," Jessica said.

Callie said, "Oh, honey, you're too big a girl to do things like that."

"Why? What's wrong with riding in a wagon?"

"It don't seem ladylike."

Jessica slid off Matthew's lap. "I don't want to be a lady. Ladies can't have any fun."

Leonie spoke up again. "Ladies don't climb trees, if that's what you mean. And they don't hold a croquet mallet between their legs when they shoot, either!"

"It's easier that way," said Jessica. "I can't hit the ball when I hold the mallet way over to one side."

"Yes, and you spraddled out the other day, shooting between your legs, and tore the hem of your dress!"

"I know it. I already told Mama."

Callie said placidly, "I don't know why you can't keep your clothes neat, like Leonie. Leonie, stop holdin' your mouth like that. Makes you look prissy."

Callie sighed to herself. In spite of her efforts, Jessica had not quite domesticated. She was a good girl, certainly. She did everything she was told, and she didn't stop to argue with you as Leonie so often did. But there was just something about her that Callie couldn't quite manage. Jessica was good help around the house; but she would rather dig potatoes than peel them, or clean the henhouse rather than the house. Leonie, for all her questioning and back talk (because Leonie always knew better than you did), practiced her piano lesson, finished her embroidery work, and had some dignity. But the minute you turned your back on Jessica, she was reading a story, or out in the barnloft with Mathy, sliding down the hay. And now she wanted to ride on the wagon, like a tomboy.

"Well," Leonie said, "I'm going to ride down in the Ford—if we have to go." She gave Matthew a black look, which escaped him, since he had gone back to grading papers. "You and Mathy just go ahead and ride on the wagon if you want to."

"I haven't said they could yet," said Callie.

But when the time came, in mid-May, she relented. The drayman said he didn't mind, and he was one of the church members.

It was decided that Mathy could ride on the wagon if Jessica went along.

"Now don't fall off," Callie cautioned, "and keep your dresses down. We'll catch up with you before long. Mathy, here's your sunbonnet."

"I don't want to wear it, Mama."

"You put it on, now. You're already burnt till you're plumb black."

"Oh, all right." Mathy pulled the bonnet over her head and flung herself at her mother in a vehemence of farewell. "Goodbye, Mama darling!"

"Mercy, honey, be careful! You nearly knocked Mama down."

Jessica stood by the wagon wistfully gazing up the street. She was praying that Marvin would appear, wild-eyed with grief, running to press a rose into her hand. For this she would endure the parental wrath. As there was no sign of him, she climbed in with a sigh. But once she was settled on the piano stool, and Mathy was ensconced in a dresser drawer, she began to giggle with excitement. As the wagon drove away, they screamed and clung to the sides and waved at Leonie till she was out of sight. Leonie rode down, ladylike, with her mother and father in the secondhand Ford, wearing her gloves and her second-best hat.

3

It had been five years since Callie lived on the farm. She was back in her element, airing the house, scrubbing woodwork, gardening and canning. And with no school to distract them, her daughters were all hers. How she reveled in their presence—agile, obedient little girls running in and out of the house, down to the garden, into the chicken yard, out to the hayloft, in from the orchard, down to the creek, in a very flurry of coming and going, with their hands full of berries and eggs and fish and flowers. Callie made the honey, but she needed her drones.

No less than the days she loved the evenings, when the family sat on the front porch and night sounds wove a soft web around them. Sometimes they only visited. Sometimes they sang, their voices spread sweetly on the darkness, Leonie's soprano, Jessica's soft alto, Mathy's thin little husky tones, guided along by Matthew's unobtrusive bass. He lay on his back those evenings, relaxed and jolly, with no studies to pull him away.

Sometimes when they rose to go in, they would find that Mathy had slipped off. Then they must light the lantern and go looking for her, down through the orchard, across to the Old Chimney Place. She was never far away. But these dark excursions troubled and perplexed them. Long ago the child had begun to wander in the night, unafraid, and not all their protests or punishments had cured her. As she grew older, and especially in town, she had seemed to outgrow the habit. But now that they were on the farm again, it recurred, compelling her into the dark. The nights seemed a world of her own, which she had found ready-made and waiting. They had the uneasy feeling that in that element she took on another shape, wore fur, or dissolved into mist. But they would find her, a solid familiar shape, merely walking about or perched in a tree fork, singing to herself. Then would come the lectures and the scoldings and repeated promises, before they could settle down again.

In spite of these occurrences, Callie found the summer complete. Sometimes it seemed to her that she could ask for nothing more than this—the long busy days and the warm sweet nights, when the smell of honeysuckle filled the air and her husband sang on the porch with their daughters.

Early in the season, Matthew had planted a lettuce bed in the woods, on a spot where he had once burned a pile of brushwood. The soil, enriched by this pure compost, yielded an enormous crop. Callie sent the girls down every day or two to gather a salad. On an afternoon late in June, the three of them set out for the timber, Jessica carrying a market basket for the lettuce and Leonie a tin bucket, in case they found some ripe blackberries. All three of them wore their bonnets and half-hands, long cotton stockings with the feet cut out, pulled over their arms.

"I hate these things," Jessica said.

"Why don't you take them off?" said Leonie.

"Why don't you?"

"I want my skin to stay pretty."

"Oh pooh, you only wear 'em because Mama says to."

Leonie tossed her head. "If I didn't want to wear them, I wouldn't."

"Let's ride Old Blossie," said Mathy. Old Blossom, a Jersey

56

cow as soft and fat and harmless as a sofa, raised her head and chewed at them.

"Maybe she doesn't want to go to the timber," said Jessica.

Mathy broke off a stalk of Queen Anne's lace. "We can switch her on the butt."

"Mathy! Where do you pick up words like that!"

"I don't know. Saw, Blossie!" Mathy patted the cow's fat yellow side and hopped onto her back. "Come on, there's room for all of us."

Jessica climbed up behind her. "Come on, Leonie, you can squeeze on behind me."

"I don't want to. It's not ladylike to ride a cow."

"Nobody sees us."

"I don't care, I'd rather walk."

"Well, I guess Blossie would just as soon you did." Jessica nudged the cow with her black-stockinged knees. "Come on, Bloss, let's go to the timber!" The cow ambled down the path with a funny braiding motion of her feet. Jessica began to sing. "She'll be comin' around the mountain when she comes! She'll be ridin' on Old Blossie when she comes!" Mathy and Leonie joined in.

"Hold her tail," said Jessica. "She keeps slapping me!"

Leonie caught hold of the tail and swung along behind, the berry bucket dangling from her elbow. They sang all the way to the lettuce bed.

As they were ready to start back, Leonie said, "As long as we're this close, I'm going on to the creek and catch me a fish."

Jessica rested the basket on Blossom's back. "Now, Leonie," she said in her gentle voice, "Mama said for us to come right back."

"She said in half an hour. It hasn't been near a half an hour yet."

"I'll bet it has."

"I'll bet it hasn't. I'm going to catch a fish—it won't take me a minute."

"You didn't bring a pole."

Leonie took a coil of cord out of her apron pocket. "I've got a line and a hook. I can break me off a branch."

"Well, all right," Jessica said, "if you think we've got time. I guess Mama wouldn't mind having a catfish for supper."

They left the cow grazing in the shade and cut down past the willow slew, toward their favorite fishing hole. As they walked through the cornfield a freight train passed, a half mile beyond the creek, squeaking and laboring on its way to Renfro.

"See, I told you!" said Leonie. "There's the Katy—it's not three o'clock yet."

"Not if it's on time," said Jessica. "It's usually late."

The faint cindery smell of train smoke blew through the cornrows. "Who-oo?" said the whistle.

"Ooooh," said Jessica, "doesn't that sound lonesome!" The sound grew softer and softer, till it was lost in the rustle of cornstalks.

The creek bank was lined with thick underbrush, sumac and berry briars. The girls were about to push their way through when Mathy, who was in the lead, suddenly stopped. "What's that?" They stood still and listened. From the creek came the sound of a man's voice singing. "Is that Papa?"

"Papa's cutting hay on the Old Chimney Place," said Jessica.

They listened again. It was a sweet contented sound, but no doubt about it, it came from a man. They turned to each other, big-eyed. Here it was at last! Danger! All their lives Callie had cautioned them, "If you ever see a strange man in the timber, don't wait! You get to the house as fast as you can git, *and stay together!*"

"Run!" whispered Jessica.

Mathy stepped forward into the brush, Leonie right behind her. "I want to see!" said Leonie.

"Come back!"

"Sh!"

The singing continued, thin and lonely and contented. Mathy crept in behind a clump of sumac. Carefully, making not a sound, she pushed aside the leaves. "There!" she whispered.

Leonie and Jessica peered over her shoulders. Below them, at the edge of the water, a young man lay stretched out on a flat rock in a patch of sunlight. He was completely naked. He lay on his back, one knee in the air and his hands behind his head, singing away to the treetops.

> "In London town where I did dwell,
>   There lived a boy, I loved him well.
>   He courted me, my life away,
>   And then he would not with me stay."

He rolled over and stood up, planting his feet wide apart on the rock as he stretched his arms. The Elders leching for Susanna were no more enthralled than the three girls hiding in the bushes. Here was a man standing before them plain. They stared at his naked body with unblushing curiosity.

"Is he a gypsy?" whispered Mathy. Callie had warned them against gypsies as long as they remembered.

The young man stretched again, scratched his chest, and plunged into the water. He ducked under and out and somersaulted. His wet buttocks glistened briefly as he went over. After a moment he moved to a shallower spot and began to scrub his arms vigorously with his hands. He threw water over himself, like an elephant, and shook his wet hair and made gargling noises. The girls began to giggle. They pressed their hands tight over their mouths and turned red with laughter.

"He's funny!" Mathy whispered.

"He's all hairy!" said Leonie.

The man waded to the opposite bank, where his clothes lay, and pulled himself out. They watched him rub himself dry with his hands and a big red handkerchief.

"Let's throw a rock and run!" said Mathy.

"Oh no!" Jessica whispered frantically. "He might chase us."

She was too late. Mathy had already heaved a rock toward the creek. It landed in the water with a loud *chunk!* The young man jerked his head up, and the girls saw no more. They charged out of the brush like big game and ran through the cornfield as fast as they could go.

"Don't stop here!" Jessica panted as they came out on the other side. "He might follow us!" They scurried up the slope, into the woods to the lettuce bed.

"Blossie will protect us!" cried Mathy, throwing her arms around the cow's neck. "Good Old Blossie!"

"Do you think he's a white-slaver?" said Leonie, panting for breath.

"Oooh, I didn't think of that!" Jessica turned pale. "I don't think he is, though. They're mostly in cities and all dressed up, Mama says. Anyway, he looked too young."

"Was he a gypsy?" Mathy said.

"Of course not," Leonie said impatiently.

"How do you know?"

"He was too white. Except where he was sunburnt. And his hair wasn't black."

"It sure was awful curly," Jessica said.

"He's probably some hobo off of a freight train."

"He didn't look like a hobo to me," Mathy said. "I thought he was cute."

"Oh, Mathy! He was all hairy," said Leonie.

"His face wasn't. He was pretty."

"Men aren't pretty," Leonie explained. "They're handsome. Only this one wasn't. He looked common."

"Not to me."

"Well, he did to me."

Mathy turned to Jessica. "Did you think he looked common?"

"I couldn't tell. We weren't close enough."

"We were close enough to see that thing between his—"

"All right, Mathy, you hush, now. I declare!" Jessica turned bright red.

"I meant if we were close enough to see *that*, we were close enough to tell whether he looked common."

"I don't remember what he looks like. I wouldn't know him if I met him in the middle of the road." Jessica giggled. "I wouldn't know him from Adam!" She and Leonie shrieked with laughter. "I'd just die if I ever saw him again!"

"Me too!"

"Are we going to tell Mama?" Mathy asked. Leonie and Jessica suddenly stopped laughing. "Are we, Jessica? Going to tell Mama about the man?"

"Well, I guess we don't really have to."

"Why not?" said Leonie. She held her mouth prissy and put her chin in the air. "I think she ought to know."

"Why?"

"She just ought to, that's all."

"I don't think we ought to mention it."

"Well, why not, Jessica?"

"I don't know, it's just that—well, I don't *know!*"

"If we tell her," Mathy said, looking sideways at Leonie, "she'll want to know why we went to the creek."

"That's right," said Jessica, "maybe she won't let us go fishing any more."

Leonie's chin came down. "Well . . . maybe so." She picked up her empty berry bucket. "Let's not say anything. I won't if you won't."

"All right," Jessica agreed.

"It would only make Mama nervous."

"That's right. No sense doing that. We better get back, though. She'll come down here looking for us."

Mathy climbed onto Blossom's back. "All aboard!"

"I think I'll walk," said Jessica.

"Giddyap, Blossie!" The cow swayed off along the path, Leonie holding the tail.

Jessica walked behind them slowly, swinging her sunbonnet against the weeds. It was a funny feeling, having seen a man with no clothes on. If Papa knew—! She shuddered. But it wasn't as if she knew the man; it wasn't like seeing Papa. Or Marvin. She suddenly tried to imagine Marvin with no clothes on and blushed at the thought. She only liked to think of Marvin in his Sunday suit, looking grown-up and important. She closed her eyes and felt again that hasty kiss by the water cooler. Oh, she *wished* they were back in town, where she could see him!

Callie had come out to the gate looking for them. "Where have you children been? I was beginning to worry."

"We rested awhile in the shade," Jessica said. It was the truth. They *had* rested a minute, after their dash from the creek.

"You had a mighty long rest, seems to me. You didn't get any blackberries, I see. Weren't they ripe?"

Leonie shot Jessica an alarmed glance. They had forgotten to look. "I didn't *see* any ripe ones," she said.

"Well, I guess they won't come on proper till the Fourth of July. You girls come on now and help get supper. Papa'll be in before long and he'll be hungry. Mathy, baby, get a bucket of water for Mama, will you? Oh, Jessica, I've got a nice little job for you!"

Jessica was edging toward the stairs. "What is it?"

"While Leonie peels potatoes, why don't you and I go plant a few rows of pole beans? Wouldn't that be fun?"

"Well, I thought I ought to write Miss George. You know, my English teacher? She wanted me to."

Her mother looked disappointed. "Oh. Well, go ahead, if you want to. I thought it'd be nice, out in the garden this time of day. We could plant a few rows before supper. It's cooler out there now. And the sweet peas smell so good. I just thought you might enjoy it."

Jessica sighed imperceptibly. "All right. I'll help."

"Good! Put your bonnet on, though, honey. There's still a little sunshine down there and you don't want to get black."

4

Jessica saw him first, whistling up the road from the east, a neat bundle slung over one shoulder. He wore dark trousers that looked too small and a blue shirt and no hat. His brown hair was very curly. He came past the garden fence, and as she stared at him from under the bonnet, he turned and saw her. He stopped, the whistling stopped, his face broke into a friendly smile, and he waved.

"Howdy!"

Callie, bending over the furrow, straightened and turned around.

"Afternoon, ma'am." He came over to the fence and rested his bundle on a post. "Nice day."

"Yes?" said Callie.

"I'm a stranger 'round yere. Just come in on a freight train. My home's down south of here. Down below Cabool? That's a ways east of Springfield—maybe you know where that is." Callie nodded. "Wondered if you'd know where I could git some work."

"Well," said Callie, shifting the hoe.

The young man smiled. "I may not be the best help anybody ever had, but I'm willin'." He said "hep" for "help."

Callie shifted the hoe again. Though she knew that Matthew needed help, she didn't want to say so. But the stranger was boyish and friendly and she hated to be too brusque. "Maybe my husband could tell you if there's anybody here needs a hand," she said. "He's out in the field right now, though."

"I'd be much obliged to talk to him."

"Well—" Callie hesitated. "Reckon you can wait here if you want to."

"That'd be mighty fine."

Mathy, hearing the voices, came out into the front yard. At the sight of the stranger her mouth fell open. He turned and smiled at her.

"Afternoon," he said politely.

"Hello." She darted back into the house.

"I'll tell you now," Callie said, "you can come around back and wait. There's the gate down there." She waved toward the lane that led from the main road into the barnlot. She was not going to have a stranger just off a freight train come through her front gate.

"Thank y', ma'am." The boy tucked the bundle under his arm and walked off toward the lane.

"You get in the house," Callie said to Jessica. "I hope Papa gets here pretty soon. Maybe I shouldn't have told him Papa wasn't here."

"He doesn't look very dangerous."

"You can't never tell by that. Sometimes the ones that looks it the least are the worst."

While Callie put the hoe away, Jessica went into the house. She found Mathy and Leonie glued to the front windows.

"That's *him!*" said Mathy.

"I know it," Jessica said. "Be quiet. He's looking for work. Mama told him to wait here till Papa comes in."

"We may all be dead by that time!" Mathy said happily, her black eyes smoky with excitement. "He may cut our throats and burn the house down!"

"Oh, that's silly," Leonie said. "I'm not afraid of him."

"He seemed very polite," said Jessica.

"Hmph. He's a hired hand."

"Well, he can still be polite."

The young man climbed over the big farm gate and started up the lane. The girls rushed to the kitchen so they could see him better. Callie was watching him from the yard.

"You can wait there," she called. "Mr. Soames will be here just any minute now."

He came toward the fence. "Could I chop some wood for you, whawl I wait?"

Mathy jigged up and down. "I hope Mama doesn't let him have the ax! He'll chop our heads off!"

"No, thank you," Callie said firmly. She came into the house. "You girls get away from that window."

"Why didn't you let him chop wood?" Mathy said. "Were you afraid to let him have the ax? Is that why, Mama?"

"Oh, mercy no! I never even thought of that!" Callie paused, as if she *should* have thought of it. "I just don't want him to feel like we're obliged to him, that's all. He might get to thinkin' because he done something for us, he could get familiar around the place. You girls come on now and help me finish supper. Get away from that window!" She washed her hands in the enamel wash-

63

pan. "He seems like a nice boy. Don't see how he can look so clean, comin' off a freight train like that."

She went out to the back porch. The girls rolled their eyes at each other and choked with laughter. "He ought to be clean!" Leonie whispered. "He just had a bath!" When Callie came back, all of them had their backs turned.

Matthew came in on the hay wagon a few minutes later and they saw him talking with the boy as he unhitched. The boy helped. After a while, Matthew left him sitting on a stump by the barn and came into the kitchen.

"Mama," he said, "I think I'll let this boy help me here for a few days. How would you feel about it?"

"It's up to you."

"Well, I could use a little help right now, and seems like the boys around here won't stay home any more. Always running off to Kansas for the wheat harvest or somewhere." (Boys were always chasing off somewhere after money or girls.) "All the neighbors have their hands full, too," he went on. "Even if we trade back and forth, we still have plenty of work. This boy seems like he's honest. He's courteous, and he seems willing."

"He's kinda frail-lookin'."

"Well, I'm not going to kill him with work."

"I know you aren't. But my goodness, where's he going to sleep?"

"In the hayloft. We talked about that. It's all right with him. It's clean up there, and we can give him a quilt. It's not the worst place you could sleep."

"Well, Papa, if you want him, it's all right with me."

His name was Tom Purdy. He was one of six children born and raised on an Ozark farm. "I took out when I's sixteen," he said at the supper table. "That's about four years ago. I already been down to Little Rock and up to St. Louis. I go home ever' now and thin and stay with my folks awhawl. We have a lot of fun, all us kids. We don't always eat too good, but we have a good time."

"Have some more potatoes," said Matthew.

"I b'lieve I will. I sind my folks money sometimes—when I have any." He grinned, showing his white, slightly crooked teeth. His eyes were large and blue, with long curling lashes that gave his face an oddly angelic look. "I decided this year I's goin' out west to wheat harvest. I got an uncle out in western Kansas—he's got a big wheat farm out there, don't raise nothin' but wheat! That's

64

where I was headin'. I was goin' up to Kansas City and take out from there. You git lonesome, though, ridin' a freight, and dirty. I's ridin' along there this mornin' in that open box car, and I felt so dirty and hot. I looked out at thim green fields and the woods and ever'thing, and I couldn't stand 'er no longer. I jumped out and rolled down the embankment and started walkin'. Boy, when I come to that creek, I sure jumped in! Sure had me a good ole swim." He laughed. "I thought somebody threwed a rock at me, though, about the time I's through."

Jessica and Leonie and Mathy stared at their plates, chewing hard.

"Didn't see nobody, though," he said. "Maya been a big bull-frog."

"I bet it was!" said Mathy and nearly died laughing.

Callie frowned at her and gave Jessica a suspicious glance. "Please pass the bread," said Jessica.

"You've got bread."

"I mean the butter, please."

The boy laid his knife and fork neatly across his empty plate. "Never did work for a schoolteacher before," he said, and added modestly, "but I'm goin' to marry a schoolmom."

"Is that right!" said Matthew.

"That's nice," said Callie.

"I and her's engaged, I reckon you call it. We're goin' to git married when I go back home." He leaned his chin on his hand. "Reckon she's goin' to have to teach me how to talk good, when we're married. I never did learn how. I went through the eighth grade and then I had to go to work. I never did git around to goin' back."

"Well, you should try to do that," Matthew said kindly.

"Reckon I'm a little too old now."

"Oh no, never too old to go to school. Why, I was your age or older when I started to high school—Mrs. Soames and I were married!" He took Tom off to the porch and told him all about the good old days.

Callie and the girls cleared away the dishes. "Where did you girls go this afternoon?" she said casually.

"You didn't get this plate clean," Leonie said to Jessica.

"Well, I can't see very well. I'm in my own light."

"I thought you might have gone down to the creek," said Callie, "when you went after the lettuce." She waited. "Well, one of you answer me."

Jessica turned around from the dishpan. "Yes, Mama, we were down there. Just for a minute."

"That's what I thought," said Callie. "And I reckon you saw that boy taking a bath." Again no one answered. "I told you not to go down to that creek this afternoon."

"No, you didn't, Mama!" said Leonie.

"Well, I told you to come right on back when you'd picked your lettuce. It's the same thing. What made you go to the creek, anyway?"

"We wanted to catch a fish for supper, that's all."

"So you went down there and saw something you shouldn't."

"But Mama, we didn't know he was there!" Leonie said impatiently.

"Well, you had no business down there anyway."

"We had more right than he did. It's our creek."

"But I *told* you not to go down there today!"

"No, you didn't!"

"All right, Leonie, that's enough out of you! If your Papa finds out you were down there, you won't feel so smart."

"But Mama," Jessica said, "we didn't *mean* to see him!"

"Well, I know, but— Which one of you threw the rock?"

"I did," said Mathy.

"Whatever possessed you to do that?"

"I thought it was funny."

"Well, I don't think it's very funny." Callie sat down and fanned herself with her apron. "Bad enough you *lookin'* at him, without lettin' him *know* you were!"

"He thought we were a bullfrog!" Mathy threw herself in a chair in a fit of laughter. "He doesn't know it was us."

"I don't want him to know it, either. He might get the wrong notion about you girls. I want you to be awful careful with a boy around. Keep your dresses down and behave yourselves. And don't let your Papa know anything about what happened this afternoon. If he finds out he'll be so mad he'll pout for the rest of the week. He'll be mad at me for letting you go."

Jessica said, "It wasn't your fault, Mama."

"Well, we won't fuss over whose fault it was. But I wish it'd never happened. You've been bad girls and I want you to go right upstairs and ask God to forgive you."

"Can't we sit on the porch a little while first?" said Mathy.

"You may not. You go right upstairs and go to bed. All three of you. Mathy, you remember to wash your feet."

As Jessica sat at the dresser brushing her hair, Mathy wandered in in her long nightgown.

"Jessica?"

"What, honey?"

"I don't know what to ask God to forgive me *for*."

Leonie, sitting on the bed with her New Testament (she read a chapter a day), said, "Neither do I. What did we do that was so awful?"

"Well," Jessica said slowly, "Mama said to come right back and we didn't do it. I guess that's what we did wrong, really."

"Is that all!" Mathy fell backwards onto the bed and waved her feet in the air. "That's such a little bitty old sin. Leonie, you were the one that wanted to go. Why don't you ask God to forgive us all, then Jessica and I won't have to?"

"Oh, don't think you can get off that easy!" said Leonie. "You went, didn't you? I just thought of it first, that's all."

"We'll all ask him to forgive us," Jessica said. "Just say, 'Forgive us for our sins, whatever they are,' and that ought to take care of it."

Mathy went off to her own room and after a moment called back, "I said 'em."

"What?"

"My prayers. I said 'em."

"That's good."

"I just said a little one tonight, because I couldn't think of very much to talk about. It's too hot. I wish we could sleep in the yard."

"Go to sleep and forget about it. You'll cool off pretty soon." Jessica went on brushing her hair. Through the warped mirror she could see the picture on the opposite wall, a gift from her parents. It showed a girl clinging to a stone cross in a stormy sea. Whenever she looked at it, her conscience bothered her. She braided her hair in one long tight braid and got into bed.

Leonie finished her chapter, blew out the light, and knelt down by her side of the bed. Jessica didn't quite want to pray. Not down on her knees, anyway, saying real words, as Leonie was doing. She stretched out on the feather mattress and tried very hard to feel sinful.

At last Leonie finished and climbed into bed. "All that trouble just for a hired hand!" she said. "My land, they're still talking down there. I wouldn't think Papa would care much about talking to anybody so ignorant."

"He's not ignorant."

"He is too. You heard the way he talked."

"Well, Mama talks kinda like that, and she's not ignorant."

Leonie didn't answer. They lay in the dark, listening to the voices from the front porch. The scent of tobacco smoke rose through the window.

Leonie said haughtily, "He *smokes!*"

After a while, Matthew and Callie came upstairs to bed, and they heard the boy go through the gate to the barn. The house grew quiet. Suddenly Jessica raised herself on one elbow. "What's that?" she said.

Leonie lifted her head. "Somebody's playing a French harp!" The sound came from the barn, faint and sweet and far away. "It's *him!*"

They sat up and listened. It was a sorrowful tune, made more so by the lonesome tones of the harmonica; and played in the boy's simple manner, it was as ungrammatical and beguiling as his speech. The sound rose and fell, lost now and then under the scrape of the crickets or the snuffling of a horse in the barnlot, but emerging again to drift in softly on the warm air. Jessica thought it was the loneliest sound she had ever heard. She lay back on the pillow, melting with sympathy—for the boy, for herself, for Marvin bereft of her, and for all the lonely, wandering, homeless souls in the world. It was a nice sorrow. She fell asleep at once.

5

Tom's few days stretched into two weeks, and still Matthew said nothing about his leaving. Though Tom had his faults (he stacked hay carelessly, forgot to lock the corncrib door, and had to sit down in the shade now and then and smoke a cigarette), he was as good-natured as the day was long and took orders as if they were some sort of special dispensation. He behaved himself around the girls. His attitude toward them was avuncular, and he paid them no special attention except a harmless teasing. The schoolmarm, looming vaguely in limbo, consoled both Matthew and Callie.

All of them admired Tom's cleanliness. Callie had set him up a washstand against the house, just outside the back door: a wash-pan on an upended box, a nail for the towel, and a cracked saucer for a cake of soap. Tom added a toothbrush and a razor. Every morning he borrowed Callie's teakettle for hot water so he could shave. And every night when he came in from the fields, he stripped to the waist and scrubbed away till Callie said it was a wonder he had any skin left on his bones.

One day Mathy found a piece of broken mirror in the smoke-house and propped it up on Tom's washstand. He thanked her kindly and occasionally chipped a little piece off the edge, just to prove that he was ugly enough to crack a looking glass.

Of all Tom's virtues, there was one which particularly endeared him to Matthew. Tom loved music. And aside from a natural aptitude and a good ear, he knew nothing about it. Matthew loved to teach. They began, therefore, in the evenings after supper, to have music lessons in the parlor. Sweating by lamplight, Matthew taught Tom to read notes. Leonie assisted at the piano. Leonie played without much inspiration, but she was very correct; she planned to be a concert pianist. With haughty patience, she went over and over and over the simple exercises with Tom. Tom blew diligently on his harmonica and sometimes, with Leonie's help, played the piano. After a while he was able to read a little, and they played duets. Matthew beat time with his hands like a conductor, singing an occasional *do re mi* or a *fa fa sol* to keep them in line.

Sometimes Callie said, "I wish they'd hurry up and learn a new piece. I'm getting tired of that one."

But the three perspiring musicians in the parlor went over and over the same simple notes, exclaiming with pleasure when they finished without mishap.

Jessica, listening from the kitchen where she helped with the dishes, felt left out of the fun. She began to wish she had practiced her piano, like Mama said. Now and then during the day she sat down and worked for half an hour. But her fingers were unruly, her timing erratic. She usually wound up thumbing through old *Étude* Magazines, which their music teacher had given Leonie, and engaging in mortal combat with some composition that had a romantic title. Callie never let this go on for long.

Sometimes at night, when Matthew and Tom were too tired for lessons, they joined the others on the porch. Mathy wouldn't rest until Tom played the harmonica, and he wouldn't play unless she agreed to sing. The musicale usually opened with a wild rendering of "Three Blind Mice," Tom making the harmonica squeak and Mathy carried away with laughter. After that, everybody sang together. Sometimes they sang "The Butcher Boy," the ballad Tom was singing that day when they found him in the creek. He had taught them the words. It made them laugh at first, remembering where they had heard it. But it was a lonesome tune, full of backcountry woe, and now when he played it they joined in softly. On those evenings Jessica floated upstairs in sweet melancholy and gazed dreamily into the mirror, remembering Marvin. Evangeline parted from Gabriel. It was all so beautiful and tragic.

One hot humid day, shortly after noon, Tom collapsed in the hayfield. Matthew brought him to the house in the wagon and drove off in the Ford to get a doctor.

"A little too much heat," the doctor said and suggested that Tom take it easy for a couple days.

Callie put him to bed in the parlor. "Can't let the poor little thing be sick in the barn," she said. She spread clean ironed sheets on the spring cot and propped him up on pillows. During the hot part of the day, she kept the blinds pulled, so that the room looked cool and deep. The girls thought the whole affair marvelously dramatic. They ran in and out with potato soup, glasses of water, and lumps of ice in clean rags. Mathy brought him ferns and colored rocks and read him stories. Leonie played the piano for him and now and then allowed Jessica to join her for a duet. Jessica could manage the bass without too much trouble.

One afternoon while Tom was sleeping, Jessica tiptoed in to lower the blinds. When she turned around, Tom had opened his eyes and lay watching her thoughtfully. "Jessica," he said in a musing tone.

"What?"

"Nothin'. Just 'Jessica.' I never did know anybody named that before. I knowed a Jessie once and a boy named Jess. But that's not the same thing." He went on looking at her with that same serious, thoughtful expression. "You look like a Jessica," he said.

She laughed self-consciously. "What does *that* mean?"

"I don't know. You just do."

She fussed with the window curtain, making the gathers even. "You want a piece of ice?"

"I'd be much obliged."

She brought him the ice and went upstairs to her room, where she stood at the mirror and considered herself. She turned her head sideways, lifted her hair and let it down again, pushed up the tip of her nose, and stared at her eyes for a long time with a little frown of concentration. *You look like a Jessica.* Now what did he mean by that? She smiled coyly into the mirror, like some girl on a calendar. Then she made a horrendous face at herself and turned away.

"Jessica?" came her mother's voice from the kitchen.

"I'm coming."

By Saturday night, Tom felt well enough to go to town with them. The ladies of the Renfro Methodist Church were giving an ice-cream supper that night, and Callie was taking ice cream and cake. Tom sat in the back seat between Mathy and Jessica, with the freezer between his feet.

"You girls treat me right good, I might buy you a disha ice cream," he said.

"Better save your money, boy," said Matthew.

"Why, I've got to buy this here Mathy a disha ice cream! If I don't, she's going to write a letter to my schoolmom and tell her I been chasin' other gals!"

"I am not!"

"Why, didn't you tell me you was? Didn't you chase me up a tree with a corn knife yesterday and make me promise to buy you some ice cream?"

"I did not! Papa, he's making that up!"

"Well, I'm going to buy you some anyway, to be on the safe side. I don't want you spillin' no beans to my gal."

Mathy beat him with her fists. "I bet you haven't got a girl."

"I bet I have."

"Why doesn't she write to you then?"

"She don't know where I am."

"Why don't you write and tell her?"

"'Cause I can't write, that's why!" He laughed. "That a good enough answer for you, Miss Priss?"

At the church, Tom unloaded the freezer and left them. He came back presently, wearing a new straw hat, hunted up Mathy and escorted her to a table, where they ordered two kinds of ice cream and cake. Callie, who was helping serve, came up and shook her head. "I declare, you'll be sick, both of you."

"No, we won't, Mrs. Soames," Tom said. "Soon as we finish here, we're goin' right over to the drugstore and buy some castor oil."

"Oh, Tom," said Mathy, "you're so silly!"

71

Callie laughed at them. "Well, don't eat any more tonight. Tom, you hadn't ought to spend your money on her."

Mathy ran off to play with the other little girls. Tom went around to help the ladies. As he came up from the street, where he had emptied a freezerful of ice water, he saw Jessica standing at the edge of the lawn. "Hi!" he said.

"Hi. Where's Papa? I want to ask him for some money. I need a new hair ribbon."

"He's around here somewhere. Come on, I'll buy you a disha ice cream."

"Oooh," said Jessica, patting her stomach, "I've already had some. I'm full."

"Aw, you can eat another dish. Come on!"

Jessica lifted one shoulder. "All right. I reckon I can always eat more ice cream." She slid onto a bench at one of the sawhorse tables. "My, but it's hot!" She lifted the hair off her neck and fanned with her hanky.

"Here, I'll help you." Tom unfolded his pocket handkerchief and flapped it at her. "You got perty hair."

"I hate it. I wish mine was yellow, like Leonie's."

"I like it brown and shiny, like yours."

"Oooh, I don't." Jessica wiped the sweat off her forehead. "Whew! I guess you need ice cream on a night like this!"

"They got some mighty good-smellin' banana ice cream back yonder. I opened the freezer for Mrs. Latham."

Jessica made a face. "If it's hers it's liable to have eggshells in it. Or chicken feathers or something! She's kinda messy with her cooking."

"Glad you warned me. How about Mrs. Barrow's? Hers looked pretty good."

"Hers always tastes thin. She's too stingy to use separated cream. That's what Mama says. Mrs. Buxton always has good ice cream, though. Let's ask for hers." She waved at the lady coming toward them. "We want some of your ice cream, Mrs. Buxton. I hope there's some left."

"Why, I think there is," said the lady. "I'll fix you children a nice big dish."

Jessica went down the list of church ladies and the quality of their cooking. Mrs. Sells's devil's-food was always four layers high and the icing tasted peculiar; Miss Serena Hicks put raisins in her ice cream; and so on. She and Tom had barely finished when

Callie appeared in front of them. "Jessica, you come back here and help us awhile."

"All right, Mama. Thanks for the ice cream, Tom."

"You're welcome." He went off down the street.

"Tom bought me some ice cream, Mama. Wasn't that nice of him?"

"You stay back here with us, now, and help us out. We're gettin' busy."

"Mama, do you think Papa would let me buy a new piece of ribbon? I need one real bad."

"I don't know, but I want you to stay around here with me. We'll see about the ribbon later."

The stores closed before Jessica could get away. But she didn't care. She had nibbled at cake and ice cream all evening and wasn't feeling too well. When they got home the house was so hot she insisted she would never go to sleep. Mathy was of the same opinion. After some amount of wheedling, Callie allowed them to drag the spring cot out to the yard.

Tom had already gone to the barn. When he started his nightly serenade, Jessica and Mathy joined in, singing. The three of them yelled back and forth and the girls acted silly and Matthew had to speak sternly to the whole lot of them from the upstairs window. They quieted down at last, and when Callie glanced out, a half hour later, the girls were fast asleep with the sheets pulled up to their chins.

Toward morning, when the moon had set and the sky begun to gray, Callie awoke and glanced again out the window. There was only one girl on the cot below. Jessica was nowhere to be seen. Instantly a kind of fear shot through Callie that had an old familiar taste. She threw a shawl around her shoulders and slipped downstairs.

"Mathy?" she whispered, shaking the little girl's shoulder. "Where's Jessica?"

"I don't know," Mathy said sleepily.

"Did you hear anyone—was Tom—"

"What's the matter, Mama?" said Jessica, behind her.

Callie whirled around. "Mercy, honey! Where'd you go?"

"Down to the toilet."

"You scared me to death!"

"Where did you think I was?"

"I don't know. I didn't think. Go on back to sleep now, both

73

of you." She tucked them in and, stooping quickly, kissed Jessica's cheek. "Mama loves you," she said and went back to the house.

"Where did she think I *was?*" Jessica murmured.

6

Jessica hated Sunday afternoons. The mornings were fine. She liked the hustle-bustle of breakfast and dressing for church. Sunday clothes were a nuisance, but they looked nice even if they were uncomfortable. (Callie often fretted because Jessica so resisted ladies' clothes; she still clung to her girlish dresses with easy skirts and nothing that bound her or cut off her breath.) It was pleasant to sit in Sunday School with your friends and gossip between Sunday School and church and settle down then for the sermon and feel a hush come over you. The minister was an old man, dry and thin as a page in the Bible and full of fine words that made a good sound through the church. Brother Ward didn't holler and pound like a lot of preachers; he merely leaned across the big open Bible and talked, and you listened and felt better.

And then to come out into the bright Sunday noon with that exalted feeling. You were so clean and so light and the sky shone; everyone was friendly, and there was ice cream for dinner! Jessica liked Sunday morning.

But Sunday afternoon was a different day. It was a lonesome time. The farm no longer seemed like home. Nothing looked familiar and nothing was real. You were caught up, stunned, in the heat and stillness; you couldn't get out and no one could get in. And you were lonely in a way you could not describe.

The people around you changed, too. They took naps. They sat on porches and rocked and fanned, read Sunday School papers and stared at the road. Now and then a buggy, and once in a great while a car, passed by, raising a cloud of dust that hung in the air for a long time before it fell back to earth of its own weight. The house was under a spell, like the castle that slept for a hundred years. Even the spiders slept in their webs. A floor board creaked, a fly buzzed, a page rustled. That was all, except for the dismal sound of the locusts in the trees.

On Sunday afternoons Leonie wrote letters to friends and cousins, she studied her lesson for the following Sunday, and she practiced piano—all with a frowning seriousness of purpose. But Jessica was too miserable to do anything that mattered.

On the afternoon after the ice-cream supper, she wandered through the house for a while and at last sat down in the back yard with a volume of Longfellow's poems. The wind mourned around the barn. She thought she would perish of longing, though she wasn't sure what for. Except that she longed for Monday. Dear Monday, with its cheerful coming and going and people *doing* things.

Inside, Leonie had begun to practice piano. Up and down the scales she went, heavy-handed but accurate. Up and down, up and down, as monotonous as the locusts. Mathy came with her pencil and Big Chief tablet and sat under the tree. She was drawing a picture of a ladybug. As she drew she sang to herself.

> "*You spotted snakes, with double tongue*
> *Thorny hedgehogs, be not seen;*
> *Newts and blind-worms do not wrong;*
> *Come not near our fairy queen.*"

"Where did you get that song?" said Jessica.

"I made it up. Not the words, just the tune."

"Where'd you get the words?"

"Out of a book."

"What book?"

"I don't know—one of those books in there in the bookcase. What's a newt, Jessica?"

"I don't know. We'll have to ask Papa."

"Listen!" said Mathy, raising her hand. "I hear an air-a-plane!"

They jumped up and ran to the barnlot, scanning the sky. But there was nothing in sight. "You probably heard the locusts down in the timber," Jessica said.

They sat down again under the tree. Mathy tried to draw a picture of a plane, and Jessica went back to "Evangeline." The afternoon seemed endless. *Do re mi fa sol la ti do*, went the piano . . . *do ti la sol fa mi re do*. Tom, who had been asleep in the front yard, came around to the well.

"Pump me a fresh drink," said Mathy.

"Git the bucket and I'll fill it up."

She brought the bucket and dipper and they both had a drink.

75

Then she pumped while Tom washed his face under the spout and ran his wet hands through his hair.

"Here, I'll help you," she said. She dribbled water on his head.

"You watch out now, Miss Priss." Tom flicked a few drops in her face.

"That feels good!"

"Have a little more." He splashed her again.

Mathy lifted a dipperful out of the bucket. Tom ran and she chased him. Just as she took aim, he dodged around the tree and the cupful of water struck Jessica. She jumped up, laughing, and ran to the house for another cup. The three of them began to chase each other around the yard. They laughed and yelled and got wetter and wetter. Hearing the commotion, Leonie came out to see what was going on. She got a cupful of water full in the face.

"You stop that!"

Mathy screamed with laughter. "I didn't mean it! I was trying to hit Tom."

Leonie dived for the water bucket and joined the fight. The girls' hair began to stream wet and stick to their necks. Their cotton dresses clung to their bodies, molding their legs and little breasts. Tom's shirt and his Sunday pants were soggy.

While Mathy and Leonie fought it out by the pump, Tom hurdled the back fence to get away from Jessica. She darted through the gate and they faced each other across the water trough.

"I'll throw you in!" he panted.

"No, you won't either!" Jessica lifted a double handful and threw it across at him. Tom bounded over, hooked an arm around her neck, and forced her head back on his shoulder. With his free hand he scooped up water and splashed it in her face. Jessica screamed and struggled, but he held her fast. The air was full of shrieks and laughter and flying water. Sunday afternoon had burst open like a jail and there was riot in the back yard. Into the midst of it, Matthew's voice snapped like a bull whip. "Here now! That'll be enough!"

Mathy, chasing Leonie with the water bucket, turned and saw him and with a look of manic glee flung the whole bucketful over his head.

It was in the evening after lamplight when Callie came upstairs. The insurrection was long since over. Wet clothes hung on the line; Mathy had been spanked and Jessica and Leonie sent up to their room for the rest of the day. They were lying on the bed laughing when Callie appeared in the doorway.

"Jessica, will you come in here a minute, please?"

Jessica went into her mother's room, and Callie closed the door. "Sit down, honey. Mama wants to talk to you."

Jessica felt suddenly as if she had swallowed a grindstone. If there was anything that filled her with dread and gloom, it was one of Callie's heart-to-hearts.

"It's about Tom," Callie began.

"What about *him?*"

"Last night. I don't think it looked nice, him buying you ice cream."

"Why not? He bought Mathy some ice cream."

"I know. But that's not the same thing. Mathy's just a little girl. You're getting to be a young lady now, Jessica, and you have to be more careful around boys."

"But that was just *Tom!*"

"That's it, honey. I don't think it's very nice, you settin' up at a table in public like that, with the boy we hire to help us on the farm."

"Oh."

"People'll start thinking you're his girl."

"Oh, Mama!"

"Well, they will. People talk, no matter how innocent you are. And I don't want 'em thinkin' the superintendent's daughter has to go around with no hired hand. It's embarrassing to Papa."

"I never thought about it that way."

"I know you didn't. But I don't want *him* thinkin' about it that way, either. Now, this afternoon, when you children was having the waterfight—I saw him with his arm around your neck."

"We were just playing!"

"I know *you* were. But I don't know about him. Mama wants you to be awful careful, now, not to let him get a-hold of you like that again or get too close to you. Boys get funny notions. And I wouldn't want him to get any notions about you." Jessica hung her head, grateful for the darkness in the room. "Tom's a nice boy, but he's just a hired hand, a kind of a tramp, I reckon. And Mama wants you to have somebody fine. Somebody from a good family, that can take care of you and treat you good."

"But Mama, who said anything about—"

"I know you don't think anything about Tom, but I want you to be careful. You shouldn't get too familiar. When boys and girls get too familiar, bad things can happen. You have to watch out about things like that now. You're at the age."

Callie went to the window and tied the curtain in a loose knot to let in more air. Jessica thought she was going to be sick. "Can I go now, Mama? It's awful hot in here."

"Yes, you can go now," she said.

Jessica ran down the stairs and out to the yard where it was dark. She would have liked to run to the woods and hide and never be seen again. Folded into the shadows by the smokehouse, she put her head on her knees and distorted her face for crying. But no tears came. She was too mortified. What made her do it, she asked herself. What in the world made her sit there last night with the hired hand! How could she be so dumb? And what made her get into that waterfight—and chase after him—and let him touch her? *That* was the thing she could not forgive. The hired hand had put his arm around her and held her head on his shoulder and she liked it! She dug her nails into the ground, furious with herself.

But then—why shouldn't she like it? Why did everyone look down on Tom? He was nice. If he was born common, was that his fault? She was suddenly so sorry for him, and that brought the tears.

7

In the first place, Tom was not bad-looking. He was clean and good-humored and as mannerly as he knew how to be. Though unschooled, he was bright. But above all else, he was *there*. Proximity is often the greatest virtue. By the time Jessica fell asleep that night, she was head over heels in love. Ashamed or not, she had to admit it. She had loved him since that first afternoon when she saw him walking up the road.

She woke up next morning with an aching head and stayed upstairs till Matthew and Tom left the house. All day she went about quietly, enduring her shame. Constantly, without a moment's peace, she thought of him. She looked at him from her mother's vantage and from Leonie's, and thought, what if her friends in town should see him! He was poor and shabby, a hay-

78

seed with bad grammar and crooked teeth. A nobody. Then she saw him through her own eyes—a laughing, blue-eyed boy with white teeth and a sweet way about him—and she loved the very barn and the water trough, the pump and the parlor couch, because of him.

But Tom had a girl back home whom he was going to marry. Remembering this, Jessica's heart sank. There was nothing she could do. To Tom, she was only a little girl, a plain gawky girl with a big nose. She couldn't even play the piano. She bit her knuckles, vowing to practice every day. But even if she did, what good would it do? Even if Tom *should* see her—even if he did begin to notice—Mama and Papa wouldn't allow it. Not for one minute. And anyway, he was shabby and common and couldn't talk right and what did she care! Except that she did.

She ran upstairs and looked at herself in the mirror. A thin face with a nose that stuck out like a beak, light brown eyes with a scared look, straight brown hair. He said he liked her hair —he couldn't have meant it. He was teasing. She began to cry, and seeing her distorted mouth and red eyes in the mirror, buried her face in her hands. "You're so ugly!" she said. "You're so dumb."

A week later they were sitting at the table when her mother said, "What's the matter with you, Jessica? You've been just pickin' at your food. You got no color at all. Don't you feel good?"

"I feel all right. I'm just not hungry."

"Oh foot, not hungry!"

"It's so hot."

"Well, yes, it is awful hot and sticky." Callie pulled out the front of her dress and fanned down her bosom. "And it's going to get worse. Awful hot day to be gettin' ready for company."

"I wish they weren't coming," said Jessica, thinking with distaste of aunts, uncles, and her Cousin Ophelia, and anybody else who wasn't Tom.

"What do you mean? I thought you were so anxious for company."

"I was, but—"

"I'm *glad* they're coming," said Leonie. "I can hardly wait till they get here."

"Well, we've got a lot to do before they get here," said Callie. "If you girls are going to wash your hair, hurry up and do it, so you can help with the work."

They washed their hair in the back yard, at Tom's washstand, using a big snowy cake of lye soap. Jessica and Leonie pinned up each other's hair in curl papers. When they'd cleaned up their mess, Callie set Jessica to making cobbler. By the time it was ready for the oven, everyone else had gone outside. Jessica slipped off to the parlor to read *Lorna Doone*.

She had barely got started when Callie looked in. "You're not watching your fire very good," she said.

Jessica sighed and closed the book. "I'll go see about it."

She emptied the coal bucket into the fire, which promptly went out. Now she would have to get corncobs and start all over. Taking the bucket, she set out for the corncrib. The sun was hot and stung her scalp between the tight rolls of paper.

"You sure look funny," said Mathy, coming in from the barn. Mathy's hair was cut short with straight bangs, and she couldn't be bothered with curlers.

"I don't care," said Jessica.

But as she reached the corner of the barn, Tom appeared, climbing over the pasture gate. "Boy, if you ain't a perty-lookin' sight!" Jessica walked on doggedly, blushing right up to the curlers. "You look like you's decorated for Christmas!"

"Maybe I am. What are you doing up at the house, anyway?"

"I come back for the pitchfork. I forgot it this mornin'."

"You forgot to lock the crib door, too." She walked in and pulled the slatted door shut behind her.

"Did I do that agin? Shucks!"

She sat down on a pile of yellow corn. She wasn't going out again till Tom had got whatever he came to get and gone on back to the field. Idly she dropped cobs into the coal bucket.

"Hey!"

She looked up, startled by the soft sound of his voice. He stood inside the crib, smiling at her.

"What do you want?" she said crossly.

"I didn't mean to make fun of you."

Jessica couldn't think of anything to say. She went on dropping cobs in the bucket.

"But you do look some comical," he added, grinning.

"You shut up!"

"Aw, Jessica! A gal as perty as you can look funny and it don't hurt."

"I'm not pretty. I'm ugly."

"Now whatever give you that notion?"

She turned around to say something sassy, and before she knew

80

it, he had kissed her full on the mouth. "There!" he said. "I'd a-done that a long time ago if I'd ever got you by yourself."

She hung her head, trying to hide the smile that stretched her mouth out of shape. "You shouldn't have done that."

"Why not?"

"It's not nice."

"I thought it was."

"Well, it's not. Anyway, you're engaged."

"No, I ain't."

She looked up to find him smiling broadly. "What about that schoolteacher," she said, "the one you're going to marry?"

"There ain't any schoolteacher."

"You said there was."

"I just made that up."

"You're not engaged to anyone?"

"Nope."

"Why did you say you were, then?"

"Figured your Pa would feel safer. Him with two grown-up daughters, he wouldn't want no unattached feller around."

Jessica pursed up her mouth the way Leonie was always doing. "I think that was deceitful!"

"Maybe it was. But I wanted to work and your Pa wanted me. So what was the harm?"

"You don't—" She tried to say "love," but the word wouldn't come. "You don't *like* anyone, then?"

"Yes'm. I like someone." His fringed blue eyes smiled steadily into hers, and she felt her heart flip like a little fish.

"*Jes-sica?*" came a voice from outside.

Tom straightened up. "Perty gals always have little sisters. Reckon I better git on down to the field." He stepped out of the crib. "Hi, Mathy. 'Bout time you's comin' to help your sis." He climbed over the gate into the pasture.

Mathy peered into the corncrib. "Jessica? Oh. Mama was wondering where you were."

"I'm just getting some cobs for the fire."

"It went out a long time ago."

"I know it. That's why I came out here. Tom forgot the pitchfork—he was only here for a minute. We were just talking and—"

"Jessica?"

"What?"

"I won't tell on you."

They considered each other a moment in silence. "What do you mean?" said Jessica.

"I won't tell, if you and Tom kiss each other."

"Oh honestly, Mathy!" Jessica ducked her head, blushing and startled.

"Didn't you kiss him?"

"Well, no! I mean I didn't kiss *him*—"

"Well, why didn't you!" Mathy looked at her impatiently. "You're so silly, Jessica. *I'd* kiss Tom if I had a chance. I *love* Tom. But I'm not old enough and it makes me so mad! Jessica, I can't marry him, so you've got to!" Her face burned with earnestness, and Jessica burst out laughing.

"Who said anything about getting married?"

"Don't you want to marry him, Jessica?"

"Oh Mathy, I declare!"

"Well, don't you?"

"I'm too young to get married."

"You're eighteen. That's how old Mama was."

"But I'm going to college and everything. Anyway, Tom doesn't want to marry me."

"Did he say so?"

"Of *course* not—we didn't talk about it!"

"I'll bet he does—I bet he'll ask you."

"I bet he won't."

"Do you want him to, Jessica?"

"Oh *honestly*, Mathy!"

"Do you?"

"Well, I don't care if he *asks* me—"

"Let's make him do it!"

"Mathy, I just declare! I never heard such silly talk! If you aren't the—" Jessica stopped, looked at Mathy in exasperation, then flung her arms around her. "You're the cutest little sister in the whole world!"

The two of them rocked together, squealing with laughter. They crept out of the corncrib feeling giddy and important. For the first time in many days, Jessica didn't feel guilty.

That afternoon when the relatives arrived, she greeted them with open arms, loving everyone. She had never seen such a beautiful day.

From then on, Jessica lived in a state of siege. There was nothing she could do without the feeling that Tom watched her. Washing dishes she thought how she might look to him (how gracefully she lifted the pot!). When she worked in the garden she no longer stood jack-knifed between the rows with her rump in the air. She squatted, ladylike, her skirts neatly tucked under. Drying her fresh-washed hair in the sun, she let it float loosely over her shoulders, the better to feel like Lorna Doone. She had given up curl papers.

One day, bathing in the washbowl upstairs, she looked at herself in the good side of the mirror, where the image was less distorted. She had a long thin body, but it was a nice color. Creamy, without freckles. She studied the little constellation of moles on one shoulder. Would he mind them? The thought of his seeing her undressed made her redden. She looked away, and immediately looked back, emboldened by a curious joy. She thought of his naked body that day at the creek, and began to long for him in a way that frightened her. She understood it without wanting to. As she stared at herself, she saw over her shoulder the picture on the opposite wall—the girl hanging to the cross in a stormy sea —and abruptly turned away from the mirror.

In all those days, all they had of each other, she and Tom, was the one kiss and now and then the touch of their hands as they passed through the house at night. She found it almost enough. It was an exquisite taste, dangerous, not to be risked in gulps. It was the sharp, provocative, green taste of grape leaves, which one chewed but did not swallow. More than a taste was bitter.

She worried, too, that alone with Tom she would disappoint him, not knowing what to say or do. But when at last they did find themselves alone, she was neither awkward nor afraid.

Matthew had sent her one evening to shut the chickens in. The sky was barely dark, still very blue, and a new moon hung over the orchard. Jessica stopped and made a wish. Then she lifted her face and turned slowly in a full circle, feeling the lovely world spread out on all sides and herself at the very center. As she went back toward the gate, Tom stepped out of the shadows. The back of the house was dark; from the front came the sound of voices on the porch. Jessica went to him like water downhill and they clung, too greedy for each other even to kiss. It seemed all her senses opened and took him in—she felt, tasted, breathed him—his heartbeats, his throat, her mouth crushed against it. *Here I am!* she cried to herself. As they stood like this, grafted, a voice from behind struck them a hammer blow. They split like a rock and turned to find Matthew.

For a moment, all three of them stood speechless, Matthew's

rage radiating through the darkness. Finding his voice again, he spat out a stream of bullets. There were words like "sneaking" and "rotten," like "insolent," like "betrayal of trust." At the end of it, Tom said quietly, "I'm sorry, Mr. Soames. I didn't mean to cause no trouble."

Another volley followed, directed at both of them, and Matthew ordered Jessica into the house. She went, unprotesting. The last thing she heard was ". . . and see no more of you!"

In the morning Tom was gone. His name was not mentioned.

8

Though Leonie was sorry for Jessica, she found the whole affair hard to understand. "He was so common," she kept saying, by way of consolation. "You wouldn't want to marry *him*. You ought to marry a teacher or somebody like that."

But to Mathy, as to Jessica, the loss of Tom was disaster. They grieved in secret, wondering endlessly where he had gone. Jessica felt sure he had taken the first freight west. "He was always talking about Kansas," she said, "going to wheat harvest."

Mathy believed he was still close by. "He'll come back and get you," she promised. Jessica cherished the words, but without hope. Tom didn't love her very much, or he wouldn't have left without her in the first place.

However, on Saturday night they saw him in town. They were walking into the Mercantile just as Tom came out. Jessica thought she would die of joy—as well as of fright. Her father's mouth froze solid. He could barely eject a chilly "Good evening" to Tom's casual "Howdy." She prayed that he hadn't seen the look that passed between her and Tom.

"You stay here with me," Callie murmured to the girls—as if Jessica had the nerve to go chasing after him!

She did not see him again all evening. Ordinarily, she and Leonie walked around the square with their friends and had soda pop at the drugstore. Tonight they couldn't get two feet away without a sharp look from their mother. Mathy managed to slip out once before Callie missed her, but Jessica and Leonie never got out of the Mercantile. As soon as the groceries were bought and the eggs sold, they had to go home. They made the trip in silence, their father sulky and scowling, mad at Tom, no doubt, just for being alive. Jessica didn't mind. As long as Tom was still close by, nothing else mattered.

She could hardly wait to get home so she and Mathy could exult. They were still spending the nights outside on the spring cot. They had scarcely hit the bed when Mathy pulled the sheet over their heads and hissed into Jessica's ear, "He sent you a message!"

Jessica gasped with joy. "What did he say?"

"He wants you to meet him down in the orchard."

"When?"

"Tonight at midnight!"

Jessica smothered a squeal in her pillow. "Does he really? How do you know—what all did he say?"

"He just said to meet him down there at midnight. I saw him on the street when I was walking around the square."

They whispered excitedly under the sheet, Jessica terrified, Mathy trying to give her courage.

"What if Papa finds out?" said Jessica.

"We'll wait till he goes to sleep."

"How will we know?"

"He snores."

"But Mama! She'll wake up and look out the window and find out I'm gone!"

"No she won't," said Mathy.

"Why not?"

"She never knows it when I go away."

"Mathy Soames! You've been walking around again in the dark!"

"Just once in a while."

"That's dangerous. Mama and Papa told you not to!"

"They don't know it. You didn't even know it and you were right here."

"You better not do it any more. If Mama ever looks down here and finds you gone, she'll spank you and me both."

"She won't know even if she looks. I got a system." Mathy rose quietly—not a spring creaked—and ran across the yard to the smokehouse. She came back with a small round crock. With a quick and practiced hand she laid it on the pillow, pulled the sheet over it, and made the quilt lumpy. In the darkness it looked reasonably enough like a figure under the covers. She laughed softly. "I do this every time I wake up and want to go for a walk."

"You're just terrible!" said Jessica. They lay under the sheet smothering their laughter in the pillow and trying not to wiggle. Once in a while they poked out their heads to listen. It seemed the murmur would never end in their parents' room. The moon rose over the orchard, prying into the darkness.

"I'm scared," said Jessica.

"I'm not," said Mathy.

After a long time the voices upstairs fell silent. Crickets chirred, leaves rustled, the darkness was loud with all sorts of mysterious noises. At last a long rough familiar sound drew once and back across the soft cacophony, like a dull saw across the grain, and the night seemed still as death.

"He's asleep," said Mathy. "You can go now."

Jessica sat bolt upright, clutching the sheet to her collarbone. "I'm not going."

"You've got to. Be careful, don't squeak."

"He won't be there, I just know he won't."

"Well, you've got to go down and see!"

"It's dark down there!" Jessica whimpered.

"Oh, Jessica!" Mathy said impatiently. "If you're such a fraidy-cat, I'll go with you!"

"You can't—we've only got one head."

"I'll get another one." Mathy ran to the smokehouse for another crock and arranged it on the pillow. Together they crept out of the yard and took out running through the orchard.

Jessica's heart pounded. "I just know he won't come."

"Yes he will."

They trotted on between the cherry and peach trees into the apple grove. Ahead lay the strip of open ground dividing orchard from woods. They could see it plainly in the dusty moonlight, and no figure in sight.

"He didn't come!" said Jessica.

"Boo!" said Tom, stepping out from behind a tree.

"I told you," said Mathy.

Jessica squealed and folded her arms across her chest, remembering for the first time that she was in her nightgown.

"Hi, Jessica."

"Hi." They smiled at each other awkwardly.

"I sure am glad to see you," said Tom.

"I'm glad to see *you*."

"I sure was surprised to get your message."

86

"What message?" said Jessica.

"Didn't you send me a message—by Mathy?"

"Why, no!"

"She told me you did—she said you wanted me to meet you."

"She *did*? Why, I never! She told me *you* were the one that wanted *me* to— Mathy, what do you— *Mathy*?"

Mathy had taken to her heels.

"Come back here!"

The white nightgown flickered among the trees and vanished.

"I'm going to shake her teeth out!" said Jessica, turning back to Tom.

"What for, Jessica? Ain't you glad we're here?"

"Well, sure, but—"

"I'm glad." He put his hand on her arm.

"I better go, Tom."

"Not yet, Jessica, you just got here."

"I know, but I better get back before Papa finds out I'm gone."

"He's asleep, ain't he? Won't Mathy keep watch?"

"Yes, but—"

"Stay, Jessica. Just for a minute?"

"Well . . ." The air was soft and the night so pretty (an old moon . . . pale silvery light dusting the orchard) and she had so longed to see him.

"Jessica?" he said, moving closer.

"Don't."

"You ain't afraid, are you?"

"No."

"I won't do nothin' to hurt you."

"I know that."

"I won't even touch you if you don't want me to. . . . Do you want me to, Jessica?"

"I don't know." She hung her head, and they stood like this for a moment.

"I'm goin' away before long, Jessica."

"You are?" she said, looking up. "Clear away?"

"Reckon I got to. I been over at Latham's ever since I left here, but he won't need me no more after this week."

"Where are you planning to go, Tom?"

"Out west, I reckon, out to my uncle's."

"Clear out there!"

"I got to go somewhere."

"Can't you stay around somewhere closer?"

"What for? Ain't nothin' to stay around here for. Except you. . . . Jessica?"

"What?"

There was a long pause. "I don't guess I'll git to see you no more. Will I?"

"I don't know, Tom."

"Don't reckon your Pa would ever let me come on the place again."

"Not unless—he changes his mind."

"I got a picture of him doin' that!" He picked up a little apple, bounced it in his hand and tossed it away. "I reckon this is about the last chance we got, ain't it, to be together."

"I guess so."

"Well, then . . . We ought to make the most of it, oughtn't we?"

Her heart set up a hideous pounding.

"Jessica?" he said, laying his hand on her arm.

"I'm afraid," she said in a small voice.

"Not of me. Please, Jessica. Jessica—I love y'."

"Do you?" she cried.

"Sure."

"You do, really?"

"Sure."

"Oh, Tom—I love *you!*" With a little cry she put her arms around him and married him in her heart.

9

Daylight, however, put a different complexion on it.

Though her absence had not been discovered (Mathy kept faithful watch), her escapade could still proclaim itself, and in a most horrific way. A few days later, when her body reassured her, she took some comfort. But only momentarily. Discovered or not, she had broken a Commandment, of all Commandments the most awesome—not the greatest, according to the Bible, but certainly the greatest to her mother. Jessica saw the Commandments as ten marble slabs, old tombstones in an old graveyard, sprouting from the grass in a neat white row. When one fell, all the others toppled with it. Day after day she stood in the wreckage of the Decalogue and felt herself damned. Tom was her only refuge and salvation.

"I've got to see him," she said to Mathy, "I've just got to! He's *got* to come back."

"He will."

"I don't know when."

"Maybe on his way back from Kansas."

"But that's a long time. Maybe he'll stay out there."

"I told you you should have gone with him!" Mathy said.

Jessica tried to explain that you can't just go off like that, in your nightgown. "Anyway, he didn't ask me," she said woefully.

"He'll come back. Don't worry, Jessica."

Mathy tried hard to distract her. Every day she brought little gifts: bouquets of grasses, the blue half shell of a robin's egg, a long brown thorn as glossy as polished wood, an oriole's abandoned nest (brought down with some difficulty from a high branch). She invited Jessica to her secret cave above the creek. Jessica was grateful, but nothing helped very much.

One night after everyone else was asleep, Mathy persuaded her to go down to the woods. "I've got a surprise," she said. They slipped out of the yard and down through the pasture, two small ghosts in bare feet and long white gowns. The moon had not yet come up. Sometimes Jessica could barely make out Mathy's figure on the path ahead. Now and then she stumbled, trying to keep up. Mathy flitted through the darkness, skimming easily over a path whose every bump and turn her feet had memorized. They passed through the walnut grove to the foot of the long slope. There they turned, taking an old road that led into the woods.

"Where are you?" Jessica called softly. "I can't see."

"Here—this way."

Jessica felt her way in the direction of the voice and rounded a bend in the road. There before her, in a black hollow under the bluff, thousands of tiny lights pricked the darkness.

"Here it is!" cried Mathy. "All the lightning bugs in the world!"

The darkness was alive with them—a great swarm, a freshet, an explosion of fireflies. They pulsed and swam, floated and fell, and rose as high as the treetops. The air was filled with their delicate acrid insect odor.

Mathy jigged with delight, beating her hard little feet on the ground. "They stayed for you, Jessica, they waited!" She plunged in with her arms outstretched. "Come on, Jessica! Dance!" Around and around she went, her joy like a whirlpool reaching out to take Jessica in.

"Oh, Jessica—" Mathy stopped abruptly. "Don't you like it?"

"Oh, yes, I do!"

"Isn't it pretty?"

"It is—it's beautiful!"

"I thought it would cheer you up." Mathy's voice brimmed with disappointment.

"It does, honey! Sort of—I mean—why, it's beautiful!"

Mathy walked back, and they stood watching the fireflies. "I guess you want to see Tom awful bad," she said. After a moment they started back to the house.

10

Jessica woke up on Sunday morning with an aching head. Dressing for church, she felt worse by the minute. Her stomach was queasy, and she felt feverish. After some consultation between Matthew and Callie, it was decided that the girls should stay home.

"What's the matter with her?" said Matthew.

"She's just got a little upset stomach," said Callie.

"You don't think— She and that boy couldn't have—"

"No," Callie said firmly. "They couldn't. I know for sure."

"I only wondered. What I saw out by the gate that night was enough to make you suspicious."

"There's nothing the matter with her except what's supposed to be. . . . I reckon you kissed me a time or two before we was married." Matthew made no comment. "I still think you were a little hard on her. And on him, too. I reckon he didn't mean any real harm."

"I could hardly let him stay here after that!"

"I guess not. But I'm glad Jake let him work over there awhile, so he didn't go hungry."

"You think she knows he's there?"

"I doubt it. Anyway, he's gone by this time. Fanny told me he was going out to Kansas."

"Good riddance," said Matthew.

Callie put on her hat. "For a little I'd stay home myself this morning. It's so hot, and I've got a kind of headache. But I guess I'd better go."

Leonie was sulking in the parlor. "Who's going to play for Sunday School, I'd like to know?"

"I reckon they'll find somebody," said Callie. "That little Barrow girl, maybe. She takes lessons. Be nice to let her have a chance at it once in a while."

Leonie stomped on the loud petal and banged the piano keys.

"Now, missy, you straighten up, do you hear?"

"Why can't Mathy stay? She and Jessica have so much business together."

"She's staying."

"By herself, I mean."

"I want you to stay, too. And you just get that look off your face. Mama's sorry you can't go, but it can't be helped this time. Mathy, you behave yourself and don't go running off."

Matthew and Callie drove away. Jessica lay upstairs in her petticoat with a wet washrag on her head and listened to the lonely sound of the locusts. Leonie was playing the piano. After a bit Jessica heard her go to the door and call Mathy. She called out the front and out back and came to the bottom of the stairs.

"Is Mathy up there with you?"

"No."

"Where'd she go, the little brat!" She yelled again a time or two and went back to the piano.

Jessica lay back with her eyes closed. A few moments later Mathy tiptoed in. "Sh!" She put her finger to her lips and crept cautiously across the room. "Tom's here!" she whispered.

Jessica jumped up, letting the washrag fall to the floor. "Where?"

"Down in the orchard."

"What'll I do—what about Leonie?"

"You wait here—don't go downstairs till I tell you to." She crept back down without a sound. Then the back door slammed.

"Mathy?" said Leonie.

"What?"

"Where have you been? I've been yelling at you."

"I was outdoors."

"Where outdoors? Didn't you hear me?"

"Huh-uh."

"I'm going to tell Mama on you."

91

"Tell."

"Where are you going now?"

"Out to the well. I'm going to pump a bucket of water. Want a fresh drink?"

"I guess so."

Jessica began to dress, barely able to manage her buttons. She brushed her hair and tied it up with a fresh ribbon, splashed cold water in her face, and pinched her cheeks to give them some color. Still the signal hadn't come. Leonie went on playing. Jessica sat trembling on the edge of the bed. Now and then her glance strayed to the picture of the girl and the cross and she turned away with a shudder. Down in the kitchen the clock struck eleven.

Leonie finished the song she was playing. Jessica heard her go out the back door and across the yard. A moment later there was a loud thud, a scuffling noise, and a banging of fists, and Leonie's voice rose in muffled fury. The back door slammed again and Mathy dashed up the stairs. "Come on! I locked her in the toilet!"

"She'll die!" squealed Jessica. "She'll knock the door down!"

"No, she won't—I put a board against it. She won't get out till I let her out."

"Are you sure?"

"Of course I'm sure. Come on, Jessica!"

She grabbed Jessica by the hand and dragged her pellmell down the stairs. They raced through the orchard, Mathy two jumps in the lead. "Tom?" she called as they reached the bottom of the orchard. "We're here—it's safe!"

Tom peered cautiously around a tree. "Hi," he said, grinning.

"You came back!" cried Jessica.

"Yeah," he said. "How are y', Jessica?"

"I'm fine!"

"Are you—all right?"

"I'm fine, Tom! Really!"

"I'm sure glad to hear that!" He hesitated, still with the foolish grin on his face. "Mathy said you wanted to see me."

"I went and got him," said Mathy.

Jessica turned slowly, her smile fading. "You did?"

"I thought maybe he was still over at Latham's, so I went and looked."

Jessica turned back to Tom. "You're still there? I thought you were going to Kansas."

"I was—I ain't left yet."

"Oh."

"Gee, I—sure am glad you sent for me. I been wonderin'—"

"I didn't send for you," Jessica said quietly. "I didn't know Mathy was going."

"She didn't, Tom," said Mathy. "She didn't send me—I just told you that."

Tom laughed uncertainly. "Well—I reckon it don't matter what she said. I'm glad to see you anyway."

"Are you?" said Jessica.

"Sure."

"Then why didn't you come back last week, Tom?"

"Well, I—"

"Without having to be brought?"

"Gosh, Jessica, I wasn't sure—I didn't know if you'd have the nerve to sneak out again."

"I would have come."

"I didn't *know* that. Don't be mad, Jessica."

"I'm not mad!" she said, blinking back the tears.

"Oh, stop fussing about it," said Mathy. "There isn't time. Hurry up and decide."

"Decide what?" said Tom.

"About getting married."

"Married!"

"You're going to, aren't you?"

"Well, I— My gosh! I reckon we never got that far, did we, Jessica?"

"I don't think so."

Mathy said, "Well, you like each other. I just thought—"

"I don't know much about gittin' married!" said Tom.

"You just go to the preacher," said Mathy.

"I don't guess it's as easy as all that."

"Why not?"

"A feller's got to have something to git married *with*."

"You mean money?"

"Yeah!" said Tom. "And a job and a house to live in."

"Oh, who needs a house!"

"Married folks do, that's who. You got to have a place to live."

"Can't you live with your folks?"

"Mathy, hush talking like that!" said Jessica. "We can't get married—Papa wouldn't let us."

"Don't tell him," said Mathy. "Just do it. *Elope!*"

"Oh, Mathy, hush that!" Jessica giggled.

93

"Would you be scared to?" said Mathy. "Would *you*, Tom?"

"I don't reckon I'd be scared, but—"

"Don't you want to get married?" said Mathy.

"I hadn't thought much about it."

"*I* think about it," she said. "I'd just love to get married. I think it would be fun!"

"Sure!" he said with a scornful laugh.

"I think so, too," said Jessica softly. "Tom? I could go with you to Kansas. I'd go anywhere you want to go and do what you said—I wouldn't be any trouble."

Tom stared at her in alarm. "I ain't got much money, Jessica."

"I don't mind that."

"Or no job or nothin'!"

"I don't care if we have to stay with your folks awhile—they sound real nice."

"Well, Jehosaphat! I ain't got enough money to get us there!"

"You can use the egg money," said Mathy. "I'll get it for you."

"That's stealin'," said Tom.

"Not if you pay it back."

"We could pay it back," said Jessica.

Tom backed up against a tree, his shirt damp with sweat. "I don't know nothin' about elopin'!"

"You catch a train," said Mathy.

"Yeah? How do we get there?"

"Next Sunday—when we go to church—Jessica can sneak off and meet you at the depot!"

"I could," said Jessica. "We could go down to your folks—"

"What if your Pa was to catch us?" said Tom.

"He won't," said Mathy. "He'll be singing in the choir."

"He sure would be mad when he found out."

"He'd only holler a lot. What do you care—you won't be here."

Tom looked at Jessica in terror.

"Could we, Tom?" she said.

"Gosh, I don't know—"

"Well, make up your minds!" said Mathy. "I've got to let Leonie out of the toilet."

Tom wiped the sweat off his forehead. "Oh boy," he said.

"Please, Tom!" Mathy cried. "We love you so much!"

He stood with his back against the tree, facing his loving adversaries—both of them soft and young and sweet, the one earnest and determined, the other shy and adoring, and both of them as deadly in intention as a shotgun. A slow, defeated grin came over his face. "Well," he said, looking at Jessica, "I reckon I'm game if you are."

"I'm game! Oh, Tom—" she cried and stopped short. "Really and truly, Tom?"

"Yeah."

"You'll meet me Sunday at the depot?"

"Yeah."

"You promise?"

He nodded soberly. "I promise."

"Well, good!" said Mathy. "Now come on, Jessica, before they catch us."

11

If Jessica had not been obsessed with first love, if she had not been so smitten with guilt, she might never have believed Mathy's assurances; she might never have left home that Sunday morning with her heart in her mouth and the egg money in her pocketbook.

If Tom had had a temperament less easy and affable, and, above all, if he had made any other plans, he might never have met her at the depot.

But she was, and he hadn't, and they caught the noon train.

About the same moment, the family was coming out of church. Mathy conveniently lost herself in the crowd until she heard the whistle far down the track, at which point she produced the letter which Jessica left. They were standing by the car, waiting for Jessica to appear. Matthew didn't finish the first page even. "Get in," he said, and they drove off lickety-split to the depot.

"Was that *yore* daughter?" said the stationmaster with a faint trace of a smile.

Matthew jumped back in the car and killed the engine. He had to get out and crank. Sweat poured from his face, and his shirt stuck to his back. On the way home, the engine died again and he had to clean a sparkplug. No one uttered a word. Callie cried all the way.

They never did find out how Tom and Jessica met. Mathy swore innocence. But she had her punishment. Papa wouldn't let them come home any more.

In spite of him, Callie sent Jessica's clothes. "I don't care what she's done, I'll not have her going around in somebody else's old rags." She packed dresses and underwear and pretty ribbons, all of them salted down with tears and exasperation. "I can't hardly stand it! Her goin' off down there with those hillbillies! I wanted her to have someone nice."

"Water seeks its own level," said Matthew.

He could not forgive her the degradation. She had wrecked his standing in the community. And why? In his good Protestant manner, he would have accepted the blame and made a virtue of acceptance. But he could not for the life of him see where the blame lay. He had given her an easy life, a good home, an education. Sitting one day in the timber in a fine August rain, he cried out to the Lord, "You know how hard I work, winter and summer! You know how I have tried! What could I do that I haven't done?"

But no bush burned and there was no answer. Only the soft sibilance of the rain in the oak leaves.

12

Tom and Jessica spent the winter with his family, a hilarious brood who simply moved over and made a place for her at the table. They were a trout-fishing, squirrel-hunting, hill-farm family who lived happily from hand to mouth. They nipped a little home brew when it came handy. On Saturday night they dressed up in the best they had and clapped and sang at play-parties. On Sunday morning they put on the same clothes and clapped and sang in church. Piety was pleasure and vice-versa, and Jessica was shocked and delighted by them.

There was very little these days that did not shock and delight her. She lived in perpetual astonishment, finding herself there and with Tom. She liked him more and more as they got acquainted. Even his illnesses—colds, fever, the attacks of weakness which he seemed prone to—even these endeared him to her. She lavished affection all over and around him, and the two of them lived in that warm radiant bath like a pair of goldfish in a bowl. Everyone around stared in and smiled indulgently.

Her one worry was financial. They were not contributing. Seeing no way for Tom to earn much of a living, she got herself a job teaching the local school. She taught by ear, remembering what she could and revising the method where she thought permissible. It was a small country school with a small enrollment of jolly children. They adored her. They coasted together at recess and sang and played games. They put on frequent entertainments, and everyone in the neighborhood came. One night, at a pie-supper, Jessica won the box of candy for the Prettiest Girl. Tom was as proud as she was. "I told you I'd marry a schoolmom!" he said.

She had written home the moment she got the job, sure that Papa would be pleased. Papa did not answer. Leonie and Mathy wrote. Leonie's letter dutifully conveyed her mother's message of sympathy: What a shame that Jessica had to support her husband. Jessica was more than disappointed, she was indignant. Here she was as happy as a lark, and all Mama did was feel sorry.

As summer came on, Tom's health improved, his worst affliction now a recurrence of wanderlust. He talked again of going west. Jessica encouraged him, thinking a change of climate might be beneficial. Only this time he was not to go alone, hopping freight trains. She had saved a little money through the winter, and both of them would go. They would put on their good clothes and ride decently in a coach. "Your uncle won't mind if I come along, will he? I can help your aunt cook for threshers. I'll work hard." Tom allowed they'd be glad to have her, and so would he. They sent off a postcard, and late in June they packed their lunch in a shoebox and boarded a train.

Jessica had been to Oklahoma City once, to visit her rich Aunt Bertie (Matthew's sister, whose husband had done well in the wholesale grocery business). The boxcars had carried Tom around the state a bit. But neither of them had made this long a journey, and Tom never in such style. They made friends with other passengers, ate fried chicken and cake out of the box, and picked cinders from each other's eyes. They rode two days and a night and arrived in a small town in western Kansas to find that the uncle had moved away. No one knew just where. He had lost the wheat farm.

Tom was astounded. Hadn't his oldest brother gone out to work for the uncle only three summers ago? No, they hadn't heard from the uncle since then. But he had just always been there, taken for granted. Tom guessed there was nothing to do now but turn around and go home.

But it did seem a shame, said Jessica, now that they'd come all this way. There must be other wheat farms around; why couldn't they work for someone else? It was worth a try. They had an ice cream soda at the drugstore to bolster their spirits, and began to ask round the town—a forlorn gritty little town huddled around the grain elevator, whose silvery towers rose in defiance of the plains. "Why don't we ask there," said Jessica, "at the elevator?" And that was how they found Mr. Olin.

He was a small sandy-haired man burnt to the color of the landscape, all but undistinguishable except for the bright blue eyes. He had a ferocious manner, a kind heart, and six hundred acres of wheatland mortgaged to the lightning rods on the barn. He also had a small tenant house where Tom and Jessica could live. They rode home with him delightedly in the big grain wagon.

Mr. Olin was a threshing machine by long association—busy and chuffing and full of noise, but purposeful noise; and he could separate the wheat from the chaff. They liked him, though he paid his help poorly (there was never enough left over from payments to the bank) and worked them hard. He asked no more of them than he did of himself, and he had a dry good humor.

They also liked his wife, and she and Jessica became good friends. Mrs. Olin, a flat weary little woman, had a winsome quality that seemed out of place in this stubborn country; a sweetness brought with her, like a pressed bouquet, from some green and juicy land. Jessica marveled that she should have kept it all these years, existing day after sunburnt day in that sandy acre that contained her life—her house, her yard, her piteous small garden.

It was a frightening acre. The house so tiny and wretched, the barn as huge and overbearing as a coffin in the parlor. There was no denying the import of that barn; this was a man's farm run a man's way, and the house and the woman got along in any way they could. Between house and barn stood the machine shed, spewing tractor parts, axle grease and tools; the water trough for the cattle; corrugated iron granaries flashing in the sunlight; the silo, a blind turret without a castle; and the windmill, creaking and complaining as it dragged up water from deep underground. Except for the great barn, everything looked flimsy and impermanent, like a child's cardboard farm set up on a floor; nothing could put down roots in a ground so unyielding.

No grass grew anywhere. In the distance a grove of catalpas drew a dusty green line along the edge of the wheatfield. But in Mrs. Olin's one acre, nothing grew except pithy vegetables, the hoodlum sunflowers, and a cottonwood or two—rough, gray trees that filled the yard with their useless cotton. The wind made a death rattle in the leaves.

Often Jessica stood at the door of the tenant house and stared across the fields, thinking of home. Green grass and roses in the yard, and Little Tebo flowing cool and gentle; the whispering green orchard, Mathy wading in the branch. When she and Tom sat on the doorstep after dark, she thought of those evenings on the porch last summer and could almost smell the honeysuckle. Sometimes Tom played his harmonica and sang "The Butcher Boy," and sometimes she cried. But they were comfortable tears, soon spent.

Many evenings Tom went straight to bed, too exhausted to sit up. He was so pale, even with his sunburn; there were blue hollows under his eyes, and he steadily lost weight. The Olins worried, urged food on him and made him take it easy. Tom grew thinner and wearier. One night he collapsed. No one thought too much about it, since that was the night the wheat stubble caught fire. In the heat and frenzy men frequently collapsed. Tom was driving the wagon with the water tank. At one point he climbed down to help beat the creeping blaze with wet gunny sacks. That was when he fell. One of the men dragged him back to the wagon. After a few days in bed, when he had gained strength, they took him to the doctor. The doctor peered and prodded, mumbled vaguely, and prescribed a tonic. As they were leaving, however, he called them back, and in his tentative manner, suggested a hospital forty miles away. Jessica was terrified. "Sweetheart, I ain't goin' to no hospital," Tom said. "Ain't nothin' the matter with me but the heat and orneriness."

"You stay in bed awhile," Mr. Olin said, "and take that tonic. We'll feed you up good and get you back on your feet."

But Jessica was not convinced. Something was wrong, and she linked it in her mind with this brimstone country. Tom needed rain. And she thought of the rain that comes in August in Missouri, sweeping away the fevers of midsummer. She thought of the farm—her father's farm—where the yard was green, the house white and orderly, and her father the Almighty. In her mind she turned again to him. "We're going home," she said.

Nothing else would do for her. On a blistering July morning Mr. Olin drove them to the train. Tom lay in the wagon on a canvas cot, Jessica shielding him with a ruffled parasol (exhumed from the trunk where Mrs. Olin had buried her girlhood). All the way in, Tom kept up a brave banter. But when the train arrived he sagged between them, barely able to stand. The little plainsman, cursing with sympathy, hustled them down the platform to the baggage car.

"This man's too sick to set up," he said. "Let him lay back here on a cot—I got a cot in the wagon."

The conductor said, "You can't do that, mister."

"Sufferin' Jesus!" said Mr. Olin, throwing the cot through the big door. "Can't you see the boy's sick?"

"He's got to set up front. It's regulations."

Mr. Olin bruised the air with his outrage. "What's he goin' to hurt, I'd like to know? If folks can take part of their baggage up front, I reckon part of the folks can take the place of the baggage."

"I can't let you do it."

"Well, I'm doin' it, and they've paid their fare and you can't put 'em off."

He dragged Tom into the baggage car, Jessica pushing from behind. Tom lay back on the cot, among the crates and boxes, too exhausted to care where they put him. The bell clanged. Jessica put her arms around Mr. Olin and cried.

"You'll be all right," he said. "He won't put you off. You can ride right here clear to Kansas City. They'll meet you there, I guess?" Jessica shook her head. "Didn't you write and tell 'em?" he said in dismay.

"I didn't think I should."

"Tarnation, girl!"

"I'll call when we get to Renfro—they'll come and get us."

" 'Board!" sang the conductor. Mr. Olin jumped down and ran beside them, shouting encouragements as the train heaved itself out of the station. He waited till it disappeared on the hot windy reaches of the plain, then hurrying back to the wagon, he drove directly to the telephone office and placed a long-distance call. He waited more than an hour, draining cup after cup of water from the big glass jug, while women's voices ran along the wires, through Salina, Abilene, Topeka, into the snarl of Kansas City and out again through the Missouri woods, till at last the phone rang in the dining room of the farm near Renfro.

Mr. Olin roared his message over the interference. "I put 'em on the Union Pacific this morning," he shouted. "Mister, I got an idea they ain't goin' to be very welcome back there. But you won't have to put up with him very long. It's none of my business, but I've got to say one more thing—whatever they done, they've had enough trouble. They don't deserve more. That's all I got to say. Except that I hope there's somebody to meet 'em when they get to Kansas City."

The connection went dead before he finished. But Matthew had heard enough to know that Jessica was coming home and Tom Purdy was dying. He stood for a moment with his forehead against the mouthpiece, trying to arrange his feelings. The Lord's judgment, he thought grimly—and with some pity, too. Poor girl. But then, she had to learn.

The train crawled and shuddered through the long afternoon. Jessica sat on a crate, fanning Tom and wiping his face with a wet handkerchief. She tried to feed him from the lunch Mrs. Olin sent with them, but he had no appetite.

Once he looked up in weak distress. "I'll make it up to you, Jessica," he said.

"There's nothing to make up."

"All this trouble," he murmured and closed his eyes. "I'm goin' to get well and I'll make it up to you."

"I know you will, honey."

After a while he said, "I'm glad we got married."

"So am I."

"Are you?"

"Oh yes, Tom!"

He looked up with a bright smile. "Reckon we never would have had the nerve if that little Mathy hadn'ta egged us on." Jessica laughed. "She's a caution," he said.

"She sure is."

"I'm thankful to her. . . . We did right, didn't we, sweetheart?"

"Yes, we did."

He smiled peacefully and closed his eyes. He slept for several miles. Presently he awoke, murmuring, rolling his head from side to side. She bent over him. "So thirsty," he said. Then, helplessly, looking up at her with pleading in his eyes like a small sick animal, he died.

The hot wind blew cinders through the door of the baggage car. Jessica stood up, wondering what to do. She sat down again and began to fan him. Then she stopped and put both hands over her mouth, while the train whistle screamed and screamed at a crossing.

13

Matthew had another call that day, from the town where they took Tom's body off the train. He caught the next train out. Jessica had not cried until she saw him.

They took Tom back to his own people and buried him in a country churchyard. But the grass there was brown and brittle; and grasshoppers rose out of it, whirring. Already the leaves, yellowed by the dry summer, had begun to fall, and the locusts scraped and droned, crying wearily that all, all was lost. Jessica stood bewildered. She had forgotten the dry seasons and remembered only greenness and deep shade, cool water, and ripe fruit on the trees. What had happened to make the summer like this? And where was Tom?

Dazed and docile, she went home to the farm, and as she went about the old tasks and visited with her sisters, the hurt slowly mended. Grieving was no pleasure to her, and she let it go. The weather broke, too, at the same time. After the long dry spell, the August rainstorm arrived. The grass turned green again, the days flowed cool and blue and golden and the nights cold and white. The house lost its hush and filled with noise again, laughter and singing and screen doors slamming. The rhythm changed, the tempo increased. Since the time was near when they must move back to town, Callie rushed to put into jars anything that survived the drought. Her runners plied back and forth between house and garden, grapevines and orchard, and the kitchen steamed with rich smells.

It was a happy convalescence. Everyone was kind. Papa held her on his lap; Mama kissed her good night. They had taken her back, opened their arms and received her like the prodigal son, all love and forgiveness and forgetting. Jessica was miserable. For no matter how good they were, no matter how much she loved them, she was going away again. And she didn't know how to tell them.

It came about one day at breakfast. They sat at the kitchen table laughing their heads off. Everything was funny that morning. Papa was cute and funny as a clown. The fire in the cookstove gave the room a pleasant warmth, and the table was be-jeweled with fresh jams and jellies. Buttering a hot biscuit, Mat-thew paused and beamed a misty smile around the table. "Isn't this just fine!" he said, turning to Jessica. "We're so glad to have you home."

"Thank you, Papa."

"We missed you, honey," said her mother.

"I'll say we did!" said Mathy. "Everybody was always crying."

"All right," said Callie, frowning at her.

"I've just been thinking," Matthew said. "Of course, we'd like mighty well to keep you right here with us this winter, but I know you wanted to go over to Clarkstown last year for some college work. And I've been thinking, if you'd like to go this term, I believe I can manage to send you." He leaned back with a smile. "Now how would you like that!"

"Why, I— My goodness, Papa, I'd like it just fine! But—"

"I thought you and I would drive up there this Saturday and get you enrolled."

"That sure is nice of you, Papa."

"We'll find you a nice room at one of the boarding houses—"

"And you can come home every weekend!" Callie gave it the crowning touch and sat back in triumph.

"My *goodness!*" said Jessica. "That would be just awful nice. I always wanted to go over to Clarkstown. But I thought this winter, now that—"

"Oh, you don't *have* to go to school," Callie said hopefully. "Not if you'd rather stay home."

"Well, it's not that, Mama. I'd like to go to school, or stay home, either one. But I can't."

"Can't what?"

"Do either one."

Matthew's hand paused with a lifted coffee cup. "Why can't you?"

"I'm going to teach school again."

"Oh? Where?"

"Down there."

He set the cup carefully back in the saucer. "I see."

"Down there with *his* folks?" said her mother. "I thought you gave up that school."

"I did," said Jessica. "But while we were down there for the funeral, they came and told me I could have it back. All I had to do was say the word."

"And you accepted the offer," said Matthew.

"Not right then. I thought it over first. I didn't let them know till last week."

"I see," he said again.

There was a chilly silence. Mathy and Leonie stopped eating.

"I thought you'd want me to teach school," Jessica said timidly.

"Not without a little further preparation. That's why I proposed sending you to Clarkstown."

"But I've already given them my word. I could hardly go back on my word."

"Circumstances would seem to warrant it in this case."

"Honey," said her mother, breaking in with a cozy smile, "you don't want to go back down there and live, do you? When he ain't there?"

"I've got lots of friends down there."

"You've got nice friends up here."

"I know, Mama. But I kind of feel like that's my home now. Oh, I know," she added quickly, seeing the look on their faces, "this is my real home. But since I lived down there when I was married, and that's Tom's home, I thought—"

"You ain't plannin' to live with his folks?"

"They want me to."

"Well, so do your own folks!" Callie burst out. "Why do you have to go running back to his!"

"I'm not, really—"

"Rough ignorant folks that don't know nothin', can't hardly make a living—"

"But they're nice—they've been awful nice to me."

"I thought we'd been pretty nice, too!"

"You have been, Mama," she said, her voice trembling. "You and Papa have been so nice!"

"Then why do you have to go runnin' back to them!"

Jessica began to cry. "I don't know," she said, knowing only that she had to.

Through all the storms of tears, accusations, and common-sense appeals, she held her ground. She had gone away before, risking everything, and she had not lost. Though Tom was lost, his love was not. Death is not the greatest disappointment in the world. And having succeeded once, she might again. But it took more courage this time, far more than running away with Tom. For she knew, though they had forgiven her that leaving, they would never forgive her this.

Seeing that her head was set, they accepted martyrdom with a grudging grace. No more was said. She was treated with elaborate politeness, like a stranger. Fun and laughter fled the house, leaving an air of gloom. Her mother sighed regularly; her father sulked. Even Mathy failed her. Mathy, who had cheered her into womanhood, failed to see now that she must stay there. She couldn't come back and be a little girl. Though she waded in the branch and they slid in the hay and had long talks, it wasn't the fun it used to be. She pretended it was, for Mathy's sake, but she could hardly wait to be gone.

As the time approached, however, she dreaded it more and more. When the day finally came, she woke up with real nausea. She choked down some breakfast and promptly lost it. Her head hurt like a conscience. Everyone went about in a muted frenzy. They dressed in their solemn best as if they were going to a funeral and drove solemnly to town. Jessica chattered all the way, hearing herself and loathing the sound. It was only, she said, for a little while; she would be home for Christmas. Next thing you knew, school would be over and she'd be home for the summer.

"Yes, that's right," her mother said sadly. "It won't hardly seem like no time."

"I'll write to you every week."

"That'll be nice."

"Maybe you can come down sometime and visit."

"Well, we'll see."

At the station they stood in a huddle, waiting for the train. Conversation sputtered and died. Jessica's head throbbed and she began to shake. Away off down the track a whistle blew, driving a spike clear through her. "Well, here it comes," she said with a crazy laugh.

Mathy screamed. "Don't go, Jessica, don't go!"

Leonie looked at her in tearful reproach.

The train chuffed into the station and the conductor swung down with the little step stool. "You're the one that's goin', young lady?"

"I'm the one."

"Well, hop right on," he said, taking the suitcase as Matthew handed it up. He stepped down the platform a little way. "'Board!" he shouted.

Jessica swallowed hard and turned around. The family was lined up like a firing squad. "Well—" she said.

"*My baby!*" Callie fell against her in agony, her body jerking like an epileptic. Her sobs hissed in and out her nose and made a storm in Jessica's ear. Mathy and Leonie clung together, wailing. And there stood Papa with his face all twisted and tears pouring down his cheeks.

Jessica's face knotted like a fist, and a lump the size of a locomotive formed in her throat. She tore herself loose and threw herself on her father. "I love you!" she cried, her voice a hideous squeak, and bolted up the steps—sick with the knowledge that this was how it would be all the rest of her life. She couldn't stay, but she couldn't stay away, and she would come back time after time, doomed forever to come and go and endure these ghastly partings. This was the price of her freedom. This was how it was going to be.

Matthew

1

It was the Friday before Easter. Butting a cold north wind up the slope to the schoolhouse, Matthew wondered by what stretch of whose imagination the day was known as Good.

His youngest daughter skipped beside him, prattling of miracles. "I'll bet he put something in it," said Mathy. "He didn't turn that water into wine—he dropped something in the pitcher while he was pouring."

She referred to a staged miracle that had taken place the night before in the Baptist church, during the annual revival meeting. Matthew and his family were Methodist, but in Shawano, denominational lines, though strict, were often crossed. For the past week, Methodists, Baptists, and Campbellites (everyone but the Hard-Shell Baptists and the Dunkards) had gathered together to hear a visiting evangelist harangue lost souls to Christ. He had done so with a number of tricks, not all of which Matthew thought necessary.

"He said the Lord gave him the power to do it," said Mathy. "Do you believe that, Papa?"

"Well—" He could hardly come right out and say the man was a charlatan. Doubts in the mind of a child . . .

"Everybody else did."

Unhappily, she was right. The gentleman was no St. Paul and not a very skilled magician. But he worked up enough hysteria in the congregation so that they swallowed his miracles like the sacramental wine. Matthew privately deplored his method and wished he made the Easter story sound less like a lynching. Even if that's what it was. It seemed a pity to paint the agonies on the Cross more vividly than the joy of the Resurrection. That was downright Catholic! But then, he reflected, the Roman love of the dramatic is with us still, in spite of Calvin and Wesley. And no amount of life everlasting makes such good drama as death.

"I didn't believe it," said Mathy and skipped on ahead.

The wind blew straight off the polar icecap. Easter came early this year. Matthew's bones ached with the cold. He was sick and tired of the winter grind and not yet caught up in the excitement of spring. Track meets and county contests, class plays, exam papers, and all the hullabaloo of Commencement.

Mathy sang aloud to the tune of "Here We Go 'Round the Mulberry Bush":

> *"When all aloud the wind doth blow,*
> *And coughing drowns the parson's saw,*
> *And birds sit brooding in the snow,*
> *And Marion's nose looks red and raw."*

"Where did you get that?" said Matthew.

"It's Shakespeare."

"I know. Is that part of your assigned reading?"

"Huh-uh. I just read it for myself."

"You'd better be spending your time on your assignments. Have you finished your W.C.T.U. essay?"

"Oh, Papa! Do I have to write that thing?"

"Just why do you think you should be excused?"

"Because I hate it, that's why."

"That's hardly an excuse. You have to learn that we can't always do just what pleases us."

"Boy howdy, I'll say we can't!" She hopped up on a stump and flung out her arms. "The winnnnd!" she shouted. "I love the wind! I'm going to fly-y-y!" She leaped off, arms waving, coat flapping open, and fell flat on her face by the Dunkard church.

"For the land of living, child, get up!" Matthew seized her arm and his hat blew off. Mathy gave chase and retrieved it. As she stooped over, her skirts blew over her head, revealing the black sateen bloomers and a strip of long underwear. Matthew winced.

"I got it, Papa, I got your hat!"

"Thank you. Pull up your stockings, for pity's sake."

Some girls of twelve were already young ladies. But not this spidery tomboy of his. She liked pole vaulting. Boy howdy, indeed! They went on up the slope in silence.

The Shawano public school stood at the far edge of town. Across the road lay a pasture; behind it, another pasture; beyond it, open country. The building was a tall brick box, as graceless a structure as ever rose in the name of education. Red and gawky as a farm boy, it stood on its ten-acre tract and endured the elements. No tree or hedge or kindly lay of the land protected it from the weather. Sun and sleet battered it, and the wind blew down the little trees which Matthew planted each Arbor Day with ceremony and hope.

Inside, a flight of noisy wooden stairs led down to the basement floor. Another flight led up to the second floor and the grade-school rooms. The third floor, a large open area with a platform at one end, was the high school.

Matthew ruled this kingdom from the superintendent's office on the second floor, a small room at the end of a long central hall. With the door open, he could see all coming and going. The office window faced west, overlooking the back schoolyard. Outside, within easy reach, the big bell hung from a tall wooden rack, a sort of bell tower, which children were always climbing. In fact, the climbing of a stout rope tied to the rack was part of their athletic program. At any recess, Matthew might be confronted by a red puffing face and triumphant cries at the window.

A table sat in the center of the room, a rolltop desk in one corner. Three or four folding chairs, a swivel chair, a filing cabinet and a bookshelf completed the furnishings. A telephone hung on the wall. Matthew's ninety-hour diploma, framed in gilt, set the seal of authority on the room, and George Washington according to Stuart looked down on all with disdain. In this area Matthew coped with the budget and the school board, counseled teachers, gave first aid, administered discipline, graded papers, and caught his breath.

This morning, after hanging up his coat, he stood for a moment gazing out at the landscape, which gave no hint of spring. The schoolyard sloped off toward a fence marking the edge of Seabert's pasture. Beyond the pasture, perhaps a mile away, a little woods began. A stand of maple, oak, and sumac grew up the side of a long hill crowned by the town graveyard. Tombstones showed bone-white above the trees. Matthew often looked out on this view. From his tiny office, secure in the matrix of familiar sounds, he could contemplate with comfort the pleasures of easeful death. They were sensuous pleasures, having nothing to do with extinction. They were "old, unhappy, far-off things," and they filled his soul with delicious melancholy. He indulged himself for a moment. Then his gaze, retreating homeward from the hill, snagged on the two weatherbeaten toilets which stood in the schoolyard. Romanticism dissolved on the reminder that he must somehow get money out of the school board for some kind of decent plumbing. He turned with a sigh and began the day's work.

Teachers ran in and out with their problems. Two boys were brought in for discipline; one had hit the other with a hard-boiled Easter egg, and they fought on the playground. In the calm that followed the nine-o'clock bell, Matthew shut himself in and managed to do a little desk work. He had risen to go upstairs and teach his second-hour class when Mrs. Delmore Jewel arrived. He opened the door into the bosom of that portly lady, who had her hand up reaching to knock and almost struck him in the face.

"Professor Soames," she said, putting a period after the name. "Could I have a little talk with you. It's about Delmora."

It always was. This time, Delmora's part in the junior-class play was far too minor to suit her mother. "You know, we take her over to Clarkstown every Saturday for elocution lessons. I should think that someone as *trained* as she is . . ." And so on.

Matthew was late to his class. He was used to the likes of Mrs. Jewel; he despised her and could not with much principle give in to her constant demands. Still, she was the public, and he didn't like to displease her. It made him nervous.

He came down from the class to find another visitor waiting in the office, one Garney Robles, a local carpenter and paperhanger. He was also, by no qualification Matthew could discover, a member of the school board. Garney slouched in a chair and didn't bother to stand up.

"How're y', Prof. I was just passin' this way and thought I'd come in for a minute. Thought we could have a little talk if you're not busy."

"We're always busy around here," Matthew said with a prim smile.

"Wanted to talk to you some more about that Latin teacher."

"Oh yes." Matthew's brows went up ever so slightly. Garney had harped on that subject since last spring, when Matthew fought for a Latin course in the curriculum and insisted they hire another teacher. ("Prof and his new teacher, sayin' sweet things to each other in a forn tongue!" Vulgar comments of that sort.) "Well, I think that had best be discussed at a meeting—"

"You're not actually rank for keepin' Latin in the crickulum, are you, Prof?" said Garney. "I understand there ain't but half a dozen kids takin' it."

"There are twelve," said Matthew.

"Half a dozen—a dozen—what's the difference, out of seventy kids? It costs us a lot of money for a teacher, just for that handful."

"She also teaches English," said Matthew.

"Yeah, but somebody else could do that. Wouldn't we be better off with a real keen basketball coach next year?"

"It seems to me that the study of the classics is of far greater value than—"

"Hell, Prof—pardon my English—we need something that'll raise our standing in the county!"

"For a school our size, we stand first in the county scholastically."

"Well, I don't understand all that scholastic stuff. But I know we sure don't have no standing in basketball. We haven't won a tournament in three or four years. We got some good boys on our team, boys like Ed Inwood—can that kid jump!—but they just don't know how to *win*."

"It's the sport that counts," said Matthew, "playing a good clean game. It isn't necessary to win every time."

"Where's your school spirit, Professor? The community wants a winnin' team. Now I know you do the best you can, coachin' the boys. But hell, you got plenty to do without gettin' out there on the court. If you don't mind my sayin' so, Prof, we need a younger man. I don't mean no insult, but you know there ain't any of us gettin' any younger. We need some fella with a little fire in his ass, that can get in there and fight!"

Matthew was grateful for a knock on the door at that moment. The janitor looked in. "Professor, I've got a touch of the flu. I wonder if it'd be all right for me to go home."

"Sure, you go ahead," said Matthew. "Get to bed and take care of yourself. I'll take care of the furnace."

The janitor thanked him and went away. Matthew looked at his watch. "I'm going to have to excuse myself, Garney. I have a class to teach in a few minutes. I'm sure we can take this matter up at the next board meeting."

"It'll come up," Garney said, rising. "But I thought we could save time if you and me had some kind of understanding."

What an affront to education, Matthew thought, watching Garney slouch away. Goodness knows, the school board was never any Continental Congress, but most of the men were decent and earnest and they tried to do right. How had a man like Garney Robles gotten himself elected? Bullied himself in, no doubt—as he would bully the rest of them into hiring a coach. *Sic transit* the Latin course, he thought sadly. He was proud of that course; it added a certain luster to the school. He would have liked to go into the class himself and study with the pupils. He had had very little Latin in college, and his ear for languages was none too good. But how he revered the classics! He had tilled his fields to the tune of the *Georgics*, a few remembered phrases singing in his head. The loss of the Latin course would be a personal loss.

What's more, he would lose his ball team, too! He enjoyed coaching and prided himself on his agility. He could still dribble a ball down the court as nimbly as boys not half his age. But as Garney bluntly pointed out, he was getting no younger. He climbed the stairs wearily to his class.

2

The events of the afternoon did nothing to improve his spirits. He was used to such crises as a baseball through the window-pane and a child throwing up in the hall. But for the furnace to smoke in the janitor's absence seemed an outright insult. Then came the special Easter assembly, and the students finished his patience. They were normally a well-behaved group—as well as you could expect at that age—but it didn't take much to set them off, and today something set them off. They whispered and squirmed and coughed in unison. Waves of suppressed laughter rolled through the room. He managed to keep it under control until he rose to direct the glee club. Then he had to turn his back, and what went on behind it he could only imagine. It was all he could do to get his singers through their anthem (which he had rehearsed so lovingly for the last four weeks).

He returned to the office thoroughly out of sorts. "Behaving like Hottentots!" he said, standing at the window. "No respect at all. And look at the trash!" The wrapper from somebody's lunch blew across the yard, followed by scraps of tablet paper, a page from a notebook. And someone had left a kite tied to the back fence. It flopped about on the ground like a chicken with its head off. Matthew turned in disgust and strode out of the building, picking up scraps of paper on his way to the fence. Taking out his pocketknife, he cut the string and began to reel the kite in, noticing as it bounced toward him that it bore some sort of decoration. He pulled it up and turned it around. It was quite a large kite, made of brown wrapping paper, and on one side, drawn rather skillfully in red ink, was the figure of Christ, crucified on the kite's crossed sticks. The other side bore the legend: "Shame on you, Pontius Pilate!"

Matthew looked at it in a kind of despair. He hadn't enough trouble this day—now this had to come along, condemning him automatically to a session with the culprit. And who the culprit was he knew full well. Only one boy in school had the audacity to make a crucifix of a kite. That was Ed Inwood. Sighing inwardly, he carried the kite back to the office. For a little, he'd drop it into the wastebasket and pretend he had never seen it—the wind blew it away. But every kid in school knew about this, and maybe the teachers, too; the story would spread all over town. He was forced to call Ed on the carpet, no more for Ed's sake than his own. He closed the office door and sat down at the desk to gather strength.

Ed Inwood was a senior by the grace of indulgent teachers—the ladies, not Matthew. He read a good deal but studied nothing and knew too little about too much. He had a mind as inquiring as a pup's nose and about as discriminating. He was forever smelling around among familiar dogmas and sniffing the backside of the Almighty at the most embarrassing moments. Many was the time he had snarled a class discussion with his irrelevant questions. "Mr. Soames, if the theory of evolution is true, does that make Adam and Eve a pair of apes?" "Mr. Soames, if Christ were alive today, wouldn't we call him a Bolshevik?" Mr. Soames this and Mr.

Soames that, till Matthew lost his temper and tripped over his own arguments.

At Halloween, Ed had tarred a *KKK* on the flank of Matthew's cow. He admitted it next day and offered to remove the brand. Matthew set him to work with turpentine, only to find later that Ed had shaved the patches, leaving the letters plainly incised. Ed swore he had to do it to get the tar off.

The boy was as governless as air! Clamp down on him, and he escaped like wind from a paper bag, with a loud explosion—more noise than damage, but he was a terrible disruption. It was the fault of his upbringing, thought Matthew—brought up by a married sister (the parents were dead), allowed to run loose and do more or less as he pleased. (Play basketball, drive cars, and chase girls. Many was the time Matthew had flushed him out of a parked car at night, up by the schoolhouse.) And it was too bad, for he had a good mind. "Ed," Matthew said to him time after time, "Ed, why don't you apply yourself! Settle down and study a little. You could amount to something." The answer was always, "I don't want to amount to anything—I just want to have fun!" Fun! That's all he thought about. And this was typical of his "fun"—to crucify Christ on a kite!

Matthew rose, rang the closing bell, and opened the office door. Children stormed out of the classrooms into the hall. He had tried to make it a rule that they march out quietly. But maybe it was too late in the year to expect much order, even of the teachers. Besides, it was Friday. As he watched, a tall well-built boy descended from the third floor two steps at a time, hugged a girl, goosed a boy, and trotted down the hall toward the office, his handsome face as brightly eager as if he expected a prize. Big basketball star, thought Matthew! At the door he paused politely. "You wanted to see me, sir?"

"Come in, Ed," said Matthew. "Close the door, please." He pointed to the kite. "I assume you're familiar with this?"

Ed leaned over the table. "Yes sir, I believe that's mine."

"You're certain?" Matthew said dryly.

"Oh yes, sir. No mistake."

"And you drew this picture on it?"

"Yes sir. I'm pretty handy that way."

"I'm aware of that." (Oh, the years of comic Valentines, of cartoons drawn on the margins of books, the tattooed arms of Venus de Milo!) "Ed, what prompted you to do a thing like this?"

"Well," Ed drawled, "I was making this kite the other day—"

"In the first place, is this a fit pastime for a boy your age?"

"Look at Ben Franklin!"

"Never mind Benjamin Franklin."

"Well, like I said, I was making this kite, and I got to thinking how the sticks made a cross— Mr. Soames, do you think the kite had religious significance at one time? Like you were saying in class the other day, how some nursery rhymes had political meaning in the beginning—do you think maybe the kite—"

"We are not here to discuss the history of the kite."

"Yes sir. Anyway, I noticed that a kite is built on a cross. And this being Easter, I thought I'd keep the whole thing in the spirit of the occasion. I thought it worked out pretty good."

"There is no doubt of your ability. It's your use of it I'm questioning."

"Is there anything wrong with drawing a picture of Jesus?"

"It's not the drawing of a picture—"

"I copied it out of a Sunday School paper. I believe the original was a painting by Van Dyck, the great Dutch artist."

"Ed, it is not the painting of a picture that's at fault! It's where you put it. A kite is no place for the image of Christ. Putting the Lord on a frivolous plaything makes a mockery of Him. And your caption," he added, "is impertinent to a high degree!"

"You don't think Pilate should have been ashamed of himself?"

"Certainly—and so should you, for treating a sacred matter so lightly."

"Mr. Soames, would you say that this comes under the heading of sin?"

"Your action? Well, no," he said, softening a bit, "I would not call it a sin. But it is highly disrespectful."

"Who to?"

"To the Lord. It's blasphemy."

"What if I don't believe He *is* the Lord?"

"Most of us do believe it. I, for one."

"Then it's disrespectful to *you*."

"And all who believe."

"But is it disrespectful to the Lord—if I don't think He *is* the Lord? What I mean is, Mr. Soames—well, my sister has one of these things you call an incense burner. It looks like a statue of Buddha—you know, you burn some kind of stinkin' stuff in it and smoke pours out of his mouth? Now a lot of Chinamen think Buddha is God. So we take their god and make him into a trinket and burn incense in him. But we don't mean any insult—we don't consider it blasphemous, because we don't think he *is* a god. So if I don't believe Christ is—"

"Ed, I will not excuse you on the grounds of your atheistic views! If you persist in your mistaken notions, there is no way I can force you to change them. But I will not tolerate your flaunting them in or around this school."

"Well, all right. But all I did was draw a picture. I don't see why I'm any worse than Van Dyck and those other guys."

"It's your attitude, Ed! Attitude makes all the difference between reverence and profanity. You can say 'My God,' and it's one thing or the other, depending on your attitude. By your attitude you have profaned the image of Jesus Christ. It's exactly the same as taking the name of the Lord in vain." Matthew finished eloquently and leaned back.

"That's one of the Commandments, isn't it?" said Ed.

"The third," said Matthew.

"Yeah . . . So in that case, I reckon I've busted a Commandment wide open."

"One might put it that way."

Ed looked at him innocently. "But you said it wasn't a sin, Mr. Soames."

"Well, what I meant was—"

"I thought breaking a Commandment was a sin, to you Christians."

"If you'll recall my words, Ed—"

"Maybe the Ten Commandments are out of date—I know some people say they are, but I sure didn't know you thought so. I'm surprised!"

"Young man—"

"I guess a lot of folks are going to be surprised!"

"Now see here!"

"But don't worry about it, Prof." Ed leaned forward with an air of malevolent complicity. "I won't tell on you!"

"Now you listen to me!" said Matthew, his voice rising. "I'll not have you go out of here and say that I have refuted the Bible. Do you understand that? You have twisted my words, and I want you to know— *Stop laughing, Ed!*"

"I'm not laughing at you!"

"Then what do you find that's so comical?" Matthew glanced over his shoulder. Pressed against the windowpane was a horrendous little face, the eyes crossed and the tongue stuck out as far as it would go.

He sprang to his feet and flung open the window. "What in the name of goodness are you doing here?"

"I'm practicing my rope climb," said Mathy.

"You get down from there about as fast as you can get and go straight home!"

Mathy dropped out of sight. A prolonged *Wheee!* rose upward as she slid down the rope.

Matthew slammed the window shut and turned around. "Now let's get this straight!" he shouted.

Ed was smiling at him in pure malicious delight. "Ah, forget it, Prof. I was only joking."

"If this is your conception of a joke—"

"Not a very good one, was it?"

"It certainly wasn't."

"I shouldn't have made that kite. It was a pretty fresh thing to do."

"Typical of your behavior."

"I know it. I apologize, Prof."

"Well—" said Matthew.

"I'm sorry I did it and sorry I got you all riled up. I didn't really mean to. I don't know what gets into me sometimes. But I'll try not to let it happen again."

Matthew sat down. "Very well, Ed," he said after a moment. "We'll forget about it this time."

"Thank you, sir. I'll try not to desecrate any more religious symbols, even if I don't believe—"

"All right, Ed. That's enough. You may go now."

"Yes sir. I think something ought to be done about those incense burners, don't you, Mr. Soames?"

Furor loquendi! "Good night, Ed."

"I wonder if the Chinese burn incense in little statues of Jesus Christ!"

"I don't think we need to discuss—"

"I'd like to see that, wouldn't you—smoke pouring out of all the nail holes?"

"Good *night*, Ed."

"Right." He rose and opened the door. " 'Night, Mr. Soames. Happy Easter," he added cheerfully and closed the door behind him.

Matthew leaned wearily on the desk. His head had begun to

ache. He propped it on his hands, rubbing his temples with his thumbs. He felt old and defeated. Maybe Garney was right. Maybe they needed a younger man.

Gradually he became aware of singing in the distance. Girls' voices singing Mendelssohn:

> *"The moon shines bright, the stars give a light*
> *A little before 'tis day . . ."*

It was a guileless and healing sound.

> *"For the Lord knows when we'll meet again*
> *In the merry, merry month of May."*

The girls' trio, rehearsing its number for the spring contest in Clarkstown. Matthew lifted his head, remembering guiltily that he had instructed the girls to stay after school so that he could help them. He started to the door, but he had delayed too long; he could hear them coming downstairs. He sat down again at the desk. A moment later there was a knock.

"Come in?"

"It's me." Leonie stepped inside, looking as righteous as the Little Red Hen. "I saw you were busy, Papa, so I went ahead and rehearsed the trio for you."

"Well. Thank you, Daughter."

"I had each one sing her part alone, first with the piano and then *a capella*, just reading notes. Then I had the alto and second soprano sing together and after that the soprano and alto. After that, we all ran through it once together. And then—"

"Yes, honey. You don't have to give me the whole story right now."

"But I thought you'd want to know how we did it."

"Yes. Well, that's fine. You run on now, dear. I'm busy."

"Aren't you about ready to go home? I'll wait and walk with you."

"I've got a lot of things to do first. You go on ahead."

"But I can go upstairs and study till— Oh, all right. Shall I close the door?"

"You can leave it open."

She went away. Matthew rose again and went to the window. Everyone else had gone, the building was quiet. He could hear it settling after the long day, its old joints creaking, the echoes sounding through the empty halls. His shoulders slumped. He was cross and tired, worn out by the day's vexations. As he stood there gazing absently toward the graveyard hill, his hot forehead pressed against the glass, the office began to fill with golden light. Shreds of cloud caught fire one after another, and the flame and tumult of a windy sunset spread over half the sky. Slowly, as it engaged his senses, it drew him forth to some godlike vantage from where he looked back on himself—a solitary figure in a deserted schoolhouse, and he felt like a general abandoned on the darkling plain, all his warriors fled. (Lear on the heath . . . sad Henry on the field at Yorkshire.) How lonely I am! he told himself. Lonely in his battle against ignorance, in his love of wisdom, truth, and order. Lonely in his love of beauty, too. He wondered if in all the town there was one other who stopped now to behold the sunset. That great slow soundless splash of color in the sky! Its beauty pained him, it called him to respond—one was *obliged* to beauty. And he wished with all his heart, that moment, for a way to answer, a way to praise it, for some *one*, even, to say to simply, "How beautiful it is." Someone to listen.

As if in answer, the front door opened and someone started up the stairs. Turning, he saw a golden head rise into the sunlit hall. Aphrodite emerging from the foam! A girl came toward him nimbused in gold, her eyes as warm and blue as the sky in summer, and paused, smiling, on his threshold. His heart stood up in welcome. "Come in!"

She came, carrying her English book; a fair presence in a middy blouse and skirt, her tawny hair bound with blue ribbon. They stood at the window side by side and watched the sunset. He told her how beautiful it was. She clasped her hands, said *Oh!* and looked at him with a shy, glowing face. Then they sat down together and opened the book and he spoke to her of literature and of learning. She listened eagerly. He read poetry aloud.

> "Thy hyacinth hair, thy classic face,
> Thy Naiad airs have brought me home."

"You make it sound so beautiful!" she said.

He talked on and on. His voice, calm and wise, bore them gently o'er a perfumed sea, while the room brimmed with golden light pouring from yon brilliant window-niche. Suddenly the girl looked up at him and said, "I love you!"

"My dear," he said smiling, "it is poetry you love."

"It's you!"

He looked into the blue eyes and faltered. "I think," he said, turning nobly away, "I think you should go now."

She protested. He was firm. She pleaded. He smiled gently.
Then she lifted her soft pink mouth and kissed him and ran out of
the room, leaving her English book behind. He heard the front
door slam.

Matthew stared down at the open book. *Helen, thy beauty is to
me* . . . He tried to straighten his desk but found it cluttered
with unfamiliar objects—papers, pencils, notebooks—and he could
not think where to put them. He turned again to the window
and found, looking out, that all he saw was her face.

3

In reality, the girl had not said, "I love you."

In reality, she had merely come in with her English book and
asked him please to explain a poem which she did not understand. Her name was Alice Wandling. She was a senior, who sat
in his history class each afternoon, next to the window where the
sunlight fell on her hair. This had not gone unnoticed. She was
also the girl chosen to represent Shawano High School in the elocution contest. For the last week or so, during study hall periods,
Matthew had helped her with her dramatic reading. He realized,
only as she walked into the office that afternoon, that he had enjoyed those sessions considerably—rather more than seemed war-
ranted by having to listen over and over to "The Lost Word" by
Henry Van Dyke.

He and she had, indeed, stood at the window together and admired the sunset. Then Alice (no doubt observing that the out-
door toilets made up part of the view) had turned away with an
embarrassed smile.

"Our assignment for Monday," she said, "is a poem by Alexander Poe. He's my favorite author, but he's so *deep!*"

So they had sat down and opened the book to "Alexander" Poe.
Matthew talked of the beauties of literature, forgot himself, and
talked on and on. He read "To Helen" aloud. Once the girl
touched his arm. "Gee, Mr. Soames, you sure make it sound beautiful!" She went on to say what a splendid teacher she thought him
and how young he looked to know so much.

Every ripple of her mature little body, the scent of her rose sachet, every soulful blue glance, were comfort and solace to him. The longer she sat, the more eloquent he became. He was having a wonderful time. Here at last was someone who listened, and he was so grateful he could have seized her in his arms. Not daring, however, he half hoped that she would relieve him of the affront by seizing him in hers.

He wondered briefly why she had come back to the building after everyone else had gone. It couldn't be (could it?) that she had come deliberately, hoping to find him there? But that was nonsense. The girl only needed help with her lesson. But why from him? He wasn't her English teacher. Why didn't she go to Miss Coppidge? Because Miss Coppidge was stupid. God forgive him, but she was; the very tone of her voice befouled poetry. And besides, Miss Coppidge had long since gone home for the weekend. Then what was this girl doing here now, smelling like roses and smiling at him with her little red tongue between her teeth? Was it out-and-out unabashed dalliance?

Certainly not, he told himself firmly. It was rapt attention. Alice Blue-Eyes loved literature, that was all. ("Oh, Mr. Soames, I love the way you talk!") She admired him for his mind.

Yet for all his reasoning and for all the girl's decorum, she might as well have flung herself upon him and declared undying passion. By the time she thanked him and went away, forgetting her English book, he was in reality, for the moment at least, quite mad about her.

It was a habit he had, this falling in love with a schoolgirl; an affliction, like epilepsy, quiescent for long periods and cropping out unexpectedly, throwing him into fits. Wild palpitations, sweating palms, uncontrollable levity, and hallucinations of brilliance, personal comeliness, invincibility—in short, of grandeur. All of this was part of the forbidden, secret rapture of having a young girl look upon him day after day as if he were the rising sun, that he should shine upon her. It renewed him, filled him with excessive wild delight.

And it appalled him. This habit, disease, this aptitude of his, which was his secret joy, was also his anguish. It made him feel some sort of monster. With desperate honesty he tried to probe its depths, wondering even if it rose from the deep and hidden evil of incestuous desires. But for the life of him, he could not believe it was that! What resemblance did his daughters bear to the girls who took his heart—the lovely ripe knowing girls, clearly a different breed!

Whatever caused it, it troubled him enormously, for it made him betray not only Callie—that was bad enough!—but his other true love, learning. These seizures of the heart used up his thought, distracted him from his proper pursuits. He was almost glad when they were over. Then, like a convalescent, he read books. He read avidly, making up for lost time. He took correspondence courses or went off to summer school again. Lectures, research papers, long summer hours in the library (sweating, itching in his woolen trousers, his shirt peeling the varnish off the chair)—all these nursed him back to his senses and healed his soul.

He had found a line by Francis Bacon, which he wrote on a slip of paper in his best Palmer hand: "Seek ye first the good things of the mind and the rest will either be supplied or its loss will not be felt." He kept it in his desk, and each time he came across it he was filled with reverence for that noble imperative. For he loved the good things of the mind. As he grew older he loved them more and more. And he thought they had cured him of his old, recurrent folly. Yet here he was—past forty, now, solid, established, a power in the community—steaming like an adolescent over a schoolgirl the age of his second daughter.

Matthew looked out on the darkening sky from the office window. "O Lord," he said, "I've done it again."

4

Carrying his lunchbox, he walked home across the pasture opposite the school. The path was always deserted by the time he reached it. He liked this walk under the open sky. It gave him a space of solitude between the pressures of school and home. Tonight he crossed slowly in the windy dusk, recalling the hour in the sunset office. He went over and over it, savoring each look, each word, trying to interpret every innuendo. The thought of Alice sang loud inside him, and he wondered how he could keep it quiet in the presence of his family. With a shudder he thought of all the ears and eyes and intrusive female voices waiting for him at the end of the street. He wished there were somewhere else he could go. But there stood the house, baited with supper, and he was trapped.

Saucepans steamed on the back of the stove. Mathy, looking under a lid, dropped it with a clatter and threw her arms around Matthew's middle.

"Papa! At last you're home! We're starving to death. I'm weak —I can't stand up! Oh! Oh!"

"Don't do that," Callie said. "Papa's tired."

"He's been awfully busy all day," said Leonie, who was ironing in a corner of the kitchen. "I had to rehearse the girls' trio for him."

"Take off your coat," said Callie. "Here, baby, go hang it up for him. Sit down, Papa, and put your feet on the oven door. I know they're cold. I made you some sassafras tea. Thought it'd taste good. Hand me a cup, baby."

Leonie set a flatiron on the stove. "I ironed your good shirt, Papa. Doesn't it look nice?"

They fluttered around him, plying him with hot tea, house slippers, and welcome.

"We better eat, soon as you warm up a little," said Callie. "We'll be late for church."

"Church?" said Matthew.

"The special Easter service. Had you forgot?"

He had. Since Ed Inwood had bade him a happy one, Easter had slipped his mind.

"Well, come on, everybody," said Callie. "Let's set down."

They bowed their heads while Matthew returned thanks. Callie looked up and ran her hand over her smooth forehead.

"Whew!" she said. "I've pretty near got a sick headache from waitin' so long."

There, she had said it! It was the little light blow he always knew was coming but never knew when to dodge. He caught it broadside and winced. She would fuss over him and be kind and good and make him feel mean as a horsethief. And then, when she had softened him up, she'd deal him the blow—some little sly thing to let him know that he had done wrong and that, although she excused it, she had not overlooked it.

"Why didn't you go ahead without me?" he said peevishly.

"Mama made us wait," said Mathy.

"Well, of course!" said Callie. "We don't like to eat without Papa." She turned to him. "Seems like we don't never get to see you except at the table."

She studied him for a moment, resting her elbow on the table with her chin on her hand. There was love written all over her pretty face, open and obvious as if the children weren't sitting right there. Matthew looked away. It made him miserable.

5

While the Baptists climaxed their revival week with trumpets of doom and colored slides, the Methodists, who were smaller in number, went off by themselves to nurse their dignity and hold a quiet service. They sang a hymn, the minister led them in prayer, and then without any shouting, which he enjoyed as much as the next one, he read them the story of the Crucifixion according to the Gospel of St. Luke.

" 'Now the feast of unleavened bread drew nigh, which is called the Passover. And the chief priests and scribes sought how they might kill him . . .' "

Matthew sat with his family near the front of the church and tried very hard to listen. Christ and Alice competed for his attention.

The minister read on. " 'And he took bread, and gave thanks, and brake it, and gave unto them, saying, This is my body which is given for you: this do in remembrance of me.' "

Yes, thought Matthew, reading himself a lecture, I would think you might have remembered, at that hour if no other, when He was dying for your sake.

" 'And truly the Son of man goeth, as it was determined: but woe unto that man by whom he is betrayed!' "

Matthew felt as damned as Judas. You are that man, he said; there's no getting around it. You could not watch with Him one little hour. You had to be lusting after the flesh.

He flinched at the thought.

Yes, you were, he went on. You wanted to hold her in your arms. You wanted to kiss her. You thought of it, all right. Don't tell me you didn't.

And he thought about it again, deliberately, as if it were evidence in court, and found it so pleasurable that he was shocked at himself. With a great effort he turned his attention again to St. Luke.

" 'And there followed him a great company of people, and of women, which also bewailed and lamented him.

" 'But Jesus turning unto them said, Daughters of Jerusalem, weep not for me, but weep for yourselves, and for your children.' "

On his right hand sat Leonie, erect and attentive, her hands folded in her lap. Her face was smooth and guileless, a child's face. She looked so much younger than her eighteen years. And she was pretty, when you caught her like this, unguarded.

With a jab of conscience he recalled how urgently she had begged to enter the elocution contest. "I'd like to represent the school just once before I graduate. Why can't I, Papa? I can win —I know I can. When we gave our readings in assembly, a lot of the kids thought I did my reading better than Alice Wandling." But of course he couldn't allow it. Alice's parents—someone— would be sure to cry foul.

And anyway, he thought, glancing at Leonie again, she was not blessed with much dramatic ability. She had a fine memory and a voice that carried, but that's about as far as it went. He felt a kind of pity for her. He was sorry he did not like her better. She was a tiresome child and stubborn as a hedgeroot. But she worked hard and she meant well. She was a good girl. She had done nothing to deserve a father who was false and lecherous. Nor had that little one over there. Nor had their mother.

Forget that girl! he pleaded to himself. You're an old fool and there's none like 'em. Now behave yourself. I don't want to hear any more about her.

He squared his shoulders and lifted his head bravely.

Besides, he added, she doesn't care a thing about you.

The minister read to the end of the chapter. "And now," he said, closing the Bible, "will you all rise, while Brother Soames leads us in prayer."

Matthew rose to his feet and asked the Heavenly Father's guidance and forgiveness. Inside he prayed fervently to mean what he was saying.

The service was over by a quarter till nine. Down the street the Baptists were still singing.

"May I go down there and wait for Genevieve?" said Leonie, whose best chum was a Baptist. "We can walk home together."

"I'll go with you," said Mathy.

"Mercy no," said Callie. "Both of you stay right here. There's always boys hangin' around outside the church."

"Well, they're not going to hurt me," Leonie said. "They're all too scared of Papa."

"I don't care. You come on now."

The two girls tagged along behind Callie and Matthew. It was a restless night, full of wind and shadows. They looked up at the big clouds blowing across the sky.

"The sky is a custard!" cried Mathy and fell over backwards with glee.

"Oh, it is not," said Leonie. "You're silly. Get up before Papa sees you."

Ahead of them, Callie tucked her hand under Matthew's arm. "It don't feel much like spring, does it?"

"Not much," he said. "Oh, shoot!"

"What is it?"

"I left my papers up at the school building. I wanted to grade them tonight."

"Can't you do them tomorrow?"

"I've got to go down to the farm tomorrow and see about things. Meant to get those papers out of the way tonight. I'd better go up there and get them."

"Oh," said Callie in sympathy, "and you're so tired, too."

"I'd better do it. It won't take but a few minutes." He turned off at the corner.

"Where's he going?" said Mathy. "Wait, Papa, I'll go with you!"

"You come on with me," said Callie. "He's got to go up to the schoolhouse, he'll be right back."

Matthew took the shortcut through the pasture, following the familiar path easily in the dark. A blast of wind across that wide open space almost took his hat off. He pulled it down and bent his head. He was halfway across when there came the sound of running footsteps, and a figure pounded out of the darkness, coming toward him on the path. In its haste it was upon him before it could turn.

"Mr. *Soames!*"

Alice Wandling had run smack into him. She backed away and stood staring, her hair ribbon in her hands and her hands to her mouth. Her long hair hung loose, splayed on the wind. For a moment that was the only movement and the wind the only sound, seized as they were by the rigor of surprise. Alice recovered first. The hands came down from her mouth, still clutching the ribbon.

"It's really you!" she said.

"What are you doing out here this time of night?"

Alice hesitated and hung her head. "I was looking for you," she said in a low voice.

"For me!"

"Yes." She looked up at him, moving closer.

"What did you want to see me about?"

"Nothing. I just wanted to see you. I thought you might be up at the schoolhouse, like you are sometimes."

"Alice, if there's something you want to talk over—"

"It's not that."

"Then what is it?"

"I just wanted to *see* you!" she said again.

There was a moment of silence before she blurted out, "Because I'm crazy about you!"

The words burst like a rocket in his head and showered colored lights.

"Didn't you know that?" she cried. "Did I have to tell you?"

The hair ribbon snapped in the wind and the scent of rose sachet drifted over him. He didn't know that his hat had blown off.

"Please don't scold me," she said in a soft voice. "I can't help it. You do like me, don't you? Just a little?"

"Alice—dear girl—" He lifted his hand and brushed the hair back from her face. That was all; only his fingers against her cheek.

"You're not mad at me?" she said. "You're not going to bawl me out?"

"No."

"Oh, thank you!" she cried.

And then she put her arms around his neck and she kissed him quick and hard and it was real. He knew it was. He felt and smelled and tasted her. Not at the moment, but the moment after, when he stood weak-kneed as a new colt and heard her run away down the path.

He never did find his hat.

6

Then the spring came and the air turned warm and salvation was here and now on the earth. Flowers shot up overnight and green stripes ran down the garden. Jonquils and radishes overran the town. The yeasty fragrance of peach bloom streaked the air. In the pastures the cows fattened on new grass, and their cream rose thick and yellow on the milk. Wild greens came to the table, and lettuce, and long-headed mushrooms picked in the woods. Women hung quilts in the sunshine and lingered there, calling to each other across the garden plots to congratulate the weather. There was a humming all over town, and in the evening, a rustle of sound—light, furtive, exciting. It was laughter, it was screen doors slamming, it was light running footsteps, a greeting under the street lamp, and the little comic kissing sounds that birds make at dusk in the spring.

Matthew moved through the exquisite days with a special pride in them. He commended all gardens for their behavior, the very grass because it grew. He looked on the world and was well pleased, as if the spring were his own performance.

The thrill of the infatuation toned up his skin and brightened his eyes. His mind quickened. He taught classes well, did his work faster, was good-natured even at home (where he appeared only long enough to eat and sleep). Neither rampant mothers nor Ed Inwood disturbed him. Ed played pranks and hooky, and when he did bother to come to school he lolled on his spine, staring dreamily out of windows.

"I'm sorry, Prof," he said one day when Matthew told him to sit up. "Guess I'm not hittin' on all my cylinders. Maybe it's spring fever—maybe I'm in love!"

Breaking a precedent, Matthew laughed. "Well, boy, it's the season, I suppose." For once in his life he was in sympathy.

In the mornings he could not wait to be off to school. He approached the building in a happy torment, wondering if all this were his imagination. But soon, there she stood, in a crowd of students, turning her blue eyes on him in a soulful glance or flashing him a quick secret smile, and his day was assured. He had never found her again on the path through the pasture, though he went that way hopefully each night. But in the afternoons they met in the office during study hall to rehearse the dramatic reading. They did not commit themselves to each other in so many words, but no words were needed—looks, laughter, the playful touch of hands, once even a hasty kiss, said all that was necessary. Not for a long time had Matthew coped with such sensations, the sudden joyful lurch of the heart, the dry throat, the palsied hands. She was indeed beautiful. The prettiest girl in school, sought after by all the boys. Yet she loved *him*. She turned pink in his presence, pouted adorably, and sighed. How dear and piteous he thought her. He should in all fairness discourage her affection; that would be kindest. But for a little while, it would do no harm. She would outgrow it soon enough. And so would he. While it lasted he might as well enjoy the daylights out of it.

He began to look forward eagerly to the county contests, held annually in Clarkstown. Alice would be there with her dramatic reading. He too would be there. Unfortunately, twenty more of his students would also be there, and he would spend the day riding herd. (No one was ever at the right place at the right time. Sopranos lost altos; the relay team lost each other. The spellers waited patiently on one floor while the match began on the next. Delmora Jewel threw up from excitement. And the girls' trio invariably were watching the boys on the track field when it came their turn to sing.) But maybe in all the confusion he and Alice could slip off from the others for a little while and be alone. In the library, perhaps; that should be safe enough! Or on some remote part of the campus, where they could stroll together, boy and girl, as he had seen others do. (Having gone to college by bits and pieces and already married, he had never had time for the classical light campus loves, and had sometimes envied the younger men idling on the summer lawns with the pretty girls.)

He began happily to plot their escape.

On the Monday before the contests, he arrived at school before the janitor. He unlocked and went up to his office. He had barely hung up his hat when he heard the front door slam. He glanced up eagerly, hoping to see Alice's red-golden head rise into view. Instead, up came the brown little braided head of Delmora Jewel. Almost anyone else would have been less of a disappointment. Poor Delmora couldn't help being her mother's daughter, but neither could Matthew help holding it against her.

"Hi, Mr. Soames!" she called.

"Good morning, Delmora."

She started up to the third floor, hesitated, and came back down. With her toes turned out, looking like a small elderly eccentric, she tripped down the hall toward the office.

"Mr. Soames, did you hear the news?"

"What news, Delmora?"

"Didn'tcha hear?" Her eyes glittered behind the gold-rimmed glasses. "Alice Wandling ran off with Ed Inwood!" She stared up at him with her mouth wide open in a horrible ecstatic grin. "They run off to Springfield and got married!"

"When—" said Matthew without any voice. He tried again. "When did all this happen?"

"Last night, I s'pose."

"Don't you know for sure?"

"Well, all I heard was they run off."

"Are you sure you aren't repeating idle gossip, Delmora?"

"Oh, no sir! It's the truth. It was on the line this morning. My mother heard it."

"That doesn't necessarily mean it's true. Lots of ugly stories get started that turn out to be false."

"Oh, I don't think it's ugly! They were crazy about each other. Everybody knew that."

Matthew cleared his throat. "Were they?"

"Sure. Alice's folks couldn't stand Ed, though. They wouldn't let him in the house. She used to sneak out and meet him all the time. She was terrible!"

"All right, Delmora. I don't think it's necessary to discuss it."

"I thought you might like to know."

"The less said about it, the better."

"Yes sir. And I heard that—"

The front door slammed again and a crowd of girls ran up the stairs. With a squeak of delight, Delmora darted away.

From the end of the hall the babble of voices pelted against him like handfuls of pebbles. He went over and shut the door.

7

Alice and Ed ran away in the night and drove all the way to the Ozarks in Ed's secondhand Overland. They were married the next morning by a Holy Roller preacher who had a wife a little younger than Alice and didn't bother to ask their ages. They had left a trail, however. Alice's parents caught up with them by noon; caught them in a hotel room in Springfield, so the story ran, with Alice sitting on the bed, mother-naked, eating a ham sandwich. They fetched her home and set about to have the marriage annulled. The following Monday, chastened and humiliated, Alice was back in school.

Ed came back, too, just long enough to pick up his sweater and quit. Matthew didn't even have the satisfaction of expelling him.

Meanwhile, there was the matter of the elocution contest. When Leonie found out that Alice had abdicated, she rushed directly to Matthew and begged to take Alice's place. Since there was no time to prepare someone else, Matthew consented. Leonie went to work with a zeal that would have moved a house and declaimed all over the place. Each afternoon she insisted on declaiming for Matthew. He listened doggedly, ruefully remembering the afternoons with Alice. The contrast between those and these was almost more than he could endure.

On Saturday morning at the college, Leonie represented Shawano High School. She delivered her reading in a clear confident voice and did not win so much as honorable mention.

That evening, as they met at the car to go home, Matthew said, "I'm sorry, Daughter. But that's just the way things go. Not everyone can win."

"I could have," Leonie said firmly, "if I'd had as much practice as Alice Wandling had."

Matthew held his tongue. She was mistaken, but he had no right to say so. Leonie climbed into the back seat with Mathy and said no more. All the way home she kept quietly blowing her nose. By the time they got there, Matthew was so filled with sympathy that he was speechless with rage.

Alice paid him no more visits to the office. She sat in class with swollen, downcast eyes. When they passed in the hall they did not speak. Yet the faint scent of roses as she went by tormented him with reminders of what he had lost. The image of himself as poet and lover, brilliant and chosen, crumbled around him, revealing the same old armature at the core, the plain, humdrum, everyday man. He went about his business sullen with chagrin. And still the maddening, beautiful spring weather continued.

Graduation time approached. Matthew plodded through the annual festivities with no pleasure. That too had been taken from him.

"It is my punishment," he said aloud, sitting at his desk one night in the empty schoolhouse. He had come back, as usual, after supper, to grade papers. "This is what I get for it. Oh, I know it, Lord. I broke the Commandment. I committed adultery in my heart, as it says in the Bible. If she was false, that doesn't excuse me."

He thought about it for a moment and added, "And I've been a damned fool, besides."

He was not a swearing man, but the word was too felicitous to be profane. Indeed, it was the foolishness more than the sin that rankled. One can repent of a sin and have done with it; but the wages of foolishness is the eternal recalling of it.

He opened the window and leaned out. The night air washed softly against his face. In the west, over the graveyard hill, the sky glowed deep-blue. Thus he had stood, that golden afternoon when she first came to him. She with her soft pink mouth and her dissembling glances. *Because I'm crazy about you!* That's what she had said. Oh, it was a clever stratagem, when he had caught her running home from a lovers' tryst. He thought of Ed, that arrogant, insolent boy. He thought of the two of them together, meeting in dark places in secret, holding each other, kissing; the frantic hands, the hot whispers. Oh, the things she must have said to him, the things she must have let him do. Matthew groaned.

"And all the time you thought it was you she wanted!" He lifted his head and laughed wearily. "Old fool," he said. "Old, homely, sinful old fool."

He slammed the window down like a guillotine, turned out the light, and left the building. A full moon hung halfway up the sky. Crossing the schoolyard, he stepped over the fence into Seabert's pasture and walked on, with his hands in his pockets, into the grove of trees, and through them up the long slope of the hill, till he came out on top among the tombstones. They stood white and peaceful in the moonlight.

"Good evening," he said aloud, as to old friends, and moving among the familiar furniture of the dead, he began to feel calmer. Up here the things that troubled him seemed to matter less. When he was dead they would matter not at all. He sat down behind a headstone, facing the moon. Looking out into space, where man had found other suns and planets but had not yet plotted heaven, he began once more to contemplate the puzzle of himself.

8

On another night, many years before, Matthew had sat alone in another graveyard. Young and troubled, he had stopped in Millroad Churchyard in the late October dusk. The sun had gone down, bleeding red along the horizon. He watched the light empty out of the sky and darkness blot up Missouri, all he could see from that high slope: Carpenter's fields, Clarence Oechen's timber, and the rocky pastures of his own father's farm. In the deepening dusk the land withdrew beyond possessing. Matthew flattened his back against the headstone and, looking out across the unclaimed landscape, he tried to feel the turning of the earth. He began to think round, holding the awareness of the moment in his head, as one would hold a pumpkin in the hands, and tried to memorize its shape and smell and color. His senses expanded to take the whole thing in: this moment in October toward the end of the century, on this hill in America upon a spinning globe, which at this very moment bore him on a journey around the sun. He moved ahead in time and looked back on the moment, to evaluate the significance of now. Around and around he went and to and fro, trying to realize time and the world and his own place in it.

Under his feet lay the bones of his ancestors. In other lands, in older graves, other forebears lay. He wondered what sort of men they were. Whose blood had come down through the conduit of his ancestry? Musing in the clear cold air, Matthew said to himself, "Who am I?" and wondered for the thousandth time how he happened to be born himself and not his brother Aaron or some girl or any one of those who lay under the ground around him. He might have been born an Indian before the time of Columbus, or one of the Children of Israel. Yet here he was in America in 1896, sitting behind his grandfather's grave with the night-damp seeping through his woolen britches and his nose in need of blowing. And how was he to know if this came about by plan or by some helter-skelter flinging of lives into time and place?

However it came about, he was not happy with it. He did not wish to be himself, eighteen and timid, nor to be here alone in the dusk instead of attending the penmanship class, down the road at the schoolhouse.

For the last three weeks, Mr. Kolb from Sedalia had conducted a class in the Palmer Method. Five nights a week the neighbors had gathered at Thorn School, each with a coal-oil lamp, ink and pens and foolscap, to improve their handwriting. Crowded into the small seats, they filled page after page with careful strokes: upper loops, lower loops, right curves and left. Tonight, since this was the last meeting, there would be a contest and, for the one who wrote the finest hand, the prize of a silver dollar.

Matthew wanted that prize. He lusted for it so steadily that it seemed the symbol of his future. It was not the dollar that counted (though he dreamed of buying a derby hat, or cufflinks that rattled); what really counted was the courage which winning would give him. If he won, he had made up his mind to go away to school. He was going to Sedalia with Mr. Kolb, if Mr. Kolb would have him, and find some kind of work. He would go to high school and earn a certificate so that he could teach.

The decision frightened him. For he had not been out of the township more than a few times, and then only as far as the nearest county seat. He had no money and not an idea in the world how to behave in any other environment except the one he was born to. The rest of the world baffled him. Though he read all he could about it, this was little enough. The books at Thorn School, where he had gone for a dozen years, were the same books year after year. And though he borrowed books wherever he could, few of the neighbors owned more than a Bible. One of them, however, lent him a book about the earth. He read with an excitement almost painful about glaciers and inland seas and centuries of rainfall. He thought of it constantly. This information was not quite compatible with Genesis, and he took to reading the Bible in a spirit of quest, with a sharp eye for clues. But all he learned only plagued him for more.

From these books, and from peddlers, circuit riders, and

itinerant teachers, he had pieced together some notion of another way of life. He knew there was something more than what he found in his father's house (a house of homemade brick, crowded with older brothers and younger sisters; a Christian house with Grace but no graces, loyalty with little affection, and little time for anything except hard work). Since Matthew was the only one who had this unsettling suspicion, it followed that the others should be suspicious of him. They could seldom find much to hold against him, in all honesty. But he wanted something more than they wanted, and that was enough to arouse them. He made them uneasy, like an omen of bad luck. And so they destroyed him each day with their counterspells of cheerful derision. He was made to feel guilty for aspiring to more than Divine Will had seen fit to give him. In a thousand little covert, even unintentional ways, they implied that he was a freak and an ingrate, and he believed them.

He knew, because he could look around and see, that he could do things as well as his brothers and do more kinds of things. He could plow more ground in a day, hitch a team faster, break broomcorn as well as a much heavier man. He could also read, write, spell, and do fractions. And he knew something of music. There was never a teacher who came through, recruiting pupils for a singing school, who didn't get Matthew's dollar. And he earned the dollar himself.

Yet none of these things gave him confidence. All they gave him was egotism, which is less the conviction of one's worth than the desire for that conviction. He was ill at ease among others, afraid of them and resentful of his fear. And he did not like the way he looked. He had grown up too suddenly to be accustomed to himself. One day there he stood, a pale-haired young man nearly six feet tall, with a high thin slice of a nose and big bones bulging under his skin like potatoes in a sack. All his joints were too large —his knees and elbows and knuckles. His brown eyes were intelligent and his face had a restless compelling look that redeemed his features, knitted them together in some harmony, and gave them a kind of comeliness. But Matthew had no way of knowing. His older brothers were ruddy and big-chested like their father, and he was different, and that was blemish enough. Even when the rest of his body began to fit with his knees and elbows, he took no comfort from his appearance.

Moreover, he had been taught humility. In the rigid mold of his upbringing, self-respect was tantamount to vanity. "For whosoever exalteth himself shall be abased; and he that humbleth himself shall be exalted." This teaching, however, could not put down a certain pride that he was born with. And so, having humility imposed upon that pride, he turned out not so humble as humiliated.

He kept a good deal to himself, taking refuge in the things of nature, which he loved for their own sake as well as for the protection they gave him. He knew all the woods and creeks around the countryside. He knew where to find the first wild grapes, the biggest hazelnuts and the greediest fish, and what day of spring the button willows showed their first green. He could stand for a long time so still that the wood doves gathered in the branches around him, while their soft plump syllables fell through the leaves like ripe fruit.

And yet, protection was not all he wanted. His nature cried out not to be lonely but to sing and laugh and kiss the pretty girls. He had a right to such enjoyments. Reason told him so. But he did not dare to presume, unless he could hold up to others some proof of his worthiness, some tangible evidence—say, a silver dollar. And that is why he had to win the penmanship contest. If he wanted to go away to school, he had to prove he deserved to go.

Everyone said he would win tonight. But they had said it last year, too, when someone else taught the class. When the night of the contest came, his heart had beat like a chopping ax, his hand shook, and the letters wavered. When he copied the proverb from the blackboard, he left out a word. And wanting so much to win, he had lost to Ben Carpenter, who didn't care much, one way or another. This year, Matthew told himself, things would be different. But the time had come, and his small store of confidence was all used up before the sun went down, like a small boy's bread when he runs away from home.

Everything had gone wrong all day. When his father called them, before daylight, Matthew had gone back to sleep and the others had eaten up all the breakfast. His father said it was justice. He had to get along with a handful of persimmons. Then the mules took it into their heads not to go to the cornfield; he had to fight them all morning. The harness broke twice. At noon he was cross and hungry and lost what was left of his temper when he found that his sister Bertie had hidden his pen and ink. She produced them, after their mother had spoken sharply. But before Matthew could get his hands on them, Aaron snatched them up.

"Don't," said Matthew. "You'll ruin my penpoints."

"I ain't hurtin' 'em. I'm just gonna show you what real writin' looks like." Aaron sat down at the kitchen table, shoved back a plate, and wrote out his name on a sheet of foolscap. "There you are, Deacon. Don't need to think you're so smart. I can write better than you and I don't have to go to no school to learn how!"

He was right. Aaron couldn't spell—much more than his own name. But he had a natural way with a pen, and the letters came out round and flowing. It was as easy for him as spilling ink. He wrote even better than Ben Carpenter.

Aaron expanded his big chest and scratched it. "Reckon I'll just drop around to the schoolhouse tonight and win that dollar myself."

"You can't," said Matthew. "You're not a member of the class."

"And ain't you glad!" Aaron gave him a playful poke. "If I ain't there, maybe you can win! Without you play out again, like you did last time. What come over you, anyway?"

"He got scared," said Bertie.

"I did not."

"You did too. I'll bet you do it again this time and let old Ben Carpenter win again."

"I bet a dollar I don't!"

"You ain't got a dollar."

"I will have, when I win it."

Bertie gave him a shrewd look. "You willing to bet me a dollar you win?"

Their father pulled his chair to the table. "We'll have none of that talk in this house," he said. "I'll tolerate no talk of betting."

"I was only joking, Pa."

" 'Avoid the appearance of evil,' " he said and bowed his head for a long inventory of temptations from which the Lord should in His mercy deliver them.

Matthew went back to work, bound around with weariness and futility. He was restored very little by the appearance of Phoebe Oechen, who had come down to the field, cutting through her father's adjoining woods, in order to wish him luck. At least, that's what she said as she poked her calf face through the underbrush and stood there grinning at him. He could always count on Phoebe. He put up with her because she liked him. But secretly he rather despised her. He gave her no credit for good judgment. Since he disliked himself, the very fact that she admired him was a mark against her. Certainly none of the pretty girls were guilty of such aberration. The pretty ones—small shiny girls, like the Grancourt sisters, with the tickling laughter and honey in their claws—such girls were so out of his reach that he hardly dared think of them. He held them in such awe that it was a fear and hated them out of shyness. But since he wanted a girl, there was left to him Phoebe, of whom he was not afraid because she was neither beautiful nor clever. She was a solid caryatid of a girl, under an entablature of dark auburn hair, and much given to stumbling over things such as heating stoves and little chickens. Matthew did wish that she'd look where she was going and that her gums didn't show so much when she smiled. In public he was ashamed of the feeling her big firm body gave him in private. But the feeling was nothing he cared to control, and he liked being liked, even by her.

On this particular day, however, Phoebe seemed to him a summation of disappointment. He wished she would go away. But there she stood at the edge of the woods, plump as a pawpaw, and a kind of desperation seized him. He needed in the most urgent way to prove himself at something. And there was Phoebe, waiting. He climbed down from the wagon and walked over to where she stood.

"I sure hope you win tonight," said Phoebe.

He put his hands on her arms and a feeling like hot molasses began to run through him. He had touched her before and put his hands a few places where they shouldn't have been, but not like this—out here by themselves in the woods, with the sun halfway down and the trees behind them in shadow. He pulled her up against him.

"You hadn't ought to do that," she said.

"Why not?" He pushed into the thicket, taking her with him.

"You better stop. Somebody might see us."

If *that's* all you're worried about, thought Matthew. He guided her back into an open space among the scrub oak. His heart beat so hard he thought it would strangle him. Now that the time had come, he was scared to death and didn't know how to begin. Phoebe conveniently stepped on a stick, caught her other foot under it, and went crashing to the ground. Instantly, he was on her, and they rolled over a time or two before he discovered that she wasn't fighting. She was clinging to him with all her might, which was considerable. When he stopped threshing about, he lay on his back, Phoebe on top of him like a sack of corn.

"You're chokin' me," he said.

She laughed and slid off to the ground. "Matthew Soames!" she said cozily. "You're a sight!"

He turned over and lunged at her with his big bony hands, and there began a steady rhythm of pawing and pushing, while the dry leaves cracked beneath them. All the time, Phoebe giggled. She was willing to play, all right, but not to get down to business. And the more she fought him—lazily, defter than he was—the more determined he was to go through with it and get the whole thing over. A man has to start somewhere. Over he went on top of her. Over she went, spilling him off. In the heat of the game, her skirts worked up, exposing bare white flesh. He took hold. But she was too solid; he couldn't get a grip on her. She slid away, picking his hands off as if they were burrs, while all the time bumping her teeth against his, trying to kiss him. At last she planted a hand against his chest and sent him sprawling. He landed on his back and lay still, pulling the cold air into his lungs out of the far blue sky. It burned all the way down.

From a safe distance, Phoebe made a soft snickering sound. "My goodness! I didn't have no idea you's so anxious."

Matthew sat up and brushed his clothes. Both of them were rolled in dry leaves like fish in cornmeal. "Let's go," he said and started out of the clearing without looking at her. He was sick of himself. He couldn't do anything right.

"Matthew?" She hurried after him. "You ain't mad, are you? Just because I didn't let you? You didn't expect me to, right off, did you? You didn't think I's that kind of a girl, did you?" Matthew kept walking. "You know if I's the kind that did that, I'd do it with you. You know that, don't you?"

"You better get home," he said at the edge of the field. "Somebody'll come looking for you."

"Nobody seen me go," Phoebe said with a smirk. She stood as if she expected him to kiss her.

"I got to get back to work," he said.

Phoebe picked leaves off her arms. "Guess I'll see you at the schoolhouse tonight?"

"Reckon so."

"I sure am hopin' you win."

"Much obliged."

Maybe she never would go away. Maybe she'd just stand there till she took root and put out branches and a squirrel made a nest in her head.

"I sure do admire your handwriting," she said.

"You better go on, now."

"Reckon you're goin' over to Carpenter's afterwards to the taffy pull?"

"I was figurin' to go."

"So am I. Well—" Still she lingered.

"I got to get to work, Phoebe," he said desperately. "I'm sorry I—well, I'm sorry!" He turned and plunged through the brush to the cornfield.

He had no more than reached the wagon when a voice called to him from the woods. "Hey! Matthew!"

It was a girl's voice and it wasn't Phoebe's. He froze like a cornered rabbit as Callie Grancourt came out of the sumac close to the spot where he left Phoebe. Callie was his brother Aaron's girl, more or less. She must have crossed the creek a little way down, where it was rocky and shallow, and come up the path through Oechen's woods. Unless she was blind as a mole or a branch had hit her in the eye, she was bound to have caught sight of Phoebe.

"Can I ride up to the house with you?" Callie called out. "I'm invited over for supper."

"Come on," he said. "Climb in."

She picked her way across the stubble. She was barefoot and carried her button shoes in her hand. As she reached the wagon she stopped and looked straight up at him with a cool quizzical look that all but chilled his blood. If she had seen Phoebe, he was in trouble. For nothing was sacred to Callie Grancourt. She lived with a feather on her nose and everything was funny. Her cool look turned into a smile. Yes, she had seen Phoebe and she would tell his sisters about it.

"Get in," he said.

She wiggled a couple of times, like a fish flicking its tail, and nipped up over the sideboard. She sat down on a pile of corn and began to put on her shoes. Her feet were rusty and chilblained.

"Mercy!" she said. "That water was some cold! I come across the creek down yonder at the ford."

"You should have come around by the road and wore your shoes," he said, wishing to goodness she had done so and stayed out of his sight.

"It's closer this way. And I wouldn't'a wore my shoes, anyhow. I ain't got only this pair and I got to keep 'em nice. I sure don't want to get no taffy on 'em tonight." She licked her finger and polished one toe. Then she wriggled herself deeper into the heap of corn, settled her shawl, and said quietly, "Your back's just covered with leaves."

Matthew turned beet-red. He reached around and tried to brush himself off. "I fell down," he said.

"There ain't any doubt about that! Here, let me do it. You can't reach."

Now she'd wonder *why* he fell down. "I tripped over a stick," he blurted out. "It was hid in the leaves." And what was he doing out in the brush? "I heard something out there—something made a noise and I went in to see what it was." For the life of him he couldn't think what it was.

Callie studied him for a moment. "Maybe it was a cow," she suggested.

"Reckon it was!" he said gratefully. "That must have been what it was! A stray cow."

"One of Oechen's maybe."

His mouth snapped shut and he gave her a quick glance. She was looking up at him with solemn eyes.

"I think I heard it myself," she went on. "Something was trompin' off through the brush as I come up from the creek. *Must* have been a cow."

"Musta been."

"I don't know what else it could have been."

"It was a cow."

He slapped the reins across the mules' backs. His face felt puckered; Callie was a green persimmon.

"You and Phoebe going to the taffy pull tonight?" she said suddenly, and he jumped as if she had yelled at him.

"I figure to go. Don't know what she's aiming to do."

Out of the corner of his eye he looked at her again. If he could be sure she had seen Phoebe, he might try to explain. But if she hadn't, anything he said would only make things worse. There wasn't much he could do about it one way or the other, except grit his teeth and wait. He looked forward to supper as to an inquisition.

Mealtime was always a trial with Callie around, and she was around often, in and out like a household pet. She was a fyste-dog, little and sassy, always taking a nip at you when you weren't looking. The rest of the family liked her, and with her in the house, everyone acted different. When she walked in the door, the rules they lived by went out the window. Her very presence said

King's X, and as long as she was around, they played her way. Matthew, too self-conscious to play, was swept into the game in spite of himself. He was always *it*—caught, discovered, left without a chair. No one made him more uncomfortable than Callie Grancourt.

She was frivolous, she was irreverent, and she was arrogant. And who was she to be so proud of herself—an ignorant little girl who couldn't write her own name, and her father as poor as an Arkansaw pig!

At one time the Grancourts had had some stature in the neighborhood. They had come up from Kentucky a generation or so ago and settled on four hundred acres. Matthew could still remember the old grandfather, lean as Lincoln and wearing a tall silk hat. He used to drive down the road in a buckboard behind a black team, with his gold-headed cane standing up in the whipholder and shining in the sun. He had a fancy attitude for this part of the country, the neighbors used to say. Still, they liked old Hugo Grancourt; he was kindly and lighthearted; and though he had too much pride for their comfort, there was not much providence with it, either on his part or the Lord's. They were not obliged to envy him. Whether he had once kept slaves and no longer knew how to function without them, or whether initiative had been bred out of him, no one knew. At any rate, he had not done well. The four hundred acres crumbled away like hoecake, and all that his sons inherited were a few rocky acres and the light heart. Most of them had sold out and moved away. But Mitch, the eldest, still lived on his eighty with his second wife and five children, all of them threadbare, energetic, and hungry. It was no wonder they went visiting as often as they were asked.

And no wonder at all, Matthew thought as he sat across the table from Callie, that she had come visiting on this particular night. Nothing good had happened all day. He chewed his food with a dry mouth, waiting for her to give him away.

She sat on the long bench wedged among his sisters, eating with a quick and delicate motion, her knife and fork held just so and her elbows in, while pork and potatoes, apple preserves and hot biscuits vanished down her small gullet in astounding quantity. Conscious of her every move, even without looking at her, Matthew suddenly forgot his fear and lifted his head in amazement. How did she do it, he wondered—put away all that food, and her about as big as a minute! The look that met him was serene as, deliberate and ladylike, she ladled a river of gravy onto her plate.

Matthew choked down the last bite of sidemeat and climbed out over the bench. "Excuse me, please," he murmured, hoping to slip away unnoticed.

"You're excusable," said his mother. "You didn't eat much. You ain't sick, are you?"

"No'm."

Everyone looked up at him.

"He's nervous," said Aaron. "He's worried about the contest."

Silent under the fusillade, Matthew rolled up his pens and paper and took his lantern off the wall. It needed trimming but he couldn't take time now. He wrapped a muffler around his neck and pulled the wool cap down over his ears, wishing that Callie would stop looking at him. He had almost reached the door when she spoke.

"Matthew, reckon that cow got home by milkin' time?"

Aaron raised his head, catching the scent. "What cow?" A leer crawled over his face.

Callie lifted one shoulder. "Ask him. He said there was a cow lost down in Oechen's woods this afternoon."

Aaron snorted. "Yes, and I bet its name was Phoebe!"

Everyone howled, his father shouted for order, and Matthew bolted into the frosty dusk. The rude sound followed him clear to the barn.

Clutching his bundle, he ran through the pasture in the direction of the schoolhouse. The lantern squeaked as it bumped against his thigh. He ran blind and muttering until he reached the woods, where he slowed down and took deep breaths to calm himself. He wished he were already at the desk and the contest begun so this dread would be over. He had to win this time, he had to! And this necessity welling up within him, he began to shake. His hands were sweating and he felt sick. He knew that he would lose again. Flinging the parcel to the ground, he cried out, "I won't go! Let him win, I don't care!" And he pounded a tree trunk with his big fists until they hurt.

After a while he gathered up his bundle and the lantern and walked on slowly till he came to the road. There was no longer any need to hurry. And so at Millroad Churchyard he turned off and sat down against a gravestone, trying to reduce the prize to its proper small place in a vast and timeless world. He would wait there until the contest was over.

In the graveyard the silence was tangible, filled with sounds remembered, Sunday voices and the insects of summer, and it was comforting. He felt easy here. He did not have to compete with the dead. If there were those under the brown October grass who once wrote a finer hand or plowed a straighter furrow or sang notes better, it was of no importance. He was their superior, being alive.

Matthew moved around from behind the tombstone, lighted the lantern, and spread out his sheets of paper. The grave mounded gently, like a fat man's stomach as he lies asleep, and the matted grass made a firm enough surface to write on. He fitted a penpoint into the nib and began to make rows of marks on the paper. Left curves, right curves, upper loops and lower. He copied the inscription from the headstone. "Gabriel Soames, 1812–1890, Asleep in Jesus." With his elbows resting on the grave, Matthew wrote it out carefully.

"Amen!" said a hoarse voice above him.

Matthew's heart rose like a bounced ball. Peering down at him in the dim light was a crooked yellow face with a jaw like a growth on a tree trunk and an arc of white over the eyes.

"Mercy goodness, Johnny Faust! You like to scared me to death!"

The wild eyes blinked and a smile like the grimace of fear twisted the big jaw.

"I come up quiet," said Johnny Faust.

He was small and bony and made Matthew think of a forked stick with a lopsided jack-o'-lantern on top. He was perhaps thirty years old, though it was hard to say. His mind was old in its slowness but young in its innocence and you couldn't truthfully hang any age on him at all.

"You a-prayin'?" said Johnny.

"Not exactly."

"You'd ought to pray, every hour. Kneel with me now."

Old Johnny dropped to his knees and they faced each other across the grave. Matthew felt a cud of laughter form in his throat. The look of enormous piety spread over that witless face was as preposterous as butter spread on a board. The mannerisms of worship had fixed themselves on Johnny, along with the image of God as an old man with a blacksnake whip in one hand and a cherry pie in the other, the source of punishment and reward.

"Almighty Father," Johnny began, rolling his eyes upward.

Again Matthew felt hilarity forming deep inside. It was all so senseless. Down there at the schoolhouse, everybody was visiting and laughing, shaking Ben Carpenter by the hand, and having a good time—while he sat with an idiot in a dark graveyard, writing epitaphs on his grandfather's stomach. He bowed his head, so as not to laugh in poor Johnny's face. After listening a moment he sat back on his heels and put the cork in the ink bottle.

"Amen, Johnny," he said kindly. "I reckon we've prayed enough for tonight."

Johnny rolled his eyes down from heaven. "Reckon we have?"

"I think so. If you did anything wrong today, God's already forgiven you. He can see in your heart." It occurred to him that God could see in his heart as well as in Johnny's and must have been well aware of what he'd had in mind for Phoebe. He profoundly hoped God *did* forgive him.

"What you doin' with them papers?" Johnny said.

"Nothing."

"There's writin' on them. What does it say?"

"It says, 'Asleep in Jesus.' "

"Amen!" Johnny leaned over and peered at the paper upside down. "You write good," he said.

"Not so very good."

"You been to the schoolhouse learnin' to write, ain't you?"

"Now and then."

"Why ain't you down there now?"

Matthew rolled up the sheets of paper. "Why aren't *you*, Johnny? Or maybe you write so good you don't need any learnin'."

Johnny laughed with pleasure. He always welcomed teasing in the beginning; it flattered him. He had learned, however, to be wary of it, since he was never sure where the teasing left off and torment began.

"Guess you're on the way to the taffy pull?" Matthew said.

"That's where I'm a-goin'. To the taffy pull." He grinned. "You goin'?"

"Reckon I might," Matthew answered, wishing he had the good sense to stay away. He was no good at parties, but he kept going, much as you keep looking into mirrors, hoping to find there something better than you expect.

"We better get on," Johnny said. "We don't want to be late."

"Yep, I guess it's time." The class would be over now and everyone climbing into wagons to go to the party.

They rose and went down the slope toward the road. In front of the church Johnny stopped. "Had we ought to pray?"

147

"I don't think so, Johnny. You can pray in your heart as you walk along."

"Amen," Johnny said reverently. "I shore like molasses taffy."

Their shadows bobbed beside them, taking the shape and texture of weeds and the rutted road.

"Johnny," said Matthew, "you're my friend, aren't you? I want to ask you a favor. Will you do a favor for me?"

"Sure I will, Matthew. I'll do it for you. I'm your friend."

"Well, then, don't say anything about this. I mean about us stopping in the graveyard. Don't say anything to anybody about it."

"You don't want nobody to know?"

"I don't reckon it's any of their business."

"That's right. Not any of their business."

"If you and me want to sit and rest awhile by the church, that's nobody's business but ours."

"That's right, Matthew."

"So you just forget all about it. Forget we's there."

"I'll forget it, Matthew. I won't say nothin' about it."

"Much obliged, Johnny."

The bonfire was blazing in Carpenter's yard and molasses bubbled in the big kettle. Matthew hoped to slip in unnoticed. But Johnny Faust liked to shake hands. He walked into the crowd with his hand out and crooked smile agape.

"Here's old Johnny!" someone shouted.

Two girls joined hands around Johnny, as in a game of Needle's Eye. As they danced around him, others joined them, and a howling, galloping circle formed, with Johnny, Matthew, and the bonfire in the middle. If the two of them had been tossed into the cauldron, Matthew wouldn't have been surprised.

Someone yelled out, "Where were you tonight? Why weren't you at the schoolhouse?"

Ben Carpenter yelled, "What happened to you?"

"Hi, Matthew!" Phoebe's grinning face went by.

His brother Aaron and Callie Grancourt passed in a blur as the circle gathered speed. It broke at last, and the boys and girls pelted across the yard like beads from a broken string. They picked themselves up and came back into the firelight, laughing. The molasses had boiled down to a thick golden syrup. They rolled up their sleeves, buttered their hands, and began to pull taffy. Already Matthew was forgotten.

He hung back in the shadows, watching the others pair off and work the tawny mass together. They stretched it and looped it, shaped and slapped it, as the stuff grew whiter and whiter and firmed to satiny brittle bone. After a while Matthew moved over to the kettle and helped himself to a molten handful. It felt good in his cold hands, and it smelled good. He had forgotten he was hungry.

Johnny Faust also stood alone, working a handful of taffy. Now and then he pinched off a bite. The crooked jaw worked vigorously and the warm cane juices ran down his chin. He looked around for someone to talk to.

"Listen here now," he began, walking up to one of the couples. But they had dropped their taffy and caught it in mid-air, shrieking with laughter, and they ignored him. Aaron passed him on the way to the kettle.

"Howdy, Aaron," said Johnny, but Aaron went on by.

Johnny sidled up to another couple, grinning hopefully. "Say there, Virg!" he said.

The boy called Virg glanced over his shoulder. "Hi, Johnny."

"Me and Matthew was down at the church," Johnny said proudly.

"How's that?"

"I's walkin' through the graveyard and Matthew was settin' there by a tombstone—" He stopped abruptly as a piece of taffy hit him on the cheek. "Who done that?"

Matthew was making furtive signals at him.

"You throw that taffy at me?" Johnny asked mildly. At that moment another wad struck the back of his head. "Hey!" he said, turning around.

"What's the matter?" said Virg. "Somebody pickin' on you?"

Johnny pulled the taffy out of his hair. "They better watch out, that's all I got to say."

"You tell 'em, Johnny."

Johnny dutifully raised his voice. "Whoever hit me with that taffy better watch out!" As he spoke, another lump landed on his ear. "Watch out, I said!"

"Come and get me, Johnny!" shouted a voice across the fire.

"Here y'are, Johnny, take a bite!"

Wads and strings of candy began to rain on him from all directions. "You-all quit that now!" cried Johnny. "Y'hear me? You better watch out."

Matthew stood in the background guiltily. He had started it, but he never meant it to turn into this.

149

Pursued by his tormentors, Johnny retreated across the yard till he reached the smokehouse. He backed up against the wall, trying to laugh, and shielded his head with his arm as the sticky lumps landed—plssh!—all around him. Suddenly out of the crooked mouth came a wailing sound like a howl of pain. Johnny had begun to sing.

> "This is my story, this is my song,
> Praising my Saviour, all the day long."

It was all he knew to do, sing to the Lord for help, for the Lord hands out punishment and reward and His eye is on the sparrow. A lump of taffy the size of a dollar struck him in the mouth.

"Stop it!"

The crowd turned in amazement at the sound of Matthew's voice.

"Stop teasin' old Johnny!" he shouted. He pushed his way through to the smokehouse and stood in front of Johnny to protect him.

For a moment there had been quiet. Now a howl of pleasure went up as they took aim at a fresh new target. Taffy flew thick and fast, sticking to Matthew's face and in his hair. And out in front stood Phoebe Oechen, laughing like a lunatic, too foolish to know that this was no longer a game.

They had begun to throw other things—clods and wood chips —when Callie Grancourt darted out, coming toward him with such ferocity that Matthew thought she was coming to kill him. She seized him and Johnny by the hand, and standing between them with her head held high, she started singing. Her voice was small and thin, but she sang with all her might and its aim was as true as David's. The barrage ended abruptly like hail in summer. The boys and girls turned away sheepishly, and nobody spoke.

"You'd all ought to be ashamed of yourselves," Callie said in a quiet voice, and there wasn't a person in the yard who didn't hear her. "Come on now, Johnny. We'll go and wash our faces. Matthew, you come, too."

The three of them stood in the breezeway drying their hands when Callie spoke again. Looking straight up into his face, she said, "I declare, Matthew, don't you *like* me? Why do you have anything to do with that old Phoebe!"

And she turned on her heel and walked off, swinging her little rear end in the fancy way she had. When Matthew breathed again, he felt he had come up from a long spell under water.

9

Matthew did not go to Sedalia with Mr. Kolb or think any more about it. After the night of the taffy pull, all he could think of was Callie. Her face moved before him day and night. It dazzled him, like the flash of a mirror in the sun, which prints its image so vividly that you see it with closed eyes. Never had a feeling so engulfed him as this one did. He was upside down and feathered with it, tall as a mountain or turned into air, so bewitched he was by being chosen.

And chosen he certainly was. Callie Grancourt had marked him as her own. When she ran out of the crowd that night pity and anger impelled her. All she had ever consciously felt for Matthew was a casual sympathy. But having rescued a person, one often goes on to love him. He has, merely by getting into trouble, allowed you to be heroic. Overnight, Callie's pity kindled to passion. She woke up with her love for Matthew in full blaze. He was illuminated by it and, like a shadow thrown on the wall by firelight, enlarged to several times his size. He filled her world.

She had known instinctively that he suffered a good deal behind his sullen manner. Now she began to romanticize him. With no way of defining them, she gave him the dark humors, the tragic longings and melancholy of the romantic poets. She would have thought of him as Byronic, had she ever heard of Byron. He had the appeal to her of storms to one who is safe inside. Though she was by nature a very teakettle for being cozy, busy, practical, and merry, she took to suffering in sympathy and mooned and sighed as she pummeled the featherbeds and dug salt pork out of the barrel.

This sighing was for the most part pure self-indulgence. For Callie was shrewd, and she very well knew that far from being a tragic figure, Matthew Soames was a bright, industrious young man who would get ahead. He was probably the best catch in the county. It pleased her that she had been clever enough to find him out before anyone else suspected.

There were other sons of other families who had more money, land, and cattle. Even Aaron, whom she had thought of marrying, was handsomer; and almost anyone was better-natured. But Matthew was smarter than the others. And there were things he wanted. It was these things which Callie found irresistible; they were a symbol of his excellence. She had only the vaguest notion of what these things were; her knowledge of the world was too limited to tell her. But she knew without a doubt that they were the right things to want, and having Matthew, she would have them, too. She set out at once to get him.

This was not as easy as it might appear. Matthew, so accustomed to thinking himself unworthy, could not get out of the habit. Though starved for admiration, he refused to take it when it came. He couldn't believe it was honest. It could not be that anyone so beautiful as Callie, so desirable in every way, could want him.

He had long since forgotten her faults. His love turned them all to virtues. What had appeared complacency in her he now saw was courage. She was not insolent but spirited. And her lofty opinion of herself he now recognized as healthy self-respect. Even her ignorance endeared her to him. She had gone through the *Fourth Reader* at Thorn School and that was the sum of her education. But hers was not wilful ignorance. It was merely the nature of girls. Their mothers kept them busy with housework; no wonder they had no time for learning. He felt sorry for the little thing. In this one way he felt superior and therefore worthy of her. But all her other virtues threw him into panics of awe.

Callie couldn't for the life of her see why, if you loved someone, you couldn't come right out and say so and act accordingly. But Matthew must hang back or skitter sideways, run for cover and dart out again, all the time so crazy for her that he didn't know whether he was hitching a team or a brace of turkeys.

Callie coaxed him with the gentle wariness of a keeper in a cage. In a hundred subtle ways, and sometimes right out bluntly, she told him he was the inheritor of the earth. He wanted so much to believe it that he didn't dare to. But when at last she persuaded him to see himself as she saw him, the vision entranced him. Not for all the world could he let go of that. He forgot about going away and getting educated. All he wanted now was money enough to marry Callie, a house to put her in, and some ground to cultivate so that he could feed her.

That winter he chopped wood, hauled it to town and sold it. He trapped muskrats and sold the skins. In the spring he bought a calf from his father and fattened it to sell. When summer came he hired out to a farmer in an adjoining county, for fourteen dollars a month, plus the keep of his mule. He milked and plowed and harvested flax. Every Saturday after sundown he climbed onto his mule, Pharaoh, and rode most of the night to spend Sunday with Callie.

Late that summer he went south and followed the broomcorn harvest. He was a cutter, whacking the broomcorn heads with a heavy knife. On good days he could cover an acre and earn a dollar. He often thought, as he followed the breaker down the rows, of the dollar he didn't win. It would have been an easier dollar than this, if he'd had any faith in himself. But having faith was sometimes harder than swinging a broomcorn knife ten hours a day.

The following winter, when farm work slacked off, he found a job in Kansas City in a packing plant. He was put to washing beef shanks in icy water. The blood and the smell, the bawling of frightened cattle and the whack of axes on their skulls, horrified him. And he was afraid of the city. He stayed with it for two months, till he knew that down in the country, under the snow, rumors of spring were abroad. He fled the city in relief, glad to go back again to a world where he had at last begun to feel at home.

By this time, Matthew had amassed some sixty dollars and a cow, besides his mule, and had found a farm to rent. It was forty acres on Little Tebo, in the next county north. It had good pasture land for cattle, good bottom land for corn, and a two-room house. It rented for $1.50 an acre per year. He and Callie were married in March and moved in in time for spring planting

10

The seasons were good to them at first. Matthew bought another mule and paid the rent for another year. He tilled the fields with love, as if they were his own, and in his mind they were. He began to talk of buying the place. He found endless things to do. He cleared brush, patched fence, and diverted the branch to protect the bottom fields. He chopped great piles of wood; he butchered pigs and cured the meat over a hickory fire in the smokehouse. In the mornings he went forth singing, singing for love and the glory of God, singing the roses on the fence. At night he came home to the warm kitchen tired and contented, so aware of his own happiness that it frightened him. Who was he that so much had been given him? He felt half guilty, as if he had come by it unfairly. It must certainly be deceptive and would be taken away.

Meanwhile, the nineteenth century came to a close and the twentieth dawned—on Little Tebo as on the rest of the world, though not much was made of it down there, except to ring the churchbells and set off firecrackers left from Christmas.

Matthew thought about it, however, and about the passing of time. And he was comforted, in a way, when a vague discontent asserted itself again. Longing and discontent were familiar to him, and he felt safer. Through the haze of his happiness he recalled that there was something more he wanted than a tidy, well-run farm. There was something he wanted to be besides a good farmer. He wanted education, the kind you get from books and teachers in a real schoolroom, with maps and charts and encyclopedias, all the precious orderly receptacles of information.

The more he thought about all this, the more he desired it. But the time had passed. Mr. Kolb and Sedalia had been his last chance. Now he had forty acres and a wife and responsibilities. His lot was cast. He pondered the futility of his life: planting and harvesting, season after season, in a constant rhythm of depletion and replenishment, and all of it on a creature level—while away off somewhere things were happening and you couldn't find out what they were. Worse still, you couldn't find out what had already happened. Rumors reached you of ancient worlds and new planets, of voyages and wars. But down here in the bottom field, riding the A-harrow made out of logs from your own hedgerow, there was no way of learning about them.

He went about his work brooding in silence till one day Callie said to him, "I declare, Matthew, what's the matter?"

She wormed it out of him, little by little. It took her nearly a week. "My goodness, honey," she said, "I always figured on you bein' a teacher. Why don't you just go on and do it?"

"I can't," he said and gave her the reasons.

"Oh pshaw!" she said. "You can too." She proceeded to tell him how. "For one thing, we can sell off the stock."

"A team and two cows," Matthew said sourly.

"Well, one of 'em's calving. She'll bring a good price. How much money will it take, anyhow?"

"More than we've got."

"Couldn't you get some work in town? Clerk in a store or something?"

"I don't know nothin' about clerking."

"Well, you could learn. You're smarter'n any clerk I ever saw. I declare, Matthew, you're so timid about things! Why couldn't we take the chickens with us and sell eggs to the town folks?"

"Eggs don't bring anything these days."

"They sure ain't down to five cents a dozen like they was three or four years ago. And I hear they're goin' up every day."

She kept at him, sweet and persistent, until his self-pity gave way to hope. But it was hope shot through with misgivings. Maybe he was too old, he said; maybe he wasn't smart enough to catch up. She had a time with him. He always resisted the thing he wanted most. But she had married him, and she could get him off to school.

They were all set to move to Clarkstown for the winter when, at the last minute, Matthew refused to let go of the farm. These fields and woods were his by virtue of love, and he could no more let them fall into careless hands than he could loan out his wife. Seeing that what he wanted was everything—the farm, education, and her—Callie sensibly decided that two-thirds of what you want is plenty and she was the expendable third.

"I'll stay here," she said, "and keep the place. Thad and Wesley can come and stay with me part of the time, and I reckon we can make out." Thad and Wesley were her younger half-brothers.

So Matthew went off to school alone, riding away one gray October morning on old Pharaoh. A change of clothing hung in a sack slung over the saddle. Behind him, on Pharaoh's rump, lay a bag of provender—onions, potatoes, a side of bacon, and two loaves of bread still warm from the oven. Callie watched him up the hill till the cold mist closed behind him, thinking her heart would break. He would be gone for six months. She would miss him every minute, and worse yet, he would miss her. How would he sleep in the long winter nights without her to warm him, and what would he do among strangers when the black moods came on him and he lost faith in himself? He was going to be so lonely for her! Yet he knew this, and still he went. She cried a little more, out of vexation.

Matthew did miss her that winter. He was lonely and home-sick. He found it hard to catch on to new ways, and it seemed to him that no one in this town did anything the way they did back home. This was largely true. For though he had come north some forty miles as the mule traveled, Little Tebo was half a century away in time. He took refuge in his studies, where he felt safer. Though new means and manners came hard to him, book learn-ing came easy. He accomplished a full term's work and left for home before the term was out. It was April, and he had to put the spring crops in.

All summer long, Matthew studied at home. He read Emerson and Hawthorne as he rode the plow. He sat at noon on the creek banks, coping with algebra. In the evenings he studied history at the kitchen table, while June bugs landed like fat pebbles around the lamp and Callie swatted moths, pausing now and then to fan him and heave a deep sigh of boredom.

Late in August he took an examination at the county seat and received a certificate. Bitterwater School hired him for the winter at twenty-five dollars a month. He was a teacher at last, and once again he was so happy that he felt guilty.

Callie's happiness was unblemished. She was the wife now of the neighborhood's most accomplished member. Her husband had fulfilled her faith. And brilliant and beloved, he had given her a child. Sometimes when she felt it move inside her, there seemed no way to contain her joy. She would sit down and look about her, blessing the walls, the furniture, the very churn and broom and buttermold, the quilts and dishes of her house. Other times she walked outside and stood quite still, looking at her healthy garden, at the big trees and the sky and in the distance the high pastures catching the sunlight, and said to herself in some manner, "Praise Him!" meaning both God and her husband.

11

Their first child was born in March. They named her Jessica, be-cause Callie thought it had a fine aristocratic sound. She had a great aversion to names that sounded common. Matthew hadn't cared much whether he sired a girl or a boy, but he was disappointed, since it was a girl, that she didn't resemble Callie. This was his child; there was no mistaking that, from the first. However, she was a good, winsome baby and ever so grateful for having been born. Not every baby is, as they were to find out two years later when the second one came along.

Leonie was cranky. She threw up Callie's milk, broke out in rashes, and screamed half the night. At rare moments they could see that she was an exquisite-looking child. And after a while she seemed to accept the fact that she must put up with living, whether she liked it or not. She settled down and became a very tolerable member of the family.

In the next years, Matthew and Callie got ahead little by little. They were able to buy the farm and some ground adjoining and add more rooms to the house. They worked diligently in order to do it and lived frugally. There were many hardships—drought and flood and other plagues of nature. And there was sorrow. Matthew's mother and father died and the family scattered. For a while his youngest brother came to live with them. Later his brother Aaron, who had never married, came also, ill now with consumption, that huge ruddy man. Shielding the children from him, they nursed him through one winter until, as a last desperate measure, he betook himself to Colorado, where he too died. Matthew, tall, gangling, and pale, was the toughest of them all and he endured while the others sickened, one after the other. He buried them in Millroad Churchyard, one per winter, till only a brother, his sister Bertie and himself were left.

Callie's father, widowed again, came to stay with them a month or two at a time—in and out, disconsolate, restless, his high spirits dipping to a sort of plaintive humor. He was sick from one thing and another and at last was taken ill in a boarding house in Sedalia. Matthew went on the train and brought him home to die.

They were not easy years. But death and uncertain weather were the way of life. Matthew went on steadily, working his farm, teaching his school, studying and learning.

After a number of years at Bitterwater, his academic efforts were rewarded with a new position. Renfro, the nearest town, decided that the community should have a high school. Accordingly, they built a new room onto the grade school building and hired a professor. Two weeks before school began the professor suddenly died.

In complete innocence Matthew said, "I wonder what they'll do about it. Where will they find another teacher this late?"

"I know where," said Callie. "Matthew, you can teach that school. Why don't you go over there and see about it?"

"Mercy goodness, Callie, I'm not qualified!"

"I'll bet you're as qualified as he was or better."

"Well, now, I'm not so sure of that."

"I am. Why don't you go see about it, Papa? It wouldn't hurt nothin' just to go see."

"Aw, I kinda hate to do that. Mr. Motherwell was just buried yesterday. I'd feel like a buzzard—couldn't hardly wait for the body to get cold."

"Somebody's going to do it. And they can't wait all year. School's startin'."

"Yes, and so is my school. If I went over to Renfro, who would teach *my* school?"

"The one that's otherwise going to teach in Renfro and make more money. That's who."

"There are some considerations more important than money," Matthew said loftily and went off to the barn.

That was the last that was said about it until two days later, when the school board in Renfro came looking for him.

They hired him over his own protests, at what seemed to him a mighty fancy salary. He would not accept until he had gone to the county seat and found another teacher to take his place at Bitterwater. This moral obligation discharged, he embarked with tremorous zeal on his new assignment. Within a month the tremors ceased, the zeal increased, and he was as happy as he could be.

Or nearly so.

There was something that troubled him a little at home. It was not that Callie had become a mother only, forgetting to be a wife. Not that at all. In spite of her busy-ness and the frequent presence of relatives, she found time to be alone with him. Made time, in fact, as on rainy days, when she made the children play indoors. Then she would run to the barn or the smokehouse, wherever he was working, and bring her pan of beans to string or potatoes to peel and sit on a box nearby so they could visit. And at night after the children were put to bed, she was his girl again, soft and solicitous, her small body obedient to his.

But somehow, in spite of this, a gap had opened between them. Nothing wide, but wide enough that he felt it. He knew that in part he was to blame. He had so many kinds of things on his mind. What with farming, teaching, and studying, he was simply too busy to devote much time to her.

And yet, in a way, he had tried. Loving the facts, theories, ideas which he found in books, he had tried to share them with her. He had tried, early in their marriage, to teach her to read. Although she had a good mind, and though she had gone through the *Fourth Reader* at school, he was shocked to find that she had trouble even with simple words and could read little more than a primer. Naturally what she was able to puzzle out bored her. He set about to teach her longer words and how to write and spell them. Sometimes he gave her exercises to do, as he would a child at school. Dutifully Callie recited her lesson and drew the words on paper with a stiff hand, until at last she began to yawn and stretch and complain of her eyes.

"I reckon I've learned enough for today," she would say. "Didn't I do pretty good?"

"Not good—*well*."

"Oh pshaw! Good or well, what's the difference! They amount to the same thing. Let's go over across the branch and pick them wild grapes. I'll make you some jelly."

Smiling a little ruefully, he would go with her. She was so sweet, so gay, so pretty and beguiling that he hadn't the heart to be cross.

Sometimes he told her stories. He recounted the wanderings of Ulysses, the romance of Lancelot and Elaine; he told her of Sydney Carton and David Copperfield, Indian wars and Benjamin Franklin. Callie listened until some convenient pause, when she would break in with a comment on the weather or the woodpile or the quality of this year's potatoes.

It was the same when he talked of his schoolwork. He found it no use to come home at night and try to communicate the day's satisfactions. If things had gone badly, why, then she was all sympathy and attention. Otherwise his work did not interest her. And apparently she figured that if he had time to stand around talking of school and such, he had time to help her. He usually ended by churning the butter ("as long as you're standin' there") or helping her stretch lace curtains; or she would entice him off for a walk in the woods to hunt the guinea's nest. He had no objection to most of this. But he did think wistfully how fine it would be if they could talk of books together.

He observed, however, that though she cared little for his scho-

159

lastic duties, she was downright vain of them to others. He heard her sometimes bragging to the neighbors. "He has to *study* tonight!" she would say, as if it were just too tiresome of him (and it was!). But she was bragging. No one else's husband had such a distinguished fault.

"Come and study with me," he said sometimes. "We'll learn some history."

"Oh, you go ahead. I'll just sit here and read the Bible."

After a while he stopped trying to teach her.

The components of his life, at first a successful amalgam, began little by little to separate, so that now he led two lives. And the more the public life involved him, the more he came to love it. It was as a facet of this life that he loved Charlotte Newhouse.

12

One morning in February of his second winter in Renfro, a tall girl in a hat and a furred cape walked into his schoolroom and introduced herself. She was new in the community, had come from St. Louis to stay with an aunt and uncle, and she wished to enroll in school. Her voice was high and elegant, a cultivated voice. Tetanized by her cool good manners, Matthew could scarcely pronounce his own name and shake the hand she offered. He assigned her to a desk and showed her where to hang her wraps.

"Thank you," she said, with a slight inclination of the head. "You are most kind."

The phrase tickled him, it sounded so formal and charming. *Most kind*, he said to himself, wanting to laugh; *most kind!* He was most kind to her all day long.

The children were most unkind. They snickered and stared, made fun of her clothes, her hair, and her name. They called her Miss Oldhouse and Skinny and Paleface. She bore it with dignity and a trace of amusement.

When school was dismissed in the afternoon, she asked if she might wait in the building until her uncle came. She sat in the back, leafing through a book, while Matthew sat up front at his desk and did his schoolwork. Neither of them spoke. The pressure of silence grew. He was conscious of his breathing; his stomach made hunger noises and he needed to urinate. After almost three-quarters of an hour, the uncle mercifully arrived.

"Good night, Mr. Soames," said Charlotte. "It has been most enjoyable."

The aunt and uncle, who lived some miles on the other side of Renfro, were a childless couple known to be well off and considered uppity. Matthew knew them only by sight. Each morning the uncle drove Charlotte into town in the buggy and each evening drove back to collect her. He was invariably late. During the waits, which varied from twenty minutes to an hour, Matthew and the girl began to get acquainted.

He learned that her mother and father were divorced, that her mother had recently remarried and rushed off to Europe on a honeymoon. Since the marriage had taken place impetuously, there had been no time to make elaborate arrangements for Charlotte. The simplest thing was to send her down to the country for three months with her mother's sister. (Moreover, Mother thought it would be good for her to breathe country air for a while and contemplate nature.) Charlotte had not wanted to come, but there was nothing else to do.

She spoke of the divorce quite openly. Matthew was shocked by her casual reference to it. But the girl seemed modest and ladylike, not at all coarsened by the experience. On the contrary she was most refined. He found out that she had studied painting, that she attended the opera and saw plays on the stage. Her mother's friend ("who is now my stepfather") sometimes took them to concerts.

She admitted serenely that she cared little for schoolwork. As a matter of fact, she had not intended to come to school at all, these three months, but to devote them to reading, which she adored, and contemplating nature, as Mother had enjoined. But after a week of books, nature, and nothing else, she had found herself hopelessly bored and had decided to come to school.

She read the novels of Scott and Dickens and spoke of other writers and books unfamiliar to Matthew—Theodore Dreiser, Edith Wharton, George Sand (Matthew was amazed to learn that George Sand was a woman), and a novel called *Madame Bovary*, written by a Frenchman. How had she come in contact with these writings, he wanted to know. Were they taught in school in St. Louis? Charlotte explained that she had read most of them at home; her mother owned lots of books. Mother herself had written part of a novel, which she had let Charlotte read.

Poetry, too, was dear to her heart, particularly that of Keats and Tennyson (how she loved "The Eve of St. Agnes" and "The Lady of Shalott"!) and a book which mother had received for Christmas, *The Rubáiyát of Omar Khayyám.*

"The what of who?"

"*The Roo-bye-ott of Omar Ky-am.* It's very beautiful. When I get back home I'll send you a copy."

Such talk dazzled Matthew. She spoke so properly, in her high fainting voice, saying the most surprising things, manipulating uncommon vocabulary as easily as the days of the week. Each day he looked forward eagerly to these late-afternoon chats. Charlotte, too, seemed to welcome them. As the door closed behind the other pupils, they turned to each other, laughing with relief, and shook hands in a playful ritual of greeting, as if they had not really met that day until this moment. Charlotte perched herself on a desk near the front, while Matthew, barricaded behind his own desk, tilted his chair against the blackboard, and they talked of books and travel and music and each other.

Charlotte often exclaimed how lovely it would be if he could visit her in St. Louis. She could show him the big buildings, the museum and the universities, and they could go to a concert together. She did miss the concerts! How nice if Matthew could go to school in St. Louis this summer! She spoke of this so often that Matthew began to consider the possibility. It had never occurred to him to go anywhere except to the normal school in Clarkstown. But why not St. Louis? The trip itself would be an education.

It became a little game with them: When Matthew came to St. Louis, they would go one evening to the show boat and see a minstrel show. First they would have dinner at a grand restaurant. They would drink champagne!

"Is champagne intoxicating?" said Matthew.

"What do you mean?" said Charlotte, looking puzzled.

"Does it make you drunk?"

"Certainly not!" She looked at him incredulously. "Champagne isn't *beer!*"

Well, and what else would they do?

Well, they would ride out to the Parade Grounds at Jefferson Barracks and watch the soldiers drill, all dressed up in their uniforms; that was very thrilling. They would go to the new Coliseum; they would go canoeing. They would visit Shaw's Garden and the buildings left from the Fair (what a pity he couldn't have

162

been in St. Louis *then!*). She would wear her hat with the roses on it and carry her pink parasol. He would wear a straw hat and twirl a cane and look so grand that everyone would think he came from New York City! They would stroll among the flowers, and people would take him for her beau! (Shouts of laughter.)

And what else?

Oh, there would be lots of splendid things to do. The city would open its arms to him.

And so on and on, until Matthew's head was turned so many times it spun like a globe map.

One afternoon as they clasped hands in greeting, Matthew suddenly bent his head and kissed her on the mouth. They stood staring at each other for a moment, and after that they couldn't think of anything to say. Charlotte sat down on the desk top, Matthew leaned against the blackboard. Neither of them could look at the other without that contraction of the face that passes for a smile. The uncle didn't come and he didn't come and at last there was simply nothing else to do but fall into each other's arms and fasten their mouths together.

13

Matthew was just past thirty that spring. The girl was seventeen and seemed far older. Her poised manner managed to obscure the fact that she was very young at love and gave her a touch of worldliness which to Matthew seemed the sum of sophistication. He felt unworthy of her, overcome with gratitude that she did not spurn him.

On her part, she was grateful to him. For she had been lonely. She had also felt sorry for herself, as she had been in love with her mother's suitor and all he had done was laugh and chuck her under the chin. She needed urgently to exert her personality upon someone who would pay attention. The tall young schoolteacher with the muscular body and nice brown eyes paid attention very nicely.

Matthew hurried to school each morning with a dry throat, in such haste to get there that he galloped his sorrel mare all the way, urging her on with apologies and the promise of rewards. At nights he rode home reluctantly, impatient for morning. Weekends were an abomination. He fled the house all day Saturday and chopped down trees, pulled up hedge, and uprooted stumps. He wore himself out trying to pass the endless time till Monday arrived again.

At school he was afraid to be seen within ten paces of Charlotte. All day he scarcely looked at her, yet he reddened with pride when in a quick glance her eyes spoke to him. In the afternoons, waiting for her uncle, they kissed in haste, greedily, in a corner of the room behind the heating stove. After that, they took their customary places, she on the front desk, he safely behind his. Sitting so circumspectly apart, they made love with words across the space between them. The things she thought of to say to him! Roses and jewels fell out of her mouth, kissed words and astonishing passion! Their voices, low and yearning, stroked and caressed each other until Matthew was in anguish.

He was not, however, so abandoned that he forgot the dangers. He cringed each time one of the students called Charlotte "teacher's pet." Since Charlotte turned it off neatly, they did it very seldom. But he wondered what whispers ran among them and what tales they carried home. At times his fear of discovery so unsettled him that he wished they had never met. What a relief if she were to go away and he could forget about her. Then he recalled that soon she would in reality leave him, and he was devastated. He looked forward to the end of school as if it were the end of the world.

Despite Charlotte's sighs and occasional tears, Matthew realized that she accepted the end more easily than he. She chatted happily of going home, of seeing her mother again and her new stepfather. All this added to his despair. He was angry with her and in turn more possessive. The thought of marrying her crossed and recrossed his mind, followed regularly by its shadow, the thought of divorcing Callie. His wife came strangely to mind; he felt he had scarcely spoken to her all spring. Yet the cataclysm of divorce was out of the question. Besides the scandal, which could do him irreparable damage, there was the formidable inconvenience, both physical and emotional, of arranging another life. And when he faced it squarely, he could not imagine a life totally and permanently without Callie. (He tried to imagine Charlotte on his farm, and it occurred to him to wonder if in spring she would come running to tell him that the lettuce was up—as Callie did; or greet a new calf with such gentle cries; or if she would butcher a chicken—which Callie always had to do; he didn't have the heart.)

He could, on the other hand, imagine a life without Charlotte. Though it was painful, he could do it. He could accept the inevitability of being without her. But not now, not quite yet. He wanted to hold on a little longer. And it bled him that she seemed less eager to hold on than he.

As the weather warmed and the new leaves came out, he grew more and more distraught. With great effort he taught his classes. At home he was cross with the children and sullen in Callie's presence. Because he treated them badly, his conscience hurt worse than before. He began to suffer from insomnia, lying tense and feverish through the night, too guilty to pray for sleep. He thought of Charlotte swept away in the various life of the city, leaving him behind. Though he had often envied the cultural advantages of a city, and though he sometimes longed to see its parks and monuments, historical shrines and famous buildings, he distrusted the people who made up a city. He had always looked with disapproval on their habits and attitudes, and considered them, at best, frivolous and pleasure-ridden. Charlotte had opened to him new Elysian vistas, and he thought with a physical thrill of gracious, learned gentlemen and ladies, of beautiful speech and elegant manners, libraries, paintings, music, and contemplation—*otium cum dignitate*. In all this he had some share as long as he held on to Charlotte. But with her going, this would go. In contrast to her world, his own seemed unendurably drab. In spite of himself, he was filled with resentment against Callie and the children. He cared for them, therefore they shackled him and held him back.

The possibility of spending the summer in St. Louis, with the excuse of school, tantalized him. He thought of it constantly, how he might manage to get away, what arrangement he could make for the family (who would stay behind, of course) and for the farm work. There were things he could do; and St. Louis was not the ends of the earth. Somehow he could afford it. One evening he made so bold as to mention it to Callie, in an offhand way. He thought he had better sound her out, prepare her. She said very little at the time, but the next day she was sick, and he felt to blame. Prone to nervous headaches, she came down with a monstrous attack. He found her prostrate when he came home. She lay across the bed with a wet cloth on her forehead and a basin on the floor to catch whatever vile liquid was left to boil up from her tortured entrails. Her lips were blue, her sunny, brown-toned skin bleached to the pallor of seed-sprouts. He nursed her through it, till she fell into a sleep akin to coma, the last stage of the illness.

He suffered, during these attacks of hers, both sympathy and aversion. They were a female trick, a protest, a reproach. They were self-engendered. Yet he felt he had caused this one with the mention of St. Louis, and he smarted under it at the same time that he felt her pain.

He left her still sleeping the next morning. When he returned (late again, in spite of his good intentions; Charlotte had driven him mad that day), Callie was somewhat revived. She even suggested that he give her a penmanship lesson, something she had not done before.

"Oh," he said, having no heart for it, "it's late. I've been teaching all day."

"But I've been wantin'—"

"I've got to get to bed. Some other time, maybe."

He could not look at her. He went on to bed and lay there, pretending to sleep. Callie and Charlotte, two kinds of a life; they tore him apart. At last, worn out by his yammering brain, he rose and pulled on his clothes. Careful not to waken Callie, he crept down the stairs and out to the moonlit yard, where he stood for a moment perceiving the night.

The stillness, the sapid air . . . flavors of green, dew, new-turned soil, the pure breath of leaf and weed and grassblade. The soft cows collapsed in the moonlight . . . his mare whiffling in her stall and the comment of her deft hoof against the manger. Walking to the gate, he looked out across the silvery woods and the pasture, and it seemed to him that he had not seen all this for a very long time.

He crossed the barnlot and walked on through the walnut grove. To his left lay an open space of meadow. A little distance to the right, a line of oaks and cedars and the white thin trunks of paper birches marked the crooked gully of the branch. Leaving the path, he cut across to the banks and looked down at the water. It flowed over sandrock and pebbles and flashed moonlight at him. A spring bubbled in the darkness below. He descended along a path made by the cows and scooped up a double handful of cold water. It had a clean medicinal taste, suggesting minerals and herbs.

On the other side of the branch, the arrangement of fence, woods, and the gully made a small triangle, a patch of ground good for little else but grazing and which he seldom visited. He thought now that he might climb up and have a look. He drew himself up the bank by a root and pushed through the bushes into the open. There he stopped in amazement. Alone, almost in the center of the plot, stood a hawthorn tree in full bloom. It had the shape of a great pine cone, round at the base and tapering to a point. And from midway up the base all the way to the top, its small white flowers rose in a solid luminous mass of white.

Matthew drew his breath in a low whistle. He had forgotten about that tree. He had never seen it in bloom like this. He walked all the way around it, marveling. After a while he went off a way and leaned against another tree (it seemed all the others had drawn back on purpose) and watched his hawthorn burn in the moonlight. It would have burned as whitely, still and impersonal, had he not been there at all. He thought of all that loveliness which might have passed unseen. And it pleased him that he had been granted the privilege to see. Pondering this, he suddenly felt humbled. Not half an hour ago, he had decried his lot. In scorn and discontent he had denied the good of his life, of all the Lord had seen fit to give him. And yet, ingrate that he was, adulterous and deceiving, he had been led to this tree. God had set it as a sign between them. This tall flowering tree was the gentle and divine rebuke.

"Forgive me, Father," he murmured aloud. "Forgive my ingratitude." And he felt a little better.

He slid to the ground and sat for a long time, half drowsing. When his eyes were saturated with the beauty of the tree, he would glance at the dark woods behind him or up at the sky, and then back quickly at the tree, with fresh vision, as if to see it again for the first time. In that white blaze, the burdens of the spirit seemed consumed. He felt purified and exalted, in a sort of holy trance, like the ecstasy of saints.

But after a while, the potential calm wore off, and the thought of Charlotte returned, wracking as before. It jolted him from grace and he moaned softly as he tumbled back into longing and despair. He thought of her cool skin and her eyes and the taste of her mouth, and his desire for her, being futile, was the same as anger. He cursed himself. Must he bring her even here, into the sanctuary of his own woods? Rising to his feet, he plunged through the woods behind him, numb to the branches that sliced across his face and the dewberry vines that sawed his ankles. Up the slope he went and down again to where he started, and it did no good. The need of her clung like burrs. And the hawthorn tree mocked him with its beauty. He slumped down again against the oak tree.

As he sat there, a sound reached him from the direction of the branch, a rustling, as of something pushing its way through the brush. A clod rolled down the bank into the water. Matthew lifted his head and peered across the open space of moonlight. Perhaps one of the cattle had followed him, or an animal had come to drink. There was more rustling, a movement in the brush, and a white figure stepped out to the edge of the clearing.

"Matthew?"

It was Callie in her white nightgown.

"Matthew?" she called again in a timid voice. "Are you there?"

"What are you doing out here?" he said from the shadows.

She gave a little startled cry that ended in a laugh. "My goodness! I *thought* you was here, but you scared me." She came out into the open and hesitated. "Where are you? I can't see you."

"Here." He stepped to the edge of the shadow.

With a murmur of relief she ran toward him. She wore a shawl over her shoulders and her long straight hair hung loose.

"I thought you were asleep," he said gruffly.

"I was, for a while. You're all right, ain't you, Matthew? You're not sick?"

"No, just tired. Seemed like I couldn't get to sleep."

"I knowed you couldn't."

"I thought I'd take a walk. Maybe the fresh air would help me."

"It's nice out. Not hardly cold at all." She pulled off the shawl and shook her hair back. "Such a pretty night! And the tree, Matthew! Oh, the tree!" She ran toward it. "I never seen anything prettier, did you?"

"No," he said, begrudging her presence. "We'd better go back."

"Not yet!" She ran back and took his hand. "Just a little bit longer. Please?" Shy as a schoolgirl, she dropped his hand and looked down. "Seems like I don't never get to see you any more," she said. The moonlight made an arc on her bent head. When he made no answer, she looked up and smiled again. "But I know you been awful busy. It's no wonder you're tired out." She turned away, breathed deeply, and flopped down on the ground. "Sit down, honey." She spread out her shawl for him.

"You better get up from there. You'll catch your death of cold."

"No I won't. Come on." She tugged at his hand.

"What if the girls wake up?" he said, still on his feet.

"They'll be all right. They sleep good, once they get at it." She took off her shoes and dug her bare toes in the grass. "It feels nice!"

"Aren't you worried about the gypsies?" he said. "There's some around."

Her feet stopped moving. "Yes, I heard there was."

"I thought I saw their campfires this evening, over there by town, in the woods. I don't think they'll be out this way, but I wouldn't want to take any chances."

"No," she said and was silent for a moment. "Well, they couldn't get in, anyway. I locked the house good when I come out. The key's in my shoe." She lay back on the grass with her arms stretched over her head. "My, the moon's big tonight." The front of her gown had come unbuttoned and the round dark eye of one breast stared at him.

"Come on, Callie. You'll take cold."

"Matthew?" she said softly.

"Let's go back."

"We will. Come and lie down a while first."

"I don't want to lie down."

There was a silence, as he stood scowling across the clearing. Then Callie stood up, facing him.

"Matthew," she said in a small voice, "love me."

He turned away. "Not now, Callie."

"Why?"

"Not out here."

"Will you if we go home?"

"I don't know."

"Please."

"It wouldn't be any good," he said desperately.

"I'll make it be. Oh, Matthew."

"Maybe tomorrow. I don't know. Come on, Callie."

She slipped around in front of him again, and before he could move, she had begun to pull her nightgown down off her shoulders. Her arms came out of the sleeves and the garment slid to the ground.

"Put it back on," he said.

"No!"

She stepped out of the gown and, with an odd smile, lifted her chest so that her plump breasts stuck out. Muttering, he picked up the gown and flung it at her and strode off across the clearing.

Callie ran after him and caught his arm. "Don't leave me, Matthew!"

"Let me alone!" he cried.

"I *have* let you alone!"

They faced each other in silence there in the moonlight by the hawthorn tree. Then with the quick slippery movement of a minnow, she was against him and her arms had gone around him and the hands were working at his shirt.

"What are you doing?"

With a sudden wrench she tore the shirt open. She put her breasts against his bare body.

"Take off your things," she whispered.

"I'll hate you!" He could hardly speak.

"No you won't."

Her body moved and her hands slid up and down his back and in a voice like warm rain she said some things that he had never heard her say before, shocking, titillating things. His heart was pounding the breath out of him. And moaning, as if in grief or terror, he seized her buttocks in his hands and pulled her up against him. Clinging together they fell to the ground.

Afterward he lay on his back with one arm over his eyes to shield them from the moon. The ground was cold, but he was too tired to stir. He had made love brutally, biting and gripping, as if it were a punishment he was forced to give her. (He found later that he had left great bruises on her.) It had given him no pleasure beyond a bitter satisfaction, like that of revenge. This had never been his way of loving. It disgusted him, both with himself and with her.

Callie leaned over him, stroking him with her long hair. "It was good, wasn't it?" she said.

He drew a long breath and let it out. "I guess so."

"Shall we go back now?"

"All right."

But he lay without moving. After a while, Callie brought her shawl and covered him. She sat for a long time without speaking. Once he thought she was crying. He looked at her from under his arm. Her head was bent and the hair fell forward, hiding her face. She held one breast in her hand.

"I didn't mean to hurt you," he said.

"I know you didn't. It's all right."

He closed his eyes and he must have fallen asleep, for when he looked again she was gone. His clothes, which he had flung helter-skelter, lay neatly beside him. He dressed and started toward the house. As he reached the thicket above the branch he paused and looked back. The hawthorn tree stood tall and serene, beautiful for its own sake, and he felt that he had in some way betrayed it.

14

When Charlotte went away, they kissed goodbye tenderly and often and vowed to see each other again, someday, somehow. Matthew was desolate. But in spite of himself, he soon found it a pleasure to wake up in the fresh May mornings and stay at home all day. He discovered his farm again and busied himself about the place with the little girls at his heels. Later he would go up to Clarkstown for a few weeks of summer school; though that was not the same as St. Louis, he looked forward to it. Meanwhile he had no lessons to study, no papers to grade, nothing to do except work in the open air and sing loud and fall asleep the minute his head hit the pillow. Such freedom came each year as a complete, refreshing surprise. He could not think of Charlotte without pain. But he could go a full day sometimes without thinking of her at all.

Callie, of course, was pregnant. This surprised neither of them. Though she was happy about it, he was gnawed with guilt. He could not help feeling this child was begot in adultery. For he had used his wife—that was the only honest word—while wanting another woman.

And yet, he had also wanted Callie that night, because she made him want her. And she had done so since. He was a little resentful of the way she contented him. Because of her, the well-bred Charlotte was fading, and with her, the concerts and museums, the fine speech and the cultivated manners.

Well, let them go. They were too far beyond his reach anyway. How could he, with his humble beginning, presume to such attainments? And what if he didn't have the concert hall, art galleries, the company of scholars? He had the birds; they made music that lifted the soul. He had the sky, whereon God painted. For company he had all of Nature. The books weren't written that could teach men more than she could! He looked at his acres with a light heart.

But oh!—as he picked up the reins again—oh, the books that

were written and the people who could read them! Oh, the things that were happening in the world, and all the seas, the mountains, craters, castles, forts and ships and statues, jungles, pageantry, and all the graceful fair-skinned girls that he would never know!

15

The child was born in January in the midst of an ice storm, when the world outside snapped and splintered and tree boughs crashed on the roof.

It was so bad that morning that Matthew almost stayed home from school. Callie didn't expect the baby for a few more days, but she didn't see why Matthew had to go out in all that weather.

"Ain't any of the children gonna be there," she said, "not on a day like this."

"Well," said Matthew, "I've got the key, and I wouldn't want any of them to get locked out."

"Can't they get the preacher to unlock—if they're silly enough to be out in all this? Ain't he got a key?"

"Yes, but I hate not to be there."

"It wouldn't do no harm to miss once."

"I know. But the stores and the bank will be open. It wouldn't look well if the school were closed."

"Well, my land! All them men live in town."

"Maybe they think I should live in town, too, so I could give better service."

"You're over there all the time, the way it is."

"Well, Callie, that's my job!"

"All right, go on then!" she said. "If you're so anxious to please everybody, go ahead and go. You and your horse can freeze solid—they ain't gonna think any more of you. But anyway, leave Jessica at home."

Jessica, who was by this time nearly seven, had started to school in the fall. She rode in the saddle with Matthew each morning and he dropped her off at Bitterwater on his way to town. But this morning he rode off without her, sulking because Callie had no understanding of his obligations.

Two or three of the town children appeared—enough to make him feel righteous but hardly enough to justify building a fire. He sent them home at noon and soon after started on his precarious journey to the farm. The mare slipped on the icy roads and they had to dodge fallen branches. It was dark by the time they reached home.

The house, too, was dark. Matthew put the mare in the stall and hurried inside. No fire burned in the range; no lamps were lighted.

"Callie?" he called.

"We're all right." Her voice came from the front room. "We're in here."

She lay in the bed in the dark, with the new baby beside her. The little girls sat close together by the heating stove.

"It's all right, honey," she said. "You've got a new daughter!"

Matthew dropped to his knees beside her without speaking. The little girls came over and he held them in his arms.

"Don't cry," Callie said. "It wasn't so bad. Jessica helped real good. She brought me things and put wood in the stove and kept us warm." She reached out and touched Jessica's head. "I don't know what Mama would have done without her."

Matthew kissed her and kissed the children and still could not speak. Laughing and crying, he knelt there, stroking Callie's forehead.

She laughed. "Now go on, Papa, and light the lamp. Don't you want to see your new baby?"

She was a tiny thing with lots of dark hair.

"Hello!" said Matthew gently, bending over her with the lamp. "Good evening, little girl!"

Callie's dark eyes shone up at him. "Her name is Matthew," she said.

"But she's a girl—she looks like you!"

"I want her named for her father." She kissed the new little head. "We'll call her Mathy."

16

Now, years later, sitting in the moonlit graveyard above Shawano, Matthew thought of Callie waiting down there, lying awake perhaps in the dark house, listening for his footstep . . . waiting, always waiting, with the warm supper, the warm bed. Waiting for him to come home, knowing that he did not always bring his heart home with him. She must have known. Not every time and not everything, but enough to hurt. Without any facts or names, she knew about Charlotte. And so she followed him to the woods that midnight. And so Mathy was born. Mathy was Charlotte's child. But Callie had borne her, saving Charlotte—and him—the trouble.

She had saved him more than once by her loyalty and long-sufferance. He was grateful to her—and a little resentful, too. Sometimes a man didn't want to be saved. But then, he did, really. No matter what he did to her, he couldn't live without her, and he wouldn't want to.

"I love her," he said, wishing sorrowfully that he loved her only. He hadn't quite. And probably he wouldn't. For the girls kept coming on, year after year, a new crop every fall, ripening girls lined up before him for his delectation. And he would in sorrow, he supposed, eat of the apple all the days of his life.

Mathy

1

By her first act—arriving early as she did, that day when he was gone—Matthew's youngest daughter put him in an unfavorable light. (Sometimes he thought her mother had her early on purpose, just to spite him. Whether it was her fault or her mother's or no one's, it irked him.) He might have forgiven her this, however, if she had behaved differently thereafter. She was a likable child, part of the time; bright and funny, often appealing. But she had a positive talent for getting him into trouble—a talent which flowered luxuriantly about the time they left the farm.

This was a little before the first war, when Matthew first accepted the position in Shawano. He wasn't at all sure it was the right thing to do. The greater prestige and responsibility, while attractive, frightened him. Callie too had her doubts. Though for years she had dreamed of living in town, she began to look at her blunt hands and listen to her speech, and her cool practical courage faltered. Even so, she knew as well as he did that they had to go.

In spite of the natural shyness of farm children, the two older girls looked forward eagerly to the move. People, stores, excitement! They thought of life in town as one perpetual Saturday afternoon.

It was the youngest who resisted all the blandishments of change. Mathy was five and a half that summer and as busy as she could be. She didn't have time to pack up and move. Seeing the preparations go on in spite of her, she hid all her clothes. She buried the doll in the orchard. She climbed the tallest tree on the place and refused to come down. She ran off to the neighbors' and pleaded to live with them. Finally, on the morning of departure, she vanished entirely. Why in creation, said Matthew, hadn't someone tied her to the fence! White-lipped, he struck off through the pasture toward the willow slew, where he had often found her knee-deep in the marsh grass. Callie looked through the house and the girls searched the grounds. Jessica found her at last in the garden, under a polebean vine where the three crossed sticks made a little tepee. There she sat, all charcoal eyes and ferocity, ready to scratch and bite.

Nobody had the heart to spank her—least of all Matthew, who, no farther from home than the barnlot, was so homesick he could have died. Grim and silent, he drove away in the big wagon, his best cow tied to the back, his family huddled behind him among the furniture and chicken coops, and that child screaming her head off.

To his relief, Mathy bowed to necessity soon after they were settled. Before long, neighbors and other novelties seemed to take her mind off the farm. The older girls were blissfully happy. They hadn't been in town two weeks till they had been invited to three birthday parties, something new to them. And every afternoon Mama let them walk to the post office and ask for the superintendent's mail. The only thing Leonie regretted was that Papa made her take the fifth grade over. She was eleven and should have been in the sixth. But she had had tonsillitis the previous winter and missed a lot of school; furthermore, Papa didn't think much of the teacher she had had, down home at Bitterwater. Though she wept and argued and kicked the door, there was no getting around him. She went back to the fifth grade, bitterly ashamed to be the oldest one in the class. However, there was a piano teacher in Shawano, and Papa let her take lessons. This helped considerably. She felt that she had come into the cultural advantages for which she was destined.

As for Callie, she hardly had time to decide whether she liked the new life or not. Living in town took more washing and ironing and much more sewing. There were new curtains to make; the girls needed new dresses; and the week scarcely went by when she wasn't making a costume. A witch's hat, a Pilgrim suit, wings for a Christmas angel. She never saw the like of programs and exercises that went on at the schoolhouse. She complained to Matthew and said there was plenty going on at the church without so many doings at school. But he said the community expected it of him, it stimulated community spirit. She supposed this was true; though there was hardly a mother she talked to who wouldn't have welcomed a little less spirit if it meant a little less sewing.

She was glad to be busy, however, as it gave her a good excuse not to socialize. Among these people situations always arose in which she didn't know how to act, situations she couldn't anticipate. On her own ground she would have known exactly what to do and done it or not, as it pleased her. But you can depart from the rules only when you know them well, and since she had not yet learned the new ones, she was not always sure what was expected of her.

There was, for example, the situation with the delivery boy.

Matthew had a telephone installed, one of the few in town, and it was Callie's special pleasure, when she needed groceries, to call up the store and order them sent out. Within half an hour they would arrive at her back door, delivered by an angelic simpleton so grateful to have been of service that you felt you had done him a great favor by ordering a sack of flour. This cheerful minion, whose last name was Dumpson, was known throughout the town as Clabber, because of the albino tint of his hair and eyebrows and the faint fuzz above his lip. He drove a small two-wheel cart drawn by a horse named Maude, an animal as stiff and slow and dependable as her master. You would hear them for minutes coming down the street, the creaking of wheels, the leisurely clop-clop of Maude's hooves in the dust. Then Clabber would shuffle around the house, whistling to himself, and summon you with a light knock. You would find him waiting beyond the screen with a smile of beatitude.

Callie's heart opened to him on his first visit. She went so far as to allow Mathy to ride with him to the end of the block. She was afraid, however, that she had been too friendly, for on subsequent trips Clabber showed a tendency to stay and visit. Oh, as polite as you could ask for, not sitting down or getting in the way, merely standing there, just inside the door, cap in hand, nodding and smiling and now and then getting out a comment that made remarkable sense. She hadn't the heart to send him right off, and didn't really want to. But she was not sure the neighbors would think the association proper. Only when she learned that Clabber Dumpson visited lengthily in every kitchen in town did she accept him formally in hers. She began to ply him with cake and cookies. He brought her news from downtown. They exchanged opinions on human nature and the weather and enjoyed each other comfortably in the manner of good servant and master, each of whom knows where the boundary lies.

Callie found such a relationship completely to her liking. It roused her sense of noblesse and restored to her, brighter than before, her dream of living in style some day in a fine white house on the corner, with a woman to come and do the wash and a boy to trim the hedge.

With his family and himself happily adjusted, Matthew dared to conclude that the move had been a wise one. He thought of it gratefully one noon hour early in the fall as he walked to town. It was a beautiful day, crisp and golden and soft in the middle, like a fried apple pie. Moreover, it was payday. His first check from Shawano lay in his inside pocket. Buoyed by sunlight and a sense of well-being, he walked down the street with a light step. A pretty woman, mother of one of his pupils, came out on a porch to greet him. A merchant on his way home to dinner stopped to shake his hand. Waving and smiling—prosperous, accepted, consequential—Matthew made his way to the bank.

Having deposited his check, he crossed the street to pay the grocery bill. For the first time in his life, and only at the grocer's insistence, he had become a credit customer. It still puzzled him that charging things was looked on as a sign of affluence and not indigence, and he was relieved to find the store empty except for the proprietor.

"Good morning, good morning, Professor!" The grocer came forward from the cool brown depths of the store, up the aisle between the bean sacks and pickle barrel and the glass-lidded cookie boxes tilted in their racks. "What can I do for you, Professor?"

"Well-sir-now!" said Matthew, shaking hands. "You can tell me what I owe you, Mr. Henshaw. If the wife hasn't run up the bill too high, why, maybe I can pay it!"

"Yessir, yessir now! I declare!" said Mr. Henshaw, still wringing Matthew's hand. "These women keep us humpin', don't they, Professor!" He clapped Matthew on the shoulder.

"Yes, yes, they do."

"That's right. Got to get up and go to keep the womenfolks supplied. Why, I tell my wife, where does it all go! She sends me to work ever' mornin' with a list as long as your arm. Clabber's old horse can't hardly pull the load. And *I* don't know what she does with all of it. I'm sure *I* don't eat it!" He slapped his solid round belly.

"Why," said Matthew, "anyone can see that!" The two of them laughed. "Well, let's see what she's cost me."

Mr. Henshaw took the sheaf of bills off a wire hook. "Here you are, Professor. You run over these figures now, to see if I've added right. I wouldn't want to cheat a schoolteacher—not the first time, anyway."

Matthew smiled. "I'll take your word for it, Mr. Henshaw. I'd never question it. Well, now, this doesn't look so bad. I guess I can afford it this time."

He walked back to the meat block to write a check, while Mr. Henshaw collected lagniappe from the candy case—gumdrops, lemondrops, and long coconut strips starred and striped like a flag. A farmer in straw hat and overalls came through the door. "Howdy, Orville," said Mr. Henshaw.

"Christamighty, Walt," said the farmer, pushing back his hat. "What'd you let it get so hot fer?"

" 'Tis right warm for this time of year."

"Let me have a sack of Bull Durham, Walt."

The screen door opened again and a big-boned woman in crackling skirts and a monumental sunbonnet strode in. "Walter?" she said in a deep musical voice that rang through the store —one of those voices you can hear in a crowd, even when it murmurs. "I've come for my groceries. Isn't that boy of yours back yet?"

"Not yet," Mr. Henshaw apologized. "My goodness, Mrs. Gunn, I'm sorry about this. I kept thinkin' Clabber'd be back any minute, and I was going to send him right out with your order. Tell you what I'll do—I'll fix you up another one right now. It's a shame you had to come and get it yourself."

"Oh, it's not far. I'd a-waited, but Roy's home, waitin' dinner, and I'm plumb out of lard."

"Well, let me get busy here and fix you up." He started toward the back. "Mrs. Gunn, have you met Professor Soames?"

"No, I haven't!" said the lady, advancing on Matthew. She seized his hand with a manly grip. "I'm just mighty pleased to meet you. My children are out of school, but everybody tells me we've got a mighty good man up there this year."

"Well, now, that's mighty pleasant to hear," said Matthew.

"You wanted three pounds, was it?" said Mr. Henshaw, dipping lard.

"Yes," said Mrs. Gunn, "that's enough, this kind of weather. If I keep it any time at all, it gets old-tastin'."

"My boy lost his horse this mornin'," Mr. Henshaw explained to Matthew.

"I'm sorry to hear it."

"Oh, I don't mean she died! She's lost—strayed, stolen—something like that. Anyhow, she ain't around. Must have wandered off somewhere while she was waitin' for Clab. You know how long it takes him to get in a house and get out again. Clab's been out lookin' for her more'n an hour. I haven't got any order delivered since ten-thirty this mornin'."

"Is that right!"

"That's why Mrs. Gunn has to come down and carry her own. I sent him out, right after she called. He had another stop to make on the way, and when he come out, old Maude was gone, wagon and all. He can't find hide nor hair of her."

"Well, what do you know!"

"He hasn't seen hide nor hair of her since."

"Walt?" said the farmer, leaning against the candy counter rolling a cigarette. "That boy of yours drives a little two-wheeled contraption, don't he?"

"That's right."

"With a old bag of bones hitched to it?"

"You're insultin' a mighty good horse," said Mr. Henshaw, grinning.

"For sausage, maybe. Well, I think I know where she's at."

"Pete sake, you seen her?"

" 'Bout three mile south of town."

"Three mile!"

In the brown gloomy depths of the store, bright daylight flashed as the back door opened and Clabber Dumpson shuffled in.

"Here y'are, Clab!" said Mr. Henshaw. "Looks like we've found your horse." He turned back to the farmer. "Can you beat that! I reckon the old rascal just taken it in her head to go to pasture."

"Nupe, I don't think so," said the farmer. "Looks more to me like she was stole."

"Stole? Old Maude? Who'd want her!"

"For mercy sake!" said Mrs. Gunn, walking toward them. "Maybe we ought to call the sheriff."

"Ah, nobody wants to steal old Maude," said Mr. Henshaw.

"Looks like somebody did," said the farmer.

"Who'd do a thing like that!"

"A hossthief."

"Go on! Ain't been a horsethief around here in twenty year, not since Ezzer Clark give up the trade and taken up preachin'!"

"I seen the culprit myself, plain as day, settin' up there on the seat, holdin' the reins."

"I'll call the sheriff," Mrs. Gunn said firmly. "Anybody that would do a thing like that to Clabber!"

Mr. Henshaw looked worried. "I'd hate to think it was anybody around here. Didn't recognize him, did you?"

"Nupe. Stranger to me."

"What'd he look like?"

"Wasn't a he."

"A *woman?*" said Mrs. Gunn.

"Nupe," said the farmer, "a little gal. Little dark-headed gal about the size of my thumb—wouldn't hardly tip them scales of yours, Walt."

"Well, what do you know!"

"*Isn't* that disgraceful!" Mrs. Gunn, arms akimbo, blocked the aisle with her righteous bulk. "Some children are allowed to act just any way! Who do you suppose she belongs to?"

Back by the meat block, Matthew stood in shame, the bright day yanked from under him. Heaving a great sigh, he started up the aisle. "She's mine," he said. In the shocked silence he walked forward, avoiding Mrs. Gunn's stare. "If you have some conveyance, Mr. Henshaw, that I may hire from you, I'll go and bring them back."

Angry, hungry, humiliated, he drove off in Mr. Henshaw's buckboard, Clabber Dumpson seated beside him. Together they rode through the noon streets where people were walking back from dinner. Clabber hailed them all.

"Found my horse!" he called out left and right. "We found her. She was stole!"

Merchants and schoolchildren stopped on the sidewalks and housewives ran to the door, staring at the new superintendent of schools, who was, apparently, taking the afternoon off with Mr. Henshaw's delivery boy.

They caught up with Mathy several miles from town.

"I was only going back home!" she insisted. Going home was not the same as running away.

"Your home is here," said Matthew.

"Well, I was going to come back tomorrow."

They jogged down the dusty road toward town, followed at a steadily increasing distance by Clabber and Maude and the two-wheel cart. Mathy sat beside her father, as erect and prim as he, each of them outraged with the other. Matthew's mouth drew a pale line, like the seam of a wound, across his red perspiring face. If his reputation was not permanently damaged, he would be much surprised. How could the people trust him with their children, when he couldn't control his own? On top of all else, Mathy was costing him money. Mr. Henshaw wouldn't let him pay for the use of the buckboard. But Mrs. Gunn's groceries were another matter. The stolen goods, though recovered, were hardly returnable. Under the soft midday sun, three pounds of lard had overflowed into sacks of soda crackers, coffee beans, and sugar. An astounding number of gingersnaps was missing, along with a quantity of sweet pickles. An oatmeal box had been broken open. Mathy had an inexplicable taste for rolled oats eaten raw. She still held a few grains clutched in her fist.

"In the name of goodness, child, throw that away! Wipe your hands. Not on your dress!"

"I'm going to vomit, Papa!"

"Not here!" he shouted. "Wait till you get home!"

"I can't!"

A hideous gagging sound rose out of the little green face. He barely had time to tip her over the side, clutching the bottom of her sateen bloomers. She hung there heaving and gasping, while he tried not to look.

"Are you all right now? Is that all?"

"I think so."

He wiped her face with his handkerchief. "I hope you will learn now," he began—but she leaned against him limp as a lettuce leaf, her eyes closed, and he knew he was wasting his breath. She'd never hear him. By the time they got home she was fast asleep.

2

For a while after that Mathy behaved herself. Now and then she enticed someone's puppydog to follow her home (Matthew allowed them no pets; an animal earned its keep or it didn't live there); and along in spring he caught her wandering in the yard after midnight. ("I never saw a child that never would sleep!" Callie fretted. "She don't even get sleepy in the daytime.") But these were, for Mathy, minor infractions. Then in the fall she started to school and trouble began anew. Mathy was a born hooky player. Every few days the teacher had to report to the superintendent that his little girl was missing. Matthew would then send Jessica or Leonie looking for her or call Callie on the phone. Then came the spankings, followed by long lectures, which Mathy listened to soberly and forgot at once. She continued to escape periodically until the weather turned cold.

After that she settled down and did extraordinarily well. In fact, at the insistence of her teacher, Matthew allowed her to skip a grade—an indulgence which Leonie never forgave him and he himself quickly regretted. For no sooner had Mathy sailed into the third directly from the first than she lost interest and became a most indifferent scholar. "Things come too easily to her," said Matthew. "It's not good when they come too easy." He sometimes made her sit in the office during recess till she had done the work to his satisfaction. Sometimes he had to spank her. Under such duress she managed to get through the year with "provisional promotion" to the fourth grade.

That "provisional" irked Matthew's soul. What a condition for the superintendent's daughter! As a penalty he set her a course of study for the summer, requiring that she do a little work each day and go over it with him on Saturdays. As he was away all week at the teachers college, Mathy had a tendency to leave her work till the last minute and do it all at once. Callie tried to keep her to the schedule, but Mathy pleaded to go outdoors and play and Callie felt sorry for her—she was only a little girl and it *was* summer. She wished Matthew would be a little easier on her.

It was probably for this reason, in recompense for his obdurate attitude, that she allowed Mathy to ride around town that summer with Clabber Dumpson. She let her make two or three trips each morning. It did no harm, she supposed. Clabber Dumpson was as good as gold, if not quite as bright. And as long as Mathy promised to do her lessons by Friday evening . . .

The two of them became a familiar sight that summer along Shawano's leafy streets—the gentle halfwit and the little bright-eyed girl, creaking along in the two-wheel cart at the speed of moss. On their first trips, Mathy stayed outside while Clabber delivered the groceries. "So no one will steal old Maude," she said. But she soon grew bored waiting for Clabber. Thereafter, she jumped down and helped carry the sacks. She chatted in kitchens with all the ladies, gravely discussing the world and the weather, and accepted with pleasure all gratuities. They gave her strawberries or grapes, bread and butter and the season's jellies, numberless cookies and drinks of water. She never wanted any dinner.

"I wish you wouldn't eat all them things at people's houses," Callie said one day. "It ain't nice—it's like you was askin' for a handout. You shouldn't take things, even when they're offered."

"Clabber does."

"That's different. You and him's different kind of folks—you'd ought to know better. I declare," she went on, talking to whoever was in earshot, "seems like she don't have any judgment at all. She'll take up with anybody. Talkin' to that tramp the other day that come here to the door! You'd have thought it was her uncle come to see her! If I hadn't caught her when I did, she'd a-had him comin' right in to spend the night."

Mathy was pressing nasturtiums in a wallpaper sample book and paid no attention to her.

But next morning she did not ask to go and join Clabber. She played in the barn and pasture and Callie noticed her at the back door frequently. She had a half-gallon syrup bucket and kept pumping it full of water.

"What are you doing with all that?" said Callie.

"Nothing."

"Now don't you story to me. You're doing something with it; now what are you up to?"

"Oh, I'm playing mudpies."

"Where?"

"Behind the barn."

186

Callie looked skeptical. She looked pretty clean to be playing mudpies. "Well, you stay around close. Don't go running off somewhere. Dinner will be ready before long."

At noon Mathy ate no more than if she had panhandled all morning. Callie supposed the child had filled herself up on sheep sorrel and pepper grass. As soon as dinner was over and she had dried dishes, she went out to the barn again.

Early in the afternoon, an elderly gentleman who thought highly of Callie came to pay a short call. Jessica and Leonie hid upstairs. Brother Cottrell had fought in the Civil War, and they had heard all they cared to hear about Andersonville Prison. They found his ante bellum witticisms very tiresome. On his departure, they tumbled downstairs full of giggles. "What did he bring you today, Mama?"

"Oh, plums!" said Callie in the same tone of voice she used for "Oh, foot!" "And dead ripe. If I don't work them up right now, they'll rot. What did he have to bring 'em on Friday afternoon for? We won't hardly get 'em done before Papa gets home."

"They'll keep," said Leonie, biting into one.

"I'm afraid not. Where are you going?"

"I have to practice my piano lesson."

"You can do that after a while. You come on here now and help. It won't take long."

"It will too. It'll take all afternoon, it always does."

"No, it won't," said Callie cheerfully. "We can get these out of the way real fast, all of us workin' together."

"We've already got a whole smokehouse full of plum jelly."

"I know, but Brother Cottrell would be disappointed if I didn't work up his plums. I'll give most of the batch to him."

"Why couldn't we just give him some of ours? He'd never know the difference."

"I wouldn't want these to go to waste."

"We could give them away."

"That wouldn't be very nice."

"Why wouldn't it?"

"Oh, it just wouldn't."

"I think it would."

"No, we can't do that."

"Why not?"

"*Leonie, stop arguing!*" Callie jammed her hands against her hips. "I never saw as stubborn a child in my life. When you get your head set, there's no unsettin' it. Now you march yourself out to the smokehouse and fill the sugar jar. And don't slam the screen!"

Leonie went off muttering and came back with the jar half full.

"I told you to *fill* it," said Callie.

"That's all the sugar there was."

"What?" said Callie, mildly surprised. "I thought I had more than that. I knew we were gettin' low, but this ain't hardly enough to do. You sure you emptied the sack? Did you jostle it down good?"

"That's all there was, Mama. I guess I know whether a sack's empty or not."

"You don't have to get so uppity about it. Well, I need some other things, anyway. I haven't ordered all week. I'll just call up the store."

"Let me do it, Mama, please!"

"Oh, all right. Talk up good and loud. . . . Jessica?"

"I'm in here," Jessica said from the front room.

"What are you doing?"

"Sewing lace on my ruffles." Jessica hastily closed her book and picked up the needle and thread. "You want me to do something?"

"Can you come and fill the jug, honey? I don't want to get coal oil on my hands while I'm workin' with fruit."

The three of them milled about the kitchen, washing the fruit, scalding jars. "I wish he'd come on with that sugar," Callie said, glancing at the clock. "I reckon we'd better start with what we've got. We can get one kettle on and cook the rest when he gets here." They divided the plums into two kettles and put one of them on the fire. "I really like to make jelly," Callie said, dropping down in a chair for a minute. "It smells so good while it's cooking. I just wish Brother Cottrell had brought these plums yesterday. But he didn't know. My land, where's that boy with the groceries? It's been nearly an hour! Look out front and see if you see him. Oh, here he is!"

Clabber Dumpson appeared on the back steps, smiling and bobbling and saying, "Y'welcome, y'welcome," before anyone had time to thank him.

"You're slow today," Callie said pleasantly, taking the sack of groceries.

"Yes ma'am, I'm slow today!"

"Well, it's all right. It didn't do no harm. Have a plum, they're nice and ripe."

"Take a lot," said Leonie.

"No ma'am," said Clabber, eyeing the basket regretfully. "I come afoot," he added.

"Afoot?" said Callie. "Where's your wagon?"

"It's home."

"What are you doin' afoot? Is your horse sick?"

"No ma'am." He smiled in unconcern as they stood looking at him, waiting for some explanation. "She's gone," he said at last.

"Who's gone? Maude?"

"Yes ma'am."

"Where to? Did she get lost?"

"They was going to take her away!" Clabber burst out, suddenly coherent with feeling. "They's going to take her away and shoot her!"

"Shoot old Maude?" said Jessica.

"Ah," said Callie in sympathy. "Who was it was going to do that?"

"Some men come after her for her hide and bones." Clabber's pale eyes filled with tears. "Mr. Henshaw said he's gettin' me a new horse."

"Well, what a shame! Did they come and get her this morning?"

A faint craftiness brightened his face. "They come for her, but they didn't git her. She wasn't there."

"Well! Where was she?"

"I don't know," he said. "Feller come with the dray, he's mad."

"I imagine he is. What do you suppose happened to Maude?"

"Ma'am?"

"I said what do you suppose happened to Maude?"

"I don't know," he said airily.

"Don't you know where she is?"

"I don't know," he said again, smiling.

Callie studied him for a moment. "You didn't hide her someplace, did you, Clabber?"

"She's gone!" Clabber fluttered his hands, as if to dismiss the subject, and turned away.

"Well, thanks for the groceries," Callie said.

"Y'welcome, y'welcome." He shuffled off, chuckling to himself.

"He's up to something," said Callie, turning to the girls. She paused and looked at them thoughtfully. "Either of you seen Mathy since dinner?"

"She was out by the pump, last I saw of her," said Leonie.

"Fillin' that little syrup bucket again?"

"I think so."

Callie took her bonnet off a nail by the door. "I *knew* I had more sugar than that!"

"What are you talking about, Mama?"

"Horses like sugar, don't they?" she said. She yanked the bonnet over her ears. "You girls put the rest of them plums on to cook. I'm going down to the pasture!"

There was no trace of horse or child in the pasture. But just beyond the hedge she found them, old Maude tied to a crabapple tree and Mathy stretched out on a limb above her, idly fanning the flies off Maude with a leafy switch. At the sight of her mother she sat up screaming. "Don't tell 'em, Mama, please don't tell!"

"You get down from there, young lady!"

"Don't let 'em find out!"

"Stop screaming," said Callie. "I don't know how you got here with this horse, but you'd better get back with her about as fast as you can."

"Don't untie her!" Mathy swung herself down and grabbed the rope. "They'll find her—they'll take her away!"

"Let go, Mathy. I reckon it's none of your business what Mr. Henshaw wants to do with his horse."

"It's my horse!"

"What do you mean it's your horse!"

"He gave it to me!"

"Who did?"

"Clabber."

"Oh, for pity's sake." Callie tugged at the knot.

"He did! We talked it over yesterday, and I said if it was my horse they couldn't take it, so he brought it to me this morning and it's mine!"

"Well, you can't have it."

"Why can't I, Mama?"

"You just can't. How in creation did you get this rope tied up like this!"

"I want to keep her!" said Mathy, her voice rising.

"Now what in the world would you do with a horse?"

"We could take her to the farm. She could work."

"She's too old. Let go, baby."

"Please don't untie her, Mama!"

"I've got to."

"They're going to shoot her!"

"Let *go*."

"Oh, Mama!" Mathy flung herself on her mother. "They're going to make soap out of Maude!"

Hobbled by the sobbing child, Callie looked at the old horse, who looked back in dumb and infinite patience. "Oh mercy," she said limply. Mathy howled and pleaded. The old horse stood meekly. "All right," she said at last, "come on, then. We'll put her in the barn till Papa gets home. Maybe he'll know what to do."

There was only one thing *to* do, said Matthew when he had heard the story: take the horse back and apologize to Mr. Henshaw. Mathy started to howl again.

"Now no more of that!" he said. "You can't have everything just the way you want it, and the sooner you learn that, the better. I understand your feelings"—his old mule Pharaoh made a brief appearance in his thoughts—"and I'm sorry it has to be this way. But it does, and you must learn to accept it. You've got to be made to respect the rights of others."

Mathy ran out of the kitchen in tears. They heard Jessica comforting her on the stairs (where she and Leonie had hid, so they could hear everything that went on without getting involved). Matthew sat for a moment, resolving his grudging sympathy with his righteous anger. Another embarrassment!

"Well," he said, starting to the telephone, "I guess I'll just have to call Mr. Henshaw and tell him I'll be over."

"Matthew?" Callie was working at the oilstove with her back to him.

"Hm?"

"How much would they give him?"

"Give who?"

"Mr. Henshaw, for Maude's hide?"

"Oh, five dollars, maybe."

"Don't seem like so much, does it?"

"Well, by the time they make the trip down here and haul her away, I guess that's all she's worth."

"Kinda pitiful, isn't it, to think of old Maude hauled away like that and knocked in the head."

"Yes, it is," he said, thinking again of Pharaoh, who died peacefully on bluegrass.

"Shame she just couldn't be turned out to pasture somewhere."

"Yes," he said absently.

"She's no good, but I reckon the children could ride her now and then—she's so gentle."

"Wha-at?" Matthew said in slow astonishment.

"Well, I just thought that if we gave Mr. Henshaw what those men would have give him—"

"Mama, for the mercy land of goodness!" Matthew looked at her in indignation. "I'm not going to spend five dollars on a worthless horse just to put it out to pasture!"

"Well, I thought—"

"We can't humor the child that much! You're always holding up for her. Why in the name of common sense—"

"I wasn't thinking of her so much. I was thinking of Clabber. He trusted Mathy—he trusted *us*."

"She's only a child!"

"Well, so is he, in his mind. He thought his horse was safe with her, and if we make him lose it now, he's going to feel worse than ever. He's going to feel like he can't trust nobody."

Matthew exploded. "Well, what am I supposed to do! I'm just as sorry as I can be. But I have no use for the horse, I don't want the horse, I can't afford the horse, and I'm not going to spend five dollars and butt in on Mr. Henshaw's business just to keep Clabber Dumpson from losing faith in humanity!"

There was a moment of silence. "All right," Callie said quietly and went back to her cooking.

After supper, when Mathy had gone to bed, Matthew took Maude home. An hour later he came back, grim-faced. Callie was waiting up.

"My goodness," she said, "was it that bad? What did he say?"

"Oh, he was pleasant about it."

"I thought he would be. Mr. Henshaw's a nice man."

"I had to pay him two dollars."

"Two dollars! What for?"

"That's what it cost him for the men who came from the slaughterhouse. They were pretty ugly about making the trip for nothing."

"Well, I guess you can't blame them. All the way from Sedalia, and now they'll have to turn right around and come back."

"They're not coming back," said Matthew.

"They're not?"

"He said it wouldn't be worth it to go through all that again."

"Well, I'm kind of glad, for Clabber's sake. He'll get to keep his horse, after all!"

"No, he'll have a new one. Mr. Henshaw's already bought it."

"What's he going to do with Maude?"

"He's already done it."

Callie clapped her hands to her face. "He didn't shoot her *himself!*"

"No," said Matthew, "he didn't shoot her."

"What did he do with her?"

"He gave her to me," he said and started up the stairs. "There wasn't a thing I could do but accept her."

From the tone of his voice, Callie thought it best to say nothing.

Mr. Henshaw was delighted to shift the burden of Maude onto someone else's shoulders. Clabber Dumpson was delighted that Maude had a good home. Mathy was wild with joy. She had saved Maude's life and she had a pet of her own. Everyone was happy at Matthew's expense.

He brooded over it often, pondering the uncanny ability of his youngest to make him pay for her mistakes. He believed that she did it in innocence, but simply without sense of right or wrong as he tried to teach it. The child seemed to operate outside morality. Hard as he tried to bring her in, she escaped him and always through some loophole that he hadn't anticipated. Because of her he suffered inconvenience, interruptions, embarrassment in public, aggravations picayune and endless.

Sometimes it seemed to him that she was a judgment on him. Deny it he might, but he had begat her in sin. The child was the avenging angel, and from the moment of her birth she had exacted her price from him. But not in noble sums that would pay the debt quickly. She demanded it in pennies.

3

In the middle of her forty-fourth summer, Callie Soames gave birth to another child.

When Leonie, away at teachers college, first learned that her mother was pregnant, she thoroughly disapproved. She was embarrassed both by and for her parents.

Callie was a bit embarrassed too, at first. But secretly she was rather proud of herself. The bigger she grew, the less it bothered her. In private she and Matthew congratulated each other fondly, as two who had come a long way together and guessed they could make it the rest of the way.

Jessica came home to help. She had lived in the Ozarks for two years now, so happily, even without Tom, that she could hardly tear herself away. For the first time in her life, she had begun to have beaus (Tom was her husband before he'd had a chance to be her beau), and in her widowhood she was having more fun than she'd ever had in her girlhood. The year before, she had come home for a mere two weeks. But this time she came for the summer, in such high spirits that the whole household was infected by them. She and Mathy saw no reason at all why Mama shouldn't have another baby if she wanted to. They thought it was pretty cute of her. They waited on her hand and foot and, when Papa wasn't around, teased her gently. They carried on at such a rate and had so much fun that Leonie had to join in.

Callie had finally got them moved into the big Cooper house, where all of them, Matthew included, felt uncommonly grand. It was a cool spacious house with many bedrooms, a front stairs and a back stairs, and lots of porches. The yard was big and shady, full of fruit trees and maples. Petunias grew in an old stump, grapevines over the back walk, and by the barn door an inexhaustible supply of four-leaf clovers. An additional pleasantry was a grassy back-yard tumulus which, beyond its convenience, was a great comfort to Callie: in case of cyclones, which she dreaded, she now had a cellar to run to.

Sometimes on hot afternoons while their mother napped, the girls opened the cellar door and sat on the bottom steps within reach of the cool stored-up air. With their stockings rolled down and their skirts pulled up, they read aloud to each other and told naughty jokes and laughed. Sometimes they read *Good Housekeeping*—lush romantic stories by Temple Bailey, Emma Lindsay-Squier, and Queen Marie of Roumania. Now and then they horrified themselves with a tattered copy of *True Story* which Jessica had found on the train. Mostly they just visited. Toward four o'clock, Callie would amble into the yard and call them. Whereupon the pace of the afternoon accelerated, reaching a noisy laughing crescendo as the girls got supper ready.

Matthew spent most of the summer at the schoolhouse.

With Callie luxuriating in the privileges of pregnancy and all his daughters at home together, he found that home, while somewhat of a castle, was no longer a man's. Insurrection of the gentlest sort had nudged him from power. He stood beleaguered by the summer maneuvers of many women in a large house. They swept, they aired, they sewed, they canned and cooked, and most of all, they washed. They washed clothes and floors and vegetables and windows, fruit jars, front steps, sidewalks and cupboards, rugs and rags and window curtains and each other's hair. They were forever pumping water. He resigned himself to the certainty that the well would run dry by August.

He found it impossible to pursue his studies at home. Say he was trying to do a correspondence lesson, in the cool of the morning, upstairs in a corner of the bedroom. Before he was good and started, he would have a dozen interruptions. Peals of laughter from the garden, titters on the back stairs, an exasperating quantity of passing to and fro. Though they tiptoed respectfully past his door, they never failed to drop the dustpan two steps beyond, or trip on a rug and have a laughing fit. And not one of them could make a bed alone. They had to work in pairs, which led to much dialogue and inexplicable hilarity. They couldn't do anything in silence. His ears rang with the fortissimo of household instruments—washtubs, carpet sweeper, pump handle, eggbeaters—all of it overlaid by the constant piercing fifery of female laughter.

He didn't really know what had come over the girls. They had gone plumb daft, as Callie put it indulgently, having lost half their manners and nine-tenths of their modesty. They painted their faces like savages—Jessica had come home with rouge! They slid down banisters, snickered during grace, and ran around in their nightgowns with all the lights on. Though Leonie maintained some trace of decorum, there was no holding the other two. Mathy alone was bad enough; she and Jessica together were a mob. Callie merely laughed at them, with soft reproaches that only made them worse. He had to admit that in spite of their silliness, the girls were diligent. If only they wouldn't laugh so much! But they did, and he hadn't the nerve to silence them, things being as they were. And so, as soon as the chores were done, off he went to the schoolhouse, where everything was arranged as he liked it and he could hear himself think. Having begat and having provided, he was of no further use at home.

The girls were delighted to have him out of the way. They acknowledged that their father was the foundation of all this good. Because of him they could live in this estimable house and sleep serenely, one to a room. Because of him the garden pushed up beans and tomatoes and roasting ears, and the delivery boy left sacks of groceries on the back porch. Their father's hens laid eggs for them, and night and morning he brought in a foaming bucket of rich Jersey milk. They took this provender and they cooked and churned and baked and preserved it, and they sat their father down three times a day to a feast. They performed the filial rituals with willingness and grace and beamed with relief when the screen door closed behind him. It was just more fun without him, engrossed as they were in pure domesticity and the shared bearing of their mother's baby.

The baby arrived in July, another girl. The sisters named her Mary Jo and received her as a new doll with which their parents had generously presented them. They adored her, bathed and dressed and rocked and cuddled her, and poured down her all sorts of faddish things that Callie thought unnecessary. Having raised her others on bacon gravy, she couldn't see the point of orange juice, codliver oil, and such. But Leonie had bought a book and they were always running to see what the book said and that's what it said. At any rate, the diet didn't seem to hurt the baby. She gurgled and kicked in a most captivating manner.

Matthew found the new girl quite agreeable, especially as her presence made the others quiet down. They didn't shriek so loud now, for fear of waking the baby. They received him into the fold again, where he preened himself with becoming dignity, and everyone was kindly toward the others. Thus the summer passed, a benevolent season.

4

Mathy, who for nearly fifteen years had been the youngest, adjusted happily to the status of older sister. She adored the baby. Denied a cat or a dog all of her life, she had a house pet at last. As soon as the child could toddle, Mathy took her on long journeys about yard and pasture. She made up stories for her and fanciful games; they fenced the yard with clover chains and made wild hats out of flowers and clothespins. Callie found her two youngest daughters enchanting—when they weren't scaring her

196

out of her wits. They had to watch Mathy. She was always dragging the child out in the rain to look at the rainbow, or rolling her in a snowdrift, or swinging her too high. The child's influence on Mathy seemed helpful, but she wasn't sure about Mathy's influence on the child.

Mathy had grown up almost overnight. All at once she looked like a girl instead of a little boy, a comely young lady with slim pretty legs and a proper bosom. One night at a church supper, Callie observed a young man flirting with her. Oh dear, she thought, now this! And wondered what in the world they would do when Mathy got interested in boys. If Jessica, so good, so docile, could run away with the hired man, what might Mathy do! Matthew wondered himself. They tried conscientiously, however, not to levy undue restrictions. Searching their souls, they tried to avoid past mistakes.

"My land, Mama," said Leonie, "you let Mathy do things you never would have let me and Jessica do."

"I know," Callie apologized. "But maybe if we'd given you more freedom, things wouldn't have happened the way they did."

"I didn't run off with any hired man."

"I know you didn't, honey. You're a good girl and Mama appreciates it. But you know Mathy—if we clamp down too hard, no tellin' what she'd do. Anyway, times are a little different from what they used to be, I guess."

Occasionally, when a motion picture came to town, and if Matthew thought it had educational value, Mathy was allowed to attend. She and her crowd went on wienie roasts, well chaperoned. There were class parties at school. In summer they went to Sunday School parties on farmhouse lawns lit by lanterns hung in the trees. While their elders visited on the porch and set out ice cream and cake, the boys and girls played run sheep run and other games which permitted them to hold hands. On rare occasions, at fourteen and fifteen, Mathy was allowed to ride out and back with her best friend and two boys (though it nearly gave Matthew apoplexy for a daughter of his to get into a car with a boy).

There were certain places, however, where he drew a firm line. The summer Mathy was sixteen, she and her friends began to learn to dance. In spite of the general community bias, a few of the parents turned their heads and allowed the children to fox-trot in the basement. When Matthew found out, he denounced the parents (not to their faces) and forbade Mathy to go to parties in those homes. Mathy sneaked out one night and went anyway. Whereupon Matthew, losing whatever restraint he had tried to show, canceled her social life for the rest of the summer. She could go to birthday parties and the like if they took place in the afternoon with no boys present; and she could go to the picture show if Leonie went with her. Otherwise, she would stay home and behave herself.

"It's too bad, honey," Leonie said to her, "but you *would* sneak out and you'll have to pay for it."

"It was worth it," said Mathy, lolling on the bed. "I had a wonderful time! Oh, I won't do it again," she said, answering Leonie's frown, "but I *had* to do it this time—Ruthie's cousin Bobby was here from California. All I've heard out of Ruthie for ninety years has been her hot-stuff cousin Bobby! Cousin Bobby was a twerp," she said placidly. "The other girls didn't know it, though. They thought he was just gorgeous and cute and a great lover, because Ruthie always told them he was. They fell all over him. But he liked me best. I was the one that couldn't stand him." She rolled over with a smug expression. "But gee, Leonie, there's a time to dance! It says so in the Bible."

"It also says honor thy father and mother."

"Okay." Mathy grinned. "Gee, Leonie, you're so good," she said, meaning it. "You never do anything wrong or get everybody into trouble. How do you keep from it? Don't you ever want to do something Mama and Papa say not to?"

"Yes," Leonie said, "sometimes I do."

"But you don't do it."

"I try not, because I love them."

"Well, I do too, but—"

"The way I love God," Leonie said simply. "When you love someone, you try to do right for their sake."

"Oh, I'll never be as good as you are, Leonie!" Mathy flopped over on her back and waved her heels in the air. "Do you think I'll go to hell when I die?"

"I doubt it," Leonie said, smiling.

"Do you believe in hell?"

"Of course."

"I don't. I only believe in heaven!"

She and Leonie didn't see eye to eye on a lot of things, but she admired Leonie greatly for her virtue and beauty. Leonie had been away for the last two winters, teaching school. She had visited friends in the city and seen some plays, read some books and learned a thing or two, and she was full of joyous plans for the future. Having outgrown the concert-pianist stage, she was now going to be a music professor, an eminence more easily obtained. She had it all planned out: In another four winters, she could save enough money to take a year off; she was going to school at the university. Then she would get a bigger job, save more money, take another year off, and study in New York City. Then a still bigger job, more money saved, another year off, and so on and on until she could spend a year studying in Europe.

"When are you going to have any fun?" said Mathy.

"Fun!" said Leonie. "You mean chasing around with boys?"

"Something like that."

Leonie tossed her silky head. "I'll chase—when I find the right one. I'm in no hurry."

"Where do you think you'll find the right one?"

"In Europe!" said Leonie.

"What do you want—a baron, or the Prince of Wales?"

"Why not?" said Leonie.

"All right, but you'd better cut your teeth on somebody closer home."

"Who's around *here*, for goodness' sake!"

"Cousin Bobby!" said Mathy, doubling up with laughter. "No, really, Leonie, *one* of us ought to have some fun this summer. And if Papa won't let me, then it's got to be you. Anyway, it's your turn, you're the oldest. Now who can we find?"

The answer came a few days later, literally dropping out of the sky.

Leonie and Matthew were driving out of town one morning (on their way to Clarkstown, where they commuted each day to teachers college) when they saw an airplane over Seabert's pasture. "My goodness!" said Matthew, craning his neck. "I believe it's going to land."

"Watch where you're going," said Leonie.

"It is—it's coming down!"

"Look out, Papa! You're going off the road—turn the wheel, turn the wheel!"

They slid neatly into the ditch. Matthew had to get out and push while Leonie steered. By the time they got on their way again, he was greasy, sweating, and all out of sorts.

Behind them, the plane swooped into the air again, made another pass over town, and flew back to the pasture to land, drawing behind, like the Pied Piper, all the loafers on Main Street and all the children who could escape their mothers. Waving triumphantly, the pilot climbed out. He was young, broad-shouldered, burned golden by the sun, and he was dazzling. The word spread through the town, reaching a group of high school girls about midafternoon, as they sat listlessly eating birthday cake on a shady lawn. Of one accord, the organdy flock rose out of the grass and fluttered away to Seabert's pasture, uttering their innocent mating cries. The pilot was there, taking people for rides. He swept the crowd of girls with his magnificent glance and pointed a finger.

"*Me?*" said Mathy.

"You," he said. He swung her aboard and buckled her into the seat. "You're not afraid?" he said.

"No," said Mathy, as calm as a saint.

Up they went, wobbling and sputtering into the June sky, where they promptly turned upside down. Then they did a loop and a barrel roll and came sloping down into the lespedeza.

Callie nearly had a stroke when she heard. And she heard right away, because Mathy came home with the pilot. She had brought him to Leonie. She kept him there till Leonie and Matthew arrived home from Clarkstown.

"Well, for the mercy land of goodness!" said Matthew as he went up the walk.

"Hi, Prof!" Ed Inwood rose out of the porch swing and came down the steps. Profligate Ed Inwood, baiter of teachers and stealer of pretty girls. He gripped Matthew's hand in both of his. "I'm glad to see you, Prof!"

"So that was your airplane we saw this morning!"

"Yeah, she's mine," said Ed and without further ado began to recount his adventures.

Like Othello to Brabantio, he spoke of disastrous chances, of moving accidents and hairbreadth scapes. Leonie and Mathy listened in rapt silence.

Four years had passed since he left Shawano (following his elopement with Alice Wandling, though he did not mention this). In that time he had worked in Kansas City, St. Joe, and Chicago and had learned to fly. He had barnstormed with other fliers, repaired planes in Texas, and acquired a plane of his own. "Won it in a poker game—rebuilt it damn near by myself!" Since then he had skimmed about the country, dusting crops, frightening cows, and giving rides at fairs. Having won a sort of fame at this wild and private enterprise, he had come back to Shawano to regale the homefolks.

"My, my!" said Matthew, half in admiration, half in reproach (the boy was either a fool or a prevaricator or both). "What do you plan to do now?"

"I'll hang around home awhile—work the fairs in this neck of the woods and live off my brother-in-law!"

"I thought perhaps you planned to get into some line of work now."

"I kinda figured I was in it."

"Yes, I understand," Matthew said with a tolerant smile, "but isn't this more of a sideline—a sport?"

"Oh, I wouldn't say that, Prof. It's an industry. There's a lot of future in aviation. Where can I go but up? Unless I get killed, of course. And I won't," he added, stating a fact.

"I certainly hope not. Have you—uh—remarried?" said Matthew.

"Remarried? Oh, you mean Alice?" Ed laughed. "I guess you couldn't call that much of a marriage. We were just a couple of kids—a good thing her folks busted it up or we'd have busted it up on our own. She was a nice kid, but—" He shrugged. "I saw Alice a year or so ago when I was in Kansas City. She was going to business college. Her folks moved up there, you know. By golly, she's got plumb fat!" He laughed again. "No, I'm not married. I don't know—I met a lot of girls, but I never stayed long enough in one place, I guess. You land in one of those little towns, out in some pasture, and you hitch a ride in and get a room at some ten-watt hotel. You're there a night or two and you're gone. I bet I've slept with the plane about as often as I slept with a—in a bed. I remember one time up in Nebraska—" And he was off again on another tale. He talked and talked till supper had all but dried out on the back burner and Callie asked him to stay.

"Thanks just the same, Mrs. Soames, but I promised my sister. Geez, I didn't know it was so late! You and I always did have a lot to talk about, didn't we, Prof?"

He was back the next afternoon and again the day after, arriving in an old jalopy around the time Matthew and Leonie got home.

"Here he comes again," Callie said impatiently, about the fourth time this happened. "What does he keep hangin' around here for!"

"Because of Leonie," said Mathy.

"That had crossed my mind."

"Haven't you noticed the way he looks at her?"

"I guess I hadn't. My land, I hope Papa doesn't notice! He'll have a fit."

"Oh, phooey to Papa!"

"Now you stop talkin' like that."

"Well, Leonie's grown up! She has a right to have a little fun. And she'd better have—she's going to turn into a fussy old maid before she's twenty-five. You wouldn't want her to do that, would you?"

"Well, no—"

"Somebody had better loosen her up a little. If she and Ed could kind of go together this summer—it doesn't have to be *serious*—it would be good for her."

"Maybe so. But my goodness—Ed, of all people! He *is* awful cute, though."

Ed did indeed cast admiring glances at Leonie, who was lovely to behold. (She was slender, a little taller than average, and stood as erect as her principles, bearing herself with the cool grace that comes of inner convictions. Her head sat proudly on a slim neck, the fair hair pulled tight and coiled like a silken rope in the back. Her brow was smooth, the eyes soft-brown and candid, her face serene and serious, lit up now and then by the sudden paradox of her eager childlike smile.) But the bulk of Ed's attention seemed fixed not on Leonie but her father. He came in the afternoons and followed Matthew through the chores. Sometimes he came back early in the evening and talked some more. He talked of planes and radios and the insides of cars, things which Matthew knew or cared little about. He talked of travels, of people he'd met and books he'd read. (Half-read, thought Matthew; Ed always skimmed the surface, hit the high spots, only half-understood.) He had picked up new ideas and terms. Names all but unknown to Matthew and vaguely distressing peppered his speech: Mencken and Russell, Freud and Sinclair Lewis. He tossed words around glibly, as if he knew what he was talking about. Glittering bits of assorted isms and ologies showered like confetti over Matthew's cautious tenets. He got tired of defending the Kansas City *Star*. He was tired of hearing that Calvin Coolidge was the pawn of big business and Americans a race of boobs. He did not care to discuss the Scopes trial any further. (It had disturbed him considerably at the time, since he couldn't make up his mind whose side he was on.) And he had little patience with newfangled notions of morality. Psychology or no psychology, he was still responsible for his actions, and there was such a thing as sin.

Ed annoyed him considerably. Beyond this, Matthew had not quite forgiven him Alice. Not that he cared about her any more; but the old wound to his pride still pained him in certain weather. After ten or twenty minutes of Ed, he took to excusing himself, retiring gratefully to the history of the secondary school in Missouri, or how to build a course of study.

Deprived of his agon, Ed turned to Callie and the girls. He often lingered for half an hour longer, visiting with them. It was known that later in the evening he had other places to go and other girls, or a girl, to see. But these were not discussed. And in the interval between Matthew's departure for upstairs and Ed's departure for parts unknown, Mathy did her best to get Ed and Leonie together. With even more effort, she saw that they were left alone. As sure as she did, however, Leonie had to excuse herself and go in to study.

Hearing her come upstairs one night, Mathy went into her room. "My land, Leonie! Why didn't you stay down there?"

"Downstairs? What for?"

"I go to all the trouble to get Mama out of the way, and you won't take advantage of it."

"What are you talking about?"

"Ed! Why don't you give him a chance?"

"*Ed?*" said Leonie, incredulous.

"What do you think I brought him home for?"

"You brought him for *me?*"

"You should have seen the trouble I had! I made him come— I pestered him."

"Oh, Mathy! You didn't *tell* him—"

"Of course not!" said Mathy. "That would have been dumb. I used Papa for an excuse—you know how he and Papa used to fight! I told him Papa would be real proud of him now and he had to come and tell him all about it. The other girls were so jealous they could have killed me!"

Leonie laughed. "You're the beatin'est kid I ever heard of."

"I wanted you to have first chance at him, Leonie."

"Honey, what in the world made you think I'd want him?"

"Gee whiz, Leonie! He's tall and handsome and cute and *he's a flier!* What more do you want?"

"He's still Ed Inwood," said Leonie, "and he didn't even finish high school."

"Oh, you make me so mad sometimes!" Mathy banged her head against the wall.

"Listen, I remember Ed Inwood when he was a smart-aleck kid in long brown cotton stockings. Just because he's been away for a while, that doesn't make him something special."

"But he's an aviator!"

"That doesn't make him any hero. All that takes is a lot of nerve, and he's got plenty of that."

"You sound just like Papa. Gee, Leonie, he's just the right age and the right height for you, and both of you are so blond and good-looking. . . . I know he's not an Italian baron, but I thought you'd like him."

"Well, honey," Leonie said, softening, "I do, but not—that way."

"That's too bad. 'Cause he's crazy about you."

Leonie raised her eyebrows. "How do you know?"

"I can tell."

"I don't know how. I certainly haven't noticed it."

"You don't look. You're always too busy."

"Well, I have to be. I'm going to make something of myself, and I can't afford to waste my good time."

"How can you waste it if you don't have it?" said Mathy.

"Hm?"

"I don't think it wastes time to have a little fun now and then."

"Mathy, you have got to think of something besides fun! My word, I hope he doesn't get the idea I return the feeling!"

"Not if you act like this, he won't."

"I certainly hope not. He needn't get any ideas about me—I'm not Alice Wandling!"

"I guess he could like somebody different from her."

"I don't care if he could. I'm sorry, but I'm not interested."

"I gathered that," said Mathy. "Good night, Baroness."

5

A week went by before Leonie, sweating over her books one night, looked up to see Mathy tiptoe into the room. She closed the door behind her and kicked up her heels in a kind of a Charleston, singing in a loud whisper. " 'Two left feet, but ain't she sweet, That's Sweet Georgia Brown!' "

"You kids were making an awful lot of noise down there," said Leonie.

Mathy giggled. "I thought sure Papa would come downstairs and hit us with the Bible or something." She took a scrap of paper out of her pocket. "Hey, Leonie, listen to this." She read:

> *"Sing we for love and idleness,*
> *Naught else is worth the having.*
>
> *Though I have been in many a land*
> *There is naught else in living.*
>
> *And I would rather have my sweet,*
> *Though rose-leaves die of grieving,*
>
> *Than do high deeds in Hungary*
> *To pass all men's believing."*

"Where did you get that?" Leonie said.

"Ed said it to me and I wrote it down."

"Where did he get it?"

"Out of a book in the public library in Chicago. Somebody by the name of Ezra Pound wrote it. Did you ever hear of him, Leonie?"

"I think I've *heard* of him."

"We don't have anything by him at school."

"From the sound of him, I don't wonder at it," said Leonie.

Mathy folded the paper and put it back in her pocket. "I thought it was kind of nice."

"How come Ed was quoting it to you?"

"We were just talking—about books and things, and he said he liked it. Leonie, do you think Papa would let me go down to Eldon on Saturday with Ed?"

"Good land, Mathy, of course he wouldn't! What do you want to go down there for, anyway?"

"Ed's going down to some picnic and take people up for rides —he gets two dollars for everybody he takes up. He said he'd take me along if Papa would let me go."

"He wouldn't let you do that in a million years."

"Oh, I know it." Mathy flopped down on the bed. "Darn!"

"You better not let him hear you say that."

"I wish he'd let me go. It's not like it was a date or anything— we certainly wouldn't dance! And it's not even at night. It would just be for the day."

"I don't think you ought to be riding in an airplane anyway," said Leonie. "It's dangerous."

"I don't care. I love to fly! It's just wonderful, Leonie—you ought to let Ed take you up sometime."

"No, thank you. And don't you go up any more, either. Once is enough."

"I've been up twice."

Leonie looked up at her sharply. "When?"

"That first day, and then one day this week."

"Does Mama know about this?"

"Huh-uh. She thought I was over at Ruthie's. I was, but Ruthie and I went downtown and Ed was there and he took us out to the pasture and took me for a ride. Ruthie wouldn't go—she's scared."

Leonie took the pins out of her long hair and combed it with her fingers. Her face was severe as she looked at Mathy through the mirror. "I'm not going to tell Mama on you, because it would worry her to death. But I want you to promise me you won't go up any more."

"Oh, Leonie!"

"Honey, it's too dangerous. And if something were to happen, and if I knew you were going up and I hadn't stopped you— Don't you see? I'd feel responsible. I just couldn't let anything happen."

"Well . . . gee, Leonie, nothing's going to happen."

"You never know," said Leonie, braiding her hair.

"Not with Ed—he knows what he's doing."

"How can you be sure?"

"I just know."

"Just because Ed can drive an airplane it doesn't mean he's Commander Byrd." Leonie braided fiercely.

Mathy lay on her back singing softly, " 'Two left feet, but ain't she sweet—' "

"I wish you'd stop that silly song," said Leonie.

"You know what?" said Mathy, sitting up. "Ed's handsomer than Commander Byrd."

Leonie stopped, braid in hand, and peered at her through the mirror.

" 'Night," said Mathy and went off to bed.

Leonie wasted no time. Dressing for school the next morning, she called her mother upstairs. "Mama, I think you'd better keep an eye on Mathy."

"What's she done now?"

"Haven't you noticed? She's getting a terrible case on Ed."

"Oh, now!" Callie laughed in disbelief. "I know she thinks a lot of him, but—"

"I'll say she does."

"He's just a kind of big brother to her."

Leonie hooted. "She doesn't consider him a big brother."

"Why, he's so much older than she is," said Callie. "He's your age!"

"That's just the point. I don't want to sound conceited or anything, but I have a pretty good idea it's me he's interested in."

"That's what she says."

"He doesn't mean a thing on earth to me—I haven't given him one bit of encouragement."

"I know."

"But if she starts thinking it's her he hangs around here for —well, she's just going to get herself hurt, that's all. She's too young for such as this."

"I guess that's why I never thought anything about it. I don't think it's a thing but just cuttin' up. But I'll watch her. I sure wouldn't want it to be anything else."

Leonie had scarcely sounded the warning when Matthew sounded one of his own. "It looks like to me," he said, that same evening, "that boy's around here altogether too much."

"Well, he started coming to see you, and you wouldn't talk to him," said Callie.

"I haven't got time. I wish he'd take the hint and stay away. He and Mathy are getting a little too thick to suit me."

"Now Matthew, they're not doin' anything wrong. I'm right around with them all the time."

"Right or wrong, he's just not the caliber I care to have her associating with. He's wild and reckless and he always was."

"Yes, I remember when he ran off with that Wandling girl," said Callie. "But she was a fystey thing. Ed seems like such a nice boy."

"No telling what he's like when he gets away. Living the kind of life he does, bumming around the country, associating with rough characters—you don't know what-all he does."

"Folks around here seem to think a lot of him."

"Hero worship!" Matthew snorted. "Just because he's an aviator—strutting around town in those boots— What has he done that amounts to a hill of beans? He hasn't done an honest day's work in his life. All he ever wanted to do was play basketball and drive cars. This is the same thing."

"He's a smart boy, though."

"Vox, et praetered nihil!" said Matthew. "He talks big! Always thinks he knows better than somebody older."

"Seems like he has a lot of respect for you."

"Then he has a poor way of showing it. I get everlastin' tired of his opinions. And I don't want him hanging around Mathy any longer!"

"Well," said Callie, "what'll we do?"

"Tell him to stay away!"

"Oh dear," she said. "Sure as we do that, we *will* start something."

"If you ask my opinion, it's already started."

"Then wouldn't it be better, maybe, just to let it blow over by itself?"

"With Ed Inwood, you never know how far these things will go. I'm just about of a mind to tell him not to come on the place again!"

"Now, Matthew, you can't do that!" Callie faced him accusingly. "You remember what happened to Jessica!"

He did, and for the moment heartily rescinded his forgiveness of her.

For a while after that he held his peace, but with reluctance. Ed not only continued to drop in, but brought over his radio set, and the warm night air was glazed with sickly love songs and sawed with static. Matthew sat upstairs of an evening snapping books open and shut and clearing his throat with great angry harrumphs. At breakfast his sulky silence hung ominously over the table.

What he didn't know would have hurt him worse. Ed came not

208

only in the evenings but all through the day, while Matthew and Leonie were gone. Sometimes he appeared at midmorning, bright and shiny, and charmed a breakfast from Callie. She and Mathy fed him and sassed him and bossed him around. They made him carry water and beat cake batter. They washed his shirt. He and Mathy ran errands. The mornings were cozy and hilarious, domesticity spiced by the illicit presence of the lover.

Callie knew in her heart that he shouldn't be there, and because she knew it she had a thousand complaints of him the minute he left. He was never serious; he was restless; he ate and drove and moved too fast; he hadn't been properly brought up; he smoked cigarettes; maybe he drank; and who knew how many girls he had. She went on in this manner until one day Mathy said, "Mama, you're talking to yourself."

"What do you mean?"

"You're telling me all the things you think are wrong with Ed because you like him as much as I do and you don't think you should."

"Why, I don't know—" Callie began defensively. "How much *do* you like him?"

"Enough to marry him," said Mathy.

Callie looked at her in horror, knowing it was true. Ed had taken over both house and hearts, irrevocably, with that sweet gall that corrupts more women than lechery ever could. And she had allowed it to happen.

That night she said carefully to Matthew, "I've been thinking. Suppose we send her down to Jessica for the rest of the summer?"

"Not much!" said Matthew. "That boy wouldn't do a thing but fly down there after her."

"I hadn't thought of that."

"We'll keep her right here, where we can keep an eye on her."

"Yes, I suppose she'd better see him here than somewhere else."

"Why does she have to see him at all?" Matthew said indignantly.

"Well, I hate to come right out and forbid it. You can't put the lid on too tight if you don't want the pot to boil over."

"Yes, but you can turn off the fire," he said. That held her. "I told you this wasn't going to blow over—I told you you couldn't trust Ed Inwood. Or Mathy, either. Now I've stood all I'm going to stand of this, and I'm going to tell the boy to clear out!"

"Now, Matthew, remember Jessica!"

"All right! I'll remember! I'll *not* send him away. But I'll certainly see that she *does!*"

He would rather put a ring in a bull's nose than have a heart-to-heart with his daughters. Nevertheless, he jotted down some points on an old envelope, in case he needed prompting, and brought up the subject at breakfast. "Daughter, as soon as you've finished there, I'd like to see you in the other room."

"What for, Papa?" Mathy looked up with her mouth full. "You want Ed to stop coming over?"

Matthew flushed angrily and shot an accusing glance at Callie. Callie looked as surprised as he was. "We'll discuss it in the next room," he said.

"I wondered how long it would be," said Mathy.

"Now none of that!"

"It's okay, Papa. If you don't want him to come over, just tell him not to."

"At this point," he said scathingly, "I think it would be more appropriate if you told him."

Mathy reached for the syrup pitcher. "Okay—if that's what you want." There was silence, broken only by the sticky sound of syrup and butter stirred together in a voluptuous mess. She glanced up. "Was there something else, Papa?"

He hesitated, brushing a speck off his sleeve. "I suppose that's enough said. I'll expect you to keep your word."

"I'll keep it."

He walked away lamely, all the air let out of his tires.

"You shouldn't have acted like that!" said Leonie.

"What did you want me to do, argue with him?"

"You should have let him have his say."

"I thought I'd save him the trouble."

"It wasn't very nice of you," said Callie. "He might have had some other things to say."

"I can imagine," said Mathy.

"Well, you should listen to him. He's only trying to do what's right. He only wants what's best for you—that's what we all want."

"You'll get over it," said Leonie. "Don't take it too hard."

"Please pass the biscuits," said Mathy. She ate two more and topped them off with a bowl of Post Toasties.

6

In the days that followed they saw no more of Ed. He had apparently left town. Callie had Mathy to herself again. In a burst of happy energy, she did all sorts of things she had been wanting to do. They aired old trunks, made new dresses for the baby, tore up all the pillows, washed and baked the feathers and put them back in new ticks. Mathy worked diligently, quick and helpful and good and gay, as if she had never heard of Ed. No more did his old car come rattling down the street or the porch shake under his tread. No more did "Sweet Georgia Brown" ring through the house. The radio was silent. Matthew and Leonie studied in peace. Everyone went to bed on time. Quiet settled over the house.

It made them so nervous they could hardly stand it.

It got so no one could sleep at night. They were too busy listening. Mathy had slipped away in the night often enough, with less incentive than Ed.

"You suppose she *would* do such a thing?" Callie would say, sitting up in the dark.

A chair couldn't snap or a curtain whisper but what one of them turned over and listened. "Remember Jessica" became a watchword, like "Remember the Alamo."

"I don't trust the appearance of things," said Callie. "She don't seem to grieve."

They began to watch every move she made. If she escaped to the pasture, Callie went to the door and called her back. If she went downtown on a Saturday afternoon, Matthew or Leonie was likely to follow. She could not go to the garden and scarcely to the toilet without being watched. Secretly Callie examined her room for smuggled letters, any signs of packing. If Mathy caught on to their vigilance, she gave no sign.

"Why don't she talk about it?" Callie complained. She loved to discuss things, analyze and console. But Mathy gave her no chance. Serene and taciturn, she repulsed Callie's efforts to draw her out.

"I think she's got it all bottled up inside," said Leonie. "It worries me. You never know what Mathy will take it into her head to do."

"God help us!" said Callie, and kept herself awake all night ruing her foolishness. She had visions of Mathy running off to the city, walking the streets, looking for Ed . . . Mathy riding on a train, accosted by strangers . . . that little soft-eyed thing . . . By daybreak she had one of her migraines.

"Matthew," she said, waking him, "what are we going to do!"

"Oh, you're worrying yourself to death."

"I can't help it. Every time I think about her runnin' off to find him—that innocent little thing away off from home—" Her voice broke and shot upward. "I just can't help it!" She buried her face against him and sobbed.

"Don't cry," he said, patting her awkwardly.

"I'm not going to have it! I'll not have two of my children slip away like that."

"It would just about ruin me in the community."

"I've got a notion to tell her she can let him come back. Just once in a while, anyway. That way, we'd know what's going on."

"Maybe we would and maybe we wouldn't."

"We'd know more than we do now. Maybe if we'd let them be together once in a while, they'd be satisfied. Maybe—" Callie sat up abruptly and listened. She got out of bed and tiptoed down the hall.

"She's there," she said, tiptoeing back. "Every morning when I go to look, I nearly have heart failure. I reckon I'd be plumb relieved if he was to come back. Matthew? I'm going to tell her to let him—it's better than having her run away."

"But mercy goodness, Callie, we don't know that she's planning to!"

"And we don't know that she's not. You remember Jessica!"

"All right!" he said, hopping out of bed. "Have it your own way. Nothing would do but you had to let her see him. And if nothing will do but to let him come back, I guess there's no way I can stop it!"

It wasn't five minutes till the delicate morning air cracked open. Windows rattled, the bedstead shuddered. A veritable sky-quake shook the house as a plane roared over.

"Well, there he is," said Matthew with grand resignation. "Bloomin' idiot, he probably took the roof off."

A half hour later, having hitched a ride from Seabert's pasture,

Ed stood at the door singing for love and idleness and two left feet. He strode into the kitchen and sat down at the breakfast table. "Mr. Soames," he said, "I've come to marry your daughter."

7

They did what they could. Callie wept, Leonie argued, Matthew stormed and threatened. It was only "Remember Jessica!" that stopped him from turning her out of the house. He predicted direly. She would rue the day, he said, she would pay for it dearly (meaning repent; repentance and remorse were the only legal tender for the purchase of such folly). But Mathy would not listen to reason. No plea for her reputation—or his—cut any ice.

He cried out *in extremis*, "But don't you want to finish high school first?"

"Not particularly," said Mathy.

That broke his heart. He went off to the schoolhouse rejected. She was her mother's daughter, all right; no regard for education. But why, if she had to scorn her advantages and marry at sixteen, why did it have to be Ed? Ed, who had given him more trouble in more ways than any other boy he had tried to teach. But what more could he expect of Mathy? They were alike, those two. Defiant, cocksure, irreverent—you could never teach either of them a lesson, however you tried. Well, let them go. Maybe they deserved each other. Let them learn that life is not all play, all flying around in the sunshine like butterflies. Let them learn their lesson the hard way.

The front door opened. He looked up and saw Ed climbing the stairs. How many times had he watched that boy come at him down the hall, full of bluff and arrogance! He came at you like a lion tamer, less noble than his beasts but nimbler, all his arguments loaded with blanks. He jabbed and thrust with any old rickety chair of a reason. Polite and relentless, he pushed you back until, maintaining what dignity you could, you hopped up on your box and sat. Matthew felt old and weary at the sight of him.

"Hi, Prof!"

Matthew sighed deeply. "All right, Ed, go ahead and marry her."

"You mean it!" Ed shouted.

"Now go on away."

"But Mr. Soames—"

"I don't want to get into an argument."

"I'm not going to argue, sir. I only wanted to say that I love Mathy very much and—"

"I said you could have her, Ed. Now spare me the rest."

Ed hesitated, standing in the doorway. "Thank you," he said presently. "Prof, I wish—"

Matthew turned and opened the rolltop desk. After a moment Ed went away.

So they were married, one day in August, and ascended unto heaven from Seabert's pasture, witnessed by friends, relatives, and town riffraff. Mathy, in goggles and helmet, tossed her bouquet from the cockpit, while Callie hid her face and wept like Niagara and Matthew stood stiff and solemn and wondered if his debt were paid.

8

He could not forgive Mathy this final insult (even though part of the blame was her mother's). Nevertheless, now that she was gone he missed her considerably. She and Ed were in the South, where Ed did first one thing and then another. He dusted crops, flew taxi flights, taught for a while at a flying school. From the sound of things, he wasn't setting the world on fire. And Matthew worried a good deal about Mathy. Not that she had merited his concern; she chose this bed, let her lie in it. All the same he worried, wondering sometimes where she slept at night and if she was hungry. Often as he and Callie sat alone in the long winter evenings, their youngest child asleep, and heard the wind sigh in the stovepipe and the big house echo in the cold, he thought of Mathy and Leonie and Jessica, the three of them as they used to sit, their heads dark or fair bent over their books. He found himself nostalgic for those peaceful times. Now and then he smiled sadly over some remembered misadventure of Mathy's. A funny

little girl . . . who ought at this moment to be sitting here studying her lessons. And might have been, if it hadn't been for Ed
Inwood. And once again he silently cursed the existence of that
boy. What fate had sent Ed to torment him apparently without
end?

Late in July, Ed brought Mathy home. She was having a baby
in August. They hardly recognized the shiny soft girl who had left
them a year ago. Her hair was cut short like a boy's, she was
burnt like toast and swollen out to there—but as healthy and
high-spirited as a colt. A few weeks later she produced a fine boy
with no trouble at all.

Ed, meanwhile, was enjoying fulsome admiration, not only at
home (where the women made over him as much as they did
over the baby), but all around town. Lindbergh had now made
his famous flight, and the people of Shawano, keyed to hysteria
like the rest of the country, made Ed their own personal hero.
He was a flier, like Lindy; that's all that was necessary. There was
hardly a man Matthew met on the street who didn't tell him how
proud he must be of his son-in-law. "Ed's doin' fine, ain't he!"

"Yes, he's flying pretty high," Matthew always answered. That
made them laugh.

"I always knew he had it in him."

Had what, Matthew wondered. He pondered on this glorifica-
tion. Ed had flown no oceans, set no records. He had merely
risked his neck. Did that make the world a better place, help the
sick and the needy, improve men's minds? Ed gave no service.
His work was sport—thrills and pleasure. He was flashy, arrogant,
irresponsible, and reckless; he defied the laws of God and nature.
But that's what people wanted these days, that's what the times
demanded. And all his faults had become the new virtues. Matthew felt old-fashioned and discarded. Well, never mind; the
old virtues would prevail. There would come a day.

Ed and Mathy came back now and then on brief visits, sometimes flying, sometimes driving an old car which Ed had over-
hauled. Mathy wore breeches and boots, the same as Ed, and
looked like nobody's mother. The baby, for all their dragging
him around, seemed to thrive; he was an amiable, amusing little
boy. They lived from pillar to post, a few months here, a few
months there, wherever Ed's fancy took them; gypsies, actually,
with no apparent desire to be otherwise. Though they toiled little
and spun not, that Matthew could see, and lived as free as the
birds of the air, yet were they fed and in their ridiculous way

well clothed. It puzzled Matthew how they managed. "But it won't last," he kept saying, to Callie's protest. "They can't get by like this forever, flitting like butterflies. There'll come a day."

He was right. Aviation did indeed grow, as Ed predicted. Competition increased. Gone were the days when a pilot got by on charm and nerve. He needed special skills now, meteorology, navigation, technical knowledge, which Ed had neglected to get. (Why should he bother? He could fly like a bird! Better than a bird—he could fly upside down!) Moreover, the times were bad. Small banks failed. People had less money and less will to spend it. They were beginning to be frightened. Then the market collapsed and panic crept westward through the country. Times were not good for a gypsy flier.

Matthew and Callie began to sense through Mathy's letters that not all was well. No complaints, only joking remarks. But they worried. Early in the spring, Matthew wrote them to come home; they could live on the farm, where they could maintain themselves with a garden and a cow. Mathy wrote back gratefully. It would be nice, she said; she had always loved the farm. But Ed was a flier, this was his life; he would make out somehow. He hoped to get a job soon as a commercial pilot.

Callie fretted about them, but she held up for Ed. He was a good boy, she kept saying. He would straighten out soon and settle down. Maybe a few setbacks like this were just what he needed.

But the day came when her faith wavered precariously. Ed went off to California on some wild-goose chase (Matthew's deduction), leaving Mathy and the child in Texas. He was away for several months. Mathy's letters did not make clear just what he was doing—he and another flier had teamed up; something about a cargo service; later Ed was working as a mechanic at some small field. She was vague. They got the idea that she didn't always know herself what he was up to. Then in late spring their anxiety turned to genuine alarm when they learned—through Jessica, who told Leonie, who broke Jessica's confidence because she thought they ought to know—that Mathy had lost track of Ed. She hadn't heard from him in more than a month and had taken a job as a waitress to support herself and Peter. Matthew wrote in haste, telling her to come home. He enclosed a check. It came back by return mail with a note from Mathy. Ed had come home, everything was fine.

They heard no more for several weeks. School ended, and they had moved to the farm for the summer when news of the accident reached them. Ed had gone up in the night, at some Southern celebration, to put on a fireworks display. Mathy went with him to help with the fuses, leaving the little boy with a local mechanic who had helped wire the plane. Everything went fine until they started down. They crashed on landing, in a strange field, in the dark. Ed was badly though not fatally injured. Mathy was killed.

They stumbled through that day almost in silence, searching each other's faces for some sign that this was an evil dream, no more than that. "But I prayed!" Callie said, in the voice of a bewildered child. "I prayed all the time!"

Nonetheless, Mathy was dead, and Matthew went down to bring her home.

In the hospital Ed lay under heavy sedation and did not waken when Matthew saw him. Matthew stood for a long time looking down on that bandaged inert figure, and he silently said farewell. He was free of Ed now. Ed had done his last mischief. Matthew went away, taking the child.

He went last to see Mathy. She lay with a little look of brown study, a quizzical half smile on her face, as if she were appraising this new circumstance, plotting coolly what she might do with death. Matthew stood dry-eyed, his grief all but eaten away by the acid of anger—a kind of divine rage that this had happened in spite of him, that Mathy should lie there so wilfully dumb and would not come when called. Then his memory, groping blindly, altered that small face ever so slightly and gave him back the tiny dark-haired child he had looked on first one winter night in a dark farmhouse. His tears began to fall. *Good evening, little girl* . . . now, good night.

9

A few days after the funeral, a curious silence came over Callie. She had held up bravely, after her first outburst of grief, comforted somewhat by the presence of Jessica and Leonie. All of them sharing the sorrow in common, they made it easier for each other. But then she fell silent. When spoken to she seemed not to hear. She spent long periods reading the Bible. They would find her sitting with her head bent, her fingers moving along the lines. Though they tried to console her, she only looked at them, more often than not, from a great distance, as if they were indistinguishable on her horizon. She wandered about the yard alone, poking at shrubs. Sometimes she went to the garden and stood among the rows, forgetting what she had gone there for.

All this time they watched her secretly, afraid that she might harm herself. They followed her discreetly. One day she escaped them and was gone a long time before they noticed. Frantically they searched house and barn and struck out in different directions through the woods. Jessica found her at last at the Old Chimney Place, where Mathy used to play. Her mother sat in the shallow depression inside the old foundations, hidden from outside view by the scrub and high weeds that grew around it. She was talking to herself in a low voice.

"Mama?" Jessica said, soft and timid.

Callie went on murmuring to herself, and Jessica hesitated, thinking it might be dangerous to interrupt her. She could hear only a word now and then, but it seemed her mother was talking to the Lord, calmly and quite reasonably, pausing now and then as if for an answer, as if she and the Lord were holding a conversation. After several minutes of this, Callie fell silent, hugging her knees and gazing at the ground. Jessica was about to speak when Callie raised her head and said clearly, "I wonder where that old hen *was!*" And she laughed, a small chuckle of plain amusement. Immediately she stood up, dusted her bottom, and started away. Jessica drew back noiselessly into the brush and let her go unaccosted. She followed her home in dread, sure that her mother had lost her senses.

Instead, Callie seemed to have regained them. From that moment, a change came on her. Her gaze cleared like the sky after a long cloudy spell, and she was her old self again. Though she spoke tremulously of Mathy and sometimes wept, her grief came out in simple familiar ways and gradually it passed into that fund of calm endurable sorrow that all must bear.

Matthew never reproached her for allowing that marriage nor for her faith in Ed. There was no need for "I told you so."

10

June passed and July wore on. Peter, now almost three, stopped asking for his mother. Leonie had adjured them not to make him feel self-conscious. "We mustn't make too much of a fuss over him or cry and carry on. We must just act natural." Conscientiously they tried. But sometimes in the evenings when the girls were busy with dishes, Callie took him on her lap and murmured him to sleep. "Poor baby, poor little boy." Then Matthew would carry him upstairs and, if he woke, would sit beside him in the darkness till he slept again. In the mornings he and Peter rose at the same hour, dressed and went downstairs together, built the fire and put the kettle on. They washed their faces at the wash-stand and combed their hair slick with water. They had long serious chats about pigs and cows and 'coons and angels.

Mary Jo was six that summer. She and Peter played together happily. Jessica entertained them with stories and games and walks in the woods. Leonie, too, indulged him in her way. In any crisis large or small she was apt to frown thoughtfully and say, "Now what would Mathy do?" and in her earnestness try to do it.

Jessica went home the first of August. A week later, Leonie left. Matthew and Callie were alone with the children. Soon now they would close up for the winter and move back to town.

On a coolish morning in late August, Matthew was working in the loft. The children had gone with him. They were noisily turning somersaults in the hay when Callie's head rose through the hatch.

"Papa," she said breathlessly, "he's come!"

Matthew stopped, the pitchfork with its bite of hay in mid-air.

"He wants to see Peter!"

Matthew deposited the hay and turned back for another load. "Well, take him in."

She helped the children down the ladder and climbed up again. "Are you coming in?"

He swung another forkful into place before he answered. "I'll be there directly."

Callie looked at him timidly across the loft floor. "Papa, he didn't mean to do it. He feels bad, too."

Matthew made no answer, and she disappeared. He went on with his work, piling up hay for another week. Then he climbed down, washed his itching arms in the horse trough, and walked slowly around to the front of the house, dreading the encounter. But this one only, and he was through.

"Look, Grandpa, Daddy's crush!" Peter ran to meet him, dragging an unwieldy object which he thrust into Matthew's hands. Matthew held it awkwardly, embarrassed by the thing. Somehow he had forgotten that Ed might very well be on crutches.

Ed sat on the top step, one knee bent, the other held out stiffly, like a stick of wood propped against the porch. "Hello, Prof," he said with an easy smile.

"How're y', Ed?"

"Pretty good, thanks. Excuse me if I don't get up."

"Sit still." Matthew's tone was polite; the formal courtesy of treaties, the breaking off of relations between countries.

Ed held out his hand. "I'm glad to see you again."

Matthew shook hands in silence, noting the other crutch that lay on the porch. Ed saw his glance. "Looks like I'll be on all fours for a while."

"Not for long, I hope."

"I don't know. The leg's full of nuts and bolts. Guess it won't be much use to me now, except to shore me up on the left side."

"I'm sorry to hear that."

"Oh, I'm getting used to it. I'm still a little shaky, but I've learned to drive with the dadblame thing. As long as I can drive, I guess I'm okay."

Drive cars and play basketball! "How long since you left the hospital?"

"Couple of weeks. I've been up at Shawano at my sister's."

"She went down there and got him," Callie said.

There was a pause. Now he will begin, thought Matthew.

"I'm getting awful restless," Ed said. "I think I'm going up to the city in a couple more weeks. I know some guys around Richards Field, maybe they'll let me work around the hangar or something."

Callie said, "You can't go to work that soon, can you?"

"I get around pretty well. As soon as my hand steadies, I'll bet I can overhaul an engine as good as the next guy."

"I'll bet you can too," she said staunchly.

"And I'll bet I'd better try. If I sit around like this much longer, I'll smoke myself to death. I've got to get busy. Anyway," he added, turning to Matthew, "I've got to pay off some debts. I'm much obliged to you, sir, for taking care of those hospital bills . . . and other expenses."

"Well . . ." Matthew looked away, letting the word hang.

"I want to pay you back as soon as I can."

"Don't worry about that."

"I do, though." He paused and, dropping his head, went on in a low voice. "I guess I don't need to tell you how I feel about what happened. I can't make up for that. But I want to do what I can."

Matthew stared stonily at the road, where Ed's car sat by the mailbox. (Same old car; same old Ed.) Callie blew her nose softly. Along the fencerow the children had planted a crutch in the moist earth, making a wry trellis among the rose bushes. After a moment Ed began to talk of other matters. Is this all? thought Matthew. One little word of remorse? The polite apology for a casual mistake? Was this all—and Mathy dead and gone?

"I want to get a couple of rooms," Ed was saying. "Lil says she'll go up there with me till I get good and settled."

"Now isn't that nice!" said Callie.

"I thought so. I asked old George if he could stand his own cooking that long. He said he guessed he could handle a can opener as good as Lil! Lil's not the best cook in the world. She can't be bothered. She'd rather play bridge or read her movie magazine."

He and Callie chatted pleasantly. The children ran back and forth, Mary Jo busy and important, bossing her small nephew about. Peter came over and stood by his father.

"Daddy, are you going to stay all night with us?"

Ed laughed, scrubbing his hair. "No, son, I don't think so."

"Why?"

"Daddy has to go back."

"Why do you have to go back?"

"Peter?" said Mary Jo.

"Why can't you stay here with us, Daddy?"

"Well, I just can't."

"Peter, come *here!*"

"Can I go home with you?" said Peter.

"Come *here*, Peter, I want to show you something!" Mary Jo jumped up and down in little-girl fake excitement.

Peter backed down the steps and scampered away. Behind him the grownups sat in a charged silence, the point of the visit hovering perilously.

"I'd like to take him," Ed said humbly. "I'm lonesome for him."

It was in the open at last. Matthew felt a kind of relief.

Ed looked up, glancing from one to the other of them. "I guess you folks would like to keep him," he said, "and maybe it would be better that way. But I'd like awful well to have him. I'd take good care of him, you can be sure of that. Lil's going to help me. And I thought—if it was all right with you folks—I thought I'd take him with me today."

Callie sat with her eyes downcast. Matthew stared at the road. Neither of them spoke.

"Would that be all right?" Ed said. "Do you think he could go with me today? Mrs. Soames?"

She shook her head, weeping. "It ain't for me to say, Ed."

He turned to Matthew.

"I can't let you have him," said Matthew.

Ed looked at him for a moment without speaking and dropped his head.

"Come, children," said Callie. She herded them around the house to the back yard, leaving the two men alone.

Ed lighted a cigarette. The smoke drifted Matthew's way, blue and pungent. By long habit he stiffened, as when his vigilant nostrils, sniffing the schoolhouse air, picked up the odor of transgression.

"Well," Ed began, "I thought you might feel this way."

"How else could I feel, Ed?"

"I don't know, unless—well, I thought if you knew how sorry I was—"

"The word isn't big enough," said Matthew.

"I know." Ed smoked for a while in silence. "I'd like to do better now, Mr. Soames. I want to make it up to you—and to him. I'll try my best. Can't you believe that, Mr. Soames?"

"No, Ed, I can't."

"But this time—"

"I've known you too long."

Ed looked away with a sad smile. "I guess you have, Prof. But Peter's my son!" he said.

"You weren't much of a father. Did you make a home for him, provide for your family?"

"Not the way you would have done, maybe."

"Nor any responsible man. Dragging around from pillar to post, running off to California and leaving your family behind. She didn't know where you were half the time!"

"I know. . . . I'm sorry for that. I was moving around so much—"

"Always moving around! Ed, you never could stick with one thing long enough to get it done!"

"Well, maybe that's not the worst fault in the world," Ed said. "Maybe I am the restless kind, and maybe I can't help it. And maybe she wouldn't have loved me as much if I could! She loved me, Mr. Soames. Don't you think she'd want me to have our son?"

"Do you think you deserve him?"

"Not for what I've done, maybe, but for what I will do."

"On that condition," Matthew said, "in view of your past record, there isn't a court in the country that would give him to you!"

For a moment Ed didn't speak. Then he said quietly, "You'd go that far!"

"If I have to. It shouldn't surprise you."

"But I guess it does. You want your revenge, don't you?"

"I want what's best for the boy."

"Maybe. But you're getting even with me, at the same time. Am I that bad, Prof? Have I given you that much trouble?"

"It's what you did to her."

"She loved me—she was happy!"

"She's dead, isn't she?"

Ed looked away. Then he turned to Matthew, pleading. "But it's you, Mr. Soames—you never liked me, even before. I gave you some trouble, I know, but was I that bad? I never meant any harm. I liked you, Prof, I admired you!" He stopped, and a look of puzzled surprise came into his face. "It couldn't be *Alice*, could it—you couldn't hold that old grudge against me? Not this long!"

Matthew felt himself turn pale. Old fears, half-forgotten, leaped awake like faulty guards when the siege had already begun and ran helter-skelter through his head with loud alarms. Suddenly not only Alice but all the girls, all the sly smiling girls who had shined up his old vanity, swarmed upon him like avenging furies, and loudest among them Charlotte. The weakness he thought so hidden was exposed. Ed *knew*.

"What do you mean?" he said feebly.

Ed shrugged, still looking at him quizzically. "She told me about it. But she didn't need to. Everyone knew."

"Well, certainly I—I admired her," Matthew stammered. "We were friendly, as student and teacher. But if she exaggerated the situation, if she—"

"Ah, go on, Prof!" Ed said with a weary smile. "You always liked the girls."

"You can point to nothing!" Matthew cried out. "There is nothing you can say! You can spread rumors, no more than that. My conduct—" His voice dried up in his throat. Ed was smiling at him, an odd calculating smile, and Matthew felt the house of his public life, built with such earnest effort, begin to tremble. One rumor was all it would take. One rumor, the wind of a whisper, could bring his house down around him. Him that is in reputation for wisdom—oh, the stink of a little folly!

"I caught a butterfly," said a small voice.

Matthew looked around, and for an instant, in his agitation, he saw Mathy standing there, Mathy at three, bright-eyed and eager, holding something living in her cupped hands.

"Grandpa?" Peter said shyly.

Matthew looked at him—that tiny soft morsel of clay. What would Ed make of him?

He turned back to Ed. "You may do what you will," he said. "I intend to keep him."

They looked each other squarely in the eye, and Ed turned away first. In the silence that followed, Peter scurried off to the back yard. From the kitchen came the clatter of plates and pans, the dipper against the water bucket. A wagon rumbled by on the sandy road. The farmer raised his hand in greeting. Matthew and Ed waved back.

At last Ed picked up the crutch. "I guess I'll be on my way," he said, and he nodded at the other crutch planted among the rose bushes. "I'm afraid I'll have to ask you—"

"Oh, yes—the crutch!" Matthew started up guiltily and brought it back.

Ed pulled himself to his feet and held out his hand. "Well, goodbye."

"Goodbye, Ed. I'm sorry it has to be this way."

Ed merely nodded.

"Shall I call Peter?" said Matthew.

"No."

"Well . . . take care of yourself, Ed."

Carefully, avoiding the rough stones planted along the edges of the path, Ed started toward the gate. Matthew watched him in pained surprise—the tall young strong body slung between the crutches, humped and laboring, dragging the useless leg behind it. He had not thought of Ed in this way. With a sudden pity he darted forward to open the gate for him and, in his haste, brushed against Ed in passing. His toe inexplicably caught the tip of a crutch—it was not that alone—the other crutch struck a rock at that same moment. However it happened, Ed lost his balance and went down. Crutches flying, arms flailing, Matthew crying out—Ed stumbled forward and fell sprawling on the path.

Matthew ran to him, mumbling apologies, reaching to help him.

"Leave me alone," Ed said quietly.

"Take hold—let me lift you!"

"I don't want any help." Ed lay with his eyes closed. "Just leave me alone."

Matthew backed away, ashamed to watch but watching, all the same, as Ed pushed himself up on one knee and crawled forward, like an animal pulling the trap with a wounded paw. He made a grotesque and painful sight. Catching the gatepost with both hands, he pulled himself up. He balanced there in precarious triumph. There was a kind of haughtiness in his face, turning in the next instant to a look of piteous, futile rage. The crutches lay on the ground just beyond his reach.

Hastily, without a word, Matthew picked them up. Without a word Ed took them. He was crying.

"Ed—" said Matthew.

Ed turned and hobbled to the car. Neither of them spoke as he drove away.

11

He was not afraid of Ed now. He had seen Ed back down. But all day he could not forget the tears pouring down that pitiful proud face. Ed had done wrong, but he was paying for it dearly. "The Lord handed down His punishment," said Matthew. "I have no right to add mine."

He said it aloud, coming up through the pasture at sundown. And he added, stopping at a certain spot above the branch, "I have not been blameless, myself."

He climbed down the bank and up the other side to the three-cornered plot where the stub of an old hawthorn stood. Except for the farthest corner, the plot lay in deep shadow. There was a hushed and midnight air about this place. It was haunted, as he too was haunted, by old half-buried guilts and longings. He stood for a long time in the stillness, thinking of that night so long ago and of Mathy's birth.

"Lord," he said at last, "I thought when You took her from me, that was my last payment. But maybe I must pay now with the boy. And maybe that will be all."

So they went both of them together, the next afternoon. On the road to Shawano the dust lay deep—red dust at first, fading to dun as they drove northward out of the hills into level country. The sedan wheels kicked up clouds that fell back slowly onto the sunflowers and Spanish needles, the bronze and scarlet zinnias on farmhouse lawns. The air was yellow, thick with dust and the sound of locusts gloating on the death of summer. This time of year was filled with loss and sadness, and Matthew's errand was part and parcel of the season.

"Sweetheart," he said, inquiring earnestly of the child, "will you be glad to see your daddy?"

"Yes," said Peter.

"Do you want to stay with him?" he asked for the twentieth time.

The child made a droll thoughtful face. "All night?"

"Yes, all night, all the time. Do you want to sleep in Daddy's house and not go home with Grandpa?"

"Fly in Daddy's airplane," said Peter, and he made buzzing noises. "Grandpa, can I honk the horn?"

"All right, you may honk it once." (He was so little; he was only three.)

"I'm thirsty, Grandpa."

"Well, we'll get you a drink." They stopped at a country schoolhouse halfway to Shawano and pumped a drink from the well. Matthew showed him how to catch the water in his hands. The child buried his face in the cool water and laughed. In the schoolhouse yard the weeds had recently been mowed. Another week and the yard would be full of children. But now it was very quiet and empty. The wind blew around the corner with a lonesome sound. Kneeling beside the child to dry his face, Matthew suddenly held him close. They could still turn back. But the impulse vanished as it came, for he remembered Ed clinging to the gate-post, his face streaked with tears.

They drove on to Shawano. At the edge of town they turned in on a narrow, little-traveled street. Plantain and goose grass grew down the middle. The house stood at the far end, aloof in an unkempt yard. In front stood Ed's ancient car. Matthew stopped beside it and turned off the engine.

"Is this where Daddy lives?" said Peter.

"Yes, this is it. Come now, we want you to look spruce." He combed the boy's hair, wiped his face with the handkerchief, and kissed him. Then he picked up the cardboard box that held the little clothes and handed Peter the bag of cookies which Callie sent with him. "Well, let's go now."

They climbed the front steps and knocked at the door. The door was closed and the window blinds drawn against the heat. Matthew knocked again, louder, and waited. Anxiously he peered down the street. There was no sign of life anywhere around. The town seemed deserted. "Has everyone gone to Clarkstown today?" he said. He knocked again. "Well, let's try the back door. Maybe they're around there and didn't hear us."

He led Peter around the house. "The kitchen door's open, anyway," he said, climbing the steps to the screened-in porch. On the top step he paused. Ed was there. He sat at one end of the porch, slumped over a round oak table with his head on his arms. He had fallen asleep over an open book.

Matthew peered through the screen. "Ed?" he called.

Ed lifted his head and stared at Matthew. Matthew stared back in alarm. Ed was ill or had been crying. Or was it only the heat and the flush of sleep? It seemed more than that, for his eyes had a dull hot look and his unshaven face looked ravaged. Matthew hesitated, but only for a moment. Numbly he stepped inside, holding the child's hand. "I've come to bring him back," he said, and he waited for that sad broken man to accept the benediction.

A hot wind blew across the porch, and a locust set up a cry in the elm tree. Ed stared, licking his dry lips and swallowing as if trying to bring out the words. Suddenly he leaned forward and moved his hand, and Matthew saw what the trouble was. Not sleep, not illness. Ed was very drunk.

There stood the bottle on the floor. There on the table was the half-empty glass which Ed's trembling hand had picked up and abruptly set aside. Matthew looked at them, sick at heart. For now he did not at all know what to do. If he were merely angry, why, then it would have been easy to turn on his heel and go, taking the boy. But there was one thing more his shocked gaze took in. Ed was seeking consolation, and not only in the bottle. The book lying open before him was a Bible. The whiskey glass had left a wet ring on the page. Holding fast to the child, Matthew stood motionless between indignation and pity.

"Excuse me," Ed mumbled, pulling himself up with the crutches. "I'll go wash my face." He picked up the bottle and vanished into the kitchen. They could hear him splashing water.

"Sit down," he said, coming out again, looking fresher.

Matthew had not moved from where he stood. He hesitated another moment before pulling back a chair. Peter went shyly to his father.

"Hello, Peter." Ed's voice was tender. He stroked the boy's hair but made no move to pick him up or embrace him. He seemed to know how drunk he was and to impose his own discipline. Though his tongue was clumsy he spoke with care. Peter swung on the chair back, prattling. After a moment he went back to Matthew and crawled up on his lap.

"You go out in the yard and play now," said Matthew, putting him down. "Grandpa and Daddy want to talk."

Peter went out, dragging a crutch with him, click-clack down the wooden steps. Matthew watched him, painfully aware of Ed, not knowing how to begin. All the fine things he had meant to say seemed out of place now. At last Ed tipped the silence balanced so uneasily between them.

"So you've brought him back."

"Yes," Matthew said uncertainly, "that's what I came for."

"I thought you were going to keep him. What changed your mind, Mr. Soames?"

"Well, Ed—"

"It wasn't Alice, was it?" said Ed. "You weren't afraid I would talk?"

"No," said Matthew gravely. "It wasn't that. And I hope you will believe me. It was—other things. It was you. . . . I thought you had suffered enough for your mistakes. I thought after all that's happened you had learned your lesson and that you meant to do better, as you said. That's what I thought. But now—" He looked at Ed in pity and loathing.

"Now you see me like this." Ed smiled bitterly.

"Why do you do it?" said Matthew, leaning forward.

"It helps sometimes."

Matthew shook his head, grimacing.

"It doesn't help now," said Ed.

"Nor ever will! Don't you see that, can't you learn? Try, Ed, try to do better!"

"I don't know that I can."

"You can if you try! You have the choice!"

"I wouldn't know how to start."

"You have started already," said Matthew, leaning forward again and touching the Bible. "Keep it up—God will help you!"

"You're sure of that?"

" 'Ask and ye shall receive.' You'll read it right there."

"I have read it. How can I receive if I don't believe?"

"You do believe, don't you?"

Ed shook his head. "Not much."

"I know you have often expressed doubts, Ed. I remember the conversations we used to have. But through doubt sometimes we are able to work our way to a deeper faith. Now if you can only—"

"Why did Mathy die?" said Ed. "Was it the will of God?"

Matthew nodded. "As all things happen by His will."

"All things? War, famine, murder?"

"He gives us a choice. We don't always choose right."

"It was not my choice to kill Mathy."

"Then perhaps . . . it was His choice," said Matthew.

"To punish me for my sins, yes!" Ed laughed bitterly.

"And me for mine, perhaps."

Ed leaned forward, thrusting his flushed face closer to Matthew. "Why were the wages of my sin *her* death—why not mine?"

"The Lord has His reasons. Maybe she is your salvation. Maybe she died that you might atone through suffering and be saved."

"Did He have to do it like this?" Ed cried. "Am I that wicked?"

"We can't always understand His ways. We must trust Him, trust in His mercy."

"If this is mercy—!" said Ed.

"His face is veiled to us," said Matthew. "But read your Bible. There is comfort there."

Ed looked down at the book for a moment. "For the men that wrote it, maybe. 'And God said . . .' It was nice and simple. If you couldn't figure it out any other way, there was always God for an answer. Well, there've been a few changes." He flipped through the pages. "I've read the voice of the whirlwind—have you perceived the size of the earth, has the rain a father, where does the snow come from, have you searched the depths of the sea—yes, we *have* now, and we know the answers."

"Not all of them," said Matthew. "Every answer breeds new questions."

"We'll find those answers, too."

"And does that dispose of God?"

"Of this one," said Ed, closing the book.

"He is not that easily disposed of," said Matthew. "For when all the questions are answered there will be one left: Who is the author of the questions?"

"Well, who is?"

"We call Him God."

"And so do I," said Ed, "but not *this* God." He laid his hand on the book.

"But the evidence!" said Matthew. "The teachings of Christ!"

"The Son of God, born of the Virgin Mary!" Ed intoned. "In the name of the Father, the Son, and Joseph the cuckold of the Holy Ghost." He crossed himself.

"Don't blaspheme, Ed, don't mock!"

"I mock the superstition, not the man. I believe in the man. He lived a good life and He died braver than most."

"Yes—and He arose from the dead!"

"I doubt it. But He took the risk. I respect Him for that. I respect His doubt."

"Doubt?" said Matthew.

"They tortured it out of Him. 'God my God, why hast Thou forsaken me?' I am sorry for Jesus Christ! For He was forsaken, like the rest of us. I can't believe in God the Father, the family man. He didn't create us! He allowed us to happen. And it doesn't mean a thing. Why should God look after us or care one way or another? We're too insignificant, us and our little worries. Why should He care about my soul—or whether I see my girl in heaven? I'm not that important. I do not matter."

"I do," Matthew said simply.

They looked at each other for a moment in silence.

"Vanity," Ed said then with a shrug.

"No-o," Matthew said, considering. "I matter because He is great, not because I am. There is more to it than vanity."

"Yes—fear!" said Ed.

"It is always called that by nonbelievers."

"Dress up your faith any way you want to—fear holds it together. Fear is the safety pin!"

Matthew thought about it for a moment. "Well, then," he said slowly, drawing a long breath, "if it is fear, then I accept it. Maybe fear is the only lever God could find that would pry us up to heaven. And I believe He meant for us to get there. We have to work for it—nothing is worthwhile that's too easy to get. We have to work and do right, here on earth. It would be more honorable to live a good life without thought of reward. But in that case, I'm afraid, not many of us would qualify for heaven. We like the temptations of the world too well. So perhaps God made fear to help us—to prod us and goad us toward everlasting joy. I accept fear, too, as part of His mercy."

Ed gave him a long look. "I believe you," he said at last. And they were silent, gazing out at the August yard.

The little boy played quietly in the hilly country of the elm tree roots. A leaf that had hung on the tree since April suddenly let go and made its slow journey to earth, tilting this way and that in its new fatal freedom, but falling, steadily falling.

"I want you to keep him," said Ed.

"I brought him to you."

"And I thank you for what it must have cost you. But I want you to take him back."

Matthew turned to him. "You asked me what changed my mind, Ed. What changed yours?"

Ed smiled. "Alice," he said.

"Alice?" Matthew said uneasily.

"Yes," said Ed, still smiling. "I wouldn't have thought to use that against you! I'm not much good, Prof, but I'm better than that. Whatever happened between you and her, I hadn't thought about it in years. It just wasn't that important. But I saw that you thought it was. You were thinking, 'Blackmail,' and I saw you were willing to risk even that. So I thought if you wanted the boy that much, you ought to have him."

Matthew sat humbly looking down at the table.

"But that isn't the whole reason," Ed went on. "He'll be better off with you, and I know he will—better than he would with me. I don't agree with you on everything, Prof, but you're one of the few men I know that I think of as good."

"I have not always done right," Matthew said without looking up.

"But you admit it to yourself. And you try."

"I have been vain. I have counted my virtues and added them up against those of others—yours—"

"And never believed in them at all!" Ed smiled again. "But I believe in them. I have no faith in your God, but I have faith in you."

"I'm glad," said Matthew, without looking up.

12

They drove away at sunset, down the street where the goose grass and plantain grew in the middle and the dust of ancient bones rose behind them, past the trees where the locusts sawed and prophesied, away from the lonely house and the other father. Beyond the town the pastures burned in the clear still brilliance. The trees cast long shadows across the road and the air began to feel cooler. With the light dewfall, an accord of evening odors rose, hay and honeysuckle, the odor of barns and sleek cattle, and the clean acridity of Jimson flowers opening at dusk. Matthew drew it into his lungs gratefully. And he marveled, coming back into a familiar world, at the turn of fate that sent him home like this, not bereft as he had thought to go, but with the child beside him. He had thought to lose, and he had won. He had seen Ed brought down, his arrogance useless, his airy carelessness turned to remorse. Ed had paid openly for the error of his ways, and this was no more than justice.

Then why did Matthew feel no satisfaction? There was something about Ed even in defeat. . . . Defeat became him, as everything else seemed to do; he wore it with an air that made it seem worthier than triumph. Matthew puzzled on it, driving down the country road. Ed had done no good and much harm. He had ruined his life and damaged that of others. Rejecting God, he was in his own mind rejected. And yet—broken, ruined, and drunken—he still had that about him which commanded Matthew's respect, his admiration even. Yes, and his envy. For envy it was, and the root went deep as the mandrake, impossible to pull up. But in the name of heaven, envy of what?

"Daddy cried," the child said suddenly. He had been very still in his corner.

"Yes, Daddy was crying."

"Why did he cry, Grandpa?"

"Well, he was sad."

The child pondered the word. "Was he afraid?"

Matthew in turn pondered the child's translation. "No!" he said with a wondering emphasis, for there was the answer. Ed was not afraid and never had been. Matthew envied him that. His courage, nothing more. But that was a very great deal. The courage to do as you pleased, regardless. It was that—the regarding—that held Matthew captive. There was so much he regarded. Hay in the barn, the ripe orchard, the diploma on the wall, the signed contract, the opinion of his neighbor, favor with God, the perpetuation of his soul. Ed prized none of these. And there was no hay in his barn. Yet fed or hungry, accepted or denied, he was his own man. How Matthew envied him that!

He wondered if belief in God was a substitute for belief in oneself. His fear—was it as holy as he held it up to be? Perhaps it was not fear at all, but cowardice. There is a difference. And perhaps God honored courage more than quaking humility. (It was the cautious servant who incurred the wrath of the master!) Perhaps, after all, Ed was the last who should be first. The meek shall inherit the earth, but nobody promised them heaven.

And he was not sure now, thinking of his own life, that they inherited the earth. He had been meek enough; he had not dared very much. And when you came right down to it, he had not achieved much, either. A smalltown school and a rundown farm, and out of a bottomless well a dipperful of learning. That was little enough. Nor did the lack of earthly treasure mean that he laid up treasure in heaven. It did not necessarily follow that the poor in body were rich in spirit.

And wasn't it because of fear? He had tried to march forward with one foot firmly planted, afraid to give up the bird in hand for the brighter bird in the bush. He would not give up his farm for his school nor the other way around. Lusting for the girls, he would not give up Callie. Enticed by the new beliefs, he clung to the old ones. Reaching for the stars, he hung onto the grass. Always the compromise, wanting everything, giving up nothing, and having nothing to the hilt. He would not pay the price, but settled for the little, the safe, the not-quite-committed, the cautious just-enough. And just-enough is never as much as should content a man.

Perhaps this was his sin—timidity of spirit. Timidity and envy—

and not the lust of the flesh which all are heir to, the little way-ward glances. Perhaps Ed was right. Alice, all the girls, even Charlotte, were just not important. He squirmed, feeling ex-posed and foolish, a grown man caught playing with toys. His little guilts had been important to him, comfortable and pleasant, even, to fondle in secret. But now he had a real guilt to bear. The sin of envy was one of the deadlies, just as much as lust. He had only flirted with that one, but envy had thoroughly seduced him.

And not only envy of Ed, he thought with deep remorse. Of Mathy, too. They were alike, those two, and he resented them both because they were not afraid of life, and he was. Care! he told them, and they would not—not for the things he prized. Plod! he said, and they flew. He wanted them to be made to care, to suffer a little. He wanted them brought down. Well, they were down. And feeling almost that he willed it, he was sorry to the marrow of his bones.

Oh, he could make it up to Ed, perhaps. He would try. But never to Mathy. A little moan of anguish escaped him as he thought of her. It was too late.

And yet (aware of the sleeping weight against him), he had the child! He looked down at the dark-haired boy, so like his mother that sometimes Matthew forgot that it was not she. And his heart filled with a quiet joy. He had been given another chance. Blessed are the ways of the Lord. He kissed the child and drove on down the darkening road eagerly toward home.

Leonie

1

Neighbors passing the Soames place that summer, going to town and back, heard a strange sound on the land. A spongy, suspiratious, somewhat mournful sound, lonely in the torpor of afternoon when the farmhouse stood blind and still, and downright creepy at dusk, breathing after you down the hill like a wounded wolf.

It was precisely at dusk and midafternoon that the sound most frequently occurred. For it was then that Leonie found time to play her accordion. Since she could not study the pipe organ that summer, she had bought the accordion as the next best thing. It also served at the farm as a substitute for the piano, which they no longer moved back and forth. As often as possible, she retired to the parlor, and setting a hymnal on the music rack, groped her way through a song. When she had mastered one sufficiently, she taught the words to Mary Jo and Peter, and they all performed it together. They were particularly good on "There Shall Be Showers of Blessing," a number rendered frequently at the evening musicales.

Peter was nearly four by this time; Mary Jo was seven. Each morning Leonie held an instruction period for them, and it was her feeling that they should have a chance to perform the songs and recitations they learned. The musicales were devised for this purpose. They also served as a pleasant diversion for the whole family, to clear the air of workaday matters and put them in a soothed and elevated state of mind before supper (now called dinner by Leonie, and by the others as often as they remembered).

On an evening in July, the family gathered in the parlor as usual. Matthew and Callie sat side by side on the settee, while the trio showered them with blessing. At the end of the song they applauded.

"My, that was just fine," said Matthew.

"You're gettin' so good!" said Callie.

"Well, we're working hard," Leonie said. "We might be able to do our piece at church one of these Sundays."

"Now wouldn't that be nice!"

"Can we sing our new song, Aunt Linnie?" said Peter.

"Right now, darling!" She turned to her parents. "We have a brand-new song tonight. All right now, children, stand over here, like we practiced, and don't forget your gestures."

The children put their backs to the wall and stood at attention.

"Ready?" said Leonie, poised with the accordion. "Don't start till I nod." She played an introduction, gave the signal, and the song began:

> "When you're smiling, when you're smiling,
> The whole world smiles with you . . ."

They sang earnestly, reacting at the appropriate times with wide grins and horrible frowns. Matthew and Callie applauded enthusiastically.

"Now take your bow," Leonie commanded.

They bent double. Peter went down to the floor and turned a somersault.

"Oh, Peter!" she said in reproach.

The boy lay on his back kicking his heels in the air. Matthew bent over him, laughing. "Here now! That's no way to take a bow! You get up, sir, or I'll put you up." He picked Peter up by the heels and stood him on his head. Mary Jo had to be stood on her head, too, and it took Leonie several minutes to get the musicale back in hand.

"Come on now, let's all sing together. One song and we can eat dinner. Come on—'Showers of Blessing.' Everybody together on the chorus!"

> *"Showers, showers of blessing,*
> *Showers of blessing we need;*
> *Mercy-drops round us are falling,*
> *But for the showers we plead."*

"Well, I enjoyed that!" said Callie, following the children to the kitchen.

"I think it's real nice," Leonie said to her father as she put the accordion away. "I'll bet there aren't many families that take time out for music and things, like we do."

"I doubt that there are."

"Not around here, anyway."

"No, not around here," he said.

"You gave us kids such an interest in music, Dad, and I've always been so grateful. I thought we should do more with it this summer, really make it part of our lives."

"That's how it should be, absolutely."

They went into the kitchen together. Callie was setting a lamp on the table.

"Oh, not the lamp, Mama," said Leonie. "We're having the candles again."

"Oh yes," said Callie. "I forgot."

"They're right there in front of you."

"I know, I just didn't think."

Leonie lighted the candles in their silver holders—candlesticks she had given her mother at Christmas. In the dim glow, the mismatched china and glassware twinkled obligingly.

The damask stripes in the tablecloth (it was pure linen; also a gift from Leonie) made silvery runnels. "Now isn't that pretty!" she said.

"Yes, it is," Callie said, "mighty pretty. My land, though, honey, don't you get tired doin' up that tablecloth? Looks like we could just eat on the oilcloth part of the time."

"Now Mama, I've told you I don't mind. We're going to live graciously, and if it takes a little more trouble, it's worth it."

"Where's the supper?" said Mary Jo. "There's nothing on the table but dishes and nothing in them. Are we going to eat dishes?"

"Eat the dishes!" said Peter and both of them staggered with laughter.

"Hush that," said Callie. "You'll get something to eat."

"Where is it?" said Mary Jo.

"It's out on the porch. Sit down, both of you, and behave.

We're not going to pass things around like we usually do. Leonie's putting everything on our plates."

"What for?"

"It's a new way to serve, like city folks."

Leonie brought the plates in from the back porch. They were filled with fresh cold food, the *pièce de résistance* a mound of chicken salad in a nest of lettuce.

"My! Doesn't that look good!" said Callie.

"I hope it's enough," said Leonie with modest pride. "I put every bit of the salad on our plates."

"It looks like plenty—just the right amount."

"Well, it ought to be enough, with all the other things—the beets and carrot curls and the eggs à la Russe. Isn't it a *colorful* plate! Color is found to stimulate the appetite."

"It certainly looks appetizing," said Matthew. He bowed his head and returned thanks.

He had scarcely got "Amen" out of his mouth when there was a loud blast of an auto horn from the barnlot.

"Mercy!" said Callie.

"It's Daddy!" shouted Peter. He and Mary Jo jumped up from the table without so much as excuse-me-please and ran out the door.

"Why, I guess it is," said Callie, pushing back her chair. "What's he doing here in the middle of the week?"

"Oh foot!" said Leonie. "I hadn't counted on him."

"It'll be all right. We can fix a little something else to go with this."

"But the chicken salad—" Leonie said plaintively, left alone at the table. The cool lovely mosaic of her supper—so carefully wrought that one thing added would spoil the whole design. "Phooey," she said, getting up to add another place.

"Hi, Aunt Linnie!" Ed came limping in with Peter clinging to his cane.

"Hi," said Leonie. "Lose your job?"

"Ah now, Aunt Linnie!" He poked her with the cane.

"Stop that."

"I got laid off for a couple of days. Thought I'd come on down and shuck a little corn."

"This is a fine time for shucking corn," she said.

"Well, there must be something I can do around here to earn my keep." He helped himself to a drink of water. "Haven't you folks had supper yet?"

"We'd just set down," said Callie.

"I'm sorry, didn't mean to interrupt you. Go right ahead."

"You haven't eat yet, have you?"

"I had a hamburger in the city."

"That ain't enough to hold you. Set down here—Leonie's fixed you a plate."

"I don't need very much," he said.

"We haven't got much," said Leonie.

Callie laughed. "You should have run ahead and told us you was comin'! We wouldn't a-been so skimpy. Papa, bring that ham out of the smokehouse and we'll fry a few slices."

"Oh, not fried ham!" said Leonie.

"Why not?"

"Not with this kind of a supper. He can have my salad."

"I don't want to do that," said Ed.

"I'm not really hungry."

"Why, you are, too," said Callie. "We'll just have some ham on the side, honey. I know Ed likes ham."

"Don't go to all that trouble," he said.

"It's no trouble. You menfolks go out and set on the porch—we'll have it fixed in a few minutes."

A half hour later, Leonie called them in. Hot and out of sorts, she sat down to the ruins of her supper. Fried potatoes steamed in a bowl; a platter of ham smoked in the center of the table where the flowers had been. The candles had gone out. She had lighted the coal-oil lamps.

After supper the men went back to the porch. Ed smoked and they talked. She could hear them as she and Callie washed dishes.

"I don't suppose we can study our Shakespeare tonight, with him here," she said.

"I suppose not," said Callie.

"Makes me mad, too. Dad enjoys it so much."

"Yes, Papa was always wanting to read."

"I thought we could read a lot this summer. But it seems like we're having the worst time getting at it. Something always gets in the way."

"Does seem like it," said Callie.

"One play a week doesn't seem like too much to get read."

"They're pretty long. Especially when we have to stop and talk about them."

"Well, you've got to discuss," said Leonie. "You can't just *read* Shakespeare."

"No, I guess not."

Leonie dunked the skillet in the rinsewater. "I don't know why Ed doesn't take an interest in things like that."

"Why, I thought he did," said Callie. "I thought Ed was always reading books."

"Oh, he is—or says he is. I never heard him discuss any of them much."

"Maybe he just don't talk about 'em."

"More likely, he can't. Dad always said Ed just looked at the pages—didn't really read."

"Well, I don't know." Callie sighed. "I'm afraid he ain't doin' very well. Just sort of living from day to day. I used to think he'd amount to something. But I don't know. Maybe if Mathy had lived—"

"Now, Mama, don't dwell on that," Leonie said gently. "We said we wouldn't."

"I know. I try not."

"And you're doing just fine, too. Why don't you go on in the other room where it's cooler and finish your magazine story?"

"I don't want to leave you with the dishes."

"We're through, all but the skillets. You go on now and read your magazine. You haven't had time all day."

Callie hung up the dish towel. "I reckon I ought to visit with Ed a few minutes. I can't hardly read by lamplight, anyway. It hurts my eyes."

"Whatever you want to do. I'll finish here."

Callie went away. Leonie carried the dishpan out to the back porch and emptied it into the slop bucket, silently vowing vengeance on the hateful thing. What she wouldn't give for a sink and running water! She dried her hands and rubbed them with honey-and-almond cream. Then, taking a lamp, she retired to the parlor. She tried to read, but the voices on the porch disturbed her. Ed was talking about the St. Louis *Post-Dispatch* and how much better it was than the Kansas City *Star*. Matthew, loyal to his side of the state, kept trying to defend the *Star*. Then Ed got off on Pendergast again and how he controlled everything in Kansas City, including the press. Leonie had a hard time keeping her mind on *King Lear*. Ed made her so mad, always arguing with Dad.

She set her elbows on the table with a little thud, like a gavel rapping for order, and, settling her chin firmly in hand, attacked the printed page. Somewhere on the heath she must have dozed, for she roused with a start at the sound of her father's voice. ". . . the tombstone," she heard him say. "They're bringing it out next week."

"Oh," said Ed, "I didn't know you had ordered it yet."

"Yes, some weeks ago."

"I should have taken care of that. I meant to, but I just put it off."

"Well . . ." Matthew said, sounding embarrassed.

"I guess I didn't like to think of it."

"Yes, sometimes we wish we could avoid such things. They're not pleasant."

Leonie closed the book. What her father had not told Ed was that he had ordered a tombstone last summer, soon after Mathy died. Only when it arrived and was set at the grave had he realized his error. He had had "Soames" cut into the granite. Whether he liked it or not, Mathy had died an Inwood. Covered with embarrassment, he called the men back. They came with some grumbling, trampled the petunias on the grave, and took the marker away. For the rest of the year, Mathy lay with no other headstone than a Mason jar filled with flowers in season. But now, reconciled to the proper inscription, Matthew had gone again to the monument maker. After next week, Mathy's death would be final, stamped with the stern authority of her name cut in stone:

INWOOD
MATHY ELIZABETH

Wife of Edward

Leonie left the lamp in the parlor and went upstairs, frowning as she thought of the ordeal ahead. They would have to go and see the new marker. It would be a sort of pilgrimage, a private memorial service, for which she had little heart. Not that she didn't miss Mathy; she did, and the farm was treacherous with memories of her. The new tombstone would only revive them most painfully. Oh dear, she thought, lighting the lamp on her dresser. Mama would cry and Dad would stand all white and terrible, and the children would stare at them, frightened. It was going to be hard on everybody.

She thought back to the day in June, the anniversary of Mathy's death. She had had to be very clever to keep *that* day in hand. It could have been dreadful if it hadn't been for her efforts. She had to be so cheerful all day, so resourceful—keeping Mama busy to keep her mind off her sorrow; running out to chat with Dad, so he wouldn't feel lonesome; saying little things to make them smile. It was exhausting. But she had done it—they hardly cried at all— and she could do it again.

She blew out the lamp and lay down. "Ahhhh!" she said, feeling her muscles let go. It was like this every night, the sudden surprising revelation that she was tired to the bone. There was so much to do on the farm, day in and day out. Sometimes she was downright provoked. She didn't want to come here in the first place.

She thought back to early spring, when she had begged them to stay in town for the summer. The farm held too many reminders of last year's tragedy. (She could not forget those weeks after Mathy's death, when Dad went about all grim and silent, and Mama almost lost her mind.) To go back this soon seemed only asking for trouble. But her father had his reasons. In times like these, he said, they belonged on the farm, where they could provide for themselves. It cost them nothing to get there, except a tankful of gas and the time it took to walk down with the cow. They no longer had to hire a truck and move the furniture. There was plenty of that in the farmhouse, odds and ends that had settled through the years like dust.

Of course she might have let them go on by themselves. She had so wanted to go to school that summer, preferably in New York City, and take pipe-organ lessons. But Mama looked sad when she talked about it and said how lonesome they would be. And they would be—just the two of them down there, with no one around but Mary Jo, who was too young to understand, and Mathy's little boy. Leonie couldn't bear the thought of it. And if she didn't go with them, who would?

Not Jessica. Jessica had married again, two years ago. (There was no accounting for that girl. There she was, a successful teacher, engaged to a young county agent with a university degree, when all of a sudden and right out of the blue, she gave back the ring and married a backwoods farmer, a widower with four children aged ten to seventeen.)

Of course, Jessica had come home last summer, when Mathy died; she came home in emergencies. But it was Leonie who really stood by the folks, year after year, and looked after them. It was Leonie who made Mama get glasses and Dad buy a decent car and saw to it that the kids had their tonsils out and stopped eating fried pies. It was Leonie who had not run off and left them for the first man that whistled.

She could have been married that very spring, if she'd just said the word. Kenny, the basketball coach at her school, had asked her. He was handsome and ambitious and had a wonderful voice. He sang at school programs, and sometimes he and she sang duets. But he was just a little bit wild, not quite the sort that her father would approve of. Anyway, she wouldn't have dreamed of getting married so soon after Mathy's death. She had more feeling for the folks than that. And since nobody else would, she would go to the farm this summer. She would honor her father and mother. She would keep them cheerful. And they would have a good summer or she'd know the reason why.

Having taken the veil, she promptly began the office. What she would have to do, she knew, was get their minds off their grief. Goodness knows, if work would do it, there was plenty of that on the farm. But hard work was not enough. They needed recreation, new interests. Psychology taught that nothing diverts the mind like new interests. Her mother and father needed some hobbies. They ought to collect something. They needed to read. Why, Mama never read a whole book in her life, not even a magazine. She hadn't had time or encouragement. Well, this summer she was going to have both. Leonie promptly ordered *The Ladies' Home Journal* sent to the farm. Mama could read about decorating and new ideas for the home; she could try new recipes.

Dad should read more, too. He hadn't read a best seller, she guessed, since *Mrs. Wiggs of the Cabbage Patch*, and maybe not even that. He hadn't even read all of Shakespeare—and neither, she reflected, had she. They could read it together, like the Bible, read aloud to each other and have discussions! She smiled with pleasure at the thought, seeing, as a passerby through a window, the professor's family seated in their easy chairs in heated discussion of *King Lear*. They would have music, too—Dad would like that—and a really active absorbing cultural life, such as all families ought to have. In a state akin to exaltation, she packed up her new accordion and her Shakespeare and hurried home for the summer.

That it turned out rather well didn't surprise her much. She worked hard at it. They had musicales, they went on picnics. Sometimes they outdid themselves and had a dinner party. On these occasions, Leonie surprised them with a new dish (the kitchen fluttered with recipes cut out of the *Journal*). The children made place cards from construction paper, and Leonie decorated the table with flower arrangements. They laid extra forks for the salad and stacked the plates at the head of the table and made Dad serve. Everybody cleaned up for the occasion and pretended it was a formal dinner, and all in a spirit of good fun they learned just how to behave.

"How did you find out how to do these things?" her mother once asked.

"Oh, you learn a lot when you get out teaching," Leonie said, "especially in a bigger town. The people up there are so up-to-date. And our school has a lot of formal banquets. The domestic science teacher really knows how to do things. That's Carol Pokorny, you know, my best friend."

"Yes, I remember."

"She had a tea for the faculty, the last week of school. It was the grandest thing you ever saw—darling little cakes and the teensiest little sandwiches and spiced tea! She asked me to pour, you know. And as I handed out the tea, she had me put a tea *rose* on every saucer! A *tea* rose—wasn't that a clever idea?"

Her mother was so impressed by other people's ways. Leonie had not realized before how old-fashioned she was. It was a pleasure to see her look around and pick up new ideas that summer. With a little encouragement, she took time every day to sit down with a magazine. Maybe she didn't actually read a whole lot—except the recipes—but it was a good exposure, just the same.

Leonie's chief regret was that they didn't have much time for Shakespeare. Dad was terribly busy. But sometimes at night she insisted on doing the milking herself, so that he could read a little. That way, they managed to get through *The Tempest*.

All in all, it was a satisfying summer. Not very often did Leonie lose her cheer and high resolve, though occasionally this did happen. Once in a while, in the long hot days, the spirit, always brimming in the morning, tipped like a bucket on the ridge of noon and threatened to run dry. Then her emptiness would fill with a guilty longing to be elsewhere and otherwise. She was lonely, buried in the country. She missed the radio and weekend trips to Kansas City. She missed her friends. Days went by with no one to talk to except Mama and the kids and once in a great while Dad, when he wasn't brooding about something.

The only regular visitor was Ed Inwood, who came every other weekend to see Peter. You'd have thought that, living in Kansas City, Ed would know all about the shows and other affairs up there. But after all, he was only a garage mechanic, so maybe it wasn't any wonder he didn't keep up with cultural events. He was lucky just to keep up with a job, considering he was lazy. And crippled, to boot. Not that his bad leg seemed to bother him much; he got around about as well as anyone, and you got used to the way he walked and hardly noticed it. You'd hardly even notice the cane if he weren't always swinging it like a golf club or poking you in the behind. Ed never would grow up, she guessed. Mathy's death had sobered him a little, as well it might. But he was still just one jump removed from the smart aleck she had loathed in high school. It was hard to think of him as a member of the family.

Now and then a neighbor lady dropped in to visit. Leonie tried to get her mother to return the call, but she wouldn't do it. Mama never cared much for anyone who wasn't an old, old friend or a relative. Relatives were what she and Dad really enjoyed. One Sunday that summer, Cousin Ophelia, Cousin Ralph, and their boy Ralphie came up to visit. (Ralphie was eighteen and peculiar; he slobbered and took things apart, such as clocks and engines; but he didn't talk much and was no bother.) Ralph and Ophelia were about the same age as her parents. Growing up, they had lived near each other. And such a lot of laughing and talking you never heard as when they got together. The whole day they were there, her mother kept saying, "Now you folks have just got to come back before the summer's out!"

"Aw, I'd sure like to," Ophelia said. "But it's such a long trip in that old car of ours. And I hate to leave Ma too often."

"You just bring Aunt Cass with you next time."

"Well, I don't know. She's gettin' so old. I don't know how much longer we'll have her with us."

They sighed and drew long faces. Then they hollered and laughed some more, and everybody sat in the yard, burping and slapping flies, till almost sundown. Leonie thought they never would leave. They were company and all that, but they were just not the sort of people she longed for.

So there she was, eighty miles from nowhere, with no one to talk her kind of talk and no one to recognize her vision of life as it ought to be. Sometimes as she bobbed up and down on the pump handle or skinned her knuckles on the washboard, the vision rose to torment her. It was an image luminous and obscure—like the sun, too dazzling to be seen plain. It had something to do with country estates, formal gardens, lakes and swans. It had to do with passenger liners and sailing parties, beaches and tennis matches, and dancing in a striped pavilion—the pastimes of the very rich as she had glimpsed them in magazines and the roto-gravure (and which she believed attainable by righteous effort).

Then in her impatience she would kick the pump, or fix with a pyromanic eye the smokehouse, which was filled with gunny sacks and castoff books and every old crock and tool and photograph that had ever been in the family. She hated the farmhouse and all its scratched, patched, propped-up furniture. All this makeshift made her sick. The superintendent of schools ought to live better than this. And Mama, for all her pride in town, down here seemed to have no shame. One day, in a pique, Leonie stomped into the kitchen and said as much to her mother.

"I don't know why we have to live like this!"

"Like what?" said Callie.

"All this broken-down furniture! That old settee with the oil-cloth patch!"

"It's good enough for down here, ain't it?"

"Oh, that's what you always say."

"Well, ain't it? We just sort of camp out here in the summer. It's not like this was a fine house in town."

"Why don't we have rustic furniture or something—a big stone fireplace? Why do we have to live like poor white trash?"

Callie looked at her with stricken eyes. "Is it that bad, honey?"

"Oh, not really." Leonie could have bitten her tongue out. "It's just that you and Dad—well, I know you can't afford to fix it up, but if you just thought about it different—I mean, if you just wanted— Oh, I don't know what I mean. I'm sorry I said anything, Mama."

And filled with remorse she ran down the path to the toilet, where she could berate herself in private. Poor Mama and Dad had worked hard all their lives. They couldn't help it if this was an old dirt farm and not a country estate. It wasn't their fault they were born poor and brought up in the sticks. It's a wonder they'd come along this far. And they wouldn't have, either, if she hadn't brought home new ideas all along. As the Bible said, the child is father to the man.

She went back to the house to finish dusting the parlor. But for just a moment she picked up her accordion and played her piece again. "When you're smiling, When you're smiling, The whole world smiles with you . . ." And she was comforted.

Such outbursts never lasted long. For the most part, she was too busy keeping the summer cheerful. And she had done it. They had come safely through Decoration Day and the anniversary of Mathy's death. But there was one more river to cross. There was still the day of the tombstone.

Lying on her bed in the darkness, she stared thoughtfully at the ceiling, half-listening to the murmur of voices on the porch below. How she dreaded the day. But there must be something she could do. There was always something. A few minutes later she rose and closed her door. She lighted the lamp, took a box of stationery out of the drawer, and sat down on the edge of the bed. Balancing the box on her knees, she began quickly to write a letter.

2

Thank goodness, the weather was fine. Hot, which was all you could expect for July, but there was a good breeze. As they rode home from Renfro, where they had attended church, Leonie looked at the clear blue sky with satisfaction. She had prayed it wouldn't rain that day and spoil her plans. They stopped in front of the house, and Matthew left the engine running.

"You children stay in the car," said Callie, "we won't be but a minute."

Her voice, cheerful enough all the way from town, had suddenly slipped into a minor key with intimations of doom. Even the children felt it. They shut up immediately and sat very solemn in the back seat. The grownups came back from the house, carrying fruit jars, geranium plants, and a bucket of flowers picked in the garden that morning—dahlias and zinnias, cosmos, larkspur, and long fronds of asparagus. When everyone was settled again, they drove on toward Grove Chapel.

Not for a long time had regular services been held at Grove. The membership had dwindled through the years, and they finally boarded up the church and locked the door. Mathy's funeral was the last service held there. The cemetery down the slope was left to the care of neighbors, various ones who had people buried there. They came in now and then with scythes and mowing machines and kept the weeds from overrunning the graves. Years before they ever left the farm, Callie and Matthew had bought a plot at Grove, big enough for themselves and any number of children. They didn't like to think of the family broken up, even in death.

Riding toward the chapel, Leonie thought of the lonely silence of the graveyard, the long grass sighing, the moaning of wind in the cedars. Why didn't graveyards have white birches and sugar maples? Why did they have to have cedars and pines, the darkest, sorriest trees in the world! But that was the old-fashioned way; gloom it up, make death even worse than it was. She scanned the road ahead anxiously and crossed her fingers. As the car headed up the hill she breathed a sigh of relief. There at the church stood another car. A man and two women sat on the steps.

"Who's that?" said Callie. "Reckon somebody thought they were still having church here?" The people on the steps began to wave. "Why, that looks like Ophelia—it is! It's Ophelia and Ralph —there's Aunt Cass!"

"Well, for mercy sakes!" said Matthew, stopping the car.

"Howdy, howdy!" Ralph came toward them, a little burnt crust of a man, waving a straw hat.

Leonie jumped out. Smiling big, she opened the door for her mother. "Aren't you going to get out, Mama?"

"I can't hardly believe it's them! What are they doin' here at Grove?"

"It's a surprise! I wrote and asked 'em!"

"Howdy!" called Ophelia, struggling across the churchyard with Aunt Cass. "Bet you never expected to see us!"

Callie climbed out and hugged them and everybody laughed and cried and talked at once. Matthew and Ralph pounded each other on the back. Aunt Cass lost control of her kidneys and let fly where she stood. Ralphie, who had appeared from nowhere, stood grinning through his hair. It was long and straw-colored and always hung down in his eyes.

"Why, I never was so surprised!" said Callie when the hubbub quieted a little.

"We're surprised ourselves," said Ophelia. "We never thought we'd make it up here again this year, but Leonie wrote and begged us to come, so here we are."

Callie turned anxiously to Leonie. "Have we got anything for dinner?"

"You just relax, Mama. Everything's planned."

"Well, let's get on back and start fixin' it. I know you folks are hungry after your long trip, and I 'spect Aunt Cass is pretty well wore out."

"Wasn't you going to decorate the grave?" said Ophelia.

"Aw, we can do that some other time."

"I thought you's going to do it today? Leonie said—"

"Why, of course!" said Leonie. "We might as well do it, as long as we're here."

"It'll make us so late startin' dinner," said Callie.

"We can wait," said Ophelia. "We ain't that hungry. Go ahead —we can help you. I'd like to see the grave, anyway. I haven't seen it since the funeral."

"Well . . ." Callie looked skeptically at the little old woman leaning on Ophelia's arm. "What about your Ma?"

Aunt Cass, who didn't hear too well, understood the look. "I thought we's goin' to the graveyard," she said in a querulous old voice.

Ophelia put her mouth to her mother's ear. "You'll have to stay up here. It's too far to walk."

"I want to go with y'."

"It's an awful steep climb," shouted Callie.

"I can make it."

"It's mighty hot—you sure you won't wear out?"

"I want to see the grave. Let me get a-holt of you, Phelie." The little dry vine of a woman curled a tendril around her daughter's arm and reached out for Callie.

"Oh, well," said Ophelia, "we might as well take her."

Leonie and the men went ahead, carrying the flowers. Ralphie had disappeared again. Nobody paid any attention to him, since he never seemed to be there even when he was.

Mathy's grave lay at the far end of the cemetery in the thick shade of a pine. It looked very small in the big plot, like a child asleep in the parents' bed. Leonie never liked to see it. Mathy's soul was in heaven, but the little body in the white dress lay there under a few feet of earth, withering away. She couldn't help thinking of it. *They* thought of it too, poor things; she knew they did. And if it hurt her, how much more it must hurt them.

Ralph went back up for a bucket of water, leaving Matthew and Leonie by themselves. Matthew bent over to examine the new stone.

"It looks nice," said Leonie.

"Well, they didn't do a very good job," he said, frowning a little.

"No?" She bent down to look. "Oh, for goodness' sake!" The

remains of "Soames" were still faintly visible beneath the "In-wood."

"It'll never be noticed," she said. "Nobody will ever know it if they don't look for it."

"I feel so foolish," said Matthew.

"It was a natural mistake, Dad. Don't think a thing about it." She patted his arm. "Come on now and help me set these geraniums. Doesn't it look nice?" she called as the other women approached.

"It sure is a pretty stone," said Ophelia.

"Well, whose is it?" Aunt Cass fretted.

"It's Mathy's," shouted Ophelia. "I told you about it, Ma."

"Why, ain't that Mathy?" said Aunt Cass, pointing to Mary Jo.

"No, that's the baby!" Ophelia looked at Callie with a helpless gesture. "She don't remember a thing any more."

Callie wasn't listening. She had walked over to the grave and stood with her hand on the warm stone, smoothing it gently.

"Here comes the water!" Leonie said in a loud voice. "Everybody get busy now. Mama, you fill the jars. Dad can start with the planting. I'll sort the flowers—"

"I want to set down," said Aunt Cass.

"There's no place to set," shouted Ophelia. "You can stand up a few minutes."

"My legs is give out. I've got to set down."

"Oh law. Well, set down here on the grass."

"I can't get down that far."

"You'll have to, there's no place else. Unless you could—" Ophelia paused, with a glance at Callie.

"Well, let her sit on that," said Callie. "She can't hurt it."

They walked her around to the new tombstone. "There," said Ophelia. "Try not to step on the grave any more'n you can help. Now then, Callie, let me help y'all with them flowers."

Everyone had something to do, and they chattered cheerfully at their labors, Aunt Cass perched above them like an overseer in a small communal field. Leonie was glad of the distraction; it gave them something to smile about and kept things from being so solemn. When they were through, they stood back to admire their work.

"Well now!" Leonie said briskly—when Ophelia interrupted.

"Poor little girl," she said in a tone so unexpectedly mournful that it struck them like a chill. "Poor little thing. Here we are so happy together, and her layin' there cold and dead."

Leonie could have kicked her. Now what came over Ophelia! She glared at her in disapproval. Ophelia paid no attention, having assumed an attitude of profound grief. "I can't hardly stand it," she said.

There was an awkward hush, and Ralph removed his hat. Self-consciously, as if shamed into it, Matthew took off his. Leonie looked around uneasily. Her mother was gazing at the grave, her face tremulous. Ophelia took out her handkerchief and sniffed audibly. Catching the mood, Aunt Cass began to weep. Oh no, thought Leonie, not after all her efforts! They had done so well up to now! She glanced at her father. With a clutch of alarm, she saw his face begin to work. The children were staring at them in fright. Then her mother, her chin trembling, reached out for Peter, and the whole structure of the day rocked on the edge of collapse. Leonie cast about wildly—there must be something she could do, some way to save them—oh please—

As if in answer to her prayer, a frantic inarticulate shout echoed down the hill. (Glory be to God!) "What's that?" said Leonie.

Everybody looked up, startled. The sound echoed again, a loud strangled cry of distress from somewhere by the church. Ophelia started up as if kicked in the rear. "Ralph-ee!" she shrieked and scrambled up the path as fast as she could go. Ralph was close behind her. The children broke rank and ran after them, stepping all over the graves.

"What in the world!" said Matthew.

"He must have fell down the well!" cried Callie. They started up the path, Leonie following.

At the top of the hill Ralph and Ophelia were running in all directions. "Where are you, son?"

"Here I am!" came the muffled voice.

"Where at?"

"Over here! Can you hurry a little?"

They found him on the fender of the car, a squirming mess of arms and legs, minus a head. Matthew threw back the hood. From the depths of the greasy interior, Ralphie's red grinning face looked up at them sidewise. "I'm glad you come," he drawled. "I caught m' hair in the fan belt."

They had to cut him loose with a pocketknife, and they nearly died laughing. They couldn't help it, poor Ralphie looked so funny. Callie laughed till the tears ran down her cheeks. It did Leonie's heart good to see her. In the thick of it, Ophelia let out another shriek. "Oh my laws! We left Ma down there on the tombstone!"

They laughed the rest of the day, first about Ralphie, then about Aunt Cass, and back to Ralphie again. Neither of those two minded. Ralphie was off by himself most of the time and didn't hear them; and Aunt Cass, reacting like a barometer to the mood around her, enjoyed the merriment with the rest of them, hardly remembering what caused it.

Waving goodbye that evening, Leonie said, "I don't know whenever I've had so much fun!"

"Poor old Aunt Cass!" said Callie. "Left sittin' down there by herself!" And her eyes grew moist with laughter.

Matthew smiled after them and turned toward the barn. "Mercy, it's late. I've got to get the milking done. Sukie?" he called, looking into the stall. "I reckon she got tired of waiting and went back to the pasture. I'll have to go look for her now."

"I'll go with you," said Callie.

Leonie watched them walk through the pasture gate, down through the walnut grove, and she smiled with satisfaction. It was like a picture show with a happy ending—the old couple arm in arm, fading into the dusk. She turned back to the house, giddy with relief. It was over.

In a surge of good feeling, she walked into the parlor and slipped the straps of the accordion over her shoulders. The room was too dim for reading music, but she sat in the gloom groping her way through the hymn. She kept hitting the wrong keys. "Shit-a-mile!" she said out loud and chuckled. It was the only expletive she had ever heard her mother use. Normally it embarrassed her, but tonight it sounded funny. She stood up and began to play her favorite song with a reckless disregard for mistakes. "When you're smiling, When you're smiling, The whole world smiles with you . . . " She sang the words aloud, and being all alone in the house and protected by darkness, she began to dip and sway, dancing about as she had seen them do in vaudeville. At the end of the number she bowed deeply, and rose to find two small figures pressed against the screen.

"You kids get away from there!"

There was a stifled giggle. "What are you doing?" said Mary Jo.

"Nothing—practicing."

"You keep bobbing around."

"It's none of your business. You kids come in and wash your feet. It's time you went to bed."

After the usual countering and delays they came inside. She made them mashed-potato sandwiches and shooed them upstairs. Coming down, she found her parents had not yet brought in the milk. She listened at the back door but heard no sound from the barn. Could they still be looking for old Sukie? She lighted a lamp and sat down at the kitchen table to nibble a chicken wing. After a while, she went back to the door and peered out. It was too dark to see much. And they had not taken the lantern. She stepped outside and called. There was no answer.

"Now what in the world!" she said, going out to the barnlot. Something stirred in the darkness, startling her. "Sukie!" she said. The dark shape ambled toward her and Leonie put out her hand to pat the gentle old cow. She ran her hand over the smooth flank and reached down to feel the udder. "Why, you haven't been milked yet! You old rascal, they're still hunting you."

She led Sukie around to the stall. As she started out, she heard their voices at the pasture gate. She was about to speak when something they said made her stop and listen.

"We don't want to hurt her feelings," her father said.

Whose feelings?

"No," said her mother, "we don't want to do that. She thought she was doing the right thing."

Leonie shrank back into the darkness of the stall. What were they talking about? They passed close to the door and stopped a few steps away.

"But all them folks there," said her mother, "and all that goin' on. It should have been quiet and nice, just us, just the family."

Her voice sounded so strange.

"Hush, dear," said her father. "Dear love, don't grieve."

"I can't help it." The voice rose in a soft heartbroken wail. "All summer she wouldn't let us cry!"

Leonie's whole body had become one prescient ear. She stood rigid, listening to the furtive sobs on the other side of the wall. And she thought then of her mother in the churchyard at noon, the tears running down her face. Why, Mama hadn't been laughing at all. She was crying all that time!

The soft gasping sounds went on for several minutes.

"Dry your eyes now," said her father gently. "We must go in. She'll be looking for us."

In a moment, the back gate clicked. Leonie waited, giving them time to reach the house. Then, slipping out of the barn, she ran as fast as she could down the lane and up the road to the front gate. Noiselessly, she crept into the yard and sank into a chair left out from the afternoon, thinking the thud of her heart would give her dead away. She had barely caught her breath when her mother came out on the porch.

"Leonie? My goodness, you scared me. I thought you were up-stairs."

"No, I'm out here."

"I came out to get the chairs."

"I'll bring them in when I come."

"Don't you want me to help you?"

"Don't bother. I'll bring 'em in later. I just want to sit out here for a while."

"I bet you're tired tonight, aren't you, honey?"

"A little."

"So am I. We looked and looked for old Sukie, but I guess she'd already come back by herself. I better go get the separator ready."

"Mama?" Leonie paused and steadied her voice. "Did you have a good time today?"

There was hardly a moment's hesitation. "Why, yes, honey, it was just real nice."

She was lying. *Mama, I never lied to you in my life, not if it really mattered. Why are you lying to me now? Why can't you tell me, why do you keep pretending!* The thought struck her like cold water—they had pretended all summer long! They had hu-mored her, like an imbecile child. Little protests, shrugs, evasions, guarded glances began to crowd in on her. Her mind had ab-sorbed them all, but backward, like words on a blotter. Now in the mirror of recollection she saw them straight. Mama forgetting to light the candles. Papa pleading no time to read. How little he had said during their discussions—*she* had done all the talking. And their evasiveness in the evenings—how often she had to go looking for them to make them come in and sing. Their dinner parties—the way they went through the motions, forgetting their new manners, never remembering to use the salad fork. . . . And Mama—Leonie winced, remembering how often she had caught her mother, magazine open on her lap, dreamily gazing across the yard, like a dull child in school.

They didn't *want* to read—or sing—or learn or do anything that was pretty and intellectual and right! And if they didn't, why didn't they say so? All she tried to do was cheer them up. But they didn't want to be cheered—they wanted to cry! Then why hadn't they done it?

She knew why. They were afraid to. They were afraid to let her know that nothing she did would help. She could give them care and chicken salad, cheer and candlelight and music, she could love and honor and obey them till the cows came home—not all she gave them or gave up would make them give up Mathy.

3

The first thought that entered her mind was to push over the new tombstone.

It made a hasty exit as she reproached herself in shame. But she wanted to hit back—it was *them* she wanted to get at. She wanted to march upstairs in a holy fury and shout at them, "Look at *me—* I'm the one!" Why must Mathy get the attention, even now? Oh, the Bible had a word for ungrateful children, but what of the ingratitude of parents!

She sat in a tense huddle, praying incoherently for help. And in her bitterness and disappointment, she wondered if it were the same with God, if a lifetime of devotion meant no more than a last-minute confession of faith. Didn't the Bible itself intimate as much? Of the one that goes astray there shall be more rejoicing than of all the ninety and nine that go not. Why should one try to do right?

"Leonie?" said her mother from an upstairs window. "You still out there?"

"Yes."

"Hadn't you better go to bed? You'll be worn out tomorrow."

I don't care if I am, she said to herself. But she rose and began to carry in the chairs. Go to bed, get up, study your lessons, go to church, work, practice, come home, be good . . . as long as she could remember. She climbed the stairs wearily, closed her door, and lighted the lamp. The volume of Shakespeare lay on the dresser, held open by the hairbrush. The sight of it made her shudder, thinking how tiresome they had found it, her trying to force it on them. But Papa always *said—* Never mind what he said. That was only talk. She snapped the book shut and with a grimace hid it under the clothes in the bottom drawer. They wouldn't have to read it any more.

"Mama," she said, in the morning, "I think I'll go away for a while."

"Oh? Where to?" said Callie.

"Does it matter?"

Callie lifted her eyebrows. "I only wondered. I guess if you don't want to tell me, you don't have to."

"I thought I'd go up to Kansas City and pick me up a boy friend and dine and dance and go to a speakeasy and raise Cain."

"Wha-at?" said Callie, bewildered.

"I'm only joking."

"Well, I *hope* so!"

"Carol Pokorny has been wanting me to come up to Plattsburg and visit. I thought I'd go up there for a week."

"That's a little better."

"We could go down to the city to shop, it's not far, you know. And I need some school clothes."

"Why, I think that would be real nice. Go ahead, why don't you."

"I guess you can get along without me."

"I think we can. I think we'll get along just fine."

A few days later, Matthew drove her to Renfro to catch the train. Her mother was working up apples that morning, the kitchen full of steam and hot jars and pans of peelings. But Leonie went ahead. They arrived at the station early and waited in silence. Matthew drummed impatiently on the steering wheel; he was supposed to help a neighbor harvest oats that morning. At last the train pulled in.

"Have a nice time," he said, giving her a peck on the cheek. "Be good."

She leaned out to wave, but he had already gone back to the car and didn't see her. All right for you, she said, settling back. Nevertheless, remembering his habitual, perfunctory "Be good," she couldn't help feeling a little guilty. For she had lied; she had no intention of spending the week with a girl friend in some burg. Instead of catching another train in Kansas City, she was going to stay there and do as she first told her mother—dine and dance and raise Cain, the only difference being that she didn't have to "pick up" a boyfriend. She had one waiting there—Kenny, the basketball coach, who was handsome and dashing and had a wonderful voice and who wanted to see her. He had said so a number of times in his letters. She took one of them out of her handbag and read it over. "If they ever let you off the reservation," the letter said, "be sure to give me a ring. I'll show you some of the bright spots, we'll have a real hot time." It was something of this temperature that she had in mind. She was going to buy some new clothes and call up Kenny and have some fun, sophisticated fun! She was going to dine and dance and go to shows, and if he wanted to take her to a roadhouse or a nightclub, all right, she was going. Her parents wouldn't approve, but they wouldn't know about it. And they needn't get worked up if they did. Times had changed. Nowadays, perfectly respectable people went to shows on Sunday, they went dancing and played cards; lots of girls even smoked—and it didn't mean they were going to hell. Hell had shifted its location; it was farther away than people used to think.

She arrived in the city just after noon, and following the ritual of winter weekends (when she and her friends came in to shop), she went directly to Fred Harvey's and ordered a Coca-Cola. The farm offered nothing like this. It had always seemed to her that the prickly drink was the very flavor of the city—biting and bittersweet; frankly synthetic; stimulating. She drew it in slowly, taking in with it the sights and sounds around her. Fortified by the elixir, she stopped on the way out and bought cigarettes, slipping them into her bag with a quick glance around.

Across from the station, at the crest of a long landscaped slope, stood the tall shaft of Liberty Memorial. By custom, she paused on the sidewalk to look at it. This was partly in silent tribute and partly to get her bearings; she was turned around in the city. As she stood there, struggling to turn north to south, she thought of the day the monument was dedicated, when she stood for an hour, shivering with cold, to see the Queen of Roumania. Today the sun poured down the mall and made a lake of heat around the station.

"Lady," said a voice, "if you don't want a taxi, would you move out of the way?"

She looked at him haughtily. "I *do* want a taxi," she said, abandoning the streetcar then and there. "The Muehlebach Hotel, please." No skimping this time; she was going to have the best.

The rates were a little higher than she expected, but she had made up her mind. And indeed she felt very grand, sweeping into the room behind the bellhop and handing him a generous tip. It was a nice room with a thick carpet and lots of mirrors and a gleaming private bath. It was warm, but after all, this was summer.

And she didn't mind the noise from the street. That was part of the city, a welcome change from cackles and mooing. She sang to herself as she unpacked, walking about in her stocking feet, now and then surprised by her image on the bathroom door. She hadn't seen herself full-length all summer! She sat down on the bed, facing the long mirror, and took out Kenny's letter. She knew he was not at home at this hour, since he worked for his father during the summer. But she thought she might call and leave a message. With the telephone in her hand, however, she changed her mind. Perhaps she should wait and speak to him in person. Meanwhile, she could go out and buy a new dress and be all ready.

She washed her face, and for the first time that summer put on rouge and lipstick. Then, putting on her hat and gloves, she set out for Petticoat Lane, a street whose very name charmed her. After a leisurely stroll up one side and down the other, looking in all the windows, she entered one of the shops. Four or five shops later she found what she wanted—a dress of flame-colored crepe de chine, very clinging, with tiny rhinestone straps and a neckline so low in front that she felt naked. But it was the latest thing and, if she did say so, it was rather becoming. With a casual gesture, hoping the saleslady wouldn't notice, she flipped the price tag over. Oh well. You couldn't expect something like this for the price of a little school dress.

She tried it on again, back in the room, and pinned up the straps to raise the neckline. But then she took the pins out and let it stay as it was. This was the way they wore them these days. She would get used to it. By this time it was after five. Kenny would be home soon, but before she called she had time for a bath. She ran the tub full of water and made it rosy with bath salts. Sudsing herself idly, she wondered what they were doing back home. Mama would be filling the lamps about now; pretty soon she would start supper. The kitchen would be hot and stuffy and the kids cross and tired, and Papa would come in with the milk, tracking manure on the floor . . . while she lay here in a perfumed bath, waiting for a gentleman to take her out to dinner.

Though she would have to call him first. She got out at once, dried and powdered herself, and put on her blue silk kimono, saved for special occasions. As she dug into her handbag again for his letter, the package of cigarettes fell out. She considered a moment, then opened it and lighted one with a shaky hand. So that's how they tasted! She made a small face. Her heart was beating as nervously as if she were doing something wrong. Pulling the kimono tight around her, she walked over to the bathroom door and stood in a stylish slouch at the mirror, one hand on her hip, the other waving the cigarette. What would they think if they saw her now! What would old Kenny think, even! He had tried all winter to make her take a cigarette and she wouldn't do it. She frowned a little as she thought of him. A basketball coach had no business smoking, not even away from school. Kenny did a lot of things she didn't really approve of. But he did work hard and he sang well and he was good-looking. Maybe when she saw him again, she'd like him better than she thought. At any rate, she could have some fun with him. She would adore to see a night-club—with bootleggers and a Negro jazz band and sophisticated people! She took another quick puff and turned back to the telephone, reflecting at that moment that it wouldn't do to appear too anxious. She had only just got here. Perhaps she would have dinner first and call after that. If he had gone out for the evening, there was always tomorrow. She had the whole week before her.

As she left the hotel, the sun was almost down, setting due east as it always did in the city. She turned her back on it impatiently and started up the street. Her step was less resolute than in the afternoon, for this time she wasn't sure where she was going. She had not yet made up her mind where to have dinner. But it wouldn't be dark for a long time yet and she was in no hurry. She would walk awhile, till she found some place she liked, something small and friendly-looking.

Around her, people were going home from work, everyone in a hurry. They brushed past her, running for streetcars, and one man almost knocked her down. She turned up a sidestreet to avoid them. It was emptier there, and she could window-shop in peace. Pausing once to peer in at some furniture—summer furniture such as she had longed for at the farm—she was aware that a man had stopped beside her. Without thinking, she looked up. He looked back and smiled, and she moved away abruptly, reflecting that it wouldn't do to stand too long in one place, not at this hour and having no one with her.

She had never been in the city before without a companion, and she began to feel self-conscious, as if her aloneness might advertise itself. Though it was still broad daylight, she quickened her pace, looking in earnest now for a restaurant, so that she could have dinner and get back to her room. Hurrying up the street, she wished heartily for a friend, Carol or one of the other teachers, or just anyone she knew. She hated going into restaurants alone.

Alone or not, however, she had to go in somewhere soon, as she had had nothing in her stomach since early morning except the Coca-Cola. She realized now that she was very hungry, and also very tired. She had been up since five o'clock. The yard was still blue-gray when she first stepped outside, and the sun just clearing the treetops on the east pasture (it stayed in its proper place at home). The air was so cool and soft at that hour of the morning, and everything smelled fresh, and the birds in the timber sounded sweet and far away. It all seemed far away now and terribly long ago. Was it possible that she had left only this morning? Pausing at a corner, she felt a momentary touch of the loneliness that used to afflict her as a child, when she was away from home and night came and she was sleepy. It passed quickly, but it left her with a puzzling sense of what-am-I-doing-here. She glanced about uneasily. The street was almost deserted. Which way *was* the hotel? She knew she could not be far away, but having wandered into a less familiar area, she could find no landmarks to get her bearings by. Turning, however, she glimpsed some distance away a massive gray stone church which she had often noticed before. Almost involuntarily, she started toward it, as if it were an unexpected friend met on the street.

She had no idea what she meant to do there, except that she had always meant to visit the church, as one would tour the cathedrals of Europe. As she approached, she caught the authoritative growl of an organ. Thinking hopefully that there might be a twilight recital going on, she climbed the steps and listened. Was any sound in the world more beautiful and noble! She gave the door a timid push. It opened, and she stepped inside.

It was cool inside and dimly lit by the afterglow of sunset through the stained-glass windows. Her vision adjusted, she saw that the church was empty except for a figure at the organ. It was a man—a young man, as nearly as she could make out with the length of the nave between them; he was in his shirtsleeves, like any laborer, intent on his work. The slim back moved busily, the arms shot out, the hips swung as he trod the pedals, and the powerful muscular tones of the organ expanded through the church as if they would push away the walls. She watched him in admiration. How beautifully he played! And for a moment it irked her soul that it was not she who sat up there working her will on the stops and keys and pressing that glorious thunder through the golden pipes. But the pure beauty of it cleansed her of envy and she tiptoed to the back pew and sat down with the feeling of having reached a destination.

The music ended. There was an interlude of silence, and it began again, softly this time, curling out of the stopped diapasons with the sound of flutes. Serene and precise, it made a simple statement, repeated it with metaphors, and paused while a second voice made answer. Other voices joined in then, one after another, deep and benevolent, and they spoke back and forth. They gathered, thronging over one another, mingling, rising in sweet argument, until the lot of them sang together in loud accord and the flesh tingled on her arms.

> O music,
> O little word
> That more than any other word is God!

This was what she loved—music and churches and goodness and God's love! And she had thought that if you believed in these, there were the just rewards. But maybe she was wrong. (Her mother and father loved Mathy best.) Maybe God Himself neither cared nor knew what she loved. It did seem that if He cared, He might have helped her a little more, since she tried to help herself. But maybe she went about it all wrong. Maybe one didn't win the prize by going at it straight, but had to go at it the long way around, through pit and mire and degradation, till one came home to rejoicing. Home and heaven—there must be a way, she had to find it. She closed her eyes. Dear Heavenly Father— But how could she ask Him to help her to be bad!

She rose quickly and fumbled her way to the door. It was late, the church was almost dark, and outside the streetlights had come on. She hesitated on the steps, struggling with her poor sense of direction. Instinct pulled her one way, but there, in the other, shone the bright lights of downtown. She struck out doggedly, scurrying through the shadows. How far had she come? She paused at every corner, looking both ways in panic, till at last she saw the hotel. She went toward it almost at a run and reached the elevator with her heart pounding. Her hand shook so that she could scarcely unlock the door. She snapped the light on and without even taking off her hat went straight to the telephone and called Kenny's number.

"Hello?" said a voice, which she took to be his mother's.

Leonie took a long steadying breath. "May I please speak with Kenneth?"

There was a brief pause. "Honey," the woman said in a tone of patient annoyance, "Kenneth is *still* in the Ozarks. Now I told you that yesterday when you called."

"Oh, but I didn't—"

"He's gone fishing with his father and he won't be back for another two weeks. I wish to goodness you girls wouldn't keep calling him all the time. Aren't you enough of a lady to wait till he calls *you?* It's getting to be a nuisance the way—"

Leonie put the receiver down quietly, cutting off the accusing voice. She was furious with embarrassment, and red as a beet—she could see herself in the mirror. She had not called old Kenny yesterday! She didn't even want to see him, and she was glad he wasn't there. But she had staked the whole week on his promise of "a real hot time"! And what was she going to do now—wander around by herself all day and sit in her room all evening? She didn't know whether to be annoyed or relieved, whether to laugh or cry, so she kicked the bathroom door. It shut with a bang that jarred the furniture, and the full-length mirror cracked from bottom to top. Leonie stared at it aghast, her mouth wide open. Then she sat right down on the floor, still wearing her hat, and squalled.

Was there nothing in the world that she could do right? She couldn't even be bad! And she hated trying. Even if they never knew about it, she just couldn't do it. She picked up the cigarettes and flung them into the wastebasket. She didn't want to smoke or wear indecent dresses or go wild. Those things were wrong. Not for other people, maybe, but they were wrong for her. She was brought up to believe it and she couldn't change now. Let Mathy and Jessica run away and do what they pleased—what she pleased to do was be good, the way God and her father and mother wanted her to be. But she did wish they would love her for it.

She cried and cried. All the tears she hadn't wept all summer seemed determined to get wept now. And after she had cried about everything else, she cried in exasperation. Here she was, in a fancy room that she couldn't afford, scared to death to go out. And she was hungry. She began to laugh, giggling through her tears as she looked at herself in the cracked mirror. She felt like an idiot, sitting there on the floor with her hat on! Well, she'd got herself into this, how was she going to get out? She would call up Ed, that's what she'd do! The thought struck her like a flash from heaven. She had forgotten he lived in town. With a little whimper of joy she reached for the telephone.

He arrived a half hour later, in his shirtsleeves, without a tie, and looking like a well-scrubbed bum. But he was homefolks, and she was never so glad to see anyone in her whole life.

He took her down the street and bought her a hamburger and a big thick malted milk. As the last drop gurgled through the straw, he leaned back and lighted a cigarette. "All right, Aunt Linnie, what's the problem?"

"What problem?" she said, plaiting the straw.

"You look like a spanked baby. What have you been crying about?"

She hadn't intended to tell him. But she had to say something. She began with the broken mirror and worked back from there. He kept nagging and asking questions and before she knew it she had poured out the whole story of the summer. "I thought I was making them happy, but they hated it. They can't stand me!" She buried her face in the paper napkin and wept.

"Now, you know that isn't so," said Ed.

"It is!"

"You're just as mixed up as a lonesome girl can be. Don't you know they love you as much as they did Mathy? They'd act the same way about you, if it had been you instead of her."

"What'll I do—kill myself?"

"That's what you're doing." He exhaled slowly. "I've watched you down there this summer."

"I was happy," she protested, "most of the time."

"Oh, sure, sure. A pretty girl down there in the sticks with the old folks and a couple of kids—you were happy as a lark."

"Well, I *thought* I was."

"Proves how stupid you are, Aunt Linnie. You don't know what you've got—you're too nice a kid to be goin' to waste. You ought to be out and around and raisin' a little dust. What are you going to do the rest of the week?"

"I don't know," she said woefully.

"Well, you ought to have some fun for yourself. Why don't we do something tonight? Want to see a burlycue? What would you like to do?"

"I just want to go home!"

"Oh, for Christ's sake." He leaned back. "Okay, if that's what you want, let's go. Get your things and I'll take you."

"You mean clear home—tonight?"

"I can drive it in an hour and a half."

"But I can't go home, not till the end of the week! What would I tell them?"

"Tell 'em anything. Make up a story."

"I can't! Not another one! I've got to stay whether I want to or not. I can't really afford it and I don't know what to do and what am I going to do about that mirror!"

Ed laughed. "Tell you what," he said; "you go back to the hotel and tell them about the mirror. Don't say how it happened, just say the wind blew the door shut. Act like it's an insult to a paying guest—you might have been cut by flying glass!"

"Oh, I couldn't do that. It was my fault."

"You don't have to say so."

"But there isn't any wind tonight."

"Oh, for the love of Mike!"

"I'd rather just pay for it and not have any trouble."

"All right. If that's what you want to do, pay for the damn thing and pay your bill at the same time. If you think you've got to stay in town all week, you might as well stay at my place. It's no Ritz, but it won't cost you anything."

"You mean stay in your apartment?" she said, looking up with a teary face.

"I've got a couple of rooms and a kitchen. It's right on the car-line, you can get downtown in ten minutes."

"But what'll you do?"

"What do you mean?"

"Where will you stay?"

"I'll stay there. What did you think?"

She looked down, feeling herself blush.

"God's sake, Aunt Linnie!" He laughed. "You don't have to worry. I'm one of the family, whether you like it or not."

"I know that," she said primly. "But what will people think?"

"What people? Nobody's going to come nosin' around. You don't have to worry about that, up here."

"Well . . ."

"I'll bunk on the couch and you'll have the other room all to yourself. In the morning I'll be gone before you get up. The place is all yours the rest of the day. And if you're scared to go out by yourself at night, I'll be glad to go with you if you want me to. I imagine your Dad would rather you had me with you than nobody at all."

She managed a sheepish smile.

"Come on now. You go up and get your suitcase. I'll settle about the mirror."

266

"Oh no!" She looked at him in alarm. "I'll do it. I wouldn't want them thinking that I—I mean that you and I—"

Ed shrugged his shoulders. "Lord!" he said softly.

4

She woke up early the next morning, before he left for work, and lay contentedly listening to him move about. It was nice not to feel all alone and afraid, and such a relief that today she could enjoy herself. She wished he would hurry up and leave so she could get started. She would ride down on the streetcar and return that awful dress, first thing. Then she could buy some school clothes. She'd look for some little surprise for the kids and the folks, and have a nice lunch at the Forum. If there was time in the afternoon, she would go to Jenkins for sheet music and listen to some classical records. She did wish Ed would hurry!

The minute the door closed, she bounded out of bed and peered out cautiously to make sure he was gone. The living room was a terrible mess, worse even than it looked last night. Shoes and books and newspapers scattered all over, ashtrays overflowing, coffee cups and glasses on the floor. A white shirt with a tie through the collar hung on a bridge lamp. Bachelors! she thought. On a table against the wall he was putting something together— or taking it apart, you couldn't tell which. There were radio parts and various tools and gears and spools of wire, with greasy rags lying around. She tiptoed about the room peering guiltily into everything. She knew so little about him, really. She felt as if she were spying and, in a way, she was. A postcard lay on the floor, written side up. She bent down to read without picking it up. It was a note from someone on vacation, someone named Billy, and from the sound of it, she didn't believe Billy was a boy. She made a prissy mouth. Just let him bring home some flapper named Billy, and Papa never *would* let Peter go.

Ed had left coffee on the stove. When she had washed a cup and cleared the table she turned on the radio and sat down. It was nice to dawdle over breakfast with music and the morning paper. It felt citified. But as she finished her coffee and toast, her country instincts got the better of her. She could not stand the sight of all those dishes in the sink. Glancing at the clock—it was early yet, she had all day—she pinned a towel around her waist, rolled up the sleeves of her kimono, and lit in. She sang with the radio as she worked and, one thing leading to another, kept on till she had cleaned up the whole kitchen and the living room as well.

"My word!" she said, looking at the time. It was after twelve. She hurried into the bedroom to start dressing. But she was hot and sweaty and needed a bath. Before she could take it, she had to give the tub a good scrubbing, and while she was at it, she cleaned the sink and toilet and the medicine chest. She wound up on her hands and knees scrubbing the floor. By the time she was bathed and dressed and on the streetcar, it was almost four o'clock.

She had only time to return the flame-colored dress and run to the dime store for some new tea towels—Ed's were a fright. After the stores closed, she stayed on for some time, window shopping, and didn't get back to the apartment until almost seven. She found Ed waiting, all shaved and shining and dressed up in a Palm Beach suit.

"My goodness!" she said, so taken aback that she hardly knew what to say. She hadn't seen him look like this since the day he married Mathy.

"I thought I'd better clean up a little, so I wouldn't look out of place. You little drudge—don't you know how to do anything but work?"

"It looks better, doesn't it?" she said.

"It looks great, but I ought to spank you. I'll take you out to dinner instead."

"Oh, you don't have to do that."

"My pleasure. Doll yourself up, we'll go some place nice."

Leonie's eyes lit up. "Well—all right!"

She ran to the bedroom and took out her flowered chiffon, her good silk stockings, and her high-heeled sandals. She brushed her hair till it shone like the satin ribbons around her waist and, after a moment's hesitation, rouged her lips lightly. When she opened the bedroom door, Ed was standing in the kitchen. He looked around at her and whistled.

"Aunt *Linnie!* Who's this frump Greta Garbo!"

"Oh, hush," she said with an embarrassed smile.

"You look like a million dollars."

"You don't have to flatter me."

"Looking at you, who'd ever know you spent the whole day scrubbing!"

"I didn't spend the whole day."

"Well, the place looks it, and you don't." He reached out with his cane and hooked her by the arm. "Let's go."

There were crystal chandeliers in the restaurant. The rug was gold. Every table had a lamp with an amber-colored shade. And there was an orchestra playing soft music.

"This is *nice!*" said Leonie.

"You like this, eh?"

"Don't you?"

He shrugged and smiled. "It's phony."

"Oh really?" She glanced around earnestly, and he laughed.

"Don't worry about it, Aunt Linnie. If you like it, it's just fine."

He could be very nice sometimes, and much to her surprise, he had fine manners. Except for the grease around his fingernails, you'd never take him for a garage mechanic. He acted more like a suave gentleman, and she kept forgetting that this was plain old Ed whom she had seen so often at the farm, with his elbows on the table. Though come to think of it, he had never been what you might call rude. All through dinner he kept reminding her of someone she had met elsewhere, but for the life of her she couldn't think who it was. They had a lovely time. The only thing that bothered her at all was the extravagance. Maybe the place was a little phony, as he said, but it certainly was expensive. Once in a while, though, it was fun to splurge.

When the check came, she opened her pocketbook. "Now we're going to go Dutch," she said.

"Why, Aunt Linnie." He looked at her as if she had done something naughty. "Don't bite the hand that wants to feed you!"

"I always pay my share—I insist."

"You're not out with the girls this time."

"It makes no difference. I'm not going to let you—"

"Aunt Linnie!" he warned her. "A lady doesn't argue money matters in public."

"All right, then. I'll pay you as soon as we get out."

"Look," he said, leaning across the table. "I am the male of the species. I have certain functions foreordained by nature. I pay the check. You are the female. By the nature of her biology the female is receptive. So for God's sake, receive, like the beautiful specimen that you are! And don't make me ashamed of you any more."

She didn't know how to take it. She followed him out in silence.

"Thank you," she said as they reached the car. "I enjoyed my dinner very much."

"I'm glad you did."

"But I can't let you do this any more."

"Oh, for the love of Christ!" He laid his forehead on the steering wheel. "All right, if it will make you feel any better, let's say it's your fee for taking care of my kid. Tell me about him."

They drove around for a long time, talking of Peter and the folks and all sorts of things, including the depression and politics and the Russian Five-Year Plan. Ed knew quite a lot about such things, even if he didn't know much about literature. And even though she didn't agree with all his opinions, she thought them interesting. She argued, as her father did, that the world would take care of itself if people only behaved themselves, worked hard and stayed honest and took their share of responsibility. This led to her plans for the future, and they in turn to his. All he hoped to do at the moment was hang onto his job. But if he did that and times got no worse and he could work up the energy, he might go to night school and study law. She thought it a wonderful idea.

"But I don't know," he said, "whether I'll ever do it or not. I'm too lazy."

"Oh, you're joking!"

"And it interferes with my good time." He grinned and winked and she laughed. Who *was* it he reminded her of?

"Oh, look!" she said. "There's a miniature golf course!"

He groaned. "I suppose you want to stop and play."

"Don't you like miniature golf?"

"I never tried to find out."

"You should—it's fun!"

"Okay, if you want to play, we'll stop and play."

"Not unless you want to."

"I'm dying to. Come on."

They played through once. Ed made two holes-in-one and that gave them two free games, so they went through twice again. Ed was so funny and made so many wisecracks he had everyone laughing.

"My goodness!" she said, as they reached home. "If I hadn't called you, I'd be sitting up there in that hotel room all by myself!"

"What a waste," he said. "A pretty girl should never sit by herself."

"Sometimes she prefers to," said Leonie.

"Only when she doesn't know any better."

She started to retort to that, but he didn't give her a chance.

"I'm glad you called me," he went on. "Your family has done a lot for me, and it's nice to do something for you for a change."

"Well, you certainly have, and I appreciate it." She smiled from the bedroom door. "Good night."

In the morning, thinking over the pleasant evening before, she decided to take Ed on a picnic that night to repay him. She went right out after breakfast, walked till she found a store, carried home a sack of groceries, and spent the rest of the day preparing. They drove out to Swope Park and had a delicious supper. Afterward they sat on the grass and listened to a band concert.

The following night they went to the movies at a drive-in theater. When they got home, Leonie made iced tea and they sat up and talked till after two o'clock.

It was on the third day, at a quarter till five in the afternoon, that Leonie made a discovery. She was dressing for the evening, keeping an eager eye on the clock, when she caught herself smiling into the mirror. She was thinking of Ed, something he had said last night, some nonsense about her having a nice frame ("like a good car—you'd look pretty good stripped down!"). And all at once she knew who it was that he reminded her of. It was of himself, the old Ed, of high school days. Ed the big ladykiller, who soft-soaped every girl in sight. Why, that was exactly what he had done to her—soft-soaped her for the last three days! And she thought he was being so nice! He wasn't nice at all. He was leading her on—Mathy's own sister!—like any other girl. And like any other girl, she had followed. She had swallowed the bait—hook, line, and sinker. She was crazy about him.

She sat down on the edge of the bed, weak in the knees. Of all the bad things she might have done, this was the worst of all! Far and away the worst. She was too good to smoke or go to night-clubs or marry old Kenny, but she could fall in love with her own sister's husband! Strain at a gnat, swallow a camel. Well, it wouldn't do. It just wouldn't do at all.

5

She was very quiet at dinner and firm about the check. She paid it.

"All right, if that's the way you want it," he said. "What would you like to do now?"

"I'd like to go back to the apartment, if you don't mind."

"Don't you want to drive around a while?"

"No, thank you."

"What's the matter with you tonight? Don't you feel well?"

"I'm fine. I just think I should start packing. I've decided to go home tomorrow."

"Tomorrow! But you've got two nights yet."

"I know, but I think I've been here long enough."

"You're supposed to be gone a week. What are you going to tell them?"

"I'll just tell them I changed my mind."

"I'm disappointed, Aunt Linnie. I thought we were having a pretty good time."

"We are—it's been very nice."

"Then why do you want to pull out now?"

"I think I've been away long enough."

"Now they're getting along fine down there without you, and you know it. What's eatin' you, don't you like it here?"

"Well, yes, but—" She drew a line on the tablecloth with her thumbnail.

"What have I done wrong?"

"Nothing. Except—"

"Except what?" he said.

"Well, nothing!" she said, putting her hands firmly in her lap. "You've been very nice."

"Then why are you running away? Godsake, Aunt Linnie, all you do is run away from people."

"I'm not running away!"

"Are you right sure of that?"

She glanced up, startled. He was looking at her in an odd way, with a little smile at one corner of his mouth. And he was so beautiful and so sure of himself, and she was so mad at him and mad about him— She blushed furiously and ducked her héad.

"That's all I wanted to know," he said. "You don't want to go home tomorrow any worse than I want you to."

"You shut up!" she said, and began to cry with vexation.

"Come on."

He led her out and put her in the car and they drove for a long time, Leonie huddled in her corner in a sodden heap. She could have died of shame, but she couldn't stop crying. After a while they stopped.

"Honey," he said, putting his hand on her shoulder.

"Don't you touch me!"

"I'd like to."

"I won't let you—I hate you!"

"No, you don't. And I don't hate you. Can't we admit that, Aunt Linnie, and not make a big fuss? What's so wrong about it?"

"You're my sister's husband!"

There was a little pause and he said quietly, "Not any more."

"Oh, how can you act like this!" she cried out, turning on him. "You're a terrible person—she's only been dead a year!"

"It's been a long year."

"I don't know how you could forget her!"

"I haven't. I never will. But she's gone, Leonie, and there isn't a thing I can do about it."

"You could wait a while. You've got other girls already—some flapper named Billy—oh, I know you, Ed! But I thought you had more decency than this—to soft-soap her own sister!"

"Oh, God," he said. "Is that what you think I'm doing!"

"All that sweet talk—telling me how pretty I was— You're feeding me the same line you feed everybody else. You think I'm going to fall for it like they all do. Well, I'm not like the others! I'm not about to fall for your line. I'm not Alice Wandling!"

"Her again!" he said with a short laugh. "Lord, Aunt Linnie, nobody could ever accuse you of that. You're just about everything she wasn't. Except pretty, and you're a whole lot prettier."

"You shut up!"

"You were the prettiest girl in school, but you were so all-godly, nobody cared. Well, I care now. If it's of any interest to you, I care quite a lot."

"That's nothing but a line!"

"No," he said calmly, "I don't think it is. I think I mean it. I don't quite know why. Maybe it's because you're so goddam dumb

273

about anything that matters. And baby, what I'd like to teach you about the things that matter! You might be a little slow to learn, but once you got the hang of it, watch out! You hardshell virgins give it all you've got. Well, maybe that's all I want, maybe I just want to—corrupt you, because you're innocent and undefiled. Maybe that's all it is. But I don't think so. You're a good, sweet kid, Aunt Linnie, and honest to Christ, I think I love you."

"But you're my brother-in-law!" she cried.

"Oh, come off it! I never was a brother to you—you wouldn't accept me as a brother. I wasn't good enough for that. So you can stop acting like it was incest. Look, baby," he said, "I loved your little sister and I still do. But she's gone, and so is the guy that married her, in a way. What I've got left is some sort of distant cousin. I don't always recognize him, but I'm gettin' to know him better as time goes on. I may even get to like him. I think you might like him, too, if you thought of him that way. He's very fond of you," he said gently.

"He just thinks I'll make a fool of myself!"

"Oh no, he doesn't, hon. You're a fool sometimes, but not that way. You're too damn stubborn. I kinda like that. I like the way you go at things—you just go at the wrong things, that's all. Why don't you have a go at me? I'll even marry you, Aunt Linnie."

"Oh—" she wailed, "how could I marry anyone that calls me Aunt Linnie!"

He laughed and pulled her toward him.

"No!" she said, pushing him away. "If you were the last man on earth and I *wanted* to marry you, I wouldn't do it on account of my father! Haven't you done enough to him? How could you think of doing any more!"

"I could do it," he said. "I'm not that noble. And he thinks more of me than he used to."

"Not that much. And I don't think it would make my mother very happy, either. I don't care how they feel about me, I don't *care*. I love my mother and father and I just won't do this to them!"

"Not even if you wanted me bad?"

"Not even if I did."

"Je-sus Christ!"

"Stop swearing. You swear all the time."

"It's a form of prayer. Leonie—either you're a masochist or you're superstitious."

"I'm not! What do you mean?"

"Anybody that'll give up her own happiness either enjoys the hell out of it or thinks it'll get her somewhere."

"Well, I don't enjoy it."

"Then you must think it'll get you somewhere."

"I don't know what you're talking about!"

"Why do you think people made sacrifices to the gods? Why do they beat themselves with thorns or wear a hair shirt? Because they think it will get them somewhere with the powers that be. It's all self-interest. So don't think you're throwing me on the altar for their sake—you're doing it for your own, so they'll think you're a dandy kid and give you a gold star! Honey, wouldn't you rather be happy?"

"I'll be happy—you aren't the only man in the world."

"You'll find something wrong with the others, too. The way you're going, you're going to give up your life for them and find out they don't appreciate you any more than if you hadn't. And don't think you can force them to—it won't work. You ought to know by now; the harder you try, the more they fight you. That's how it is, Leonie, and you might as well face it."

"All right then, I'll face it."

"You're going to have it your way, aren't you? Okay, Leonie, you go home tomorrow. Go right on back to your chastity, poverty, and obedience, and be their good little girl. And while you're being their good little girl, you just remember this." He pinned her back against the seat and kissed her. Then he wrapped his arms around her and held her till she stopped fighting.

6

"Honey," said her mother, "you could have stayed the rest of the week. We were getting along just fine."

"Well, I had my visit out. I was ready to come home. There's a lot to do before school starts. I've got to get my clothes ready and everything."

"I thought you were going to buy some new clothes while you's up there. Didn't you and Carol get down to the city?"

Leonie turned her back. "We went in a time or two. But I didn't see anything I liked."

"Seems like there would have been something you liked, in all them stores."

"It was kind of picked over."

There was a little pause and her mother said, "You girls had a pretty good time, you say?"

"We had a fine time."

"What all did you do?"

"Oh, nothing important—just fooled around mostly."

"Didn't you have any beaus or anything?"

"Huh-uh."

"You didn't!" said Callie. "I'd a-thought Carol might have invited some nice boys to meet you. Didn't you meet any of her friends?"

"A few."

"Didn't nobody take you to a picture show or anything?"

"Well—once when we were in the city I called up Ed. He took us to a movie."

"Oh?" said Callie. "I didn't know you saw him. You hadn't said anything about it."

"I guess I—just didn't think of it."

"Well, I declare!"

There was a moment of silence, during which Leonie tried frantically to think of something else to say. All she could think of was him.

"How was he?" said her mother.

"Hm? Oh—he was fine."

"When's he coming down again?"

"I don't know."

She knew. He was coming tomorrow night. He said so. He said, "I'll come down every weekend. I won't lay a hand on you or say a word. But I'll be there, just to remind you." The thought of him turned her to putty and made her distrust the sound of her own voice. To her relief, her mother let the subject drop.

She believed now that he loved her. He had made her believe it, and believe too that he wanted her for her own sake, not merely as a mother for Peter. But even believing him made her angry. He had no right to want her, or to make her want him! A man had obligations to a woman. He owed her a home and security and a future. Ed had none of these that you could count on. All he could offer her was a lame body and a child she was caring for already. Just the same, she wanted him, and she was furious, both with him and with herself.

He came, as he had said, every weekend, and he said nothing and did nothing to give her away. But he stalked her with his eyes —she could feel them following her—and it made her drop the silver, knock things over, and sit tongue-tied in his presence, too self-conscious to speak. The more she saw him, the more she loved him, and the more she knew she must not.

She worked doggedly, trying to forget him. All day she ran and, at night, lay abed too tired to sleep. There were no more airs and graces. The time of candlelight and musicales had passed. Yet sometimes in her despair she took refuge in the parlor and played her accordion. "When you're smiling, When you're smiling, The whole world smiles with you . . ." Sick at heart, she gave the instrument a mighty squeeze, crushing out the song that had so betrayed her. Then, penitent, she played a hymn of faith. But even that mocked her, for though she could play the notes, the music never came out right. Never once under her diligent hands did an instrument give back the sounds she carried in her head, the sweet escaping tones that went on and on, like the voices that drive people mad. All her life she had heard them. What must she do to possess them? For there must be music, since all else she wanted was denied her—the love of her mother and father by their love for Mathy; Ed, by her love for them.

His name swung in her head like a clapper and her whole body rang. Edward, Edward . . . over and over. Yet no one must hear it, and her disappointment was enormous. She had always thought that when she loved it would be so proudly. Her love would fly like a flag in the open, for all who saw it to salute. But this—whatever it was—bore no resemblance to anything she had ever imagined. This was a sickness which she could admit to no one, not even to herself without humiliation. Edward her love was everything she had ever scorned. And he was her sister's husband. This was the cruelest mark against him, yet this was the one that seemed least real. (Even Peter looked different now—no longer Mathy's child, but Ed's.) Was it true that he was a different man now? Matured in sorrow and remorse, had he changed—enough? Pray God that it was so! For if he *had* changed, if he had steadied and wanted truly to do better— Oh, she could help him! She had the strength and the will. She could bring out the best, as Mathy never could have, for she was different from Mathy and he loved her for different reasons. Her thoughts went through arabesques of imagining. She saw that handsome head in a law bonnet, saw him in judge's robes, a tall figure with a touching limp. . . .

He would have a book-lined study smelling of leather and genteel tobacco. They would read together in the evenings, and they would entertain, there would be distinguished guests, conversation, music—

It was no good! He was still Ed, and he had killed her sister, and her father and mother would never quite get over that. Let them love Mathy more than her, let them think what they would. She could not marry without their blessing. And how could they ever in the world give that? Help me, her eyes said. Mama—Papa—help me!

The look was not lost on them. They saw her running through the days, silent and harried, a small eleven deepening between her eyes; they saw her grow thin and melancholy, protesting steadily that nothing, nothing was the matter. And they felt somehow to blame. They began to be thoughtful of her, enormously gentle, to make up for something they had done to her. And in their vague fear that they did not love her as they should, they loved her more perhaps than one whom it takes no effort to love—as one is often more polite to strangers than to an old friend.

Callie would say to her, "Sit down and read awhile, honey. I'll can these few peaches."

Or: "I'll put the children to bed. You go on and get some rest."

One evening she clapped her hands and said, "I tell you what —let's have the candles on the table tonight! We've been forgettin' about 'em. You fix us one of your pretty centerpieces."

"I'm too tired," said Leonie.

"I know it, honey, you look tired. Sit down—let me mash them potatoes."

"I'll do them." She turned away from her mother's searching, gentle gaze.

They began to notice her awkwardness in Ed's presence, and her brusque replies. One night Ed suggested that they drive into the village, and she turned him down with a curt "No, thanks!"

"You weren't very nice about that," Callie said as they washed the dishes.

"Well, he ought to know I'm too tired to go anywhere after a day like this."

"I think he's right—you need to get out more. Why don't you go on?"

"I don't want to."

"I thought you liked picture shows."

"Not the kind they have in Renfro!"

"Well, I know. But them old pictures are kind of funny sometimes. Why don't you go ahead?"

"I don't want to go, Mama."

"Well, why not?"

Her mother was looking straight at her and Leonie turned deep red. "I'm—too tired," she stammered. "I don't feel like it tonight —I've got a kind of a headache."

"You've got a kind of a heartache, I reckon," said Callie quietly.

"That's not so!" Leonie turned on her, irate. "You must think I'm pretty bad if I'd do a thing like that!"

"Like what?"

"Whatever you were thinking." She looked away in embarrassment. "Just because Ed asked me to go someplace— Well, I'm not that bad or that dumb!"

"Why, honey, I never said anything like that. Don't cry! Mama didn't mean to upset you."

"I just don't want you to get any such idea."

Callie put her arms around her. "What's the matter, darling?"

"Nothing!" Leonie shook herself free. "I'm all right."

Callie went on putting the dishes away and hanging up the skillets. After a moment Leonie blew her nose. "Mama," she said, "do you think I wanted Mathy to die?"

"Why, no, honey. Whatever made you think a thing like that?"

"I used to be mean to her sometimes—she always got away with everything, and things came so easy for her. I thought maybe it was a kind of punishment to me."

"No, darling. If it was anybody's punishment, it was mine."

"How could it be yours?"

"Oh . . . I used to favor her a little. She was the youngest for so long. And that wasn't fair to you and Jessica."

"Oh, Jessica never minded!"

"Well, Jessica understood her better than the rest of us. Mathy wasn't like the rest of us. But don't worry. I don't think God gives and takes like that, just to punish us. I can't find it in my heart to believe it."

"I can," said Leonie.

"Well . . . go to bed now, get some rest."

They watched her through the long yellow days, running like a hound gone daft, feverish and silent. And they watched Ed watching her. August wore on, and the locusts cried shrill and lonely, and the accordion wheezed in the parlor, till the sound became the sound of her anguish. They listened in silence, aching for this hurt stubborn child of theirs, and endured it as long as they could.

"What'll we do?" said Callie. "She's killing herself."

"I know it," said Matthew.

He was working at the bottom of the pasture, making a trench to channel the water of the branch into the slew when the August rain would come. Callie had come down to talk.

"It's Ed," she said. "I'm sure of that now. She wants him, and I think he wants her." There was a long pause. "How would you feel about it?"

He said, "I guess it doesn't matter too much what I'd feel."

"Yes, it does, Papa! It matters this time. Leonie won't go against your will."

He worked on without answering.

After a while Callie said, "I guess Mathy might want it this way, if she knew. She tried to make a match of them herself, before her and Ed . . ." Her voice trailed off. She sat on a flat rock in the shade, fanning herself with her sunbonnet. The smell of the branch was cool and sandy. The branch was low now; a good rain would help everything. "I can't help thinkin'," she said, "if they *was* to marry, where would Ed be buried—next to Mathy or next to Leonie? It would look kind of funny to put him down between 'em, one on each side."

"Well, I don't suppose we have to worry about that."

"No, I guess not. It just crossed my mind."

Matthew laid up a spadeful of earth and tamped it into place. "He says he's going to law school this fall."

"Yes, he sounds like he means it. He ought to make a right good lawyer, he's such a great one to argue."

"It takes more than that."

"But it's a start."

"It costs money to go to school," said Matthew. "How does he think he could go to school and support a family, in times like these?"

"I don't imagine they'd get married right away, not for a year or so, maybe."

"They certainly ought to wait."

"Yes, I think they ought to. But if they just knew we didn't oppose it . . . She'll be goin' back to school in another week. I can't hardly stand for her to go off like this, wantin' and wantin', and thinkin' we don't want her to have him. It ain't just what we want, I know. But I don't know how to explain it to her without her takin' it wrong, like we won't let her have something we let Mathy have."

"Mathy was going to have him whether we liked it or not."

"Yes, but Leonie won't. That's the difference—she won't do it unless we say she can. And if this is what she wants—"

"It won't work," said Matthew.

"I'm afraid it won't, either. But how do we know? It ain't our lives—it's theirs."

"That's right. We can't always tell."

"Like Jessica and Creighton," Callie said, musing. "I said that marriage wouldn't work, either—or would have, if I'da been asked. But looks like it's workin'."

"Looks like it."

"Hard to see just why she'd marry a man like him, 'specially when she had a poor one before. Creighton's an awful nice fellow, seems like, but all them big children! And that old farm of his, leanin' up against the side of the hill! Don't see how he makes a livin' at all. But land, she had a chance to do different. I guess this was what she wanted—a whole houseful of noisy kids a-stompin' and singin' and the fiddle playin' and dogs and cats underfoot! Makes me laugh, every time I think of that time we went down there to see 'em." She wiped her eyes. "Well, I guess Jessica's happy. Maybe Leonie and Ed would be, too. Like I say, it's their lives, not ours."

She sat for a moment. "But Papa," she said then, getting up, "I've always been the one that held up for Ed, and maybe I was wrong to do it. I'm not going to do it any more. It's whatever you say, this time. It has to come from you. Whatever you tell her, I'll go by that." She turned and walked back up the path.

Matthew went on digging. His shirt was damp and the sweat-bees plagued him. After a while he climbed up the bank and sat down in the shade and took off his hat. Maybe it wasn't as serious as they thought. Maybe Leonie would forget about him when she got back to school. Maybe this was only a case of puppy love. But looking back (half embarrassed, as if he were spying), he could not remember Leonie in the throes of love, puppy or otherwise. He thought of her in high school, hurrying home in the afternoons to help her mother, at night bent over her books at the parlor table or practicing her music . . . and later, coming home from college or her teaching job, weekend after weekend and faithfully every summer. Not in all that time had there been one boy whose face he could remember, nor any sign from Leonie that life was not all business. Was it possible that she had never been in love before? This was worse than he thought! First love at her age—what was she now, twenty-five, twenty-six?—was a serious affair. Youngsters might come through unscathed, but older persons—why, it could ruin them, like the mumps! If Leonie had waited all this time— Oh, and she had a hard head. "Hard as a rock," he said, kicking a chunk of sandstone out of the ground. If she had set her head for this one, she would never give him up, whether she married him or not.

And what of Ed? He had grown fond of Ed now, trying earnestly to make up for the years of rejection. But he hadn't thought that he would have to make it up like this. He picked up the rock and brushed it off. Suppose he said no? It might be best. For even though they loved each other truly, they were bound to have trouble. They differed too much from each other. He could see Ed's way now; he could, by a little understanding, accept it. But he doubted that Leonie could. Ed was not likely to give her the things she set such store by, the fine house and travel, the cultural life, all the medals of success. Leonie needed prizes, as he did. Ed and Mathy never needed them at all.

He sighed, bouncing the rock in his hand. How could he ever tell her that? No one can tell anyone anything, not even how much you love them. That was the hardest of all. And he loved this stubborn bewildered child whose nature was so much his. Perhaps the only way he could say it now was to give her what she wanted.

He wondered suddenly if he had ever given her anything she wanted before. Oh, he gave her a good home and an education (though she paid for part of that herself). The girls had always had presents. But Callie had seen to that, not he. Coming home from a trip, had he ever brought one of them a toy, a souvenir? He could not think of one. And time, that great gift that he had given so charily! He dropped his head in shame. The sins of omission. Perhaps his girls had needed more from him than food and moral instruction. Dolls and chocolate drops and frivolous doodads—perhaps if he had given these sooner . . . Well, he would give her what she wanted now, even though she suffered from it, as a child from too much candy. What a pity if she had none at all! And maybe she would find her own cure. Maybe she was the only one who could make Ed amount to something. Lord knows, she was determined.

He stared absently at the rock in his hand. Sandstone . . . probably argillaceous. He licked his finger, touched it to the rock, and sniffed. It had that smell. Clayey. He turned it this way and that, noting the infinitesimal particles that glittered in the coarse brown surface. Bits of mica mixed with sand, which was itself particles of quartz, all of it granite once, and in the beginning, magma. Everything began in fire. He dug into the small crater in one side and blew out the clinging soil. The walls inside were striated, fossil-like. Though probably erosion caused the grooves, some chemical action on the stone. Shale and limestone were better for fossils, limestone being itself solid creature. He thought of Cambrian and Silurian seas sweeping over his land and receding, each one leaving a stria of sea creatures crushed, pressed, made into stone. And after the seas, the tropical jungles decaying slowly into the ooze and hardening there through millions of years, until he dug them out of his own hill and took them home to burn. Paleozoic forests going up in smoke from his own chimney. As it began, so it ended, in fire. Yet not ended, either. The mineral ash lay on his garden, blending with earth again, renewing itself in another form, and going on. There was always a going on.

But he digressed. He looked up at the heat waves that shimmered over the bottom field. It was very still down here, so still that he could hear an accordion playing in the distance, a distressing sound, like someone trying to laugh through tears.

With a sigh, he fitted the rock back into place, picked up the spade, and started toward the house.

Callie

1

The redbird said *Richard!* three times in a row, making clean cuts in the stillness. Callie opened her eyes. It was morning. The wallpaper's satin stripes glowed in the pale light. At the windows the white lace lapped the air slowly. More birds awoke. Bluejays, a mockingbird. There was a scurry of wings in the cedar and the nasal *chrk-chrk* of a robin. The day came alive with such grace, unhurried and sweet and certain. Nothing remained of night but the still feeling, and that was not properly of the night at all, but of the morning. Night was full of murmurs and stirrings, itchings in the grass, and the tired mind talking and talking endlessly to itself. At night the mind said *I am old* and mumbled long-forgotten tiresome sorrows, until sleep crumbled like an old wall and buried the sound. Peace and stillness were part of the early dawn, with only the birds to say how quiet it was.

How she loved the summer, when the nights passed quickly and the mornings were long—summer, when the children came home. She allowed herself to think of it at last. Today they were coming! She had held the thought back, saving it up to make it last longer. They had such a little time together. Even the looking forward must be prolonged, savored a little at a time. In two weeks they would go away again, taking the summer with them. Each time it was a death to her. But now, at the start, she would close her mind to that and pretend they would stay forever. The pain of their going was never so great as the joy of their arrival.

Matthew had not yet wakened. He lay with his lean old body curled inside his nightshirt, his knees drawn up. Even in sleep he seemed alert. He slept so busily, wearing his little frown of concentration, the eyes closed with effort, the brows drawn together. All their daughters wore this same look. Not any of them cared much for sleeping; daylight and doing were important to them.

She pulled the sheet over his shoulders and got out of bed. At the washstand she poured water into the bowl and dropped her nightgown to her waist. Her body was thin and old but firm enough even yet and smooth, except where one breast had been cut away and the flesh stitched together in a fine seam. She washed the spot gently, wincing at the touch of the cool water. The scar no longer spread fear and resentment through her. It had become a sort of medal on her chest, a decoration for bravery, which she could think of now with a certain satisfaction and even a touch of wry amusement. Matthew, half suspecting a judgment on him, had suffered all her pain and a good deal of his own. He had been a little foolish in his day and he felt guilty. Poor Matthew. So easily led on, always losing his head and his heart. She knew him well. He had been faithful, she was sure of that. But a good part of his loyalty was caution. Timid, foolish, aggravating man. And yet (turning to look at the gray head on the pillow) when she thought of God, she saw Him in Matthew's image. Loving him, she stood for a moment watching him sleep, then folded the towel and began to dress.

The fresh-air, hot-ironed smell of her clothes filled her with pleasure. She combed her short white hair and put on her glasses. The alarm had not yet gone off. She took the clock from the whatnot shelf and turned off the button. Matthew would wake up in good time. The shelf held a collection of little vases, doll dishes, dime-store bric-a-brac, which the girls had given each other long ago. Among them were two hounds and a fox, three separate figures carved in wood. As she set the clock down, she gave the little fox a nudge, widening the distance between him and the hounds. The clock said twenty till six.

Downstairs, the kitchen lay cool and shadowy, still asleep. She thought of the jostle and hullabaloo that would fill it later. The children were coming home! As she stepped out on the back porch, she caught the faint odor of tobacco, an effluvium alien to this place. She shot an anxious glance at the screen door to see that it was hooked. Reassured, she looked out, wondering what man could have come here at this hour. But there had been no man. On the doorstep sat a stone jar covered with clean muslin. She smiled in relief. A friend had come and gone. Miss Hagar had been here, smoking her little pipe. She opened the door and looked inside the jar. There were two plump pullets dressed to the last pinfeather. Miss Hagar must have been up since dawn, with a fire built in the back yard under the kettle, and her cow waiting to be milked; she had walked the two miles with her offering before anyone should be awake to thank her. The good old woman, with no one of her own. She wanted to be part of this homecoming. And so she should be. (Though, guiltily, Callie wondered when; she was so jealous of the children in the short time they were home.)

She carried the chicken inside to the icebox. She could save her fat hen and bake it later on. Maybe they would have chicken salad. That would please Leonie. Fixy fussy Leonie, wanting everything just so. Callie smiled to herself. Well, everything was just so, the linen tablecloths done up, the candles bought, and the silver holders polished till they gave back the kitchen stove. You couldn't find the food in front of you, by candlelight. But it would make Leonie happy.

She went outside and down the path, pausing by the smokehouse to count the moonflower pods. Another day or two and they would be ready to bloom. The flowers were so lovely, and they lasted so short a time. It was almost like the children's visit, something you looked forward to all year, then it came, and you enjoyed it so much, and then it was over, in no time. Maybe that's the way it should be. She thought she wanted them home all the time, but maybe she didn't, really. Everything in its own season. If they were always here, she wouldn't have so much to look forward to.

"I must give Leonie some seeds," she reminded herself. Leonie could plant them next summer alongside her new fence. That fence! Callie shook her head, smiling. Started two years ago, abandoned halfway across the yard; Leonie had pieced it out with hollyhocks, to hide the mess behind it—the wrecks of cars that Ed hauled home from the garage and puttered with in his spare time. It made Leonie so cross. They had had their troubles, those two. (The depression, Ed out of a job, Soames on the way, Peter back home with his grandparents most of the time. Then the war, Ed in Kansas City again, working in the plants; and Leonie teaching a country school, living in a rented room with little Soames.) But they were doing better now. Mismatched though they were, Leonie and Ed seemed to need each other, like a churn and dasher. They got along all right. But Leonie and Soames were a different matter. It was a pitiful thing; Leonie liked her sister's child more than her own, and Soames knew it better than she did. It made them do things to each other that neither of them could forgive. But across the gap that lay between them, they loved each other. Now Soames was going away, and he was afraid. Yet he had to go. He had to fly the planes. It was something his father had done and Peter hadn't. And there was Leonie, seeing him slip away, trying to reach him before the time ran out.

Poor Leonie. Poor little boy. Callie sighed as she passed the garden (making a mental note that the beans needed picking). Children want to love their parents, but parents make it so hard sometimes. She was guilty of that herself, no doubt. Looking back, she could see mistakes. Still and all, maybe she hadn't done too bad. The children had left, but they found their own way back. Like the old nursery rhyme, "Leave them alone and they'll come home." The hardest thing in the world was to leave them alone.

She had learned that first with Jessica. She was still learning, with Mary Jo. She thought of her youngest daughter and felt again that familiar need to reach out and protect her. But Mary Jo was the hardest of all to reach. The years between them were so many, and the child felt so worldly wise. Such a knowing child, so full of reasons and argument. "But Mama, you're so old-fashioned! Times have changed since you were a girl. . . . But Mama *darling*, that's so middle-class! You just don't understand. . . ." And all sorts of fancy words and notions out of books. She was worse than Leonie, that way. Sometimes Callie felt like a stranger to her youngest. Every year there was less they could say to each other.

What the child did away off in that city, how she lived, who her friends were—all this surpassed Callie's understanding. The dangers alone she could imagine clearly, and she feared for her lamb. The girl was smart and educated and all that, but she was also a little foolish, like her father; easily taken in; no judgment at all; as happy as a lark if someone admired her, even some poor squinting boy; so eager to be loved. She could be hurt so easily, and maybe she had been, and there was so little Callie could do.

"But today she'll be home!" she said joyfully to a rooster, who had pranced down the path. "Today we'll see her and know she's all right! Get out of the garden, you scamp. Shoo!"

She flapped her apron at him and walked back through the yard. In the barnlot the cows lay big and soft in the morning shadows. One of them rose and came toward the fence, chewing thoughtfully.

"You'll be milked pretty soon," Callie assured her. "Though I don't know where I'll put all the cream," she went on, counting in her head all the crocks of milk waiting in the icebox. "I'll have to churn again this morning. Maybe we'll take some butter to old Mr. Corcoran. We haven't looked in on him all week. Well, good morning, sir!" she said, as a glossy bull strolled through the lot. She watched the rhythmic sheen of his plump flanks. Matthew was proud of his fine red bull.

Away to the south, beyond Little Tebo, a high meadow had caught the sunlight. It glowed above the dark line of the woods. Soon now the sun would take the walnut grove and send yellow runnels among the trees. It was pretty down there. "I'll go and pick berries," she said aloud. Matthew liked them with thick cream for breakfast. It wouldn't take long, and he had not yet come down.

Taking her small berry bucket, she set off through the pasture. The blackberries ripened late this year, due to the rain. But now they were fat and glossy and tumbled off the stem at a touch. Though her bucket filled promptly, she did not turn back at once, but wandered farther down the slope, considering the fine green morning. The broad leaves of the oak trees glistened; the willows made a soft haze down by the slew. Beyond them the cornfield rippled as she imagined an ocean might. Little Tebo had flooded in the spring, but who would believe it now? She recalled the thick brown water spread in a sullen lake on the bottom fields; it retreated slowly, leaving fences down, and bundles of drifted trash, sticks and cornstalks and dead perch. It had been a cold wet spring and a wet cool summer. But now it had turned fine. And better too much rain, she thought, than the droughts they had had in the thirties, when the sun flooded the land day after day, washing away the green, leaving its residue of burnt leaves, brittle grass, withered fruit, and dust. Hot autumn by the middle of July. Nothing came in reasonable measure, it seemed, not water or sunshine or sorrow. But joy, too, is immoderate sometimes, and that makes up for the rest.

She walked on slowly, musing on joy and sorrow, the seasons, and the passing of time. Odd memories slipped through her mind half-heeded . . . Mathy, no more than three, finding a new calf in the thicket, its eyes no softer or more surprised at the world than hers (twenty years now since Mathy died, yet she seemed still to be here—among those trees yonder or just across the hill). She thought of Jessica and Leonie, tiny things gathering flowers for their Maybaskets . . . bluebells, Sweet William, and verbenas . . . the time the crazy cow chased her up the branch; a poor lunatic of a thing, who bucked and kicked, when they tied her up, and finally hung herself in the barn. . . . Early like this, things came back to you—your childhood, the old hill farm, an empty house.

She stopped on the path, puzzled by a vague feeling of sadness. A little wind had passed through the oak leaves, recalling . . . what? Echoes of voices all but forgotten, children's voices . . . *'way down in the pasture, we can hear them sing.* What was it? So lost and long ago. She had cried. Someone she had loved . . . *'way down in the pasture*— Two little boys, that's who it was, two lonely little boys at a pasture fence, straining their ears for the sound of singing over the fields and far away.

A sob escaped her as she stood there on the path. Her little brothers, brown-eyed boys like puppies, tumbling and awkward and underfoot and wistful; half-brothers, they were, children of the bitter woman her father married late. Callie had helped raise them. And she loved those little boys. But she had gone away and left them, she and all her sisters, left them with a mother who didn't want them and a father too distraught to care. *Ma won't let us go to church* . . . Sunday and friendliness, laughter, and children to play with! *Ma won't let us go . . . but 'way down in the pasture, we can hear them sing.*

Fifty years gone by, and she was weeping for them still. Thaddeus was dead now and Wesley an old man. And the Lord knows if either of them had ever got nearer the singing. Maybe that was the way it went, that all your life you heard the singing and never got any closer. There were things you wanted all your life, and after a while and all of a sudden, you weren't any closer than you ever were and there was no time left.

She looked up at the bright sky. I am seventy, she said to herself. Seventy was *old.* How many more years did she have? Ten? Her mind ran backward over the ten years past. But ten was no time at all! It was so short—over, like that! Was another ten years all she could expect? She would be eighty then, a very old lady. In just that little time. And where was the fine white house on the corner, where her mind had lived all these years? And the trim green hedge and the rock garden in the yard? How—in just ten years?

And was this all, then? All she was to have? She turned slowly. Branch, field, creek, timber, the long slope of the pasture, the barn roof beyond. This and a few small towns were her world, all she was likely to know.

"I always meant to see the ocean!"

She said it aloud and in some surprise, as, for the first time, it occurred to her that she might *not* see the ocean, or do a number of things which she had intended to do.

"I never learned to read," she said, and alone there in the pasture, she dropped her head in shame. She could make out no more words than you found in a recipe, and not all of those. She had never really read the Bible. She only looked at the pages, reciting to herself the verses which she knew from much hearing, taking comfort from the feel of the big book in her hands. She had never let them know. Soothing her deception, she had promised herself that next week she would learn to read, just as soon as the house was cleaned and the ironing done. She was always so busy. And now she was seventy. In the time left, she was not likely to read, no more likely than she was to see the ocean. The future lay suddenly blank as a prairie. From here there was nothing to look forward to. Nothing but heaven.

And for all she knew, there might even not be that! She stirred uneasily. Oh, there was a heaven, all right; she was sure of that. But now that she'd come bang up against it, she was not at all sure she would get there. Always before, she had thought she would; she had taken it for granted, trusting her prayers and penitence to save her. But they might not. On the Day of Reckoning, heaven too could dissolve away, like the ocean and the fine white house.

She stood in the still pasture, thunder and lightning of the Last Judgment rumoring around her. Awed to silence, the mind stopped making words, and an old, old memory rose softly, as fresh and living as if it had not lain buried these many years. In its presence, the woods around her changed to a spring woods, and the air took on a tenderness felt only now and then in a lifetime. She remembered it clearly. And that was forty years ago.

2

It was April. School had not yet let out. Matthew rode off each morning to Renfro, where he was the high school teacher, and home again after dusk. The longer the days, the longer he stayed in town. Though he had plenty to do on the farm, he seemed to take little interest. Ordinarily, in the spring, he bloomed like a tree and went about full of new vigor and singing. This time he did what he had to in a dogged manner. He was gloomy and silent, cross with Callie and the children. They hardly dared speak to him half the time, and when they did, he didn't half hear them. He had had spells like this before; they often came at this time of year, when he had lots on his mind. But this time there seemed something more. Callie thought of his brother who had wasted away of consumption, and she was terrified that Matthew had caught the disease. It made little difference that he protested he was well. She continued to worry and watch him closely for any fatal sign.

Something was the matter, of that she was sure. He was changed in some way. He took no pleasure in the children and none in her. In fact, he seemed to go out of his way to avoid her. It came to her at last, with a wounding surprise, that there was another woman. Someone he saw every day. It had to be that. What else but a woman could have taken away her husband and replaced him with this stranger?

She was as curious as she was hurt. Who in the world could it be? She went over in her mind every woman and girl in the countryside, convinced by plain reason that it was none of these. Though she was not precisely vain, she knew her own worth; she was as smart as any female of their acquaintance and prettier than most, and she had a way about her. No girl had ever taken a man away from her. If any taking was done, she had done it. Who could it be who was turning the tables on her? Some town woman, no doubt; a silly creature who would turn his head and just as quickly drop him. She knew that kind of woman. Men caught them like spring colds. But they didn't last. Come summer, he'd get over it. She was certainly not going to make a fuss.

That's what men hoped you would do. It made them feel important. It also gave them something to hold against you. And she wasn't going to give him that! If he had to stray, it would be his own doing; he could not say that she drove him.

Sometimes, though, when he felt guilty and took it out on her, it was hard to keep quiet. She wished she could dress him down proper. But she held her peace and did what she could, with sassafras tea, wild greens, and patience, to thin his blood, keep his bowels open, and hasten his return.

Jessica was seven years old that spring, in her first year at school. Each morning Matthew dropped her off at Bitterwater on his way to Renfro. In the afternoons she walked home across the fields or a neighbor gave her a lift. Leonie, who had just turned five, had begged to go to school all year. And on a morning in April—a particularly warm fine morning—she was allowed to go with Jessica to "visit." Matthew was cross, having to drive the buggy that day; it delayed his getting to school. But Leonie had run them ragged and he supposed he might as well take her.

Callie waved them out of sight and hurried in to start the morning's work. Since the day was fine, she put the bedding out to air, hanging the quilts on the line and spreading the featherbeds on the grass. Reluctant to go inside, she decided to go looking for her broody-hen. The cantankerous thing, she had hidden a nest somewhere and they hadn't been able to find it.

She walked down through the pasture thinking of the hen— the soft, plump, stupid thing, hidden away somewhere on the warm eggs, drowsing and waiting out her time, till she should come out, a fussy old biddy with yellow puffballs cheeping after her on their twiggy feet. She smiled to herself. Even a hen took pride in her babies. And a hen didn't know the half of it. How much prouder it was having babies because you loved someone. "Oh, Matthew!" she said aloud, woefully. What was the matter with that man, and why didn't he act like he used to! She missed him. She missed her chickens, too. She wished she had kept Leonie at home. It was lonesome with no one there at all. These days, it was lonesome even with them. She sighed and, after a desultory search, went back to the house.

She was working in the kitchen when a sound from the front caught her attention. Hoping it might be a neighbor passing, she ran eagerly to see. To her alarm, a strange man was coming through the gate. He was dark-skinned. He wore a plume of redbud in his hat, and he jingled as he walked. *Gypsy!* she thought in panic, but was instantly reassured by the pack slung over his shoulder. He was a peddler, and though it was early for them, peddlers were no cause for alarm. Nevertheless, he was a man and a stranger, and her finger came down instinctively on the screen door hook. She would have run away and hid, except that he had seen her.

"Good morning!" he called. He came across the yard with a prancing step, a young man, rather slight of build. The jingling came from a harness bell on his shoe. Now that she saw him closer, he was not as dark as she thought; part of his color came from the sun. But his hair and his eyes were black, and there was something about him that marked him, if not as a gypsy, as some sort of foreigner. He stopped at the doorstep, slipped the pack from his shoulder, and took off his hat. "Fine day today!" he announced, looking as pleased as if the weather were his own doing. "May I present myself—Marco Polo of the wilderness, a caravan of one, with a cargo of riches—silks, laces, and jewels, the pearls of the Orient, also pins, needles and plug tobacco— and," he added, taking the sprig of redbud from his hat, "flowers for the ladies!"

He held it out with a big friendly smile. But if he thought she was going to open the door for him, he was mistaken. "That ain't a flower, it's redbud, and I got a woods full of it."

He laughed as if she had made a joke. "Is that your woods back there? Then it was yours in the first place. I stole it," he admitted cheerfully. "But since it belongs to you, I'll give it back, none the worse for wear. On second thought," he said, barely pausing for breath, "I think I won't. Since you have a woods full and I have this one little branch, I'll keep it, with your permission."

"You can have it."

"Thank you!" He stuck it back in his hatband and looked up with his bright smile.

"Ain't it a little early for you peddlers?" she said.

"As a matter of fact, yes! And I didn't intend to be here so early, or to be here at all."

"Then how come you're here?"

"I'm lost!" he said happily, flinging out his arms. "I know I'm somewhere in Missouri and a quarter hour's walk from a redbud tree, but aside from that, I don't know where I am."

"Well, my land, how'd you get here?"

"I walked."

"Where from?"

"A railway stop. Not a town, only a stop, somewhere in the wilds."

"I reckon you mean the junction, back that way. Trains that don't go through Renfro stop there sometimes."

"Renfro?"

"The closest town. Is that where you was headed?"

"I don't think so! I was headed south, to the hill country, where it's almost summer already. But yesterday—you remember what a fine day it was, like today, only this one is better—yesterday the thought hit me to get off at this—junction, wherever it is, and have a look at the countryside. It's nice around here, the sun was warm, and I was tired of riding. There would be another train to take me where I was going. So away I went! I started walking along the road, thinking that if I came to a house, maybe I could make a sale. If I didn't, then I wouldn't. The only trouble was—I got lost in the woods."

"Why didn't you keep to the road?"

"I find it hard." He smiled, cocking his head to one side like a robin, which was in fact what he made her think of, with his bright black eyes and his flickering step, and being so early in the season. "There was a path," he said. "I can never resist a path. No telling where it will lead you! Well, this one led me to a stream and left me. But that was not bad. I caught a beautiful fish! I ate him for supper."

"How did you cook it?"

"I built a fire. And I have a pan. I carry one here," he said, nudging the pack with his toe, "for I never know where mealtime will find me. After my supper, I curled up in my coat, by my little fire, and had a good night's rest."

"You stayed all night in the woods?"

"There was no place else!"

"My land, though, wasn't it cold?"

"It was! But with my fire and my coat, it was all right. I don't mind the cold. This morning I had a dip in the stream. Yes," he laughed, seeing her shudder, "I was numb to the bone. But I thawed in the sunshine. I felt good. All I had to do now was find my way back to the railroad. So I took my bearings and started out. But if you say the junction is *that* direction, then I am not a very good woodsman. I'm only a lucky fellow, delighted to be here!"

"If you're going to be lucky enough to catch that afternoon train, you better get started."

"Is there a later one?"

"Not till late tonight."

"Then if I miss the one, I can take another. In the meantime, with your permission, I'd be pleased to show you my wares."

"I'm sorry you had to walk all this way," said Callie, "but there ain't anything I need. You might as well not waste your time."

"But I have the whole day," he said, spreading his arms.

"Well, I haven't. I've got work to do."

"And here I stand, taking up your time. Forgive me!"

"Oh, that's all right."

"But as long as I'm here," he said, bright as a button again, "and if you are too busy, perhaps I could open my pack for the children—only to entertain them; you don't have to buy. You have children?"

"Two little girls. They're both at school."

"Then your husband?"

"My husband's—at work. In the barn," she added firmly. "There ain't anything he needs, either."

"Then you," said the peddler, with a pleading smile. "Why don't *you* have a look? It won't take a moment. I have silks—fine silks for pretty dresses? Ribbons? Gold buttons? Please—as long as I'm here?"

"Well . . ." She looked thoughtfully at the pack. She did love those glittering grab bags. "Well, all right, I'll take a look. Just a look, though; I can't buy nothin'."

"Don't worry about that," he said, tugging at the straps.

"Spread it out there on the porch. I can see from here."

"Yes ma'am." The pack burst open like a ripe melon, rich with color and seeded with small necessities, pin papers, needles, spools of thread.

"My, you sure carry a lot!"

"Everything your heart desires, and I know the hearts of the ladies." He began to pull out lengths of bright silk, crimson and silvery green and one with a broad purple stripe. Not a serviceable black in the lot.

"Tss!" said Callie. "Ain't them the prettiest things!"

He pulled out another and spread it open with a flick of the wrist. It was taffeta, russet and green like the feathers of a Rhode Island Red. Its restless colors glistened in the sun and made a whispering sound.

"My!" she breathed. "It's just lovely."

The peddler scattered gilt buttons across it, as if they were a handful of corn. Then he brought out loops of ribbons, pink ones, blue, yellow, and red. Callie looked at them with shining eyes, thinking of the little girls.

"How much would them cost, I wonder?"

"My ribbon is six cents a yard. It's nice and wide, good quality."

She figured it in her head, frowning. "I'd have to have about four yards."

"I'll make you a price. Four yards for twenty cents."

"Hm . . ." She held her lower lip between her teeth. Blue for Jessica, yellow for Leonie, such pretty sashes for their new dresses. But if she bought the ribbon, she would have to open the door. Though he seemed a nice young man, you couldn't be too careful. "Well, no," she said at last, "I just can't do it. I'm real sorry."

"So am I—if you want the ribbon. Make it fifteen!"

"No. But thank you just the same. I better get along without it. I'm sorry to waste your time."

"I'm not sorry at all," he said with his quick smile.

"If you hurry, you can still get to the junction by train time."

She watched him fit the treasures back into the pack, folding and tucking, his slender brown hands flickering among the silks. Scraps of sunlight lay on his bent head. The hair was thick and glossy and it curled on the back of his neck. It needed trimming, she thought, but noted that his neck was clean. He closed the pack and began to buckle the straps.

"You left something out," she said.

"I know it."

She looked at the coil of blue ribbon left on the porch, and back at him, and a glare of suspicion kindled in her eye. "What'd you do that for?"

"I'd like to make you a trade."

"What kind of a trade?" she said, backing away. The shotgun was in the kitchen, and she knew how to use it.

He went on working with the straps. When they were fastened, he straightened up, holding the ribbon. "If it wouldn't be too much to ask, could I please trade you the ribbon for an egg?"

"An egg!" It was so far from what she expected that she had to laugh. "What for?"

"I am hungry!" he said, with such a comical look on his face that she laughed again.

"Well, forever more! I reckon you are, lost in the woods all night, like you were."

"I chased a cow, but I couldn't milk her."

"Put your ribbon away," she said; "I reckon I ain't going to let you starve."

"No, no, we'll make a fair trade. The ribbon for an egg. Or maybe—it's a nice long piece, four yards at the very least—maybe two eggs?"

"I got plenty. I can fix you all you want."

"I didn't ask you for that, ma'am."

"Well, you ain't going to eat 'em raw, like a 'possum!"

"I have done it. It's not so bad."

"Ain't any use in that. I'll fry 'em for you."

"But I have taken up enough of your time—you have work to do."

"Well, yes, I do," she said, recalling her words.

"I'll cook them myself, as I cooked the fish. I can build a fire, I have a pan. I'll make out, as I always do."

"Well—" She considered a moment. "If you want to cook your own breakfast, I reckon I could let you do it out in the lot. That way, you'll be handy to water."

"That would be all right?"

"I think it would. Just be careful you don't set nothin' on fire."

"I'm always careful."

"But you don't have to unpack all your stuff. I'll give you something to cook in. Come on around to the back."

"Thank you!"

She ran through the house, hooked the back screen, and waited till he came around the corner. "You go on and get your fire started, out there by the cultivator. Don't get too close to the stump. I'll put the things here on the step and you can come and get them."

When he was safely beyond the gate, she took out a skillet and two large eggs and cut him a slice of bacon. After a moment's thought, she added a third egg, and set them outside on the step, careful as she came in to hook the screen again.

She could see him from the kitchen window. He had taken off his jacket and rolled up his sleeves. Within a few minutes, he had a small blaze going. He knelt beside it, fanning it with his hat. Seeing him start toward the house, she moved back from the window. He came to the step, the harness bell jingling, and jingled away again. Going to the door, she saw that he had left the ribbon, neatly folded on a burdock leaf and weighted down by an egg. He had taken only two.

She smiled as she stepped outside. "Thank you," she called, waving the ribbon. He waved back.

She might have given him a slice of bread. "Why didn't I think of that?" she said, going back to the kitchen. She cut a thick slice, spread it with butter, and set it on the step in a saucer. "Here's some bread for you."

She waited for him, just inside the door, not bothering this time to hook it. "Two eggs ain't much of a breakfast. I figured you'd like some bread with it."

"You've done more than enough. I shall have to give you more ribbon," he said with a smile.

"You don't have to do that. Enjoy your breakfast."

A few minutes later, she stepped outside again with a bowl of apple preserves. She started to call him, but it seemed foolish to keep him running back and forth. She walked out as far as the gate. He was kneeling at the fire with his back to her, and as he still had not seen her, she went on out. "I brought you some preserves."

"Oh, hello!" he said, springing up. "What's this you've brought me?"

He was not as tall as Matthew, but taller than she. "They're apple," she said.

"I like apples." He dipped his finger into the bowl and licked it. "Good."

"I'm partial to 'em. Some folks ain't." She stood for a second or two and, thinking of nothing else to say, turned to leave.

"Won't you stay?"

"Oh no, I've—"

"You've got work to do. Well, I know how it is. I'm as busy as a bee, myself, cooking and sweeping and dusting the furniture—" He capered about, flicking his handkerchief over the stump and the cultivator. He dusted the metal seat. "Sit down!" he said, with his boyish grin.

She couldn't help laughing. "I ought to get back."

"But it's such a fine day!"

"Well, yes, it is," she said, looking at the sky. It was as blue as she'd ever seen it.

The peddler flung out his arms. "Behold, the winter is past," he cried, "the sun shines and the birds sing and gather ye redbud while ye may, or whatever it says in the Bible."

"You've got it all mixed up," she said, laughing. "It don't say anything in the Bible about stealin' redbud."

"Why, it does," he said solemnly.

"It don't either."

He bounded to the stump and fished a small book from his coat pocket. "I have a Bible right here, I can prove it." He flipped it open and pretended to read, " 'Gather ye redbud while ye may in the land of milk and honey!' Here, read it for yourself." And he tossed her the book with a merry laugh. "Well, anyway, it sounds like the Bible, doesn't it? And it is a beautiful day. You'd be turning your back on the Lord Himself to go inside in such weather."

"Well, I'll stay just a minute." She climbed up on the cultivator and wriggled into the metal seat. It was warm from the sun and felt good to her bottom.

"Now this is jolly!" said the peddler, hopping onto the stump. He tossed the eggs into the air and began to juggle them, as she had seen a man do at a Fourth of July picnic. "I trade for an egg and I get all this—meat, bread, and apples, and good company, too." He caught the eggs and burst out singing. "Praise God from whom all blessings flow!" It was more shout than song, and if God didn't hear it, He was mighty deaf. The red rooster skittered to safety. "Behold the fowls of the air, they toil not, neither do they spin, but the Lord in His mercy provideth, and I am Solomon in his glory!" He flipped himself off the stump, heels over head, and landed on his feet.

Callie stared at him, bedazzled. He was a little daft, but whether from a secret nip in the woods or the tonic of the weather, she couldn't tell. At any rate, he was as frisky as a colt, and it made her laugh. "I don't know how you can be so lively without any breakfast," she said.

"Oh, I like to be hungry when I know I'll be fed." He dropped down by the fire and broke the eggs into the skillet. They hissed in the hot fat, curling around the edges like starched doilies. "But if I am any hungrier, I won't be able to eat. I'll be dead of starvation. And I should hate to be dead on a day like this and waste such a breakfast. To your health, ma'am, and to mine," he said, lifting the skillet. He set it on the stump. "Good bread, good meat, praise God, and I eat." And with that blessing, he fell to.

He ate ravenously and yet with a kind of niceness, not gobbling but eating quickly, with a gusto that made her almost taste the food. It was downright flattering to have fed him. She watched him curiously, fascinated by his quick silky movements. There was a luster about him, a clean healthy shine to his hair and skin. She thought he was young, probably no more than twenty, though it was hard to tell. One minute he acted like a ten-year-old boy, the next minute he seemed older than she. In spite of his nonsense, she felt he was well brought up, educated.

"My husband reads all the time," she remarked, turning the small Bible in her hands.

"Umhm?" said the peddler.

"Every minute he's not workin', and sometimes while he is. I don't hardly know what he looks like when he's in the house, he's always got his face hid in a book."

The peddler smiled. "Do you like to read?"

"Well, I don't have much time. I look at the Bible some. It's nice you carry it with you."

"Part of my stock."

"Oh."

"I read it sometimes when I stop to rest. It makes a good sound."

"You read it out loud to yourself?"

"It's the best way, especially outdoors—it sounds better outdoors."

"I don't see what difference that'd make," she said, smiling.

"Try it and see. Read something."

"Right now?"

"Of course."

"Oh—you can read it for yourself, can't you?"

"I'm busy," he said with his mouth full.

"Well . . . I don't read very *good*."

"It's no matter, as long as you read loud."

She opened the book reluctantly. The print was so fine she could barely make out the letters, let alone read the words. She turned through it and at last, staring intently at the page, began to recite, skipping or inventing where memory failed her. " 'For God so loved the world, that he gave his only begotten Son, that whosoever believeth in him should not perish, but have everlasting life.' "

"You see?" said the peddler. "Doesn't it sound better out here?"

"It sounds all right."

"Go on, read some more."

She turned several pages. " 'Judge not, that ye be not judged;

condemn not, that ye be not condemned; forgive, and ye shall be forgiven.' "

She paused and glanced up. As he seemed to be waiting for more, she leafed through the pages and began again.

" 'The Lord is my shepherd; I shall not want.

" 'He maketh me to lie down in green pastures; he leadeth me beside the still waters.

" 'He restoreth my soul . . .

" 'Yea, though I walk through the valley of the shadow of death, I will fear no evil; for thou art with me . . .

" 'Thou preparest a table before me in the presence of mine enemies: thou anointest my head with oil; my cup runneth over.

" 'Surely goodness and mercy shall follow me all the days of my life: and I will dwell in the house of the Lord for ever.' "

She closed the book and looked up. The peddler was leaning against the stump, looking at her through half-closed eyes.

"You read very well," he said after a moment.

"Oh, not so very." She accepted the compliment, nevertheless, casting about in her mind for some justification. She could accept it for her memory; that would be fair enough. She smiled at him warmly. It was pleasant, sitting here in the sunshine with someone to talk to. It did get lonesome with Matthew away all day, and even when he did come home, he didn't say much. She glanced down to find the young man looking at her with an odd, smiling gaze.

"What are you lookin' at?" she said uneasily.

"The cobweb."

She turned and saw it floating over her shoulder, one of those long fine threads that seem to hang from the sky, the filament spat out by a spider and blown loose from the web. She touched it with her finger. The peddler gave a low chuckle.

"Why do you laugh?" she said.

"Because it shines!"

It seemed reason enough.

She smiled, settling back and looking all around. The air was uncommonly clear. Green woods, blue sky, the red rooster parading in the lot, even the worn silvery wood of the granary, seemed to give off a light of their own. It was a kind of choir where everything joined with the sun and cast its radiance on the day. And everything was still. The stillness itself made a kind of music.

The peddler slid down and put his hands behind his head. "Now I am sleepy, like a dog with his belly full."

"That wasn't a whole lot of breakfast."

"It was just right."

"You may get hungry before you can eat again. I could fix you some lunch to take with you."

"Oh, thank you, but that won't be necessary."

"Ain't any more houses between here and the junction."

"Then I may have to catch another fish," he said, with his eyes closed.

"You don't seem to worry much."

"What good would that do?"

"Well, I don't know. But I'd think you might like to know where your next meal's comin' from."

"Heaven will provide, or a kind lady."

She laughed. "Do you like bein' a peddler, walkin' around from place to place?"

"I like it very well."

"Looks like you'd get awful tired."

"Sometimes I do."

"Ain't it lonesome?"

"Sometimes."

"But I guess you make a lot of money at it."

"Not very much."

"My land, then, what do you do it for?"

"So I can sit here like this in the sunshine."

"The sun don't shine every day," she said.

"It does somewhere."

He was right about that. He sat with his eyes closed, a little smile on his face, and for a moment she thought he had fallen asleep. But after a moment he sat up brightly.

"Yes, it's a good life," he said. "I have been a peddler for two days now!"

"That's what I thought," she said, laughing.

"And now I must be getting on."

"Yes, you better get started."

"How do I go now, the same way I came?"

"Well, you could; it's a little shorter that way, cuttin' through the woods. But it's easier walking if you take the road. You go up that way, up the hill, and keep on till you come to a crossroads. Then turn north, and the junction's about three and a half miles from there."

"I'll find it—if I don't lose my way again."

"Just keep to the road; you can't miss it."

"It has been very nice here," he said, putting on his coat.

"Well, I enjoyed it. I hope you'll come and see us again if you're ever out this way."

"Thank you. But I'll not be this way again, I think."

"You don't think so?"

"The world's a big place."

"I guess it is." She watched him hoist the pack onto his shoulder. "That sure looks heavy."

"It is lighter now by a length of ribbon." He held out his hand. "Thank you for the breakfast."

"You paid for it."

"All the same I thank you." With a quick little bow, he kissed her hand. Then he looked up with a smile of pure devilment. "And thank your husband—who is working in the barn. Goodbye!" he added. Clapping the hat on the back of his head, he marched down the lane like a whole parade.

Callie stood abashed, caught in a lie which she had forgotten. A silly lie, too, it turned out, seeing that the young man knew all the time that she was alone and hadn't lifted a finger to harm her. She watched him go, wishing she might apologize. She could wave, at least, if he would look back. But he went on without turning and disappeared up the hill.

She walked back slowly to the house and carried the feather-beds in, wondering what to do next. The day was quite thoroughly disrupted. For all the visitor had left her of the morning, he might as well have stayed for dinner. She wandered through the house, dusted the piano stool with her hand, opened a window, returned to the kitchen, and, seeing the loaf of bread left out, cut off a slice and ate it. She chewed absently, staring out at the bright weather. The house was cold and unnaturally still, having no children in it. She wished they were at home; she would take them on a picnic.

Out in the lot, a squawk of insult tore the air, as a hen escaped from a rooster. Watching her waddle away adjusting her feathers, Callie remembered her broody-hen. She jumped up from the table. This was a good time to look some more for that nest. Taking her sunbonnet, she set out, grateful for any task that would take her out of doors.

For most of an hour, she poked cautiously into weed patches and brush piles along the edge of the woods. There was no sign of the hen. But enjoying the walk, she went on through the trees and came out on the other side on the Old Chimney Place. The blackened chimney stood some distance away, surrounded by a thicket of sumac, buckbrush, and wild plum. "Well, I'll look up there," she said. It seemed a likely place for a hidden nest.

As she crossed the open meadow, she took off her bonnet and opened her dress at the neck, baring her throat to the gentle warmth. The sun shone from the top of the sky and the air smelled sweet. Her footsteps flushed a lark from the grass. He flew off toward the road and his whistle came back sweet and lonely in the stillness. Everything was hushed with noon, resting, like a traveler at the crest of a hill. She thought of the peddler leaning against the stump, his face lifted to the sun. She was a little sorry he had gone. He seemed a natural part of the shining day, and something was missing when he went.

The thicket rose on all sides of the old house site, walling it in, leaving in the middle an opening where the grass grew soft and thick in summer. She and the children often came here on picnics. Having searched around the edges, she parted the brush at a certain spot and stepped through to the clearing. The grass inside was already green, spangled with dandelions. And there, not twenty feet away, lay the peddler, bare to the waist and sound asleep in the sunshine.

Her mouth fell open with a soundless gasp, though, to tell the truth, she was not much surprised. She might have conjured him there by her very thoughts. The scamp! He hadn't kept to the road. She stood absolutely still and gazed at him with furtive pleasure, as she would at a robin on its nest or a lizard sunning himself on a log. He lay on his back, his hands above his head. The hair curled dark and shiny under his arms. It curled on his forehead. And the upturned face wore a little smile, as if he dreamed happily. She wouldn't want to wake him. It would embarrass them both to find her spying. She looked at him fondly for another moment, then with great caution turned away.

"Hello!" said the peddler.

She looked over her shoulder, and a queer kind of numbness seemed to creep upward from her feet.

"It's nice to see you again," he said.

"I didn't know you was here," she said in a breathless voice. "I was lookin' for my broody-hen."

"Your what?"

"My old broody-hen—she's hid out a nest somewhere."

"I hoped you were looking for me." He rose to his feet, smiling. "I've been thinking of you."

Her knees had begun to tremble. She took a faltering step backward.

"Shall I help you look?" he said, starting toward her.

"No—I can do it some other day."

"Where are you going?"

She wasted no time for an answer, but plunged into the brush, her heart pounding in her throat.

He caught her before she got through to the open. "Don't go! I'm nicer than a broody-hen."

"Let me go!"

The jerk of her arm did not free her, but only brought him up close. He pulled her against him, pressing her hand against his bare chest, and she dug her nails into his flesh.

"So we must fight!" he said sadly.

She raised her free hand to strike him. He smiled as he caught it, and they began to struggle.

They fought in silence, the only sound their breathing and now and then a soft laugh from the peddler. He fought like a boy at play. It was a sport with him, a game he knew he could win. But he fought hard because he had to. Her flesh stung where he gripped her, and one knee twisted under her as she went down. He fell with her, pinning her to the ground.

"There!" he panted. He put his hands on her shoulders and pushed himself up part way, catching his breath. "You're stronger than I thought—you are good!" He leaned down and kissed her hard on the mouth. Then without warning he let go of her and sat back on his knees. "Now I have won, I let you go."

It happened so quickly that for an instant she was too stunned to move. She stared at him in disbelief.

"Go," he said, "if you want to."

She struggled to her feet and pitched forward with a cry of pain as the hurt knee gave way beneath her. He caught her as she fell.

"Ah, you are hurt!" he said gently. He pulled her close and began to murmur in a language she did not understand but whose meaning she knew, soothing and gentle, as if she were a child. She hung limp in his arms, sobbing helplessly.

"Don't cry," he said. "Let's be happy together for a little while. You will like me—I am clean, I won't give you a disease. I am careful. Stay with me," he said, and his whisper roared like a seashell held against the ear.

3

Callie went home sobbing through the tender noon. She felt the air and heard the meadowlark, she smelled the blossoming orchard. The day had been so beautiful—it still was—but she was a blemish on it. All her life she had been virtuous; no man but Matthew had ever touched her. She had saved herself for love and she came to him so proudly, all new and unsullied for him. That was changed now. And the pure clear air and the sweet sounds broke her heart. She went inside and locked the door. Hiding her face in Matthew's old coat, she wept bitterly, weeping for him. For the harm had been done to him as much as to her. Something of his was defiled.

With no other thought than to go to him, she unlocked the door and ran to the barn, where she took down the bridle, intending to find the sorrel mare and ride into town. But as she started toward the pasture, something—some rapidly emerging apprehension—slowed her down, and, running through the barnlot, she stopped and looked back at the spot where the peddler had built his fire. Suddenly the whole scene rose before her again: herself and the peddler laughing and talking, having a pleasant time together. *How was that going to sound?*

And with that question, others came crowding in, one over another. She heard them in Matthew's voice: *Why did you let him stay, in the first place? You were there by yourself, you were asking for trouble. Why didn't you stay in the house? Why did you follow him when he left?* (She *had* followed him, in a way; the road he took ran alongside the Old Chimney Place, and she knew which way he went.) *Didn't you know something like this could happen? Haven't you got any sense at all?* Furious, accusing questions. And how was she going to answer!

She had been foolish. She could see that now. To anyone that didn't know better, it might look as though she *invited* the peddler! Matthew would know better. He could never accuse her of being unfaithful. But he could certainly, and he might, accuse her of being a fool. He was so cross, these days. Perhaps she deserved his anger; but just the same, she cringed at the prospect. Why did he have to know? She didn't have to tell everything. She could leave out the part about the breakfast and even the peddler's coming to the house. All she had to say was that she came on him unexpectedly—that was true—while looking for the broody-hen. That was all he needed to know. Unless—it occurred to her with a start—unless the peddler told *his* story! But he wouldn't —he was no fool! He would take the first train and get out of the country. But suppose, just suppose, that he stayed in the neigh-borhood a few days, and suppose that Matthew called the law! It could happen. Matthew was not a violent man, but he was a man and had a right to avenge his honor.

She sank down on the stump, her head thronging with echoes of country tragedies—jealous husbands, guilty lovers, bloodshed and disaster. Suppose he had the peddler brought to justice? The peddler would then tell his side of the story, and even if he told only the truth, that was enough to damn her. Oh, she could say that she fought him. That was true. But so was it true that she had been easy; she had sat with him for an hour or more, visiting as she might with a neighbor's wife. They laughed and talked, he kissed her hand! She could never look him in the face and deny it—any more than she could deny that she liked him.

She covered her face in shame. She wanted never to see him again, but while he was there, she had liked him. Leaning against the stump, he had shone in the sunlight. He shouted the Bible like one singing—God is love and life a praising. He was all joy and freedom and innocence. How could she see him punished, a boy like that! The thought of him locked up, beaten, or maybe worse (men hung other men for such as this) made her sick at heart. He had done wrong, and he deserved to be punished—but only for what he did to Matthew, not for what he did to her. That was the bitterest part of all. A thing that should have been shame-ful and ugly was not. Not to the peddler and not altogether to her. There was something about him, even in his trespass, that kept it from being mean. He had come down the road full of shout and halloo, drunk with the spring weather, taking the good things of the day as his rightful pleasure, and she was one more of those. He took her in high spirits, for the plain joy of it, as easily as he took a branch of redbud. And for a little time there, under the blue sky, on the new grass, she had loved him.

But it was Matthew she loved truly. Plain, earnest, hard-working Matthew, who tried to do right, even though he didn't always make it, and who had been good to her, gentle and loving. It broke her heart that for a moment, against her will, she had forsaken him.

He must never know that. "O Lord," she prayed, "isn't part of the truth enough?" It would have to be. Whatever else happened, and for everyone's sake, the peddler must not be caught.

She dried her face on her torn skirt and, knowing what she must do now, set about it. Working quickly, she gathered up the charred sticks from the fire and carried them in to the kitchen stove. Back in the lot, she scattered the ashes and carefully brushed sand over the blackened earth. When all trace of the fire was removed, the skillet and dishes put away, she took a spade and went far down in the pasture. There above the branch she dug a deep hole and buried the blue satin ribbon. The ribbon was clean and pretty, lying there. She saw the damp earth fall over it and she cried. Then she raked leaves over the spot and walked back home.

When she was washed and had changed her clothes, she went over the barnyard once more and all around the yard. Assured that no sign of him remained, she breathed easier. She would tell Matthew, but it could wait now till tomorrow. Tomorrow night when he came home from school, she would say, "It happened this morning." By that time, the peddler should be two days away.

Long before sundown she began to watch the road, longing to see him, hoping some miracle would send him home early. At dusk she gave the children their supper and put them to bed. The cows came jingling up from pasture, their udders swollen. Taking pity on them, she went out and milked. It was dark when Matthew drove in.

She ran out to greet him. "I'm glad you're home!"

"What's wrong?" he said sharply.

"Nothin's wrong. I'm just glad to see you, that's all. I was gettin' worried."

He climbed down, avoiding her. "It takes forever, driving the buggy. Did the girls get home all right?"

"They walked. You go on in. I'll unhitch."

"No, I'll do it."

311

"But you're tired," she urged. "Go on, honey, your supper's waitin'."

"I want to get the milking done first."

"I already done it."

"What'd you do that for!" he said irritably. "You'll keep on till you make yourself sick, that's the way you do."

"But you were so late gettin' home—"

"I was busy!" he snapped. "Now don't throw that up to me. I get home as soon as I'm able."

"All I said was—"

"All kinds of things come up that I can't foresee. You ought to know that. I've tried to explain it. But you never take any interest in my work." He gave the horse a slap on the rump and strode off angrily.

Callie leaned her head against the buggy. No matter what she did or said these days, he found some fault. It seemed like he was looking for it, hoping to find it. Anything to excuse himself. He felt guilty, that's why. There was somebody else, all right. She struck the wheel softly with her fist. But then (remembering the morning), she was not free of blame, herself; perhaps she had done Matthew more wrong than he did her. "I didn't mean to, though," she said. Maybe he didn't either. Some things happen in spite of you. She was sorry for him. She started toward the barn, then thinking better of it, she turned back.

He came in presently and sat down to supper. She watched him across the table. He had lost weight. The bones stood out in his cheeks; he looked hollow and big-eyed. It became him, somehow. He was beautiful like this. But pitiful, too; he looked troubled. If it was what she thought it was, he deserved to be troubled. Just the same, she was sorry for him. Her resentment shifted subtly from him to the woman. What kind of a woman was it who would do this to him, torment him till he was half crazy and couldn't sleep or eat!

"You look tired," she said.

"I am." He crossed the knife and fork on his plate and leaned his head on his hands.

"I'll be glad when school's out, so you won't have to do two things at once."

"Well, yes . . ."

"Be nice when you can stay home all day."

"Yes."

"Nice for me, too. I get afraid sometimes, here by myself."

"No need to do that," he said. "You have the gun if you need it."

"It ain't much company, though."

There was a pause. "I ought to go to school again," he said.

"This summer?"

"I've got to keep up."

"But you've been workin' so hard—you need to rest!"

"Well, Callie," he said severely, "I can't neglect my education, not if I'm going to get anywhere."

"I know you can't." She sighed. "But Clarkstown's so far away."

"I've been thinking," he said, "I'm not sure I'd go to Clarkstown this time."

Something tingled in her, a struck nerve. "Where would you go?" she said, watching his face.

"Oh, I don't know . . ." He looked up innocently (as guilty a look as she ever saw). "I'd thought about St. Louis."

"St. Louis? How ever come you to think of that?"

"They have fine schools up there, big universities. And then the cultural life of a city, the atmosphere and association—it's just as important as classroom studies."

"Would you—would we go with you, me and the children?"

"Well," he began, apologetic, "it would be expensive, I'm afraid. I don't know if I could afford for all of us to be there. I might just have to go by myself and batch for the summer."

So that's what he had in mind! Someone was pushing him. He never made a rash move in his life unless someone kept at him.

"I'd be lonesome," was all she said.

"It would only be a few weeks."

"What about the work?"

"Around here? I thought your brothers might help out. Thad and Wesley, maybe they could come and stay while I'm gone."

He had it all worked out.

"But I don't know," he said, rising. "Maybe I can't do it. We'll see." He took the lantern and started out. "I'm going to throw down some hay for the stock."

"Careful with that lantern in the barn," she said.

She sat at the table, staring into the lamp flame. He was willing to leave her. Whatever she was up against, it was more than she'd reckoned on. This was no idle, silly country woman; it was someone from off, and someone of Matthew's kind, who read books and talked his kind of talk. Someone *educated*. She passed a dazed look around the kitchen. This was the only thing she didn't know how to fight.

She could have learned to read! She was smart enough, she could have learned. "I will!" she cried out. "Matthew, I will!" But it was a little late for that. By the time she learned how to read, she could lose him. And she could not lose him now. She wanted him. He was not perfect, but she would rather have his faults than any other man's virtues. More than that, she needed him. She was in trouble. And maybe that was good, she thought suddenly. Trouble brought people together sometimes. Maybe it had happened for the best. She rose, eager to tell him, but reaching the door, she drew back. She had better wait, give the peddler a chance. Tomorrow would be time enough.

She had covered the peddler's tracks thoroughly. No trace of him remained, or of any stranger. In the morning, however, after a dream-weary night, she woke with a start, realizing that she had forgotten one small thing. The small thing was Leonie. Yesterday Leonie went to school. Today she would be at home. If a stranger came to the house, Leonie would know it. If no one came, she would know that, too. Callie despaired of her stupidity. Somehow now she had to be rid of the child. An hour would be long enough, a half hour even; but she had to have time alone, with Leonie out of earshot.

Any other time, she could have managed. The children often played away from the house, far enough that if someone came, they wouldn't know. Today, however, Leonie had a cranky spell. She was cross and whiny, worn out by the previous day's delights. Callie could do nothing with her. She set up a playhouse deep in the orchard; Leonie followed her back to the house. She sent the child to the pasture to pick spring beauties; Leonie was back in ten minutes. Sent to the hayloft, she was back in five. Callie suggested a picnic in the walnut grove, mudpies by the branch. Leonie would not go by herself. In a spectacular tantrum, she refused to take a nap. No one was fooling her—she knew when she wasn't wanted. In retaliation, she did nothing the livelong day but dog her mother's footsteps. Callie was frantic. Her nerves already strained to the breaking point, she lost her patience and spanked the child. Leonie looked up at her with a sad, red little tear-stained face, and Callie gathered her into her arms and cried with her. It wasn't the baby who had done wrong.

By the time Matthew came home that night, one of her sick

headaches had struck, leveling all memory of peddler and remorse, guilt and fear. Nothing remained but triumphant nausea and the steady hallelujahs of pain.

She slept that night in utter exhaustion and didn't wake up till late the next morning. Matthew had fed himself and the children and gone on to school. Leonie, frisky as a kitten, was dabbling around in dishwater, intent on helping Mama. She helped Mama all day, aggressively. Callie hadn't the heart or the strength to cajole her out of the way.

Two days and two nights had passed now, and her dread was doubled. The longer she waited, the more impossible it became to avoid telling the truth. She could not say it happened today or yesterday; it had to have taken place when it did. And what excuse was she going to give for waiting? Perhaps, she thought, lit by a desperate hope, she needn't tell him anything. But it was a false hope, as meaningless as lightning in a drought. With a moan, she clutched herself, as if pain had already struck in her womb. It could not be! But it *could* be, to punish her. She could not be sure for a whole week yet. Before that, she had to tell Matthew.

But when he came that night—late again, scowling and withdrawn—her courage failed her. They sat at the table together in silence, and she watched him. If he had once looked at her to see that she was troubled, if he had bothered to ask why, she would have blurted out the story in gratitude. But he sat with his eyes down, his thoughts far away. The clock ticked loud and ominous. Time was passing, and she was afraid.

It was strange and awesome how her fear had changed him in her eyes. Always before, she had viewed him from a position of virtue, from where she was unassailable. Now, in her distress, feeling to blame, she began to see him from another angle. It distorted her vision of him, diminished his humankindness, and enlarged the intolerance in him. It no longer seemed possible that he would forgive her—especially as he no longer loved her. She kept coming back to that. He was ashamed of her, because she was ignorant.

"Matthew?" she said timidly. "Soon as I clean off the table, why don't I practice my writin' again? You haven't give me a lesson in a long time."

He glanced up with a frown. "Oh, it's so late. I've been teaching all day."

"But I've been wantin'—"

"I've got to get to bed. Some other time, maybe."

He went upstairs. After a while she followed. She tiptoed into the room. "Matthew?" she said softly. There was no answer.

They lay with their backs to each other. He was no more asleep than she, but for the life of her and the peace of her soul, she could not make herself speak. Toward midnight she heard him rise and go outside. It was a bright, moonlit night, and she could see him from the window. He stood there for a long time, just standing, looking all around. Then he passed slowly through the gate, across the barnlot, toward the pasture. Taking her shawl, she followed him.

She found him in a clearing, near a hawthorn in full bloom. She could see him from the shadows. She stood for a moment with her hands against her pounding heart. It was a chance she took.

"Help me, Lord," she said and stepped out into the moonlight.

Having loved the peddler for one moment, she loved Matthew as she never had before. With all her heart she wanted the child to be his. Long before its birth she named it for him.

When the child came, perfectly formed, with her own look stamped unmistakably on it, she gave thanks to the Lord. ". . . the woman being deceived was in transgression. Notwithstanding she shall be saved in childbearing." The Lord had sent her a token of His mercy.

It was not until later, when the little girl's nature began to reveal itself, that she was once more plagued with doubts. Yet in her heart she had made it Matthew's daughter, and she would hold to that. And ever after, there was nothing she would not do to please him, nowhere she would not go, nothing she would not —however reluctantly—forgive him.

The years passed, and the small events of everyday sifted down like leaves and snow. Buried beneath them, the memory of her guilt lay quiet. Then Mathy died, and it rose savagely to haunt her. The Lord had bided His time and sent His punishment at last.

But then as she studied about it (wandering alone, standing long moments lost in thought), she came to the conclusion that this was not so. We do not die for each other's sins; Christ alone did that, and that was not to punish but to save. For the rest of us, death is a natural occurrence, like the falling of the leaves or a fire going out. Mathy's death was not a punishment of anyone, any more than her life had been. She had given them joy. Though her death hurt them, she had not died for that purpose. That was not God's way. God is mercy, He is love. It said so in the Bible.

"And I don't care what else it says, I know that's the way it is."

She was sitting on the grass, near the old crumbling chimney. She drew a long breath and looked up. "I wonder where that old hen was!" she said. And she rose and went home, easy in her soul.

4

That was a long time ago.

Now on this August morning, with seventy years behind her and eternity just ahead, she was troubled again. She was thinking that perhaps, after all, her God and Matthew's differed. She had made hers up in her head. But Matthew was smart, he could read; perhaps his God of wrath was the real one and every word of the Bible true, though some were as bitter as gall. If this were so, then Mathy's death had indeed been the warning which she would have done well to heed. Perhaps it was not enough to confess to the Lord—she should have confessed to Matthew. Told him everything and suffered the consequences, even to losing him.

Instead, she had taken a nip and a tuck in God and made Him fit her needs. She stayed in her green meadows. She kept her husband, her comfortable home. She held the love and respect of her children.

"I have been happy!" she cried woefully.

She had been, and she was. Though much had been taken and much had not come, she was happy.

"Is it a sin, Lord, considering what I did?" She stood in remorse on the pasture path, holding the berry bucket.

A flicker of white through the trees distracted her. She peered down the slope to where the branch spread into rivulets and drained into the slew. In the green light of the willows stood a large white bird. A heron, she thought. A white heron, the first she had ever seen. She stepped forward eagerly, careful to make no noise. The bird stood with his neck arched to the shallow water and took no notice of her. She moved on until she came within a few feet of him. Strange, humpbacked creature, how big and white and proud he was! He minced along, lifting his finicky feet and setting them down like a woman crossing a puddle. He was looking for frogs and little fish. Presently he lifted his head, the long neck arranged in an S, and seemed to listen. He sees me, she thought; birds didn't need to turn their heads. They stood like this for a long moment, she and the heron, contemplating each other. Then slowly he lowered his foot and spread the wide white wings. She thought he was going to fly away. Instead, he folded the wings snug to his sides and, arching his neck again, picked his way toward the slew.

What a splendid sight he was. She thought him a good omen. It would be a good day. She climbed back up the path and, recalling all the day held in store, she felt giddy with happiness. She wanted to caper on the path, cut a shine. She sang aloud in her thin old voice,

> *"If a tree don't fall on you*
> *You'll live till you die!"*

Looking about her, she thought how beautiful it was. For God so loved the world! She turned the words around—For God loved the world so! So much, so very much, as a child is loved, in pride and hope, and in pain, too. God's love is infinite, past all understanding. How great then, beyond man's comprehension, must be God's suffering. For when His children erred, it must hurt Him, as all of us are hurt.

"O God," she cried out in compassion. She had hurt Him. She had done wrong, and to tell the truth, she was not sorry. (And she had not learned to read.) What must she do now in recompense? How could she comfort Him?

She thought about it for a moment. "I love your world," she said simply. It was what she could do.

She looked around at the good things she was granted—green fields, good pasture, shining weather. The air was fresh, the birds sang, and she had seen a white heron. Matthew was waiting for her. The children were coming home. And they would watch the moonflowers bloom. Oh, if she never got to heaven, this was enough, this lovely earth with its sunlight and its mornings and something always to look forward to. (Earth had *that* over heaven!)

She looked up at the clear sky. "Thank you," she said and went home to breakfast.

About the author

About the book

Read on

Insights,
Interviews
& More…

Meet Jetta Carleton

William G. Berkeley

JETTA CARLETON was born in 1913 in Holden, Missouri (population about 500), and earned a master's degree at the University of Missouri. She worked as a schoolteacher, a radio copywriter in Kansas City, and, for eight years, a television copywriter for New York City advertising agencies. She and her husband settled in Santa Fe, New Mexico, where they ran a small publishing house, The Lightning Tree. She died in 1999. *The Moonflower Vine* is her only published novel. ᴄᴧ

The Lightning Tree

JETTA CARLETON LYON called The Lightning Tree, the private publishing firm she owned and operated with her husband, Jene, "an affair of the heart." She said the work was hard and the pay was low, but the satisfaction of keeping books alive was reward enough.

The Lyons set up their shop southeast of Santa Fe in the foothills of the Cerros Negros in 1973. They named their press for a giant ponderosa there, a landmark scarred by lightning. Jene, who had worked as a production manager for New York publishing firms, was a genius with printing equipment and served The Lightning Tree as pressman, Linotype operator, and hand compositor, in addition to his duties as designer and bookkeeper.

Having enjoyed some success as a novelist, Jetta used her literary skills to read manuscripts, proofread galleys, and do some rewriting. Until 1991, The Lightning Tree produced an eclectic list of titles, including books of poetry, regional history, bibliographies, and cookbooks, all designed and set in type by Jene.

The foregoing description, which accompanied the exhibit Lasting Impressions: The Private Presses of New Mexico, *was written by Pamela S. Smith, retired director of The Press at the Palace of the* ▶

> " [Jetta] said the work was hard and the pay was low, but the satisfaction of keeping books alive was reward enough. "

The Lightning Tree *(continued)*

Governors, Santa Fe, and author of Passions in Print: Private Press Artistry in New Mexico, 1834–Present. *Reprinted with permission of Pamela S. Smith.* ∾

The Moonflower Vine: A Timeline

1962: *The Moonflower Vine* is published by Simon & Schuster. Immediately following its publication, reviewers are already praising Carleton's work as a future classic:

"The flavor of *The Moonflower Vine* is much the same as that of *To Kill a Mockingbird*. . . . It has the same quiet feel of nostalgia, a breeze scented with bluegrass and wild roses. . . . A delightful book."   —*Denver Post*

"Once in a great, great while comes a new book that makes you thankful you know how to read. *The Moonflower Vine* is just such a book . . . written with a great feeling for beauty, human emotions and human foibles . . . filled with nostalgia, love, laughter, tears, and real people."
            —*San Francisco News-Call Bulletin*

The Moonflower Vine goes on to spend three months on the *New York Times* bestseller list.

1963: Carleton's novel is a selection of the Literary Guild and the Reader's Digest Condensed Book Club.
    Reviewing the book in *Harper's Magazine*, Katherine Gauss Jackson calls *The Moonflower Vine* an "unpretentious first novel." "The opening chapter," she writes, "is completely self-contained, but I think that no one who reads the book will fail, when he is finished, to go back ▶

About the book

to read the first chapter again for the pleasure of seeing all the disparate parts fall into place with the knowledge of the past which the reading has provided. . . . It is also that one has grown very fond of these God-fearing, strictly brought-up folk who live by a stern code even when they break it, as nearly all of them do at one time or another. And there is humor of a pleasant, quiet sort." Jackson goes on to call *The Moonflower Vine* a "deeply felt American saga, its pleasures and tragedies moving slowly like the seasons but like them containing unexpected and dramatic tensions that keep the story constantly alive. . . . Ugliness and beauty, good and evil, weakness and strength are here, and an author not afraid unsentimentally to praise love and delight, even in so quiet a thing as the magic summer blooming of the moonflower vine."

1963–1987: Editions of *The Moonflower Vine* are published in the United Kingdom, Germany, Spain, the Netherlands, Italy, Sweden, Norway, Denmark, Finland, and Poland.

1964: *The Moonflower Vine* is published in paperback by Crest Books (Fawcett World Library).

1984: For Bantam's reissue of *The Moonflower Vine*, its editor, Robert Gottlieb, writes, "Of the hundreds upon hundreds of novels I've edited, this is literally the only one I've reread several times since its publication. And every time I've read it, I've been moved by it again—by the people, by their lives; by the truth and clarity and generosity in the writing and feeling." From the editor of such literary giants as Joseph Heller and Doris Lessing, that's no small praise.

1999: Jetta Carleton Lyon dies in Santa Fe, New Mexico, at the age of eighty-six.

2005: Pulitzer Prize winner Jane Smiley includes *The Moonflower Vine* on her list of one hundred illuminating novels in *Thirteen Ways of Looking at the Novel*—alongside such classics as *Don Quixote*, *A Tale of Two Cities*, and *Anna Karenina*. Of it, she writes:

> This novel may be the most obscure contemporary novel on our list, but those who have read it, if the customer reviews at Earth's Biggest Bookstore are any guide, are very loyal to it. . . .
>
> Several American novels on our list—*The House of the Seven Gables*, *The Awakening*, *To Kill a Mockingbird*, and *The Moonflower Vine*—gain considerable dramatic tension from secrets that the characters are required to keep to maintain respectability in the towns where they live. The conflict between who a character feels herself or himself to be and what is acceptable to friends and colleagues is as constant a theme in American ▶

novels as, say, a character's relationship to the state is in German novels. In exploring the romantic secrets of each member of a single family, Carleton offers something of a catalog of ideas on the subject of secret desires—*The Moonflower Vine* could have been a scandalous novel. But by presenting each character's desire as a moral dilemma for that character, and especially by consistently depicting the bonds of love that eventually hold the family together, she succeeds in arousing both empathy and sympathy in the reader.

2006: Inspired by *Thirteen Ways of Looking at the Novel*, the editor of NeglectedBooks.com includes *The Moonflower Vine* in his compilation of "books that have been neglected, overlooked, forgotten, or stranded." (See below, in Read On.)

2008: First editions of *The Moonflower Vine*, listed for sale on BookFinder.com, begin at $98.

2009: Harper Perennial publishes the first new edition of *The Moonflower Vine* in more than twenty years. New editions are also planned abroad in countries including Spain, Russia, Korea, and Germany. ◠

A Neglected Book

Following is Brad Bigelow's review of
The Moonflower Vine. *The review
appeared on NeglectedBooks.com,
December 23, 2006.*

I READ *The Moonflower Vine* after coming
across Jane Smiley's discussion of it in
her *Thirteen Ways of Looking at the Novel*.
It wasn't so much what Smiley had to say
about it as that it was essentially the only
genuinely little-known novel she saw fit
to include in her list of 100 great novels.
In there amongst *Wuthering Heights*,
Moby Dick, and *Ulysses* was this book
with a completely unfamiliar title and
by a completely unfamiliar author. To see
a neglected book rate such high-profile
coverage alone made it worth a try.

    I can't say that *The Moonflower Vine*
would have stood much chance of a
second look from me had it not come
with such a sterling recommendation.
Its marketing, back when it was picked as
a Literary Guild selection and condensed
in a Reader's Digest edition, was
definitely aimed at a feminine audience,
and its first paperback edition featured a
small picture of a big, strong, dark-haired
man embracing a delicate young
woman—the sort of image that's become
the cliché of gauzy romantic novels.

    As Bo Diddley sang, though, you can't
judge a book by looking at the cover.
There's barely a lick of romance in the
whole of *The Moonflower Vine*. Carleton
grew up on a Missouri farm perhaps not
too unlike that described in her novel, ▸

Read on

> ❝ Its marketing,
> back when it
> was picked as a
> Literary Guild
> selection and
> condensed in a
> Reader's Digest
> edition, was
> definitely aimed
> at a feminine
> audience. ❞

and no farm family that survives a hard winter or a bad harvest has much romanticism left in its veins. The pragmatism of farm life is multiplied by the stern morality of the Midwest Methodist, with its clear-cut sense of right and wrong (and none of the Southern Baptist's taste for a little melodramatic backsliding).

The Moonflower Vine is a multidimensional tale of the lives of Matthew Soames; his wife, Callie; and their four daughters—Jessica, Leonie, Mathy, and Mary Jo. Mary Jo is probably closest in profile to Carleton herself. The youngest of the girls, she is roughly the same age as Carleton and, like her, left rural Missouri for a career in the world of television in New York. She narrates the introductory section of the book, which takes place one summer Sunday when the daughters (with the exception of Mathy, who dies before the age of twenty) have come back to the family farm for a visit. This section is gentle, lightly comic, and bucolic in its description of rustic pleasures such as skinny-dipping in the creek.

The rest of the book, however, is related in the third person. Starting with Jessica, it deals in turn with each of the other members of the family—Matthew, who struggles throughout his career as a teacher and principal of a small town school with a lust for bright young women in his classes; Mathy, the family rebel, who elopes with a barnstorming pilot; Leonie, the dutiful daughter, who never quite manages to find her right place in the world; and finally, Callie, the mother, whose brief moment of adultery mirrors her husband's own private sin.

Sin is a constant presence in the book. Everyone in the family, with the possible exception of Mary Jo, commits one or more sins, in their own eyes or those of the community, that prevents any form of love expressed in the book from being completely unequivocal. Matthew never fully forgives Mathy for quitting school and running off with one of the local renegades, nor Jessica for marrying a drifter Matthew takes on briefly as a hired hand. The Soameses are a God-fearing family, stalwart members of the Methodist Church, very much Old Testament Christians.

At the same time, though, progress makes its own changes in their lives. While Matthew and Callie refuse to install indoor plumbing, planes, trains, and automobiles all bring the outside world a little closer to their doorstep. Jessica and her new groom catch a train for his family home in southern Missouri—genuine hillbilly country—and though he dies less than a year later, she remains with his people thereafter. Ed, one of Matthew's old students, returns to town with an old biplane and proceeds to sweep daughter Mathy off her feet, only to kill her a year or two afterward in a crash landing. Sometime later, Leonie takes a trip to Kansas City, meets a somewhat reformed Ed, and eventually decides to marry him. ►

❝ Sin is a constant presence in the book. ❞

Read on

A Neglected Book *(continued)*

66 As the reviews of *The Moonflower Vine* on Amazon.com demonstrate, this novel, though long out of print, continues to hold a fond place in the hearts of readers who've discovered it. 99

Though *The Moonflower Vine* is full of lush descriptions of the trees, birds, flowers, and plants that fill the Soameses' world, it's very much a Midwestern, rather than Southern, novel. The comedy and tragedy are always moderated with a spare sense of realism. Missouri is, after all, the "Show Me" state—skepticism prevents any of the characters from leaping headlong into any of their passions for more than a moment or two. Or, rather, it makes them look before leaping, if leap they do.

As the reviews of *The Moonflower Vine* on Amazon.com demonstrate, this novel, though long out of print, continues to hold a fond place in the hearts of readers who've discovered it. Carleton never wrote another book, though she did publish over a hundred others through The Lightning Tree, the small press she founded with her husband, Jene Lyon, after she left the television business and moved to New Mexico.

Brad Bigelow edits and maintains the Neglected Books Page (www.neglectedbooks.com), which features reviews, articles, and dozens of lists of fine but forgotten books and authors. He also edits the Space Age Pop Music Page (www.spaceagepop.com), which pays attention to music most people prefer to ignore. After serving with the U.S. Air Force for twenty-five years, he now works for NATO and lives outside Brussels, Belgium. ➣

D on't miss the next book by your favorite author. Sign up now for AuthorTracker by visiting www.AuthorTracker.com.

12